Ring the Bells

CW01496767

Ring the Bells

The fifth *Stranger Times* novel

C. K. McDonnell

bantam

TRANSWORLD PUBLISHERS

UK | USA | Canada | Ireland | Australia
India | New Zealand | South Africa

Transworld is part of the Penguin Random House group of companies
whose addresses can be found at global.penguinrandomhouse.com.

Penguin Random House UK, One Embassy Gardens,
8 Viaduct Gardens, London SW11 7BW

penguin.co.uk

Penguin
Random House
UK

First published in Great Britain in 2025 by Bantam
an imprint of Transworld Publishers

001

Copyright © McFori Ink Ltd 2025

Typeset in 12/18pt Van Dijck MT Pro by Six Red Marbles UK, Thetford, Norfolk
Printed and bound in Great Britain by Clays Ltd, Elcograf S.p.A.

The authorized representative in the EEA is Penguin Random House Ireland,
Morrison Chambers, 32 Nassau Street, Dublin D02 YH68.

A CIP catalogue record for this book is available from the British Library

ISBNs:
9780857505392 (hb)
9780857505408 (tpb)

Penguin Random House is committed to a sustainable future
for our business, our readers and our planet. This book is made
from Forest Stewardship Council® certified paper.

*In memory of two amazing women – Ciara Phelan and
Aedín McDonald*

PROLOGUE

We are dead things, you and I.

Ghosts? No, not ghosts. Don't go getting ideas above your station. Ghosts can rattle chains, throw teacups, maybe even put in the occasional translucent appearance. They are spirits trapped in this world by unresolved trauma. Festering wounds on the spiritual landscape.

Us? We are the forgotten ones. Life's rounding errors. Whatever is supposed to happen after death hasn't. Not for us. Think of it like PE, only we didn't get picked for either team. It's not that in life we were good or bad, it's more that we weren't much of anything. We never mattered. Simply put, our lives did not contain enough story. It's an important word that is far too easily dismissed. *Story*. It's the force that keeps the world spinning or, at the very least, keeps us interested in seeing that it does. It is the invisible magic that binds humanity – love, hate, life, death, good, evil. They're all merely elements of the story. Most people might be worth only a paragraph, maybe just a footnote; a precious few will take up multiple volumes, but it all contributes to the all-powerful story. You and I, in life, we literally didn't manage to get a word in edgeways, which is why we're reduced to being spectators for all eternity.

It's not all bad. Ironically, we now exist solely for the never-ending pursuit of story. It's hard to find – at least the good stuff. 'All the world's a stage', as another now-dead thing once pointed out, but what he didn't mention is that most people are terrible actors, working from a bad script that the writers cranked out to fulfil a contractual obligation. Like *Battlefield Earth*, only without the special effects or the joy of seeing John Travolta dressed up like a space-age turkey.

That is what drew you here and what keeps me here. This run-down former church may look unpromising, but it is filled with story. Come inside, let me show you around.

Pass through the new front door, which is just the old one held together with chipboard and good intentions. How did it come to be shattered by a howling mob of abominations? Because story, that's why. And that was a good one, but it's not the story we are here for. That is the past, we are here for the future. However much of it may be left.

Through that door over there is the printing press, which is much more than a printing press, run by a Rastafarian who is much more than a Rastafarian. The one known as Manny cohabits his body with a scion of the old ones, tasked to remain here and protect this place. Still, while he does not know it, story is coming for him, too. He thinks he has stepped out of life to fulfil his role, but life has other plans. Even now, his heart is in the back of an ambulance screaming down Oxford Road, sirens wailing, setting in motion a story that will crash around him – but that is not for now.

It is the week before Christmas, a Thursday evening after hours, but we have a full house because the press needs to be fed, and story doesn't care about regular office hours. A deadline looms. With a newspaper a deadline always looms, but at this moment the staff of *The Stranger Times* can feel its breath on their necks. These problems are everyday ones, but do not worry, a problem that is more end of days is coming. Right now, it resides in a book sitting in the satchel of a librarian who is also hurrying down Oxford Road, past revellers on their way to festive office parties that will be full of low-level scandal and small stories involving Mandy from Accounts and Darren in Shipping.

As the players in the bacchanal stagger along the rain-soaked pavement, they diverge to give this woman a wide berth without realizing what they are doing. The woman herself does not know her own purpose on this rainy night, her mind like a waking fever dream full of a voice that is not her own. She pays no heed to the drunken merrymakers, to the beggars seeking change, to the ambulance screaming past, siren blaring. She is not feeling herself, and will soon not even be herself. Her benign purpose has been corrupted. She is now merely a domino about to fall. Hard.

Elsewhere in the city, the Founders – powerful people who have sold their souls for immortality and who now fancy themselves as the invisible hands that run the world – sit and fret.

What do the Founders have to fear? Why, story, of course. Keep up! Story is change and that is something they do not want, because maintaining the status quo is key to preserving their safety. Immortality is not the same as invincibility. Everything can die and the Grim Reaper will extract a terrible price from those who dare to put him on hold. The Founders know that those who control the story control the world, and so they worry, because it is far easier to hold back death than story. Ironically, as the slight librarian clutching her bag with the book inside walks with terrifying purpose towards her destination, they are nowhere near worried enough.

Back at the former church, up the stairs, skipping the dodgy step fourth from the top, we find ourselves in the reception area. The domain of Grace. She is the other guardian of this place, equally fierce in her own way. Her weapon of choice is a cup of tea, which might not sound like much, but you would be surprised how much can be achieved with such a thing. She is in the kitchen, brewing up, and breaking out the chocolate digestives in an endeavour to stop rancour from becoming rage as this motley crew battles to publish the final edition of the year.

Before you became a dead thing and forgot who you were, you may have come from a time when newspapers were towering institutions, feared by the powerful. Those times have passed. They are being washed away by the twin forces of technology and interpretive reality. People get to choose their own truth now, and the entire concept has been so pummelled and perverted as to be unrecognizable to itself. Here, though, this ragtag bunch fights against the dying of truth's light, for this is *The Stranger*

Times. It reports what has always been dismissed by many as fantasy, but some of which is far more real than the slanted truth to which the sceptics and naysayers cling so tightly. The world is full of magic and monsters, both metaphorical and terrifyingly real. The plastic tree in the corner, festooned with baubles and lights at Grace's insistence, attests to the fact that it will soon be Christmas, the opening of the greatest story ever told. (Or at least it is to those who have yet to experience *Battlefield Earth*.)

Through these doors we enter the bullpen – the main office space. The first person we meet is Stella, although 'person' may not be the right word. This teenager is not a teenager. She has no memory of the time before she ran away from her past life. Snippets are slowly coming back to her, and they pose more questions than they answer. A power lives within her that, in its own way, is far scarier than the one inhabiting Manny. Not least because nobody knows what it truly is, not even her.

As Stella works, trying to reorder words on a screen to make that which does not fit fit, there is a woman looking over her shoulder while trying very hard to look like she isn't. This is Hannah, the paper's assistant editor. Recently divorced, she has found a life here, a story she is happier to be a part of, but it is not without its problems. She is haunted by a recurring dream, something she is refusing to refer to as a vision, even to herself. In it, she sees sweet Stella laughing as she rains down destruction upon the world. There is that, and then there is also the fact that Hannah works for a man who is not the devil, because the devil has more charm. Or, at the very least, a better sense of personal hygiene.

At the desk behind her, typing away furiously, are Ox and Reggie. Ox, the misfit Mancunian battling his own personal demons, is a recovering gambling addict. He doesn't like his odds of making it. Reggie is another who is running from his past, and is so desperate to leave it behind that he now gladly wears the straitjacket of civility to hide the scars of brutality – his and other people's – that cover his skin.

Then, as we pass through the door on the far side of the room, we enter the lair of the beast himself. The boss. Vincent Banecroft – editor-in-chief and the first man to be banned from the corner shop for 'being himself'. He is currently half asleep, glass of rum in one hand, lit cigarette in the other. In his way, he is as content as he can be. With the deadline looming, in a moment he will get to shout at people, an anti-social habit he has somehow raised to the level of art form. Behind all of that, though, lies tragedy, too. Grief, regret. He was once the king of the world – or, at least, Fleet Street, which the British press has always secretly considered to be the same thing. How the mighty have fallen. Worse than that, though, he was once loved. Truly loved. And he not only lost that love, but he did terrible things in the mistaken belief he could get it back. Now he owes a debt to others, some of them in this very building, that he cannot repay. That is why he is still here. Well, that, and because the printing press downstairs needs feeding and, on a fundamental level, the best of him exists to feed the press.

But now, the ambulance has reached the hospital and the librarian has reached her destination, so this is as good a point as any to call our beginning. The staff of *The Stranger Times* think they are putting the last stories of the year to bed, but they are wrong. Their biggest story yet is hurtling towards them, and they cannot avoid it.

Oh, yes, I almost forgot. A ghoul called Brian also lives in the basement. You will find yourself inexplicably liking him, despite the fact he occasionally takes a poo in the corner.

Onwards.

1

Debra nodded a silent greeting to the others and opened the doors to the library. Normally, their group met on a Sunday night, after closing, but now the students were off for Christmas, the library closed early on several evenings, including tonight. The other three women filed in wordlessly behind her and she re-locked the door. Their usual chat was noticeable by its absence, instead replaced by nervous looks. If Debra had been thinking of such things, she might have seen in the faces of her friends hints of the children they once were, waiting excitedly to find out what Santa Claus had brought them.

They were allowed to be there. Debra was an assistant librarian after all and, as her boss, Maggie, had said, if a book club couldn't meet in a library, then where could they? Debra's flat was out as she had Mr Mittens, and Rose was allergic. They couldn't meet at Rose's either as her new flatmate was always there and not big on respecting personal space. Sue's husband and two kids struck her place off the list, and Michaela's was a no-go as her mother was living with her now. Besides, coming to the group was Michaela's respite and the one night a week she could leave the house while her otherwise useless sister stepped in to mum-sit for a few hours.

As Debra flicked on the lights and the group moved through reception, she clutched her bag to her chest. It was warm, almost as if energy was thrumming through it, which was ridiculous. Strangely, the book itself had been icily cold the one time she'd held it directly in her hands.

Sue said something but Debra didn't hear it. The whispers in her mind were too distracting.

Soon. Soon, now. Keep going.

She used her pass to open the gate beside the barriers, and led them into the staff room.

They really had started out as a book club. Initially, they'd attempted to skew themselves as more 'literary,' without expressly saying it, priding themselves on being a little more refined than the Richard & Judy Book Club crowd. That was until Michaela had picked a fantasy novel that had become one of those TikTok internet-sensation things. During their discussion of the book, after Rose's predictable diatribe about the sexualization of the female form, they'd moved the conversation on to the very idea of magic.

Sue was the one who'd brought in the book on modern witchcraft, in that sort of joking-but-deep-down-not-really way. Like, if the other's hadn't reacted to it well, she'd have laughed along with everyone else. They'd all taken a look, though. Rose had then found a particularly good essay online that explored how the term 'witch' was used throughout history primarily to silence any woman who dared to confront the heteronormative patriarchy. It had started with a bit of meditation, something that Michaela said her GP had been trying to get her into for years. From there, herbal remedies – the one Debra had found to help with her asthma really seemed to work, and Rose's attempt to make a relaxation concoction had given Debra embarrassingly loud wind for two days.

Still, they'd continued to dabble and research. It was amazing what you could find in a library, or order in. Nobody checked up on those kind of things, as long as you weren't ordering *Mein Kampf*. Even then, every university library worth its salt had a couple of copies of that – it was undoubtedly one of the most important books in history and needed to be available for academic study. If you tried to take it off the shelves, the staff would just spend a lot of time debating your hairstyle.

The first 'spell' they'd tried had been aimed at a man called Clive who worked with Sue at the bank. She assured them he was a very sweet guy who struggled greatly with halitosis. Unlike many fellow sufferers, he was aware of the issue, and it had steadily crushed his confidence over the last couple of years. Sue had discreetly taken a Garfield toy from Clive's desk, and together the group had followed the instructions from a book Rose had found in a New Age shop in Afflecks. They'd felt silly chanting and doing all the rest, but that was soon forgotten when Sue had reported back excitedly that since she'd returned the toy to his desk, Clive's breath had been as fresh as a summer's breeze. He was a new man. Unfortunately, the new man in question received a formal warning two weeks later for making a remark to a female customer which the branch manager deemed could be construed as being 'of a sexual nature', but they didn't let that affect their sense of achievement. Suddenly, everything felt possible.

From there, the triumphs kept on coming: Debra's cousin's psoriasis, a luck spell on Michaela's nephew who was struggling in his new school, and the cure for Sue's husband's 'little problem', which she had confided with a giggle had been a great success. So much so, in fact, that a couple of weeks later they'd performed another spell that endeavoured to reverse it.

The implosion of Rose's engagement when she learned her ex had been cheating on her was something of a watershed moment for the group. She'd found all manner of hexes to exact revenge on Callum and presented them to the others. They'd spent an entire session talking it through, and suddenly it was more like therapy than anything else. In the end, largely thanks to Sue, who was very good at this sort of thing, they got Rose to a 'living is the best revenge' headspace. The whole thing felt as if it'd brought the four of them closer together, though. Subsequently, when Rose had discovered that Callum had withdrawn all the money from their wedding savings account and used it to take his new girlfriend on holiday, there'd been universal agreement that all bets were off and they rolled out the spell they'd used to dampen Sue's husband's ardour. On this occasion they performed it with considerably more gusto. They'd been taken aback when Callum had been flown home from the Seychelles for medical treatment. Shaken, the group had held a meeting, where talk quickly turned to the whole thing being a coincidence. The spell had mentioned nothing about anything like that. The word 'coincidence' had been repeated by everyone again and again, as if they were invoking another spell that made it the truth. Still, from that moment on, they'd decided to focus on being only a positive force.

And they had. Sue's new job, Michaela's mum's anxiety, the botanical gardens at Fletcher Moss that had experienced 'incredible regrowth' after being damaged by hooligans – so much so that it'd made the newspaper. They were particularly proud of that one. It had been one positive after another. The thing about magic, though, was that there were limits on what could be achieved, given that none of the women had what one book termed 'innate talent', whatever that was supposed to mean. In practical terms, it meant that they'd needed to acquire objects with a certain power that could be harnessed.

While Debra may not have innate talent, it turned out that she had a knack for sensing which objects contained some intrinsic power. It was hard to pin down. Whatever this skill was, it had proved vital, as otherwise she would have been just another clueless wannabe buying up the tat that made up most of the stock at Paulo's Emporium in Afflecks. As they stood around in the library's staff room, a tiny voice in the back of Debra's mind shouted to be heard, reminding her that Paulo's had not been the source of this book.

What they were about to embark upon was by far and away their most ambitious project ever. A spell to open a powerful well of healing at Royal Manchester Children's Hospital. It wasn't going to cure all the patients, of course, but it would have a significant effect. It was Rose who'd first used the words 'Christmas miracle'. The timing couldn't be a coincidence. As Michaela had said, it was as if the universe had been leading them to this moment. She'd also mentioned that maybe, after this, if it worked, they could look at doing something for her mum. Earlier that day, Sue had gone down and planted a flower in the garden at the hospital, and now all they had to do was perform the spell.

Normally, before they got down to things, they'd have a cup of tea and a chat. Debra always brought biscuits because if there was one thing library staff took deathly seriously, it was biscuits. Heaven help anyone who just helped themselves. And then there was the espresso machine, gleaming like a new penny on the staff-room counter. Three members of staff had clubbed together to buy it, and it was quite the bone of contention. They'd had to have a special meeting about it and, after extensive negotiations, as the rather long and tersely worded sign on the wall beside it explained, it was for general use on Mondays and Fridays, pro-vided people brought in their own pods – with an amendment that only manufacturer-approved pods were to be used. More time had been spent negotiating a peaceful settlement around that espresso machine than had been spent resolving several rea-sonably sized armed conflicts.

Debra opened her bag. Today, it very definitely did not contain biscuits or coffee pods. She placed the book down on the table.

Rose wrinkled her nose. 'Is that leather?'

Debra found herself bristling internally at any criticism of the book. Before she could say anything, Sue – ever the diplomat – spoke up. 'Well, it's very old, isn't it? A different time.'

The only feature of the book's cover was an ouroboros – a snake eating its own tail.

Soon. Soon. Soon. Very soon.

'Right,' said Debra, feeling short of breath. 'I know we're all in a rush, so what do you say we crack on?' None of them was in a hurry to be anywhere else, but they could all feel it – the energy in the room.

Some furtive glances were exchanged. 'Have you brought the spell?' asked Sue.

'I've learned it off by heart,' said Debra, closing her eyes.

Now. Now. Now.

Without another word, she held out her hands. After a second, Sue took one and Michaela the other, both women then linking with Rose to complete the circle.

With the connection made, Debra started speaking. Something inside her was aware that the words leaving her mouth were not hers. Not only did she not know where they were coming from, but she didn't even understand them. They weren't in any language she recognized. Her mouth was forming shapes it never had before – guttural, harsh sounds that left a bitter taste in her mouth. She could feel the others tense, but it was too late now.

Something inside her desperately wanted to stop, even as the words kept coming. Pouring forth. Faster and faster. This was wrong. Terribly wrong.

She opened her eyes to see the others looking back at her in terror. The lights in the room were flickering and, somehow, inexplicably, given the absence of any open windows or doors, a wind was whipping around them, tearing flyers off the staff notice-board. Debra tried to let go of Michaela and Sue's hands but couldn't. She realized they were trying to do the same, writhing desperately, trying to break the connection but failing. And all the time, the words kept coming. Spilling forth like a torrent.

Debra noticed Rose's terrified gaze was now fixed on the book on the table in front of them. She looked down to see that the ouroboros was bleeding. Sticky, dark red, almost black blood had filled the debossing and was spreading across the rest of the cover and spilling on to the table.

And then, as her voice rose to a crescendo, her vision filled with red and every bulb in the room blew. The Christmas tree lights all popped in quick succession, like firecrackers at Chinese New Year. She found herself standing at the eye of the storm, the wind having stopped and the only light in the room emanating from the glowing book on the table in front of her. Her three friends lay dazed on the floor.

She looked around. Only 'she' didn't. She was no longer in control. Somehow, she was now a passenger in her own body. She could see through her eyes, but she wasn't in charge of where they were looking, or anything else. In her mind she screamed, but nothing came out. Instead, a jarringly deep laugh echoed round her head, before a voice growled at her, 'Silence, fool!'

She watched as her body, without any input from her, moved across the room and picked up the espresso machine, the red glow reflecting off its gleaming silver surface. She could feel her hands hold it, heft it, judge its weight.

Then, she, or whatever she was now, turned back towards the table, where she could see the other women pulling themselves to their feet. Looking around in shell-shocked confusion.

Suddenly, the tiny voice in her head was now hers.

Run! Run! Run!

She watched herself walk across the room. Sue gazed up at her, wide-eyed. 'What happened? Are you OK?'

Then, with a soul-swallowing dread, Debra watched helplessly as her own hands raised the espresso machine above her head and swung it downwards.

2

Hannah was not hovering.

Was she very close to hovering? Yes. But she felt she was a good foot further back from where Stella was sitting working to be just out of hovering range. It may've been a distinction that existed only in her own head, but it was a crucial one. She was the assistant editor, but she wanted to be one of those cool bosses who gave you space, trusted your instincts and, most crucially of all, didn't hover.

Stella stopped typing and scanned the text on the screen in front of her one last time.

When she spoke, it was in a disbelieving whisper. 'I . . . I think we're done.'

Hannah resisted the urge to lean over and start double-checking. Quite aside from anything else, Stella didn't make mistakes. She was such a natural with the publishing software that it was hard for the human eye to keep up.

'We're done?' said Ox, looking at his watch. 'It's seven fifty-nine p.m.'

Hannah had worked at *The Stranger Times* for just over nine months – although in that time it felt as if she'd crammed in a couple of lifetimes – but this was another novel experience. They had the latest edition good to go for eight o'clock on a Thursday night, the theoretical time it was meant to be ready to go to print every week. It was never ever ready on time. Never. Thursday nights always invariably turned into Friday mornings before the press started rolling. It said all you needed to know about the unprecedented nature of this event that, despite all the weird, wonderful and occasionally earth-shatteringly horrible things the staff of *The Stranger Times* had experienced together, it was one of those incredibly rare moments when they were rendered speechless.

It wasn't as if it had happened by accident. Hannah had been building up to this for weeks – ever since she'd realized how much it meant to Grace, their long-suffering office manager, to have a proper Christmas party. Admittedly, 'proper' was a relative term here. It would just be the eight of them standing around, attempting to make small talk in their office. Still, Grace did so much for them all and asked for so little in return that Hannah had become hyper-fixated on making this one thing happen.

She'd worked late several nights, making sure that many of the more general, broader pieces were done and dusted early. Reggie's yearly review of ghostly activities and Ox's euphemistically titled 'Turned Out Nice Again' piece, in which he went through all the various religions, cults, psychics, soothsayers and, in at least one case, aquatic mammals who had predicted that the world was definitely going to end this year, and how it disappointingly hadn't. Both pieces were something of a tradition now, as Hannah had discovered when she'd read some of the previous years' Christmas editions to get a feel for them. The most surprising thing was how many of Ox's runners and riders reappeared time and again. Naively, Hannah had assumed that proclaiming an imminent apocalypse only to end up with egg on your face might discourage those people from doing so again. It did not.

Along with those big articles, there was all the weekly news that made up the majority of the paper. She'd felt bad doing it, but Hannah had told Reggie that they were printing a day early, which meant he'd been able to get his habitual deadline-day histrionics out of his system yesterday. He'd looked rather hurt when he'd found out the truth, but he also knew why she'd done it.

In all honesty, Hannah had no idea why Grace had become fixated on having a Christmas party. Reggie and Ox said they'd never had one before, even in the pre-Banecroft days when the newspaper was a very different affair. They had discussed going out somewhere but rejected the idea as Manny literally couldn't leave the building and Brian the ghoul, now resident in their basement, still hadn't mastered the finer points of where and when was optimal to go for a poo. All that aside, Hannah would still rather take her chances with Brian showing them up than Banecroft. She'd spent an entire weekend trying to picture their boss in a karaoke bar or a restaurant, but her brain kept rejecting the idea, like the body would if you replaced a kidney with a sandwich toaster.

So, a Christmas office party in their actual office it would be. Grace had put on quite the spread, and with all the festive decorations, the old place was looking positively Christmassy. Banecroft had moaned about decorations being overpriced tat, only for Grace to explain cheerfully that she enjoyed making them by hand. She had a flair for it, too. She'd made baubles out of cupcake cases, glittery stars out of clothes pegs, swans out of pine cones . . . The list went on. The office was positively festooned in hand-crafted Christmas cheer and the biggest challenge in getting work done all day had been avoiding being distracted by the enticing food smells emanating from their humble kitchen. Grace had even made a playlist which Stella had confided excitedly didn't even contain that much Jesus-y music.

Now it was eight o'clock and, against all odds and precedent, this week's edition of the paper was ready to be put to bed.

'Perhaps I could—' started Reggie.

'No,' said Ox, cutting him off. 'You're done. We're done. It is done.'

Reggie bit his lip and nodded.

'Right, then,' said Stella, looking at Hannah. 'Time for you to tell Ebenezer Scrooge.'

They all jumped as Banecroft spoke. 'No need, and we're done when I say we're done.'

Hannah spun around to see him standing a few feet away from her. 'On the very rare occasions you want to be, Vincent, you can be remarkably quiet.'

'I'm like the wind,' he responded. 'Whispering softly through every nook and cranny of this place.' He emphasized his point by passing wind, an ability Hannah had long since resigned herself to accepting their editor had somehow trained himself to do on demand.

'Vincent!' admonished Grace, walking in from the reception area. 'Please comport yourself with the expected level of decorum.'

'I don't think we can consider what just happened unexpected,' said Reggie.

'I hear that we are done?' said Grace, hope shining in her eyes.

'We're done when I say we're done,' repeated Banecroft huffily. He turned to Stella. 'Did you move the graffitiing ghost—'

'To page four?' she finished. 'Yes, I did.'

'What about—'

'Alien abduction in Altrincham is now on page two, along with the picture of the survivor in question holding a copy of the book he wrote about his experiences. There's also the review you wrote, right there beside it, pointing out that he's lifted chunks of it from the script of *E. T.* and Leonard Nimoy's autobiography, *I Am Spock*.'

'The man's a charlatan.'

Hannah assumed Banecroft was referring to the alien-abduction author as opposed to Nimoy, but if you wanted to get anywhere, it paid not to ask follow-up questions.

'I've also triple-checked the crossword,' continued Stella, 'alphabetized the small ads, reworked page six as you requested, and cut the fourth line in the "Haunting at Town Hall" article.'

'That was a fine piece of prose,' sniffed Reggie.

'You're not writing prose,' barked Banecroft. 'You're supposed to be writing news.'

'He did,' said Hannah. 'We did. It is done. Vincent, can we please just say it is done and send it to press?'

Hannah locked eyes with her boss. She had also laid the groundwork with him that for once in his life, he wouldn't be awkward when it came to going to press. He hadn't agreed as such – Banecroft never actually agreed to anything – but he hadn't protested too much either, which was as good as anyone would ever get from him.

After a long moment, Banecroft relented. 'Fine.' His facial expression indicated that uttering that one word may have caused him actual physical pain.

'OK,' said Stella, as the room collectively let out a sigh of relief. 'We are ready to go. I just need to . . .'

Her computer warbled one of those irritating synth-trumpet flourishes.

'What the actual f—'

'Stella!' admonished Grace.

Stella ignored her. She pushed back her chair and pointed at the screen, upon which a skull wearing a cheery Christmas hat had appeared. 'Is this . . . Is somebody messing with me?'

'It's on my screen, too,' said Reggie.

'And mine,' added Ox.

'If this is someone's idea of a joke,' started Hannah, 'we all like a laugh, but this might not be the best time.' She was technically addressing the room while trying hard not to look at Ox.

'No,' he responded, the resentment in his voice indicating he knew precisely at whom Hannah's words were directed. 'It definitely isn't.'

They all looked around as the cackling laugh of a roughly animated skull emanated from every set of PC speakers in the room.

'What kind of bargain-bin Hollywood histrionics is this?' barked Banecroft. 'I don't like anyone laughing around here, least of all the glorified appliances.'

The skull disappeared to be replaced by a screen full of text.

'Oh God,' said Ox. 'Comic Sans. The true sign of an unhinged mind.'

'"Dear *Stranger Times*,"' began Stella, reading out the message for the group, '"the day of judgement is at hand."'

Grace blessed herself twice.

'"For too long you have refused to share the truth with the world. That ends now or you will never produce another newspaper again. You know what you have to do." And then it's signed C. A. Horntail.' Stella walloped her keyboard, trying in vain to regain some form of control.

'Don't click on anything,' said Reggie. 'It might be a virus.'

'Excellent warning,' said Stella. 'Only, a – we've clearly already got a virus, and b – this thing has already got complete control of my computer.'

'Who the hell is C. A. Horntail?' asked Hannah.

'It doesn't matter,' snarled Banecroft. 'We will not negotiate with terrorists!'

Grace sighed and Hannah felt a pang of guilt. 'Of course not, but maybe we could—'

'Never! And nobody leaves until we figure this out. First off, I would love to know how our security was compromised. Perhaps our head of IT security could explain?'

Banecroft turned and glowered at Ox, who raised his palms defensively. 'Whoa, whoa, whoa! How am I the IT guy? What? Just because I'm Asian?'

'Oh, heavens,' said Reggie. 'That is just racist.'

'Yep,' agreed Stella.

Grace tsked pointedly.

'That is a bit . . .' Hannah started without knowing where she was heading.

'If you've all finished galloping around on your high horses,' said Banecroft, 'the reason he is the head of IT is that three years ago the newspaper paid rather a lot to send him on a security course.'

'We did?' said Reggie, surprised. 'How would you even know that? You weren't here three years ago. Neither was I, for that matter.'

'It's in his personnel file.'

'OK,' said Ox, stepping up, 'now that you mention it, there was a week-long course, and I was supposed to go on it, but . . . in the spirit of honesty and making amends, I should admit that the money went to pay off some gambling debts.'

Hannah winced. Ox, as they all knew, was a recovering gambling addict, something she had discussed with Banecroft several times in an effort to encourage him to be sensitive about the matter. It was rather like trying to fix climate change by asking the sun to go easy, but she'd nevertheless felt compelled to try.

'Well,' said Banecroft, 'ironically, it seems you've gambled with our security, and lost.'

'It was years ago,' said Ox. 'Whatever I might have learned

would be useless now. Hackers are always coming up with new stuff. It'd be like trying to stand up to tanks with a bow and arrow.'

'We don't even have anti-virus software,' added Reggie.

'That's because we apparently blew the entire IT budget on the four fifteen at Kempton,' said Banecroft.

'Be fair,' interjected Stella. 'Our systems are so woefully out of date, this was inevitable. I mean, seriously, we're running something called Windows 98 on most of the computers. That's from, like, the last century.'

'Yes,' said Reggie, 'we're the only people on the planet who still get to see the Microsoft paperclip. He popped up last week and asked me why I wouldn't let him die. It was tremendously disturbing.'

'A bad worker always blames his tools.'

'As do people who have extremely bad tools,' countered Reggie.

'They have a point,' said Hannah. 'And, more importantly, the blame game isn't getting us anywhere.'

Banecroft narrowed his eyes. 'Spoken like someone who opened an attachment.'

'We all open attachments. People send us all manner of weird stuff every week.'

'Yeah,' agreed Stella. 'Pretty much everything on page nine came from an attachment.' She looked at her screen forlornly. 'Or at least it did . . .'

'Don't we have a back-up?' asked Hannah.

'Where? We don't even have a printer after last week's . . . incident.'

'Oh, I see,' said Banecroft, 'we're trying to deflect the blame for this catastrophe on to me, are we? Like somehow it's my fault that our printer could neither print nor stand up to a spirited attempt to resolve the issue.'

'Resolve the issue?' repeated Grace, exasperated. 'You threw it out the window!'

'Pressure makes diamonds,' responded Banecroft.

'What does that even mean in this scenario?' asked Reggie. 'Are you claiming it's the printer's fault that it didn't survive being thrown out of a second-floor window?'

'Nothing is built to last any more.'

'All right,' said Hannah, raising her voice. 'Enough! Everybody just calm down. I'm sure we can sort this out if we work as a team.'

She glanced at Stella to make the point that she'd both heard and not appreciated the scoffing noise. 'Hang on,' said Hannah, 'we managed to print the paper before, when the police took the computers away.'

'Yeah,' said Stella, 'but back then, Manny had the pictures already and we had the articles on my phone. I don't have any of that this time . . .'

'Hannah's right,' said Banecroft. 'Batten down the hatches. Christmas is cancelled and nobody is leaving until we sort this out.'

'Wait. What? I didn't say that. When did I say that?' exclaimed Hannah.

Banecroft clapped his hands together and flopped down into a chair. 'Grace?'

Grace shook her head. 'I'll go and get the grudge file.'

'The grudge file?' echoed Stella.

'Wait a sec,' said Ox. 'Speaking of files, can we go back to the fact that, apparently, we all have personnel files?'

'I found them in the bottom drawer of my desk last week,' said Banecroft, 'while I was searching for a thing I had mislaid.'

'Or already drank,' said Stella.

Banecroft ignored Stella's jibe entirely, as he often seemed to do. She was the only one afforded such a luxury. 'The files must have been put there by my predecessor.'

'Barry kept files on us?' asked Ox, looking horrified.

'Yes, as well as one folder full of fan fiction of an erotic nature, which he'd written about a duo of former morning TV presenters. Frankly, it's upsettingly graphic.'

'I demand to see it,' said Reggie, before blushing. 'My personnel file, I mean.'

'Sure,' said Banecroft. 'We're under attack but let's take this time to process your freedom of information request. Grace, what's taking so long?'

'As always, Vincent, no need to shout,' she said, returning to the room and holding up a large manilla folder. 'Here you go.'

'That's the grudge file?' asked Hannah, shocked by the size of the thing.

Grace gave a humourless laugh. 'Oh no, this is just A to D.' She looked pointedly at Banecroft. 'Hard as it is to believe, we have been irritating quite a lot of people recently.'

'If you're not annoying people,' said Banecroft, 'you're not doing real journalism.'

Ox sat down heavily in his chair. 'Congratulations, boss. You're a massive journalist.'

3

A phone call in the middle of the night was never good news, at least not in DI Tom Sturgess's experience. On the drive into the city centre, he'd found himself musing on what might be considered good news in such a situation. 'Congratulations, you're a grandma/grandad, mother and child are doing well.' That'd be one possibility, he supposed. Unlikely in his case, seeing as he didn't have kids and, given the current state of his romantic life, that wasn't going to be changing any time soon. Similarly, booty calls, as the kids called them, were a non-starter. He was mid-thirties, single and in decent shape. He couldn't help thinking that they probably shouldn't be beyond the realm of possibility, but the twin issues of his unhealthy obsession with work and his inability to keep a relationship going . . .

Still, no time to think about that now. If he ever was going to get good news in the middle of the night, the call would definitely not be coming from DI Sam Clarke. The pair had never got on even before Sturgess had gone into his 'area of speciality', as a senior officer had euphemistically referred to it. He knew for a fact it was Clarke who had come up with the rather more direct term of 'weirdy bollocks' that had inevitably caught on with the rank and file. Clarke had a talent for nicknames, bullies always did, and that's what the man was. Sturgess instinctively railed against such behaviour, which meant their mutual animosity had been written in the stars. Unfortunately, while Clarke was a bully, he was also an expert social climber, so despite his minimal talent for the job, he was one of Greater Manchester Police's rising stars, while Sturgess was, as far as he was aware, the only officer ever to be given their own off-site office in a determined effort to forget they existed. The force would have happily got rid of him, only his 'area of speciality' kept awkwardly popping up.

What made the phone call from Clarke even more of a surprise was the fact that it was the first Sturgess had heard from Clarke in a couple of months. Back in the autumn, using information obtained entirely by Sturgess, Clarke's highly vaunted drug taskforce had raided a farm out in Saddleworth in what they'd expected to be an easy win and a photo opportunity. Sturgess had tried in vain to advise them otherwise. Still, when they had come face to face with weirdy bollocks that even Clarke couldn't explain away, suddenly Clarke was no longer the golden boy. Two members of the armed response unit had been killed and, while the subsequent hastily convened inquiry had been an elaborate fabrication from start to finish, some of the stink had inevitably ended up on Clarke.

The call had been brief. 'We need you at the Man Met University Library in the John Dalton building right now. Chief's orders.'

And so here Sturgess was. He pulled up behind a car he recognized. DS Andrea Wilkerson was standing beside it, takeaway cup of coffee in one hand, can of Diet Coke in the other. She nodded at him. 'Guv.'

'Sorry about this, Andrea.'

She shrugged. 'Sleep is overrated. At least this way I don't have to go to the gym.' She handed him the drinks can as they fell into step together.

'You're a lifesaver,' said Sturgess, opening it.

'So they say. Any more info?'

'Nothing. Just said, "Get here now."'

'Clarke – helpful as always, then.'

If anything, Wilkerson seemed to have a lower opinion of the DI than Sturgess did, but he'd never got to the bottom of why exactly. Recently, she'd been moved over to working with Sturgess full-time, a tacit acknowledgement by somebody somewhere that in the last six months there'd been a dramatic increase in incidents that fell into his 'area of speciality'. He very much doubted there existed anywhere within the GMP machine a piece of paper that stated exactly what that meant.

Manchester Met University, or MMU, was one of the city's two major universities, or 'the other one', depending on who you asked. The institutions seemed to be expanding constantly, combining excellent reputations with the fact that kids wanted to come to Manchester because the nightlife sounded considerably more fun than, say, Hull. All of which meant the higher-ups were sensitive about anything that involved either establishment. The library building had a very seventies look to it, increasingly outdated compared to the shiny modern structures surrounding it. Sturgess had a vague recollection of reading somewhere that they were trying to knock it down and replace it with a gleaming, thirteen-storey behemoth, no doubt overflowing with knowledge.

At 3.32 a.m., the area around the campus was as quiet as a hub like Oxford Road ever got. Stragglers walking home from the clubs wandered by, against the flow of power walkers heading to jobs with early starts. Ahead of Sturgess and Wilkerson, two female PCs were standing by a line of police tape, doing their best to shoo away a handful of looky-loos that included a girl leaning against her tall boyfriend in a way that suggested she could do with lying down before she fell down.

As the pair approached, Sturgess could pick out the young lad's clipped accent, slightly slurred but nevertheless brimming with confidence as he spoke to one of the uniforms. 'I am a student at this university and I therefore have the right to know what is going on.'

'No,' said the older of the officers, sounding as weary as Sturgess felt, 'you don't, sir. Now, please move along.'

She threw a nod in Sturgess and Wilkerson's direction. Impressively, given the conversation, she held back the eye roll.

'I demand to speak to your superior,' persisted the young lad.

'Jacob,' said the girlfriend in a whine of exhaustion, 'can we just—'

'It's a matter of principle.'

Wilkerson stopped. 'DS Andrea Wilkerson, sir. I'm happy to be of . . .' She paused. 'Sorry, I can't help but notice that you have flushed cheeks and your pupils appear dilated. You haven't consumed any illegal narcotics this evening, by any chance?'

The girlfriend, with a sudden burst of energy, extricated herself from under Jacob's arm and started to walk away. The flush disappeared from Jacob's face. 'A-absolutely not,' he stammered. 'I am . . . I can see you're busy, officers. Carry on.'

With that, he spun away to catch up with his girlfriend, who appeared all set to break into a run.

Wilkerson turned back to the uniforms with a grin. 'Did that little sperm just tell me to carry on?'

Sturgess held his tongue until they'd both dipped under the police tape and started making their way towards the library doors. Even then, all he did was raise an eyebrow in his colleague's direction.

'Doesn't do any harm to keep the uniforms onside,' Wilkerson said.

'And you enjoyed it.'

'And I enjoyed it.'

As they headed down the path between the library and the park, Sturgess noticed someone in a crime scene suit through the large glass windows. Whoever the tech was leaped over the turnstiles inside with surprising dexterity and slammed through the revolving doors with enough force that the PC on duty jumped. As they spun round the corner, Wilkerson and Sturgess saw the tech pull down his mask and throw up. They exchanged another look. With his face covering removed, they spotted the highly recognizable ginger moustache of John Brooker. A seasoned vet with at least a decade's experience under his belt.

Neither of them said anything, but their shock said it all. What the hell had a seasoned pro like Brooker losing his dinner?

Sturgess caught a glimpse of Brooker pushing the on-duty PC away, but they otherwise paid him the courtesy of ignoring him entirely as they pushed their way through the revolving doors.

On the other side of the turnstiles, Sturgess caught sight of DI Clarke in hushed conversation with a DS he didn't recognize. Four other people were sitting in reception. One was a fresh-faced, terrified-looking security guard, then there was a woman in the garb of a cleaner, who appeared extremely pissed off. Near by was a woman of about sixty comforting a portly man in his thirties, who was sobbing into a hanky. As Wilkerson and Sturgess approached, the unfamiliar DS turned and headed back to the quartet of civilians.

As Clarke clocked his colleagues, he set his face into a determinately neutral expression. 'Tom. Andrea.' He jerked his head. 'It's through this way.'

Once they'd walked a few feet, Clarke stopped and spoke in a lowered voice. 'We've got multiple fatalities.'

'Right,' said Sturgess. 'Who discovered them – the cleaner or the security guard?'

'Neither. It was one of the librarians. A Richard Duff.'

Wilkerson looked back at the group in reception. 'He came into work in the middle of the night?'

'Apparently. He'd agreed it beforehand with his boss – he was due to catch a flight later today and didn't want to use up a day's leave,' Clarke blew out his cheeks. 'Along with everything else he's been through, he ain't taking that flight. Poor bastard.'

If Sturgess hadn't already been on edge, Clarke showing basic human compassion for someone who wasn't himself would have set alarm bells ringing. 'What else do we know?' he asked.

'We believe the victims are members of a book group, if you can believe that. They hold their meetings in the staff room on a Thursday evening. Normally, the library would still have been open, but Christmas holidays mean reduced hours.'

'So the members are all library staff?'

Clarke shook his head. 'No. We think a couple of them were, including Debra Brimson, who we'll get to – the others were possibly uni staff or outsiders. I've got Rhys going through CCTV now to try and identify who exactly came in last night and didn't leave. We . . .' He paused. 'We aren't sure about the number of victims. Three or four.' Clarke caught Wilkerson's confused expression. 'IDing is a nightmare, as you're about to see. The scene is . . . not good.'

Sturgess nodded. He'd never seen Clarke like this. 'And nobody noticed anything until Mr Duff . . .'

Clarke shook his head and gave a laugh devoid of any mirth. 'As daft as it sounds, neither security nor the cleaners have gone into the staff area for over a fortnight. It seems there's been quite the set-to over two-thirds of a birthday cake that disappeared.'

'For Christ's sake,' muttered Wilkerson.

'Yeah. The alarm was only raised when the cleaner heard Duff screaming.'

'But we know this Debra Brimson is one of the victims?' asked Sturgess.

Clarke shook his head again. 'No. We've got her on CCTV just over two hours ago, calmly walking out of here covered in blood.'

'So we think she's the killer?'

'I guess,' said Clarke.

'You *guess*?' said Sturgess, failing to keep the incredulity from his voice.

Something in Clarke kicked in and he bristled. 'I've got a general alert out for her and units sitting on her address. She can't have gone far looking like that. But you haven't seen the scene. It's hard to believe a woman, one woman, could do this.'

'I see. Sounds like a right mess, but you're sure this is . . . one for us?'

Clarke had been known to dump crap in Sturgess's direction if it looked as if it might damage his all-important case-closing stats, but this was inevitably going to be high profile and he already had what sounded like a locked-in prime suspect. Whatever this was, it wasn't Clarke playing politics.

'It's . . .' Clarke looked up and made direct eye contact with Sturgess for the first time. 'Probably best you see for yourself.'

With that, he led them around the corner to the crime scene.

4

'There ain't no party like a *Stranger Times* party!' At least that was what the home-made sign on the wall said. Actually, it didn't. The original version Grace had made had indeed said that, but Hannah had noticed her glancing up at it every time she passed through reception. It had survived in its original incarnation until about 3 p.m. when it was replaced with a new sign that stated, 'There is no party like a *Stranger Times* party', which was both more grammatically correct and fitting for the bleak mood that hung over the office.

Technically, many elements of Grace's plan for the evening's festivities were still present – the staff were all sitting around talking and, after a couple of hours, when it became apparent that the problem of what Banecroft kept laughingly referring to as *The Stranger Times'* 'IT systems' having been taken over by a hacker was not going to be resolved quickly, if at all, with a resigned sigh, Grace had started to distribute the spread of party food she had lovingly assembled. Hannah felt terrible about how the evening had turned out but unfortunately their current predicament had blown all their best laid plans to smithereens.

In the – Hannah glanced at her watch – good god, six and a

half hours and counting since the mysterious and massively irritating C. A. Horntail had completely taken over every computer in the building, their hacker had engaged in what could loosely be termed as communication. Every now and then, seemingly at random, the laughing skull in the Santa Claus hat on their screens disappeared to be replaced with either cat pictures or an animation of two frogs having 'relations'. It spoke to how well the staff's attempts to figure out who this Horntail person was going that Stella had spent an hour taking pictures of the cats with her phone and doing a Google image search in the hope that perhaps one of the felines was owned by somebody local. It was a monumental stretch, and one that had led nowhere, but it still constituted the best avenue of investigation they'd come up with so far.

About an hour ago, Reggie had pointed out that they should stop referring to Horntail as a man. It was equally possible that they could be a woman. While it had been a good point well made, it depressingly expanded their range of suspects from half the population of the planet to the entirety of it.

Beyond being assigned various so far pointless tasks by Banecroft, most of the staff had been sitting round the bullpen, going through the aptly titled 'grudge files'. They contained all the correspondence *The Stranger Times* had received that could be broadly categorized as complaints, which ranged from irritations at the crossword to death threats and, in one case, both of those things at the same time. It was a very disturbing collection, both in terms of the contents of the letters or emails Grace had printed out, back when they'd had a printer, and in its sheer volume. Even with several of them working their way through the pile, they hadn't even made it halfway through, and time was running out. The newspaper had to be printed and loaded on to the trucks by 6 a.m. Nobody needed reminding of that, and yet . . .

'Come on, people,' roared Banecroft. 'We've got a paper to get printed and on to the trucks by six a.m.'

'Really?' said Ox. 'I thought the first forty times you'd mentioned that you'd been joking, but I get it now.'

Banecroft narrowed his eyes. 'Of all the people to be engaging in sarcasm right now, for our head of IT to do so is a rather bold decision.'

'Oh, stop blaming him,' said Hannah. 'He didn't wind up this Horntail nutter.'

'We don't know that,' said Reggie, which earned him a glare from both Ox and Hannah. He smiled apologetically and clarified quickly, 'I mean, we have no clue what set this individual off. It could be something any of us wrote or didn't write or . . .' Reggie let his sentence trail off. None of them needed reminding about how clueless they were.

They'd been scanning the grudge correspondence for anything signed C. A. Horntail or some such variation of the name. Grace had also pointed out that the written message on the screen used a version of Comic Sans that featured a weird backwards R, so they were on the lookout for that, too. Along with any mention of cats or frogs. As Ox had rather succinctly put it, it was less like looking for a needle in a haystack and more like looking for a particular loose screw in a mountain of loose screws. It was enough to turn someone to drink except, of course, nobody dared touch any of the dozen or so bottles of wine that were set out beside the food. Nobody, that was, except for their editor, who was already on to his second.

Stella held up a letter written in a small, neat script. 'This person seems very angry about us either not taking the threat from toxic seaweed seriously enough or too seriously – it's hard to tell. They also include a hand-drawn picture of Paul Holly-wood from *The Great British Bake Off*.'

'That's odd,' said Reggie, 'I've got one here that rants about how Canada is secretly in charge of the new world order before segueing into a couple of pages about the territorial instincts of the Canada goose, then ending with a portrait of Paul Hollywood.'

Stella and Reggie held up their respective drawings.

Grace gave both pieces of artwork an assessing look. 'I think the seaweed person has captured his smile better, but Canada goose got his eyes.'

'Unless you'd like to put forward whoever this Hollywood person is as a suspect,' said Banecroft, 'then where is this get-ting us?'

'My point was,' said Reggie, 'perhaps we should start another pile?'

'No,' said Hannah quickly. 'Sorry, but by my count we already have fourteen different piles. We do not need a Paul Hollywood pile. Put the goose person in the crazy-animals pile and the sea-weed in the the-end-is-nigh pile.'

'What is the point of all the piles again?' asked Reggie.

'They're . . . We're . . .'

'Organizing?' offered Grace.

'Yeah. That.' Hannah was painfully aware of how weak it sounded. She'd been thinking the same thing herself. This all seemed utterly pointless. It was just that they couldn't think of anything else.

Ox attempted to lighten the mood by picking up an item from his plate of party food. 'These little Yorkshire puddings full of stuff are ace, Gracie. Absolutely banging.'

'They're not Yorkshire puddings, you ignoramus,' barked Banecroft. 'They're vol-au-vents.'

'What's the difference?'

'One is . . .' started Banecroft, before losing a bit of steam, 'made of something, and the other is made of something else. And besides, aren't you supposed to be working on a technical solution to this problem rather than shovelling food into your face?'

'For the last time, I've attempted to reboot each of the machines, I've restarted them in safe mode, which did nothing, and I've done a full reset and diagnostic on the network. There's eff-all else I can do.'

Stella spoke without looking up from the latest letter she was reading. 'When you say a full reset and diagnostic on the network . . .'

Ox shifted in his seat and threw daggers in her direction, which went entirely unnoticed by their target. 'I rebooted the wifi. Twice.'

'Twice?' repeated Banecroft. 'It's rare to be in the presence of a true master.'

'Stop it, Vincent,' said Grace, before turning to Hannah. 'And that computer lady you know is definitely unavailable?'

Cathy Quirke, the grandma from Salford with a certain genius for computer manipulation whom they'd worked with previously, had been Hannah's first thought. She shook her head. 'Her voicemail is very clear – she's gone on one of those week-long yoga retreats where there aren't any phones and you don't even speak.'

'Really?' said Grace. 'I've never heard of such a thing.'

'That's because they're a ridiculous affectation dreamt up by work-shy hippies,' said Banecroft. 'Who in their right mind needs that much silence?'

The rest of *The Stranger Times* staff studiously avoided making eye contact with each other as they undoubtedly shared the same thought. Anyone who spent much time in the vicinity of their boss quickly came to appreciate the value of blissful silence.

At the sound of whooping and clapping from the far end of the room, the staff all looked up to where Brian the ghoul was jumping up and down on a chair in delight. Once you got used to his gangly yet stooped appearance, his lank hair and bulging eyes, and his skin's oddly waxy sheen, there was a childlike innocence to him that was somewhat endearing.

Sitting opposite him was Manny, fully dressed, thankfully, with his long mass of distinctive white dreadlocks tied back. He gave a toothy smile and nodded at the game between them. 'Him connected four again.'

'Well done, Brian,' said Grace in her best matronly voice, 'but do sit down or you will hurt yourself.'

Brian nodded, did as he was asked and returned his focus to the game. It had not gone unnoticed that since he'd become their sort of lodger, living in the basement of the church, Grace had taken a considerable interest in him. It was she who'd tried to insist that it was unhealthy to live in a place that contained all manner of things, the least of which was a crypt, but Brian had kept returning there whenever they'd tried to set him up anywhere else. As Reggie had pointed out, given that the primary focus of a ghoul's existence was to ensure the sanctity of the resting places of the dead, the basement might seem like a natural choice of habitat to him. Comforting, even.

Ox had also been put in charge of attempting to toilet train Brian, a task he was handling almost as well as he was being the paper's head of IT security. In his defence, Hannah didn't have the first idea how you might go about training a grown, well, sort of, man to do such a thing, and she was glad she wasn't the one Grace had appointed to make it happen. While Brian never spoke, he did seem to understand certain things, just not advice about the delights of modern plumbing. Beyond exchanging a couple of knowing looks with Stella, neither she nor anyone else had said anything when Brian had turned up to the party that wasn't a party wearing a dickie bow and having apparently brushed his hair. As Stella had commented earlier in the week, Grace appeared to be trying to *My Fair Lady* him, which, if nothing else, would be a process worth watching.

Reggie held up a see-through plastic wallet containing a sheet of paper. 'Grace, why is this letter in here?'

'Do not open it, Reginald.'

'But—'

'Let me put it this way,' said Grace. 'There is a reason I always wear gloves while opening the post.'

'Oh,' he said. Then, after a moment, horrified realization spread across his face. 'Oh, good God!' he howled, dropping the thing as if it were on fire.

Ox leaned across excitedly and inspected it. 'What do we reckon – blood or—'

'There is no need to speculate, thank you very much,' interjected Grace.

'When you think about it,' continued Ox, 'it's sort of like recycling, isn't it?'

'No,' said Hannah, 'it definitely isn't.'

'I don't know what is more depressing,' said Reggie, 'the fact that it's written in who knows what or the fact that it's one of the few letters I've read so far that didn't contain any spelling mistakes.'

'What's it about?' asked Stella.

'Oh, just the standard how dare we "the mainstream media" keep peddling these lies about mobile phone masts. I've done my own research and so on and so on.'

'Where do these people get off calling us mainstream?' asked Ox. 'Last week we ran an article about a bloke in Arkansas who claimed his meat and two veg could be used to divine water. Let's see the BBC cover that!'

'It's only a matter of time before he'll be chatting it up on *The One Show*,' said Reggie. 'I am so utterly sick of the phrase "do your own research", though. Like a peer-reviewed academic study and a forum post from someone called ElvisIsn'tDead429 should carry equal weight.'

'Too right,' said Ox, stabbing a finger at the letter. 'This guy's opinion isn't worth the excrement it's written in.'

'Ox!' said Grace.

'What? I didn't do it.'

'Enough of this jibber-jabber,' said Banecroft, standing up abruptly and knocking over his chair. 'Let's recap what we know.'

'That shouldn't take long,' said Stella.

Banecroft ignored her and instead wiped the office whiteboard clean before dragging it into the centre of the bullpen. The staff winced collectively as its wheels squeaked painfully.

Reggie threw a look at Grace, who folded her arms defiantly. 'I am not buying any more 3-in-One oil until whoever took the last can brings it back.'

'Right,' said Banecroft, slapping his hands together and picking up a red marker. He sounded out 'C. A. Horntail' as he wrote the name on the board, then wrote another word below it. Or at least he got most of the way through it before Grace snapped 'Vincent!' at him. He thew her a sullen glance before rubbing it out and replacing it with the word 'bastard'.

'That is also a bad word,' said Grace.

'Can't be,' said Banecroft. 'It's in the Bible.'

Grace looked somewhere between confused and defiant. 'Well . . . it is not in any of the good bits.'

'So,' continued Banecroft, 'what do we know so far?'

'Nothing,' said Ox.

'Wrong. We know several things.' Banecroft returned to the board and began to bullet point under 'bastard'. 'We know he—'

'Or she,' interjected Reggie.

'Or she,' conceded Banecroft reluctantly.

Stella pointed at her computer screen to where the two frogs were back at it. 'To be fair, the whole thing's got a very male vibe.'

Banecroft wrote the word 'unhinged' on the board. 'We are dealing with an unstable individual.'

'That narrows it down,' said Reggie.

'We know they are tech savvy,' continued Banecroft, adding 'nerd' to the list. 'And what else?'

Banecroft looked around the room expectantly. Nobody said anything.

'Unbelievable,' he said, shaking his head. 'Room full of sup-posed journalists and—'

'Local,' interrupted Stella.

Banecroft tilted his head towards her. 'How so?'

'He knows when we print the paper and timed this to cause maximum inconvenience. So, local, or at least knows how we work.'

Banecroft nodded. 'And that's why she is my favourite.'

'And,' said Reggie, 'they've clearly got a grudge against us.'

'Or do they?' said Hannah. 'Perhaps we're thinking about this all wrong. I mean, do all hackers have grudges? Maybe they're just enjoying messing with us?'

Banecroft tapped the marker against his chin as he considered this. 'Hannah is right.'

'Wait. What? I am?' said Hannah, suddenly alarmed. If this job had taught her anything it was that when their editor said anyone except himself was right about anything it was often followed swiftly by a kick to the head. 'I mean, it might just be—'

'It could be someone who is an admirer of the paper. Grace, get the fan-mail folder.'

Banecroft's request raised a groan from the group.

Grace sighed as she got to her feet and patted Hannah on the shoulder. 'Don't worry, it's a lot smaller than the grudge file.'

Shock Clock

Experts have revealed that the Doomsday Clock – the metaphorical representation of how close humanity is to global catastrophe – has exploded. The clock, which began ticking in 1947 with the hands set at seven minutes to midnight, had edged forward to just one minute and twenty-nine seconds as of January 2025. This new development has left scientists both confused and deeply alarmed. Professor Richard Winkleworth commented, 'I know what you're thinking: how can a metaphor explode? We have literally no bloody idea, but I'll tell you now, it's not a good sign, is it? I mean, is it? We don't know, but I'm stocking up on canned goods regardless.'

5

Fifteen minutes after they'd entered the MMU Library, DI Sturgess and DS Wilkerson re-emerged through its doors, crossed the path to the entrance of the park wordlessly and slipped under the police tape. They moved over to one side and only then did Wilkerson pull out her cigarettes and, with shaking hands, light one up. Once she'd taken a couple of drags, she spoke for the first time since the pair had signed out of the crime scene. 'Jesus.'

'I know.'

'I mean . . . Jesus!'

'It's—'

'That,' she said with a catch in her voice. 'I've seen plenty in my time but that, that's . . . I mean, the writing and then . . . What the actual fuck?' She flicked some ash away. 'I've never seen anything like that.'

'Me neither. I don't think anyone has.'

She ran the fingers of her free hand through her hair. 'Sorry, Tom, I'll pull myself together in a minute.'

'Take your time. It'll take me a lot longer than that. I'm just glad I didn't eat before I came here.'

'Yeah,' she said quietly. 'Yeah.'

The pair stood in silence as Wilkerson finished her cigarette then stamped out the butt underfoot. 'Right, guv – course of action?'

'I'm thinking you head back to the office and see if you can find anything online about those symbols and that writing.'

'Like what language it's in, for a start.' She tilted her head. 'And where will you be going?'

Sturgess rubbed his palms together. 'You know where.'

'Do you really think that's a good idea?'

'I don't know. I really don't. What I do know is whatever we've just seen is unfortunately in our ballpark, and beyond looking for Debra Brimson, which Clarke already has every available resource working on, I'm out of ideas. It's not like there's a manual for this stuff.'

Wilkerson held her tongue. The silence between them hung heavy with all her previous objections to this course of action.

Sturgess for his part was keen to move on. First, because treading over that old ground would get them nowhere, and second, because while he was trying to be supportive, the smell of cigarette smoke brought back stomach-churning memories. After the morning he'd already had, a churning was the last thing his stomach needed.

He turned back towards the doors of the library and stopped. 'What the hell?'

A woman was standing on the path just to the right of the doors, staring at the sky intently. She was wearing at least a couple of coats, fingerless gloves and a rather ratty-looking bobble hat. She also had with her two shopping trolleys, both tied to her waist, each containing a multitude of bags for life, all full to the brim with knick-knacks and random objects. It was as if she'd been to a charity shop that was holding an 'everything must go' sale to clear space. As well as looking like it contained everything she owned and a lot more besides, at the front of one of her trollies perched a large, stuffed raven like a bonnet mascot.

As they ducked back under the police tape, Sturgess gave the uniform on the door a glower of disbelief that he was ignoring such a flagrant breach of a police cordon. All he received in response was a vacant expression which, even from someone who was in the midst of the sort of mind-numbingly dull duties every copper hated, could best be described as blank.

Sturgess cleared his throat. 'I'm sorry, madam, but you can't be here.'

The woman didn't reply. At least not to him. Instead, she clucked her tongue and murmured quietly, 'By the gods, would you look at that, Frank? Not even in one of the weak points. You mark my words, there'll be trouble. You see if there isn't.'

'Madam, could you—'

Sturgess and Wilkerson both jumped backwards in shock as the raven, very much alive, turned to squawk loudly at them.

'Jesus!' exclaimed Wilkerson.

'No,' said the woman, without taking her eyes from the sky, 'it's definitely not him.'

Sturgess couldn't draw his attention away from the raven that was staring back at him with a kind of malevolent intensity that shouldn't be possible from a bird. Wilkerson tapped his arm and pointed. The two officers they'd passed on their way in, manning the cordon, were still stationed in the same spot. However, both now wore vacant expressions on their faces too, and each one of them was holding an end of broken tape.

The woman sucked her teeth, bent over and started rummaging around in one of her trollies as if looking for something.

Wilkerson stepped forward. 'Love, did you hear the man? You can't be here.'

'Yeah,' said the woman, shifting a bag of what appeared to be ceramic gnomes. 'Men are always saying things like that.'

'This is a crime scene,' said Sturgess.

'You're not wrong.'

'Can you stop what you're doing and pay attention?' said Wilkerson.

'No,' came the response, delivered in a relaxed, conversational tone. 'I won't be doing that.'

'We weren't asking. Stand up and turn around now.'

This elicited no response at all. Instead, the woman looked over at the raven, who turned his head towards her. 'The doohickey is in this one, isn't it?'

The bird cawed in response.

'You know the one I mean.'

The bird cawed again.

'I'm sure it's in this one.'

'I've had enough of this,' said Wilkerson. 'Start cooperating or we'll place you under arrest.'

All this earned her was a chuckle. 'Under arrest,' repeated the woman, addressing the raven. 'Been a while.'

Wilkerson looked at Sturgess, exasperated.

The DI took a step forward and placed his hands on the side of the trolley in which the woman was still rummaging, which garnered a couple of irate caws from the raven.

'I'd be careful if I was you,' said the woman. 'Frank here can get very territorial. He also has one of them whatchamacal-lits? Problems with authority. Start touching stuff and you're going to have difficulty counting to ten without taking your socks off.'

'Right,' said Sturgess. 'You've had your fun. I want you to step away from the trolley, then explain to me what you are doing here, or else we'll be continuing this chat down at the station.'

'Got it!' said the woman triumphantly, standing back and holding a rather worn plastic trumpet in her right hand.

'Congrats,' said Wilkerson, reaching into her coat. 'Now drop it and turn around. I'm placing you under arrest.'

For the first time, the woman turned to look directly at them. She was maybe somewhere in her sixties, but it was hard to tell under all the layers of clothing and the incongruous bobble hat. 'Look, normally I'd humour you.'

The bird cawed again.

'I might,' she responded, before scrunching up her face. 'No, you're right, Frank. Good shout. I wouldn't. But I'd be at least willing to banter. Not tonight, though, as well . . .' She pointed up at the sky.

Frank cawed again.

'I know they can't, but it doesn't mean it isn't there.' She turned back to Sturgess and Wilkerson. 'The point being, I've spent decades making sure stuff like this doesn't happen. Then someone drives a metaphorical bus through the fabric of time and space, and someone has to pick up the pieces, so I'm rather busy. How about you two just toddle off and leave me alone?'

'Look,' said Sturgess, lowering his voice, 'if you can explain to me who you really are – and I mean really – and what you're actually doing here, I'm willing to listen.'

The woman tossed her head back and issued a surprisingly girlish giggle. 'Explain myself. That's a good one. Even if I could, you couldn't and wouldn't understand, and I do not have the time.'

'In that case . . .' began Wilkerson, removing the handcuffs from her inside pocket.

'Ooooh,' marvelled the woman. 'Shiny. Not as shiny as this, though.'

She twisted her left hand and something between her fingers caught the light . . .

The next thing Sturgess knew, the officer who'd been standing beside the revolving door was standing before him, clicking his fingers in front of his face.

'What the—' said Sturgess, stepping backwards, feeling lightheaded.

'You all right, sir? You and the DS were sort of just standing here.'

Sturgess turned to Wilkerson, who looked as confused as he felt. Then, he spun around so fast that he nearly fell over. 'Where is she?'

'Who?'

'The woman. The woman with the trolleys and the raven and . . .'

The PC scanned the front of the building, looking not so much for the woman Sturgess was describing as for someone else who could come and help with the situation.

'I'm afraid I don't—'

'The homeless woman,' interrupted Wilkerson. 'She was just here. We were talking to her.'

'Right. I see,' said the officer, who clearly didn't.

Along the path, Sturgess caught sight of the two officers who'd been manning the cordon. They were now locked in a heated discussion, their voices lowered, while one of them tried desperately to tie the ends of the broken crime-scene tape together.

'You must have seen her,' protested Wilkerson. 'What about—'

Sturgess put his arm on Wilkerson's elbow and, when she looked his way, gave a subtle shake of his head.

'Thank you, officer,' he said. 'Just an in-joke. Apologies. That'll be all.'

'Right.' The officer moved away quickly, looking like a man who was regretting his career choices.

'What the hell just happened?' asked Wilkerson.

'I have no idea,' conceded Sturgess. 'Absolutely no clue. But I'm definitely going to be paying a visit to you-know-where now.'

Wilkerson let out a heavy sigh. 'All right. Fine. But I'm having another cigarette first.'

She slapped at her coat pockets.

'I appreciate this probably isn't the time, but didn't you tell me you were trying to give up?'

'You're right, sir,' she said, the 'sir' laced with enough insubordination for it to have her directing traffic had it been aimed at someone who wasn't him, 'this definitely isn't the time.'

6

There are some things they can't teach you during basic police training. How to defuse an ugly pub fight when seriously out-numbered, how to get through to a seemingly feral bunch of kids on an estate and how to maintain your dignity while, most importantly, upholding the rule of law when faced with some pompous arse who claims to know the commissioner.

Some things they can teach you. Like, for example, if you hear someone roaring 'I'm going to kill him', you should probably go check that out. And so it was that DI Sturgess found himself compelled to break into a run across the darkened car park of the Church of Old Souls aka the offices of *The Stranger Times*. It being half four in the morning, he was surprised to find the front door unlocked, but it meant he was able to head straight up the stairs towards the sound of what any official report worth its salt would call a fracas – one of those words that only existed for situations such as this.

In his haste, he was also caught out by the dodgy step fourth from the top, which was why he arrived in the reception area head first, sprawled on the floor and swearing loudly. When he looked up, clutching his recently abused shin, he was greeted by the sight of Ox at one end of the room, pinned up against the reception desk by Reggie and Stella, while Hannah and Grace corralled Banecroft at the other end. Proceedings were being watched by Manny, the Rastafarian whom Sturgess had met only briefly. He was sitting with a bemused look on his face, like a pastry chef who'd mistakenly walked into a lecture on astrophysics. Hunched beside him was a weird-looking individual clasping a Connect 4 game to his chest while gawping fearfully at the confrontation. It was Ox who had shouted the death threat and who was indeed continuing to shout variations of it now. Technically, the threat in itself could be considered a crime, but seeing as Sturgess had met Vincent Banecroft several times previously, he knew it could also be construed as a reasonable response to the man's personality. Vincent Banecroft was very much a Marmite character, in the sense that if he started talking to you, the natural and correct response would be to run away screaming.

'I'm going to kill him. I mean it this time,' roared Ox.

'No,' said Hannah from the other end of the room, 'you don't.' She looked down at Sturgess and gave him an awkward smile of acknowledgement. 'For the benefit of the police officer who has just entered the building, I should make it clear that was a hyperbolic statement.'

'No, it wasn't.'

'I'd like to see him try,' responded Banecroft.

'Say another thing, Vincent,' said Grace, 'and it will not be him you have to worry about.'

'All right,' said Hannah. 'We're all tired, it's been a very, very long and frustrating night, so why doesn't everybody calm down before I have to ask Stella to Mace you all.'

'I'll do it, too,' said Stella. 'How else am I supposed to check that thing works?'

Ox, breathing heavily, held up his hands, and Reggie and Stella took a step back. 'All right, all right. I'm calm.'

'Really?' said Reggie.

'Ish. I'm fine as long as he doesn't say it again.'

'Say what?' said Banecroft, puffing out his insubstantial chest. 'Loquacious?'

Reggie and Stella grabbed Ox as he attempted to lunge towards Banecroft again. 'That's it. That's absolutely it.'

'Right,' bellowed DS Andrea Wilkerson as she stepped over Sturgess where he lay. 'Everybody shut the hell up and stop behaving like idiots or I'm arresting all of you.'

This had the effect of drawing the attention of everyone in the room and allowing Ox to reestablish a grip on himself. Wilkerson bent down to offer Sturgess a hand. 'You all right, guv? Did they assault you?'

'No,' he said, getting back to his feet. 'I did that to myself. I thought you were going to stay in the car?'

'Figured you might need back-up.'

'May I ask,' said Banecroft, 'under what legal remit is the Greater Manchester Police forcing its way into our offices in the middle of the night?'

'We didn't. The door was unlocked, and you couldn't hear me knocking on it as you were too busy roaring at each other.'

'That doesn't explain what you're doing here?'

'No,' conceded Sturgess, 'it doesn't. It also doesn't explain why you are all here or . . .' He nodded in the direction of the whiteboard in the bullpen that was clearly visible through the open double doors. 'Or who C. A. Horntail is and why they are a bastard.'

'A local nerdy bastard with a grudge, apparently,' added Wilkerson, reading what appeared to be a profile that had been established.

'That is a private matter,' said Banecroft haughtily.

'No, it isn't,' said Hannah. 'Someone has hacked our computers and we're trying to figure out who, because otherwise we can't get this week's edition printed. It's not been going well and' – she glanced at Ox and Banecroft before offering a despairing shake of her head – 'let's just say we're all on edge.'

'And some of us are pig-headed males,' added Stella.

'Well, that's just sexist,' huffed Banecroft.

Ox gave a begrudging grunt of agreement.

Stella shrugged. 'If the penis fits.'

'Stella!' exclaimed Grace, genuinely outraged.

'Have you reported this hack to the police?' asked Sturgess.

'Ehm, no. We didn't really think of that. Have you got someone who can help?'

Sturgess looked at Wilkerson. 'I'm actually not sure. Do we?'

Wilkerson didn't look up from her phone, which she was typing away at furiously.

'Andrea?'

She didn't respond.

'DS Wilkerson?'

This finally got her to look up. 'Sorry? What?'

'I was saying, do we have anyone who can help them to resolve this hacking thing?'

'That depends.' She addressed the room at large. 'Does anyone here know a Clint O'Hara?'

Grace turned around and walked into the bullpen, shaking her head.

'Yeah,' said Ox. 'He's a kid that comes in here occasionally, spouting the latest thing he's read on the internet. Is he working for the police now?'

'No,' said Wilkerson. 'But his name is an anagram of C. A. Horntail.' She held up her phone. 'Look, there's a website that can generate anagrams for you in, like, a second. Are you telling me none of you thought to check that?'

They all had the decency to look embarrassed, except for Banecroft, who, Sturgess guessed, was quite probably biologically incapable of it.

'Right,' Banecroft said. 'Where does he live? I'm going to go round there and wring his neck.'

'Isn't he eleven years old?' asked Reggie.

'Good. I'll stand a good chance of succeeding, then.'

'I'm going to help him,' said Ox. 'And he's fourteen, just small for his age.'

'While it's a delight to see you two getting on so well again,' said Hannah, 'none of you will be doing anything like that because . . .'

'You've just disclosed your intentions in front of two police officers?' offered Sturgess.

'Well, I was going to say because it's idiotic and won't help us get our computers back, but yeah, that too.'

They all turned towards the bullpen at the sound of each of the desktop machines issuing a pinging noise.

Grace was standing in the doorway, a phone held to her ear. She pointed at the receiver. 'I've just woken up Clint's grandmother. She is not happy with him.' She looked around. 'It appears we are back up and running.'

Banecroft consulted his watch. 'And we have a paper to get printed.'

As everyone rushed back to their desks, with even Manny doing his approximation of springing into action, Hannah turned back to their two visitors. 'Thank you very much.'

Wilkerson gave a shrug and made a poor attempt at not looking smug. 'It's what I do. Detective and all that.'

Hannah scrunched her brow. 'Actually, why are you two here?'

Sturgess looked at Wilkerson and then back at Hannah. 'How about I buy you breakfast?'

7

This body. He'd had more than enough of this body. Yes, it had served his purpose. The female had returned him to the world and even provided the blood sacrifice necessary to tie him to this plane of existence, but it did not mean she was a fitting vessel for the mighty Zalas. He was a god and this puny form would not do. Not do at all. He was a warrior king, not some feeble keeper of books.

Once he'd performed the ritual, humiliatingly having to do all the work himself as he no longer had any acolytes left here, he'd walked again into the world of man. How much it had changed since he had been cast into the void. The night was no longer dark – there were strange lights attached to the sky. Towers of glass and rock were everywhere he looked. Horseless chariots that moved at remarkable speed flowed between them. And nowhere – nowhere – was his name spoken. He could feel it. He had been forgotten. In his time, he'd had hordes of worshippers, and the masses were too afraid even to whisper his name. Now that name was all but forgotten.

Not entirely, though. Someone had brought him back. Part of him wondered why they had done so. Was someone daring to use him as a pawn? They would come to regret that. He would make all of humanity suffer for what it had done to him. And there was so much of it now – human beings were everywhere. Their foul stench permeated all of existence. Fetid mewling sheep in need of a shepherd. They wanted to be shown the way, whether they knew it or not. First, though, before he could do that, he needed them to believe in him. Truly believe. He was a god among men, but gods were only truly gods when lesser beings believed in them. His power was weak and he needed to find a way to replenish it quickly or he would fade to nothing.

He stopped. His wanderings had brought him to a bridge. He looked at the water below, tamed, barely moving. What had they done to this world? Even the water was a turgid shadow of its former self. So much would need changing. He had no time to waste.

And then, for the second time that night, fortune smiled upon him. He noticed a figure coming towards him. Broad. Mightily built. This was the body of a true warrior. One far more suited to be graced with the presence of Zalas. He could hear the woman's soul wailing and jabbering away in the back of his mind. If he possessed a body for long enough, its previous owner would die away eventually, but the eviction was not immediate, much to his chagrin. Still, it didn't matter now. The mighty warrior approached, and he was looking at Zalas.

'Are you all right, love? Jesus, you're covered in blood.' The warrior looked around. 'Has someone had a go at ya? Do you need an ambulance?'

He stood before Zalas, towering over this weak form. Yes, he would do nicely.

'I . . . I can't see where the blood's come from.'

He paused and looked down, noticing that the woman before him was now smiling.

Zalas reached out a hand and, in the matter of a moment, he was in possession of this new vessel.

'Oh yes,' he roared. 'This is more like it.'

He could feel his host's mind trying to fight back, pathetically weak. No match for the mighty Zalas. It may be a powerful body, but it was not a powerful intellect. He stood there and flexed these new muscles, feeling the strength in these limbs.

The woman was now before him, her blank expression giving way to one of terror as her pathetic little mind regained control of her body.

'Oh my God, what happened? The blood.' Her voice rose to a screech. 'So much blood!'

'Silence, snivelling wench.'

'You monster. What did you make me do?'

'Silence.'

He struck a blow, which sent her sprawling to the ground. Then he picked her up, raising her pathetic form above his head, and threw her over the side of the bridge. As he strode away, he heard the splash of her limp body hitting the water.

Zalas flexed the hands that were now his and grinned. Yes, this was much more like it. He looked around in the mind of his new host and images flashed up of where the man had been heading. Interesting. Interesting indeed. Things were looking up.

8

In the dim, pre-dawn light, Hannah and Sturgess watched DS Wilkerson's rear lights disappear around the corner. The DS had said she was heading back to the station to, as she'd put it, 'wake up some academics' – something about getting some bloody gobbledegook translated, which Hannah didn't understand. Hannah and Sturgess then both sat in Sturgess's car, which was scrupulously clean save for the bag for life full of empty Diet Coke cans that Hannah had known would be on the back seat. The man himself was similarly immaculate despite the ungodly hour, which made Hannah feel grubby by comparison, and, as always, he smelled remarkably good. She reckoned it was sandalwood, whereas she strongly suspected she reeked of coffee and stress. A silence hung over them for a few seconds before . . .

'I need to tell you something,' began Sturgess.

'No,' said Hannah, stopping him. 'Let me. This is my fault. We had our . . . moment and then I disappeared, and you thought I'd got back together with my ex-husband, which I definitely hadn't, but I needed everyone to think that because I was undercover, but I realize that I should have told you, only I couldn't. Or maybe I should have explained it better or just not taken you for granted or made you feel like I was taking you for granted, and I'm sorry because maybe I'm not good at being in a relationship, seeing as my previous one was with a complete narcissist, and I should have said something sooner or just been better at being better, but I'm sorry if I hurt you and I should have handled everything differently.'

Sitting there, her eyes fixed firmly on the vague outline of the climbing frame in the park's playground, Hannah was fully aware that sentence hadn't got away from her so much as fled the country, moved to Brazil and lived on the run for a couple of decades. It was too late now. It was out there and not coming back.

Inside the car, all remained silent for what could have been a couple of seconds but felt like an ice age.

'Right,' said Sturgess. 'I was going to say that I don't actually know anywhere we can get breakfast at this time of the morning.'

'I see.'

'Yes.'

'Right.'

'But—'

'No, no,' said Hannah. 'Don't worry about it. Although, I don't suppose I could convince you to *Thelma and Louise* this thing off a cliff, could I?'

'I'd love to, but this is Manchester. We don't have any cliffs.'

'Massive oversight, that.'

'Actually, I say that – we're right beside the Peak District and there are loads of them there. Or really steep inclines, at least. It's very beautiful.'

'Sounds it.'

'I mean, the views and stuff.'

'I've never been.'

'I was driving out there last week. Breathtaking.'

'Sounds it.'

'It was work. I was out there because someone found a headless corpse.'

'Right.'

'But beautiful. The views, I mean, not the . . .'

'I get you.'

'You should go.'

'I will. Might do it right now.'

'I've got work.'

'Don't worry. I'll walk.'

Silence fell inside the car again, save for the sound of Sturgess drumming his fingers on the steering wheel.

'Is it me—' started Hannah.

'Or are we both terrible at this?' finished Sturgess.

'Yeah.'

'Oh God, yes. Outstandingly so.'

'Can you be outstandingly bad at something?' asked Hannah. 'I suppose you can. Course you can. Sorry, editor brain kicking in. God, I'm tired.'

'Have you been up all night?'

'Yeah. Last night was supposed to be our Christmas party, but that monumental arsehole of a hacker destroyed that plan.'

'Oh dear.'

They stopped talking as a surly-looking boy passed in front of the car. He was being marched towards the door of *The Stranger*

Times by a woman who had evidently just thrown her overcoat over her nightie and slippers.

'Was that—'

'I assume so,' said Hannah. 'Probably shouldn't have called him a monumental arsehole.'

'Clearly you've never walked the beat. Some of the biggest arseholes I've met have been children.'

'That's very nice of you to say. Apparently, he's short for his age.'

'They're always the worst ones.'

Hannah laughed. 'I'm really hoping I'm going to wake up in a minute and this will all be a dream.'

'Maybe you're just drunk? There seemed to be a lot of bottles of wine up in the office. Sorry, that sounded very judgy.'

'Well, I've just called a child an arsehole, so I'll let it slide. But in answer – no. Not drunk, thank you very much. Grace is getting a bit obsessed about Banecroft's drinking, so all that wine you saw was non-alcoholic. She's been collecting labels and swapping them over for weeks. It's become something of a mission.'

'I didn't even know non-alcoholic wine was a thing.'

'Really? I thought with you being a non-drinker and all.'

'I guess stuff like that isn't meant for non-drinkers like me. It's meant for people who can't drink or miss it or something. Has he noticed?'

'Not so far. He smokes so much that if there's any difference in taste, I doubt he'd realize. When we all got a take-away a couple of weeks ago, Ox claims he saw him eat a wooden kebab skewer and not even notice.'

'Seriously?'

'He actually nodded approvingly and said "crunchy". Anyway, where were we?'

'I was not buying you breakfast.'

'And lucky for you, I'm ninety per cent pigs in blankets and triangular sandwiches right now, so I'm not hungry anyway.'

Sturgess nodded. 'That's probably for the best. I've just been to the scene of a horrific triple murder, so I'm all right for a bit, too.'

'Oh no.'

'That's what I'm here about.'

Sturgess then filled her in on the scene at the MMU Library and Hannah listened in silence until he'd finished. 'God, that sounds horrendous.'

'If anything,' said Sturgess, 'I may have undersold it.'

'And you're sure it's . . .'

He nodded. 'You haven't seen it. The symbols and writing are over every wall. All written in blood.'

'God.'

'Oh, and I haven't even got to the woman with the shopping trolleys.'

'Now you really have lost me.'

'There was a woman outside the library. She had two shopping trolleys and what I think was either a raven or a big crow, and she . . . hypnotized us or something. Andrea and me, plus a few PCs that were standing post. One minute she was there and we were arresting her, and the next she was gone and we were standing there gawping at each other like we'd just been in a trance.'

'By any chance, do you remember seeing something shiny?'

Sturgess gave her a sideways look. 'Seriously?'

'It's a thing. Not like the hypnotism you'd see on TV. I believe it's called a glamour.' Hannah had experienced the phenomenon herself once before and knew how unnerving it was. 'What's the last thing you remember?'

'I . . .' Sturgess concentrated. 'Andrea was about to put the cuffs on her and then, you're right, there was something shiny in her hand and' – he rubbed his brow and closed his eyes – 'I think I may remember her saying something like, "What's in your head?"'

Hannah started to cough, not deliberately but in an attempt to hide her immediate reaction. She was one of the few people who knew what was in Tom Sturgess's head, and she wasn't talking figuratively. She regularly had flashbacks to the freaky eyeball on a stalk that she'd seen pop out of his scalp when he'd been put into a trance. It wasn't the kind of thing you forgot in a hurry. The reason she'd never told him what she knew was that she had it on good authority – namely from the woman who'd put the thing there – that if Sturgess ever found out about it, the parasitic whatever-it-was would kill him. It said something that this fact wasn't even the most awkward thing about their relationship.

'Are you OK?' Sturgess asked. 'I think I've got some water here somewhere, or at least a Diet Coke.'

Hannah held up a hand and caught her breath. 'I'm OK. Sorry. Frog in my throat. Weird expression, that. So, this woman – the one with the shopping trolleys – you've no idea who she is or what she was doing there?'

'No. I was hoping you might or . . .'

'That I might know someone who would? The only person I can think to ask is the one you're thinking of and, as we both know, he's not a big fan of yours.'

'But luckily,' said Sturgess with an awkward smile, 'he is a big fan of yours.'

Hannah sighed. 'All right, let's go.'

'Thanks.'

'And you didn't even have to buy me breakfast.'

9

Grace tried not to fidget nervously. Nadine O'Hara was standing in their reception area having refused both a seat and a cup of tea. Her face was red with barely suppressed rage, her lips a thin white line. She was wearing an overcoat over her nightie and slippers, her only concession to dressing for leaving the house. She didn't live far away – just down the road from Grace. In fact, that was how they knew each other.

She had a firm grip on the shoulder of her grandson Clint, all of fourteen years old and small for his age. She'd marched him straight there and he was managing to pull off what could best be described as a defiant slouch. He wore a red tracksuit and had one of those bowl-type haircuts that, much to Grace's surprise, had seemingly come back into fashion. The three of them stood there awkwardly, the silence broken only by Nadine's occasional and barely audible growls of seething anger.

Down below them, the familiar rumble of the printing press passed through the building. Despite everything that had happened, this week's edition would be printed in time for the trucks. Just.

Nadine didn't fit the mental image that the word 'grandmother' typically conjured. She was younger than Grace for a start – probably mid-fifties – although standing there she looked older, given that being dragged out of bed in the early hours of the morning was never anyone's best time. Perhaps not older, just exhausted. By both this night and life in general. Grace felt for the poor woman. They'd never been particularly close – their friendship, if you could call it that, didn't extend to much beyond neighbourly hellos whenever they passed in the street – but Grace knew that Nadine had recently become Clint's sole guardian. Her daughter, Clint's mother, had died tragically young a few years ago and his father, her ex-husband, had been sent to prison. Grace, keen to be a good neighbour, had made offers of help several times but Nadine had always turned them down.

Clint, to put it in the politest terms possible, was a 'handful'. Only four weeks earlier, he'd crashed Nadine's car into the front of her house while trying to take it for a joyride. Then Mr Wallace from across the road had called round last week, trying to get Grace to sign some ridiculous petition to get Clint evicted from the street. Grace had given him a stern talking-to about the meaning of Christian charity, while also taking the opportunity to point out that his cat seemed obsessed with attacking her rhododendrons. Everyone could see that Nadine was struggling but she was too proud to accept help. Grace hoped she would accept it now as she was about to face one of the worst things imaginable – Vincent Banecroft when he was justifiably angry.

'He will be out in a minute,' said Grace in an attempt to fill the silence.

Nadine nodded.

'You should prepare yourself for . . . Vincent is . . . The thing is . . . What I'm trying to say is, keep in mind that . . .'

Nadine took a break from glaring at the back of her grandson's head long enough to give Grace a bemused look. Grace smiled back awkwardly. The problem she was having was that Vincent Banecroft was hard to explain, and harder still to apologize for at the best of times, never mind when you've been up for most of the night.

She decided to finish with, 'He is a good man.' Oddly, she really believed that. He was just very good at hiding it.

Clint looked around the room. 'It's a bit shit here, innit?'

'Shut up, Clint,' snapped Nadine. 'You're in enough trouble already.'

'Just saying.'

Grace could only assume the child had more than one facial expression. In their limited interactions, all she'd seen from him so far was the petulant scowl he was wearing at that moment, but he must have others.

Despite expecting it – indeed, standing there waiting for it – Grace still jumped when the doors of the corridor that led to Banecroft's office flew open and he emerged.

He favoured them with a broad smile. 'Ah, we have guests.'

Oh no, he was going for the overly polite thing. This was bad. Grace particularly disliked it when he did this. It was as if he wanted to give himself as much runway as possible before reaching a crescendo of screaming and shouting, having made several stops along the way for large servings of sarcasm.

'Vincent,' she began, 'this is my friend Nadine and her

grandson Clint.' She had thrown in the word 'friend' in an almost certainly vain attempt to get him to take it down a notch.

'I'm very sorry,' said Nadine.

'What are you sorry for?' asked Banecroft. Worse still, sweetness and light. 'You didn't do anything, did you?'

'No, but he did.'

Banecroft was now standing in front of Clint, looking down at him. 'And does he have anything to say for himself?'

Nadine poked Clint in the back.

'Yeah,' Clint said. 'Does you know that your fly is open?'

Nadine clipped him round the back of the head.

'I do,' said Banecroft, not missing a beat. 'That's because this is my home and place of business and it is nearly six in the morning. I should be fast asleep, our newspaper having been sent to press hours ago, but instead, this noble institution was the victim of an act of terrorism.'

'All right,' said Nadine. 'That's a bit much.'

'The dictionary definition of terrorism is the calculated use of violence or intimidation to inculcate fear. It is intended to coerce or intimidate governments, institutions or societies in the pursuit of goals that are generally political, religious or ideological. This evening, we witnessed an attack on the free press, making Sonny Jim here a terrorist.'

'He is fourteen,' said Grace.

'Congrats,' said Banecroft. 'He's very advanced for his age. You must be very proud.' He looked around. 'Sorry, I've just realized that our head of IT security isn't here for this meeting. I know he wouldn't want to miss it.'

'If you mean Ox,' said Grace, 'he's gone home.'

'No, he hasn't, as I told him if he did, he wasn't to come back.'

On cue, Ox appeared from the bullpen, bleary-eyed and even more dishevelled than usual. 'Don't threaten me with a good time. Sorry, I fell asleep.'

'And if we wanted a visual representation of the last however many hours, there we have it.'

'Oh great,' said Ox. 'He's doing the polite sarcasm thing. That's always fun.'

Banecroft motioned at Clint. 'Here is the criminal master-mind that outwitted you. You must be very proud.'

'Least he don't smell like three-day-old KFC,' said Clint.

Ox laughed then tried hard to cover it with a terrible attempt at a coughing fit.

'Ah, how lovely. You two are bonding,' said Banecroft. 'Maybe you can be his prison pen pal?' He glared at Clint. 'Seeing as you're talking now, how about you start by explaining to me your problem with the free press?'

'You ain't free. I seen your stupid paper in the shop. And besides, the mainstream media is bullshit. Everybody knows that.'

'How are we mainstream media?' protested Ox. 'We've got a two-page spread on demonically possessed pets, and our biggest advertiser is a company that makes Ouija boards with nothing but emojis on them for contacting dead Gen Zers.'

'Press is all full of bull,' continued Clint.

His granny sighed. 'Oh, for God's sake, is this about your dad again?'

'What about his dad?'

'He don't take no shit,' said Clint defiantly.

'Oh, like a broken toilet?' asked Banecroft.

A pause stretched out as the room considered this.

'Think about it. It's clever.'

'Whatever,' said Clint. 'What I'm saying is my pops was victimized by the press.'

'No,' countered Nadine, 'he wasn't. We've been through this, Clint. They accurately reported what he did.'

'Says you. He's a political prisoner. He got locked up for fighting the man.'

'A man,' corrected his granny. 'The man in question being a bloke whose electric wheelchair he got caught trying to nick.'

'Sounds like he stinks,' said Banecroft. 'Again, like a broken toilet.' He looked around at the confused faces staring back at him. 'I'm entirely wasted on you people.'

'I remember that story,' said Grace, keen to move the conversation on. 'The wheelchair bandit – isn't that what the papers called him?'

'Yeah,' confirmed Nadine. 'My poor Caroline, God rest her, was an angel but she had terrible taste in men.'

'Don't be dissing my pops,' shouted Clint.

'And will you stop talking like that? You're from Manchester, not South Central LA.'

'Fuck you, old woman.'

'Whoa!' said Banecroft. 'If I'm not allowed to swear in this building then you definitely aren't. My advice is don't do that when the police get here – they've not got my forgiving nature.'

'The police?' asked Nadine, alarmed.

'I ain't afraid of no fuzz. You feel me?'

'Once the Greater Manchester Police are done with him,' said Banecroft, 'I'm calling the grammar police.'

'I know he messed up,' said Nadine, 'but we don't need to involve the police.'

'He committed a crime. That is very much their bag.'

'Vincent,' Grace hissed, 'I would like a word.'

'No, thank you.'

'I would like a word in private right now.'

'I'm busy.'

'Yes, you are busy having a word with me.'

Grace locked eyes with Banecroft and did not look away, daring him to ignore her.

'Fine,' he said huffily, walking back towards his office, mumbling something that Grace chose not to make out.

Nadine gave her a pleading glance and Grace tried to look reassuring in return. 'It's all right. Come with me.' She turned to Ox. 'Ox, keep Clint entertained, please.'

Unenthusiastically, Ox moved to stand beside the young boy. As he did so, Clint peered up at him. 'You some kind of paedo?'

Ox shook his head. 'Don't take this the wrong way, but you are awful. Just awful.'

It said something for Nadine's panicked state of mind that she barely seemed to register the all-senses assault that was Banecroft's office. Grace often found herself debating internally whether it smelled worse than it looked or looked worse than it smelled. Still, touch was the clear winner. Everything was some degree of sticky and just thinking about it made her want to have a shower.

Banecroft slumped behind his desk, upon which sat two of the bottles of non-alcoholic wine he was unknowingly drinking. Grace hoped that after several days of this she might at some point use it as evidence that he didn't need alcohol. Even though she was an optimist by nature, even she thought that was a massive stretch, but the good Lord loves a trier.

'This esteemed publication was mercilessly attacked and my employer would expect me to demand that the full weight of the law come crashing down upon the perpetrator.'

Even by Banecroft's lofty standards, this was quite the conversational opening gambit.

'He is just a child,' said Grace, getting in before Nadine.

'Why do people keep saying that? You know all the worst people in history were also children at one point. We need to stop using that as an excuse to give kids *carte blanche*.'

'Nobody is saying he should not be punished,' said Grace, 'but there is no need to involve the police. He is a good boy.'

'No,' said Nadine, 'he's not.'

Grace looked at her in surprise.

'He isn't,' she insisted. 'I mean, he's my grandson and I love him, but you've seen him – he's a prize little shit.'

Grace smiled awkwardly. 'I am not sure you are helping my point.'

'It's the truth. He was a lovely little fella back in the day, and I hope he'll end up being a decent sort when he grows up, but I've been looking after him for six months and I can tell you, he's an absolute shitshow right now.'

Even Banecroft looked confused. He wasn't used to people agreeing with him and the look on his face showed he was having a hard time processing it.

'Look,' continued Nadine, 'after Caroline passed, Clint lived with his dad. His dad, as previously mentioned, is a grade-A, one hundred per cent, certified wanker. Of all the many things he's bad at, parenting might be at the top of the list. Clint has been raised on junk food, Xbox and YouTube videos of angry bald millionaires smoking cigars while explaining how they can't say anything any more and how women are property, or science is bullshit, or whatever other shite those idiots get rich spouting. You put any kid in that environment and see how they turn out. I'm trying my best with him, but he could really do with a strong male role model.'

Once Nadine had stopped talking there was an odd pause. Eventually, Grace and Banecroft realized simultaneously what she was getting at. It was hard to say who was more surprised.

'Me?' said Banecroft.

'Him?' said Grace.

'Why not?' said Nadine, turning to Grace. 'You said earlier that he was a good man.'

'He is, but . . .'

'But what?'

'But,' interjected Banecroft, 'why would I want anything to do with this demon child?'

'Because you're a good man. Grace doesn't strike me as a liar.'

'She's not that but she does have a much higher opinion of people than all the available evidence justifies. It's all that Bible – rots the brain.'

'Clint needs punishing,' countered Nadine. 'We all agree on that. You must have lots around this place that needs doing. No offence, but, well . . .' She looked around the room and her point was more than adequately made.

'I do not believe anyone has done something bad enough to have to clean this office,' said Grace.

'The rest of the place, then.'

Grace nodded. 'We have been saying how the old girl needs a lick of paint.'

'While I am old school in many ways,' said Banecroft, 'I draw the line at child labour.'

'It wouldn't be that,' said Nadine. 'You wouldn't be paying him.'

'There's an even worse word for that.'

'It'll be like one of them summer camps posh kids get to go to, only free and in the middle of the bastard cold winter.'

'No,' said Banecroft.

'Nadine,' said Grace, 'I would like to speak with Vincent in private, please. Would you mind stepping outside?'

They both waited until she had left the room.

'Vincent—'

'Don't start with me, Grace. My decision is made. Carved in stone. End of story.'

'You are an editor, not the Almighty.'

'This kid tries to destroy us and now you want me to make this into some sort of feel-good buddy movie?'

'Do you remember what I got you for last Christmas?'

'No, I don't, but unless it was a lobotomy, I fail to see the relevance.'

'Socks,' she said. 'Socks. Underwear. A new wallet. Nothing fancy but things you needed.'

'OK.'

'Do you remember what you got me?'

'Ehm . . .'

'That's right. Same thing as the year before – nothing.'

'I don't want Christmas presents,' protested Banecroft. 'I say that every year.'

'You do. And every year I get you some anyway because while you refuse to believe it, I know you are a good man.'

'This again?'

'And if you do this thing, I will give you what you want most in the world.'

Banecroft narrowed his eyes. 'While I appreciate the sentiment, I don't really believe you're going to hunt down and kill Russell Brand.'

'No,' said Grace, 'not that, but I will give you the thing you actually want.'

Banecroft's eyes widened. 'I can swear in the office again?'

'For one day.'

'A month.'

'One day. The whole twenty-four hours.'

'A week.'

'And you can pick the day. Final offer.'

'What makes you think I'll accept that?'

Ox stood awkwardly beside Clint. He didn't like silence. Something in his brain felt compelled to attempt to fill it. 'So, do you like school?'

The enquiry earned him the kind of withering look that chilled a man's soul. He was starting to remember why he hated being a kid – it turns out a large part of it was having to be around kids.

'What kind of a weirdo likes school?' asked Clint.

'Yeah, school is whack.'

'You got kids?'

'No.'

'What you doing hanging out at schools, then?'

'Ehm, what? No, I—'

'I thought you lot weren't allowed within one hundred yards.'

'No, I am. I mean, course I am. Not that I do. Don't go near the places.'

'Look at you – got your alibi all sorted out, innit? Just as well, too. Police be coming, but maybe they looking at you and not me.'

'I didn't . . . I don't . . .'

Clint started laughing. 'I'm just fucking with you, son. So, you the head of IT security for this gaff?'

Ox shrugged. 'I guess.'

'Nice one,' said Clint. 'Sweet gig.' He looked around, nodding appreciatively. 'Yeah. Nice.' Then, as an afterthought, he added, 'There's not another one, by the way.'

'What?'

'A virus. There was just the one. You got nothing to worry about.'

Ox looked down at him. 'Are you saying there was another virus?'

'No. Absolutely not. One hundred per cent.'

'Because if there was, you'd be in really big trouble.'

'Yeah. I mean, if they could prove it was me. You're right, though – your boss would go totally mental if there was another one. I mean, losing his shit, son.'

'All right, if there is another virus, you need to tell me now.'

'That's what I been saying,' said Clint. 'There's not. Far as I know. Which is a good thing as that boss-man, he seems like a ball-breaker. But don't worry. You totally fine.'

'Are you just trying to mess with me?'

'No, man. I'm telling you that everything's fine. Go home. Sleep. Do what you do.'

'Oh my God, you are such a little shit.'

'You got some of those unresolved anger issues, bro. You need to work on that.'

'So help me, if—'

The doors to the corridor that led from Banecroft's office flew open and the man himself strode out, Grace and Nadine following in his wake.

'Right,' said Banecroft. 'Ten o'clock later this morning, be here. Clint, you shall be working off your debt to society.'

'No way, man.'

'Clint!' snapped his granny. 'You're doing it or so help me, I'm going to smash that Xbox to bits right in front of your eyes.'

Clint folded his arms. 'This is bullshit,' he mumbled.

'Nice one,' said Ox gleefully. 'Seems very fair.'

'I'm glad you agree,' said Banecroft, 'because you're going to be supervising him.'

'Me? Why me? Wait – don't. I know. Head of IT security. Paying back my debt. Oh God, someone please kill me now.'

'That's the spirit. I'm not sure Clint is capable of murder but if anyone can bring that out in him, I'm confident it will be you.' With that, Banecroft spun on his heel and headed back towards his office. 'Cup of tea, please, Grace, and don't spare the Hobnobs.'

Ox looked down at Clint, who smiled up at him with a wicked glint in his eyes. 'Is you my new uncle now?'

10

It felt good.

So good.

Zalas clenched and unclenched his fists. These new hands belonging to this warrior's body. While it was an enjoyable vessel it was also confusing. Despite the mighty muscles, the hands were soft and belonged to a weakling who had never done a proper day's labour in his life. As he put the body through its paces, he sensed that while it had been built for battle, it had not experienced it previously. The feeling was backed up by the snivelling spirit of its previous owner, which he could sense cowering in the back of his mind. Pathetic.

It had been so long since Zalas had been able to exert his physical prowess, it had come as the sweetest of releases. He sucked the blood off his knuckles.

He was sitting on a stool in some kind of ring that someone had strung ropes around. Surrounding it were various machines of metal that men had been lifting or pushing when he'd come in. When he took over a host, some of their knowledge came along with the vessel. This place was called a gym. He'd never heard of such a thing, but warriors training – that he knew.

When he'd entered, two men had been sparring in this ring while a third shouted instructions. Zalas had laid down his challenge and one of them had laughed. He wasn't laughing now. He was lying in the other corner of the ring, his body bent at an unnatural angle. Zalas thought that was him, but it could be one of the others. It wasn't like he'd been keeping track. Bodies lay all around him now, mostly still alive, but all having been thoroughly dealt with. Each one had possessed a physically powerful body but lacked the warrior's instincts to go with it. There was a hesitancy, almost an aversion to violence in most of them. The pathetic worms had even tried to reason with him. Reason had no place on the battlefield. Clearly, their training was severely lacking in important areas. Not that they'd really stood a chance – this body and Zalas's instinct together with his innate power was far too much for any mere mortal. Yes, his exile had left him weak, but only by the standards of who he truly was. In his time away, humans had become pathetic. Soft. It seemed they had been smothering their primal instincts for so long that they had forgotten who they truly were. He was here to remind them.

He had been rather confused by their response. Normally, upon seeing a true warrior assert themselves as the dominant alpha, they would fall into line. People followed strength, or at least they always had before. Instead, after he'd dispatched those who had challenged him, the others had run away like scared little children. Not all of them had managed to do so – somewhere among the peculiar shiny machines there was a groaning noise, and elsewhere a pathetic sobbing. He would not have left so many alive had he known they had such weak spirits. They were not fit to stand in his vanguard. Beyond warriors, though, what Zalas needed was followers. Believers. In belief lay power, and if he was to bring this world to heel, that was the thing he needed to find.

Now, he was waiting. Inevitably, once he'd made his presence known, the lesser mortals would retreat, then send forth their champion. Initially, Zalas had thought that was what the people in the shiny yellow jackets were – the ones who had done a lot of shouting and telling him to calm down. He was completely calm. The portly one had attempted to strike him with a metal stick. Zalas had taken it away and shoved it somewhere the man would not forget. He was fairly sure he was the one he could hear whimpering like a beaten dog.

Just then came a loud bang and people started rushing into the room from various directions.

'Finally,' he said, standing up and moving into the centre of the ring, his arms extended. The newcomers were all dressed in some form of black armour and were carrying weapons. At least Zalas assumed that was what they were, given they were being pointed at him. His new adversaries were all shouting at him to get down, a clamour of voices repeating the same instruction that he had no intention of following.

They were surrounding the ring now. Zalas turned on the spot and raised his voice. 'Who amongst you has come to challenge the mighty Zalas?'

'Get face down on the floor now, Paul. This is your one warning.'

Zalas laughed. 'I am the mighty Zalas, god amongst men, and you will address me as such.'

'Fuck it,' said the voice. 'Take him.'

Some magic that he did not know struck his body and it spas-med as he tumbled to the ground.

He tried to regain his footing, but something was sprayed in his eyes, blinding him. Another jolt passed through him, fol-lowed by many hands grabbing him.

That did not go as expected.

Dead Man Twerking

Manchester's John Rylands Library has been reported as the site of an unusual form of haunting. Abridged apparitions – hauntings that feature incomplete bodies – are nothing new. Headless spirits have been recorded since records began, and hauntings featuring only the sound of footsteps are ten a penny. However, in true Manchester style, the John Rylands Library's ghost is believed to be the first of its kind. Irate head librarian Robyn Deanne Wooster explains:

'It's an arse. Just a naked arse. You'll be sorting out the Natural History and Ornithology section – which is always a mess, books put back willy-nilly – and you'll turn around, and there it is. A naked arse, right beside your head. Obviously, the first few times it's shocking, but after a while it just becomes annoying. And before you ask, yes, if you look at it from the other side, it's exactly the same arse. It's three hundred and sixty degrees of flabby buttocks.'

The apparition calls into question the theory that ghosts are the souls of the dead with unfinished business, as it remains unclear what a backside could possibly have to do that wouldn't also require the rest of the body. Attempts to identify the owner of the posterior have so far proved fruitless, as the only identifying marking is a rather unsettling tattoo of the word 'Mum'.

11

Dr Veronica Carter walked down the hallway, her trademark high heels clacking on the marble floor, then halted abruptly. With a smile, she realized she had been humming. She couldn't remember the last time she'd done that – a joyful tune to meet the morning sun. Normally, her mornings were very different. Up at dawn, two hours of arduous workouts, the treatments, the ointments, the you-name-it-she's-tried-its. Increasingly, despite it all, she had found herself staring into the bathroom mirror, day after day, cataloguing the ravages of time upon her face and body.

She had been a beautiful thing once, she was sure of it, but now, as happened to all humans, she was caught in the twisted gravitational pull of age. She hated it. Hated it. Hated it. Sure, nobody liked it, but she was aware that her hatred blazed with a zealous ferocity to which others couldn't hold a candle. She'd always been that way, even as a child. A psychiatrist would no doubt have a field day with it all, 'because of the cruel wasting disease that took her mother and blah, blah, blah'. While she had seen many doctors over the years, in her quest for longevity, she wasn't a fan of the medical community in general, and the head-shrinkers in particular. One of the many things that irritated her

about the modern world was its unhealthy obsession with why —
why we think something, why something is the way it is, and so
on and so on. She had long since realized she didn't care about
the why, only the how — namely, how to fix it. She was solution-
orientated. It was what made her good at the job she had been
doing for so long now. By her estimate, for longer than anyone
else ever had done.

When it came to fighting off the lecherous advances of Old
Father Time, she had thrown a vast array of resources at the
problem. Financial, magical, not to mention an obsessive exercise
regime. It was all just sandbags trying to hold back the rising
flood waters; there was only one way to stop it, and now she'd
done it. She'd finally done it. Or at least she would have done
it — in just a few days' time.

She regarded her reflection in the glass frame of the obscenely
expensive and largely white canvas that adorned the wall. As
with all corporate art, it had been acquired because it matched
the decor, and it had cost enough to reassure anyone who saw
it that nobody in the building needed their money and hence
could be trusted with it. The building in question belonged to
a company that actually did what the signage outside indicated.
Just not on this floor. The whole thing belonged to her employers. One of a vast and mind-boggling array of such assets. If you
came from old money and had even a modicum of sense, it wasn't
hard to watch it grow and grow, and she was working for the
oldest money there was.

Dr Carter had always been short, topping out at five foot one,
but that had never bothered her much. In fact, it worked to her

advantage, given the delight she took in wearing killer heels. She turned to check out her figure from another angle and smoothed the line of her dress. It had been a long battle but she hadn't done too badly, all things considered. She gave herself a nod of approval and started to walk on, delighting in the eccentricity of resuming her hearty hum. When she recognized the tune, she couldn't resist a giggle – 'Santa Claus is Comin' to Town'. Well, it was almost Christmas.

She nodded at her PA cheerfully and pushed through the doors to her office to find Tamsin Baladin, tablet in hand, standing beside her desk, awaiting her arrival. To say the woman was keen was the understatement of the millennium. Dr Carter could respect ambition – hell, she wasn't exactly without it herself – but Baladin was something else. The woman was an actual billionaire, after she and her odious twin brother had set up the dating-site-cum-social-media platform Fuzzy Britches, but Tamsin had still joined the organization Dr Carter worked for because it offered the chance of something all the money in the world couldn't buy – immortality.

The Founders were, by and large, a bunch of old men, even if many of them didn't look it. Identifying as forty for four hundred years didn't mean you were still middle-aged. The patriarchy's patriarchy, bathed in the certainty that they were right about everything because only those with a death wish would dare tell them otherwise. Dr Carter and Tamsin Baladin should have enjoyed a kinship, being a pair of females working for the oldest of old boys' clubs, but that was not the case.

Thanks to the Accord – the deal signed with the Folk to bring to an end the war that had been flirting with mutually assured destruction – the reality was that the old boys' club had a new rule: one in, one out. In other words, nobody could be 'made' unless one of the existing Founders died. Behind the younger woman's perfect smile lay a burning ambition that saw Dr Carter as an obstacle between her and immortality. An obstacle that needed to be removed. Dr Carter knew this because she'd have thought the exact same thing in her position. Normally, the gap between the two women – Dr Carter was a 'seasoned' member of the organization and Baladin was just in the door, after all – would mean that there would be no competition, but Baladin had been so single-minded in her money-is-no-object thirst to acquire magical abilities and knowledge that she was advancing faster than anyone could have predicted. She'd hired the best people she could find and had so many people assisting in her training that Dr Carter was beginning to suspect she didn't sleep. Still, none of that mattered now.

'Tamsin, Tamsin, Tamsin. Good morning. Season's greetings. Merry Christmas. All the above.'

Tamsin looked slightly taken aback. 'Ehm, yes. Of course. To you, too.'

'That's the spirit,' said Dr Carter, settling into her leather office chair and spinning around. 'Now, as you know, with the ceremony coming up, there's going to be a lot of Council members in town. Frankly, the amount of bad blood, and the number of grudges and centuries-old feuds we have to manage when more than one of the members is in the same place would put a class of teenage girls to shame, but I believe I have everything in hand.'

In fact, Dr Carter knew she did. For longer than she'd cared to remember she'd been the person in charge of crisis management for the Founders in Manchester. Her ability to handle all manner of sensitive and precarious situations was what had got her the 'promotion of promotions' she was finally about to receive. Tamsin Baladin could then have her job and she would be welcome to it. Dr Carter had changed her last proverbial nappy; it was someone else's turn to shovel the shit.

'As anticipated, I will have to alter the banquet plans because they all have demands,' she continued.

'I thought we had already asked about . . .'

Dr Carter laughed. 'Here is a free lesson, Tamsin. Regardless of what kind of preparation you do for something like this, the individuals concerned will have last-minute demands. It's how they prove to the world and, most importantly, themselves, that they are truly powerful. Knowing that, it's pointless to try to prevent it. Rather it's your job to plan for the plan not staying the plan. It's why I have booked four chefs and three venues, among many, many other things.'

'I see,' said Tamsin, trying to look humble. 'Thank you. I appreciate the advice. Can I ask about the timing?'

'What about it?' said Dr Carter, picking up the pink squeezable stress toy from her desk and leaning back. 'Old Franzen left us six weeks ago. They generally do these things at the next meeting.'

Anders Franzen had been one of the more powerful Founders, in all meanings of the word. He had also been an obsessive about cars since their literal invention. Even by the standards of

'petrolheads', the man had not been an engaging conversational-
ist. What's more, he clearly hadn't cared. Dr Carter's bosses were,
unsurprisingly, mostly indifferent to social niceties. It was one
of the characteristics they all shared. Another was being understandably obsessive about their personal security and so on,
given that they still had to fear anything that could be defined as
'not natural causes'. The uneasy truce with the Folk didn't stop
them obsessing about an assassin's bullet or whatever else. Still,
even the most cautious of people had their weaknesses.

Franzen had rarely left his estate, preferring to spend much of
his time in the hangars (plural) he had assembled there, full to
the brim with all manner of vehicles. Officially, the cause of the
accident had not been pinned down, but the version Dr Carter
thought most likely was that old Anders had been working away
on one of his beloved restoration jobs when he'd decided to treat
himself to one of those foul-smelling cigars he so loved. Fuel and
flame. The rest had been history, with a considerable amount of
chemistry thrown in. In fact, the explosion had been so big that
he'd ended up covering quite a lot of geography, too.

'No, not that,' said Baladin. 'I just meant it seems odd to hold
it on Christmas Day.'

Dr Carter shrugged. 'They have held a meeting then for as
long as I can remember. Don't forget, the Council isn't exactly
full of people with families with which to surround themselves at
this time of year.' In fact, as part of the Accord, Founders were
not allowed to have children, the reason being that the agreement stipulated there would be no increase in the number of
Founders, and even they might object to sitting around watching

their children growing old and dying. 'Besides, you will become painfully aware the longer you are part of it that many things happen in this organization for no better reason than they always have, and it is bloody difficult to get any of them changed.'

'Well,' said Baladin with a smile, 'now that you'll be a full member of the Council, perhaps it will be a little bit easier.'

Dr Carter spotted the shameless attempt at flattery a mile off, but she appreciated the effort. It seemed that ever since her ascension had been rubber-stamped, Baladin had decided to try to reestablish Dr Carter as an ally. That ship had sailed, but it didn't mean she was above the cheap thrill of a bit of toadying.

'I'm not there yet,' was all the response she gave. 'Any incident reports from overnight?'

Her job was still hers for at least a few more days. More than anything, the Founders treasured the status quo and the general public's ongoing ignorance of anything magical. Her role was to handle anything that threatened that. Given the chaotic nature of magical forces, it was one hell of a big ask, but then if it was a job just anyone could do, it wouldn't have earned Dr Carter the biggest of all prizes.

'Yes,' said Baladin, indicating her tablet. 'There was an incident outside a pub in Oldham.'

'Find me a night when there isn't.'

'Aha, yes, but this one ended up with a man being petrified.'

'As in?'

'Stone, yes.'

'I think we are all too aware who that was. I feel it is drinking-up time at the last chance saloon, which is probably a poor choice of metaphor given her issues in that area. Inform Alpha team and they can sweep her up.'

'Confirmed. Also, a man claims he was chased through Prestwich Forest Park last night by a massive hairy beast.'

Dr Carter waved this away. 'We get that every few months.'

'So we believe it isn't true?'

'Oh no, it's true all right, but that man will have been up to something he shouldn't have. Those woods are protected and we stay out of it. Anything else?' Dr Carter tossed her stress toy up in the air and caught it.

'I'm afraid so. There appears to have been a triple murder in the library of Manchester Met.'

'Really?'

'A book group.'

Dr Carter paused and tilted her head towards Baladin. 'Are you leading up to telling me a joke, Tamsin?'

'No.'

'And how is that a matter for us?'

'I am looking into that, but your DI Sturgess has been called in.'

Dr Carter waved this away, too. 'They're increasingly calling him in for anything. The boys and gals in the Greater Manchester Police are all getting rather jumpy after that shitshow out at the Saddleworth farm that we do not discuss.'

'Speaking of which, we did say we would come back to the matter of your' – Tamsin paused briefly and considered her words – 'direct link with DI Sturgess.'

Direct link – now there was a euphemism and a half. Dr Carter had implanted a parasitic creature in the man's head because if he couldn't be controlled, they needed to know what he knew. The man had an unhealthy obsession with the truth. Still, Carter had a grudging respect for him. Part of her was tempted to tell Baladin to go find her own pet bloodhound if she wanted one so badly.

'Yes,' she said, 'we did. We can discuss transferring him to you at a later date.'

Baladin nodded, handling her disappointment well.

'Very well, then.'

'Check in with the usual sources and keep an eye on it. Soon enough all of this will be your responsibility, after all.'

Tamsin smiled back at her. 'I just hope I can handle it all half as well as you have done.'

Dr Carter laughed. 'Keep up the shameless flattery, Tamsin. It'll get you far.'

Tamsin nodded and made for the door. Dr Carter watched her leave, then tossed her stress toy up in the air again. *Yes*, she thought, *let's see how you like it when you're no longer on the sidelines, chipping in, and when everything is your fault instead. Be careful what you wish for, Tamsin, because you might just get it.*

Dr Carter tossed the ball up into the air once more and happily resumed humming 'Santa Claus is Comin' to Town' to herself.

12

Hannah bounced up and down on the balls of her feet and, in the absence of any better ideas, she pressed the buzzer beside the door again, leaving her finger on it for longer than was necessary. She felt bad doing it, but not bad enough not to do it. What was worse, she was working on the assumption that the property behind this door, to the side of the Kanky's Rest pub, both belonged to it and would be occupied by its landlord. It seemed like a reasonable guess, not least because his battered old jeep was parked in the alley beside it. It looked out of place in the city centre but then so did its owner, who had always struck Hannah as a man more suited to living halfway up a mountain.

She considered leaving again but some part of her hated the idea of Sturgess coming to her for help and her not being able to provide any. John Mór, whether he liked it or not – and affable though he was, she was fairly sure the answer was 'not' – was her best connection to the world of the Folk. Nine months ago, she thought magic extended to slightly odd blokes asking if that was the card you were thinking of, but now, she needed all the help she could get, navigating the new world into which she'd been thrust. The Folk – people with magical abilities – were understandably reticent when it came to talking to outsiders, given their very existence was a secret. Ordinary people like Hannah rarely, if ever, got to even know of them, and their distrust for outsiders was considerable. It had been a while since anyone burned any witches at the stake, but that kind of thing had a tendency to stay rooted in the collective memory.

Ideally, Hannah would have rung John Mór, but he'd changed his number recently, and then claimed his new phone was broken when she asked for his number. Her suspicion that this was an outright lie was a strong one. Anyway, she was here now, and since she'd already buzzed three times and knocked twice, thumping loudly on the door with her fist wasn't that much ruder than she'd already been. On the downside, if someone was going to answer, surely they would have done so by now. She envisioned herself trudging back across the road to where Sturgess was parked and admitting defeat. The reason he was over there and not standing beside her was because John Mór had made clear his feelings on the police in general and on Sturgess in particular. Hannah was already in danger of wearing out her welcome, so it was best not to poke the bear.

Having said that, she found her hand hovering in front of the door again, ready to put Operation One Last Thump into action. Thankfully, it opened before she could make contact and she managed to right herself before she fell through it in a very unladylike manner.

John Mór was a striking man, broad shouldered and six-foot-eight, most of it covered in tattoos, with a salt-and-pepper beard that stretched down to his navel and an equally long head of hair that flowed down his back. He was also far too big a man for the fluffy pink dressing gown he was wearing, made from the kind of sheer material that was intended not to leave much to the imagination while nevertheless inspiring it. Hannah looked up and focused intently on his face, for fear of making eye contact with anything else.

'Hannah,' he said, leaning wearily against the wall and pinching the bridge of his nose. 'Always lovely to see you, and so early, too.'

'Hi, John. Is now a bad time?'

'What gave you that impression? The fact I didn't answer the first half-dozen times you buzzed, perhaps? Persistence is an admirable quality in a lot of murder victims.'

'Sorry, but it is almost eight o'clock.'

'Only in your world.'

'Do . . .' Hannah glanced around and lowered her voice. 'Do the Folk have a different time system?'

'No, but people who own pubs do.'

'Oh.'

'We had our Christmas party last night.' He stopped and opened his eyes. 'Wait, what day is it?'

'Friday.'

'Yeah, last night.'

'Are you feeling a bit worse for wear?'

'You know, you always hear about the fabled journalist instinct, but when you see it in action, it is still truly awe-inspiring.'

'I deserved that.'

'Oh, let's not go down the path of what you deserve.'

'I wouldn't be here if it wasn't important.'

John Mór sighed. 'I know you believe that, but "important" is a relative term. I believe conservation of the natural world is important, but I'd still drop-kick a panda right now for two Pana-dol and a bacon butty.'

'How about a triple murder?'

'I mean, I'd prefer the bacon butty, but I'll take what you've got.'

'Please, John?'

He scratched at his beard. 'Is there anything you'd like to tell me?'

'Ehm. Yes – I'm sorry?'

'Not that. And you're not. Not really.'

'Nice dressing gown?' she ventured.

He looked down then closed the door slightly to cover a little more of himself.

'Thank you, but no. Third time lucky.'

'Oh, ah, yeah . . . DI Sturgess is parked across the road waiting for me.'

'And there it is. I don't know if you picked up on my subtle hints on this before, but even when I've not got a hellscape-sized hangover, I'm not super keen on being a police source.'

'Triple murder, John. It's serious.'

'I'd imagine triple murders always are.' He gave her a look before sighing deeply again. 'All right, you can stand down, Margo.'

'Stand down, M—' Hannah screamed and bent near double. The woman called Margo, whom Hannah knew as a regular in the pub, was standing right behind her, casually picking at her teeth with one of her alarmingly long fingernails. 'Jesus!'

'This might surprise you,' said John Mór, 'but there are people we're even less keen to have drop around unannounced than you. Although you are rapidly climbing that list.'

Hannah straightened up and smiled awkwardly at Margo, who was standing deathly still as she always did. Every time she'd seen the woman, she appeared like that, only to somehow move inexplicably fast the moment you blinked. 'Hi, Margo. Sorry, I didn't hear you there.'

'That is very much the point,' said John Mór, pulling the door back open. 'Whack the kettle on, Margo, I'm going to go put on some clothing that belongs to me.' He turned around and Hannah was still so freaked out by Margo's sudden appearance that she forgot to avert her eyes. This was how she discovered that John Mór had a coquettish-looking bunny rabbit tattooed on his left arse cheek. She tried to look away, only to see Margo smiling at her.

'You should see where he's got a fox,' she said with a wink.

'Tell Inspector Clouseau he can come in,' John Mór shouted back over his shoulder, then he stopped. 'Actually, tell him he can go and get two breakfast butties with absolutely everything and then he can come in. If I'm going to be a police informant, I might as well be a well-fed one.'

Fifteen minutes later, Hannah and DI Sturgess were sitting across a small table in John Mór's rather cozy kitchen, waiting patiently as their host worked his way through the requested breakfast butty. It was really more of a kitchenette than a kitchen, which made the picture on the wall stand out even more. Initially, Hannah had clocked it as a hunt chasing deer, but when she looked at it again it was a herd of deer hunting a bunch of hunters. She was really tired, so it was possible her mind had just filled in what it had expected to see the first time. That being said, given whose apartment they were in, well, there were very probably many other possible explanations. Hannah focused her attention on the big man. Thankfully, he'd found himself a more appropriate dressing gown. It was still too small for him but at least it covered more of the noteworthy places of interest. Margo had taken her butty and disappeared somewhere, leaving Sturgess looking appropriately confused about how she had somehow done so without moving.

John Mór popped the last of his breakfast into his mouth, swallowed it and belched loudly, before rubbing a hand down his beard to check for crumbs. 'That hit the spot.'

'You're welcome,' said Sturgess stiffly.

'Yes, do pass on my thanks to the taxpayers.'

'Do you seriously think I'm allowed to put a breakfast butty on expenses?'

'Like the police haven't been known to fake a bit of paperwork.'

'Boys, boys, boys,' said Hannah. 'While I normally love nothing more than watching the two of you butt horns, could we move this along? I haven't slept in over twenty-four hours.'

John Mór raised an eyebrow at this.

'Long story,' Hannah continued. 'We got hacked.'

'By whom?'

'From what I can gather, the twenty-first century Dennis the Menace.'

'That's why I don't trust 'em.'

'Computers or children?'

John Mór gave a slight smile. 'Both.' He took a slurp of his tea. 'So, you mentioned a murder?'

'A triple one,' said Hannah.

'To be clear,' said Sturgess, 'what we're about to tell you is all strictly confidential.'

John Mór bridled at this. 'If you like, you can keep it all really top secret and bugger off out of my kitchen right now.'

'Bloody hell,' said Hannah. 'Could you two just get past this crap? I'm too tired to play referee.' She turned to Sturgess. 'Just tell him what we know.'

For a moment, it looked as if Sturgess was considering lodging some further objection but he wisely decided to comply with Hannah's request. John Mór listened in silence as Sturgess took them through what had been found in the library. It was the first time Hannah had heard it laid out in such detail and she found herself fighting down waves of nausea.

When Sturgess had finished, John Mór nodded solemnly. 'And you reckon this librarian woman . . .'

'Debra Brimson,' supplied Sturgess.

'. . . is your killer.'

'That's where the evidence is pointing,' said Sturgess, 'but I'm keeping an open mind.'

Hannah spoke quickly, in case John Mór felt inclined to comment on Greater Manchester Police's ability to keep an open mind.

'Does the name ring any bells with you. John? Debra Brimson?'

'Afraid not,' he said, then glanced over Hannah's shoulder. She turned to see Margo standing there, offering a near imperceptible shake of her head.

'Us not knowing somebody doesn't necessarily mean they're not Folk,' he said. 'It's not like we keep a roll.' His face darkened slightly. 'There is one, but it isn't us keeping it. But no, we don't know her. These symbols, were they all written in the blood of the victims?'

'That's the working hypothesis,' said Sturgess, 'but the lab is doing tests to confirm. There's a lot of it.'

John Mór nodded. 'And the victims – do you know who they are?'

This time Sturgess referred to his phone. 'We are now mostly certain their names were Sue Millard, Rose Mitchell and Michaela King. Again, subject to testing and autopsies. Identification is going to be' – he paused and a haunted look passed briefly across his face – 'challenging.'

John Mór glanced up at Margo again then gave a shake of his head. 'No bells ringing there either. These symbols and the writing you keep talking about, what did they look like?'

Sturgess scrolled through his phone. 'Wilkerson's just sent me some sketches of parts of it. She's sending it around a few academics with expertise in languages and semiotics.' He found what he was looking for and held out the device.

John Mór squinted at the screen. Hannah blinked and Margo appeared behind him, glancing over his shoulder. Beside her, she felt Sturgess stiffen, similarly unnerved. Some things you just don't get used to.

John Mór hovered a finger over the phone until Sturgess gave him the nod, then he scrolled back and forth through the images. Once done, he looked back at Margo before speaking again. 'We don't know what they are, exactly. Only seen something like that once before.'

'Where?'

'Can't tell you that.'

Sturgess turned his eyes to the heavens.

'Can't tell you that,' John Mór repeated irritably. 'You get what you get, or you get out.'

Sturgess said nothing to this.

'Is there anything you can tell us?' asked Hannah.

'They're old,' said John Mór. 'The symbols. Real old.'

Hannah didn't know what to make of this. 'Do you mean, like, I don't know, Egyptian or—'

'No, no,' he said. 'I mean *old* old. Before history books old. Ancient.'

'Do you know anyone who can tell us any more about them?' asked Sturgess.

John Mór considered this for a moment then said, 'I'll ask around.'

Sturgess took back his phone, locked it and slid it back into the inside pocket of his coat. 'What about the woman outside the library?' Hannah had noticed a shift in the big man's body language when he'd reached that part of the story. Clearly, it hadn't escaped the DI's attention either.

John Mór paused and looked up at Margo again, some form of unspoken negotiation going on between them before he eventually turned back around. 'If we did know who she was, what would be your interest in her?'

'She interfered in a police investigation,' said Sturgess.

'No,' John Mór said firmly. 'She didn't.'

'How do you know that?'

'Because I know what she is and what she does, and what she doesn't do is go around interfering in police investigations. Most people, even on our side of the fence, might have forgotten who she is, but some of us haven't.'

'We can respect that,' said Hannah. 'So, who is she?'

'I can't tell you that. And before you ask, I'm not telling you what she does either.'

Sturgess gave a groan of exasperation, which earned him a warning glance from Hannah before she turned back to John Mór. 'What *can* you tell us?'

'Nothing. But . . . provided she's treated with the respect she deserves, we'll see if we might – and I stress *might* – be able to get you an audience with her.'

'An audience?' repeated Sturgess.

John Mór folded his arms. 'I said what I said. Take it or leave it.'

'We'll take it,' said Hannah. 'When do you think that'll happen?'

He shrugged. 'Hard to say. Not like she's got an office or a number we can ring. I'll put out some feelers and let you know if we can sort something out.' He ran his hands along the edge of the table. 'Best I can do. Now, if you'll excuse me, I drank rather a lot of Guinness last night and I have to go pay the piper.' He started to stand and then stopped, looking back at Margo. 'I didn't do the thing with the axe last night, did I?'

She gave a gleeful smile and nodded.

'In the names of the gods, I told you not to let me do the thing with the axe.'

Two minutes later, Hannah and Sturgess were back on the street outside the Kanky's Rest, as the throng of early bird Christmas shoppers and Friday-morning commuters, the odd one sporting a length of tinsel, flowed past them.

'That man takes being evasive to the level of an art form,' said Sturgess.

'He doesn't have to help us at all,' Hannah replied.

'Three people are dead and I've got a horrible feeling in my gut that whoever was responsible for it isn't going to simply disappear. John Mór's got a civic responsibility just like everybody else.'

Hannah rubbed her palms into her eyes. Whatever adrenalin had carried her this far had dissipated and left her feeling utterly exhausted. 'And I'm sure he'll do all he can. He's never let us down before.'

'Hasn't he?'

'Well, me – he's never let me down before. Now, if you don't mind, my bed has been calling to me. As soon as I hear something I'll be in touch.'

13

Stella didn't even like coffee.

As far as starting points to a day went, this was pretty grim. Standing in the stone-cold kitchen of *The Stranger Times*, hugging her dressing gown to herself having just got out of the shower, preparing a drink she didn't like in order to get a desperately needed burst of artificial energy. She had a uni project due after the Christmas break and she'd decided to get it done early, because the thing about working and living at the office was that you soon learned to make the most of the quiet times. That's why, after only a few hours' sleep following last night's fiasco of a Christmas party that never was, she was up at ten o'clock on a day off, when any self-respecting student would either still be in bed or wouldn't have even got into it yet.

On the upside, while, to put it nicely, Banecroft could be mercurial, he tended to barely put in an appearance on a Friday. This week's paper was gone, next week's was a review of the year that was already mostly done, and there was a very large, stringently worded sign on the front door to the office, explaining how the newspaper only cared about your earth-shattering paranormal experience between the hours of nine and five from Monday to

Thursday. It didn't stop people knocking, of course, but it provided cover for Banecroft to treat anyone who did so to the sunnier side of his disposition. Stella's three housemates were Banecroft, the grumpiest humanoid in existence; Manny, the permanently stoned Rastafarian; and Brian the ghoul, who now lived in the basement, which on the upside meant she was the only one who ever used the shower. On the downside, she was the only one who used the shower. She was confident she could find any of them blindfolded by sense of smell alone, not that she'd want to. To be fair to Manny, he occasionally went just outside the doors and stood topless in the rain to 'let the good Lord wash we sins away'.

The kettle clicked off. With a yawn, Stella started pouring the hot water into her mug. She didn't even like the smell.

''Sup, babes!'

Boiling water splashed against her wrist as she spun around, instantly more alert than any tepid coffee shot could make her. She felt that familiar tingle as the power in her surged, her flight-or-fight response instantly activated. She was greeted by the sight of half a man leaning against the door frame, favouring her with a downright lascivious grin.

'Feisty. I like it.'

Stella took a step back, cinching her dressing gown tighter as she did so. 'What the hell are you?'

'What do you want me to be?'

'Somewhere else.' She slammed the kettle on to its base then ran her scalded wrist under the cold tap. 'You're lucky you didn't get a face full of boiling water, sneaking up on someone like that.'

Ox appeared behind the half-man. 'I see you've met Clint.'

'Don't crowd me, knobhead,' hissed Clint. 'We're vibing here.'

'Ugh,' said Stella. 'I just had a shower and now I need another one.'

'Nice,' said Clint, grinning.

'So gross. What are you, like, ten?'

'I'm fourteen.'

'He's small for his age,' said Ox.

'I'm a grower not a shower.'

'Like a fungus,' said Ox, looking as tired as Stella felt.

'Hang on,' said Stella. 'Is this—'

'The terrorist who attacked this sacred bastion of free speech? Yeah.'

'What's he doing here?'

'Same as me,' said Ox. 'Repaying our debt to society.'

'Oh dear.'

'Yeah,' said Ox. 'Merry bloody Christmas.'

'So,' continued Clint, 'how's about giving me those digits, sweetness?'

'Normally,' said Stella, 'you'd get all five straight to the face but I believe it's against the law to hit a child.'

'Kinky. I'm into it.'

Ox grabbed Clint firmly by the shoulder. 'C'mon, you little sex pest, there's a scrubbing brush with your name on it.'

Clint tried to shake him off. 'Don't cock-block me. I'm working the magic here.'

'Judging by the look on Stella's face, you're dangerously close to witnessing her work her magic, and I don't think you'd enjoy that.'

'I didn't even get a chance to neg her yet.'

'Good God.' Ox turned his protesting charge and started to march him away. 'Bear in mind I'm a man drowning in crippling debts he can never hope to pay, but is there any way I could pay you to shut up for, like, an hour?'

Half an hour later, Stella was sitting on her bed, typing then deleting the first line of an essay on the dangers of unregulated media for the twenty-ninth time. Normally, she liked to work at her desk in the bullpen, but Ox was in there losing a battle of wits with a sperm in a tracksuit. Something to do with trying to fix desks. Banecroft was quite the evil genius when it came to constructing a to-do list – only half of the desks in there were occupied but some of the unloved ones managed the feat of having all four legs shorter than the other three.

Amid the hammering and bickering, a more rhythmic noise made itself known. Someone was knocking on the front door. Stella endeavoured to ignore it but in the battle of wills between her and the knocker, the other side seemed determined not to blink first.

'Right, fine,' huffed Stella. 'I'll stop what I'm doing because you can't read a sign, shall I?' She stomped down the stairs, resigned to the fact that there was no chance of anyone else going. If Banecroft was able to sleep through the noise Ox and Clint were making, he wasn't going to be roused by this, and knocks on doors were one of the many things Manny never seemed to register. She'd often wondered how he communicated with and received supplies from his weed dealer. It was one of the bigger mysteries in a building protected by an ancient spirit with a ghoul in the basement and a dent in the back wall from where a werewolf had tossed furniture about the place.

Stella had her phaser firmly set to sarcastic as she threw the door open, but the sight of the woman standing there caused her to pause. She looked to be in her early twenties, maybe – smartly dressed, biracial with light-brown skin and black curly hair tied back with a hairband. There was something in her eyes – as if she had been crying or soon would be.

'Hi,' said Stella.

'Hello,' said the woman. 'Ehm, sorry about all the . . .' She stopped and cleared her throat. 'I'd like to speak to Emmanuel Devon, please.'

'Oh, I'm afraid there's nobody here of that name. This is the offices of *The*—'

'*Stranger Times*. The newspaper thing. Yes, I know,' said the girl. 'He's . . . You might also know him as Manny.'

'Manny?' repeated Stella, taken aback. Nobody had ever come here looking for Manny, and while Stella tried not to prejudge people, this girl did not have weed-dealer vibes. 'Well, I mean, he's here – probably.' Manny literally couldn't leave the premises owing to his passenger but she felt obliged to throw in the 'probably', in case she realized that this was something she needed to shut down. 'Can I ask how you know him?'

'I'm his great-great-granddaughter.'

'OK, sure.' Stella raised her voice. 'I assume you're standing at the top of the stairs, Ox. I'll be honest, not one of your better ones.'

'I know how it sounds,' said the girl.

'Oh, I don't think you do.'

'My great-grandmother is his daughter.'

'I can't fault your maths, and seriously, well done for committing to the part, but—'

'Listen!' snapped the girl with more than enough sincerity to stop Stella in her tracks and wipe the grin off her face. 'I appreciate it sounds crazy but . . .' She opened her bag and searched around in it for a few seconds before finding what she was looking for. She held the item out to Stella. 'This. This is them.'

Stella didn't even touch the picture. Instead, she just leaned forward and looked at it. It was a black-and-white portrait of a young Black girl of maybe seven or eight years of age in a frilly dress. She was beaming at the camera while, standing behind her, also smiling broadly at the camera, was a man in an army uniform. Stella studied the man's face for a very long time. No locs. No beard. And yet, the more she looked . . . 'Manny?'

'Yes,' confirmed the girl, taking the picture back. 'That was taken in nineteen forty, just before my great-grandma's father shipped out to fight in France.'

'But—' Stella couldn't think of a single word to say. It was like her brain was one of their PCs after it'd been taken over by the virus. All she could do was stand there with her mouth open.

'I'm aware how insane all of this sounds.'

'If that's . . .' said Stella, pointing at the space where the picture no longer was, 'then, he'd be . . .'

The girl nodded. 'Grammy Dottie is ninety-two, and I believe Emmanuel is one hundred and twelve.'

'Wow! I mean, I've heard the black-don't-crack thing before but . . .' Stella realized she had never considered Manny's age, but if she had, she'd have probably guessed late thirties – maybe forty at a push. His locs were white, yes, but she and everyone else had seen him wandering about in various states of undress on more than enough occasions to know he had a pretty athletic physique, certainly for someone who, if what this woman was saying was true, would be knocking on the door of being the oldest man alive. The paper had written an article about this recently – Stella had a vague idea the current record was something like one hundred and sixteen years old.

'I'll be honest,' said Stella, 'I'm utterly confused.'

'So am I,' said the girl. 'My grandmother, Grammy's daughter, only told me about this last week, but judging by your reaction, I'm guessing he's here.'

'He's . . . I mean, he's here all right, but . . .'

'He still looks like he does in that photo?' finished the girl. 'Only Grandma says he has white locs now. She says she saw him, from a distance, a few years ago.'

'Yeah, but . . .' Stella still couldn't form anything that felt like a coherent thought. 'I . . . I guess you'd better come in.'

'Thank you. I'm Zoe, by the way.'

'Right. I'm Stella. Ehm . . .' Stella looked at the door to the printer. 'OK, I guess I'll . . .'

She knocked on it gently. 'Manny?'

There was no noise from the other side.

Stella chewed on her thumbnail nervously. 'He might be sleeping. I'll just . . .'

She hammered on the door more loudly.

This time there was a thump and the sound of something hitting the floor in response.

'Manny,' shouted Stella. 'You've got a visitor.'

'We no have no visitor,' came the cheerful response.

'You do now.' Stella turned back to Zoe. 'Stay here a sec.' She raised her voice again. 'I'm coming in.' She wanted to add, 'Are you decent?' but it seemed like an awkward thing to say in front of her audience. Instead, she left a long pause before easing the door open slowly. She found Manny standing in front of the press, thankfully fully clothed, staring back at her.

'Hi, Manny,' said Stella, opening the door wider. 'You've got a visitor. She's . . . I'll let her explain.' Stella stepped to one side and Zoe nervously entered the room behind her.

She and Manny stood staring at each other in silence, the time stretching out. Maybe it was Stella's mind playing tricks on her but she thought she could see some form of family resemblance. Something around the eyes.

'Wow!' said Zoe softly. 'It's really . . .' She drew a deep breath and pulled the picture out of her bag again. She held it up like an ID card. 'Hello. My name's Zoe and I'm Dottie's – your daughter's – great-granddaughter. I—'

She gave an involuntary yelp as Manny slumped forward. He hadn't collapsed, though. Instead, he just hung in the air like a puppet.

'Oh no,' said Stella, who knew what this meant.

'Is he—' started Zoe.

'You should probably go,' said Stella.

'No, I need to—'

'Go. Really, because—'

It was too late. The smoke that wasn't smoke had started to billow forth from Manny, not coming from anywhere that you could see, but filling the air above him.

Zoe stood frozen to the spot. The fog of white smoke was roiling in the air now, and then, as Stella knew it would, it began to form into the awe-inspiring figure of the winged woman – the angel. Almost as soon as it appeared, the beautiful face transformed into a mask of fury as the figure swooped down. Its voice, more like a hundred shrill voices roaring in unison, screamed as it surged towards Zoe. 'He. Is. Mine!'

Zoe stumbled then crawled towards the door and was gone, the door slamming hard behind her.

'What the—' started Stella.

The angel was swirling around the room now, a frenzy of enraged motion, while Manny hung limp and lifeless beneath it. A wind whipped in its wake, picking up random pieces of paper and tossing them about in the maelstrom.

As Stella turned to leave, stunned, something small and square, picked up by the wind, stuck to her chest. She grabbed it and, with difficulty, heaved open the door. Once back in the hallway, the door slammed behind her and she leaned against it, breathless, trying to process what had just happened. Zoe was nowhere to be seen.

Stella looked down at the thing in her hand. It was the picture Zoe had shown her – Manny, some eighty-six or so years ago, standing with his daughter.

14

Sergeant Tony Morrison looked into the eyes of the prisoner opposite him in the back of the van and a shiver went down his spine. The man, shackled in maximum restraints, spit and bite guard on his head, was sitting perfectly still and staring back at him calmly. A raving lunatic, he'd been taken down with Tasers and pepper spray in a job done well, but there was something about him that didn't sit right. Unnatural. Morrison had seen people high on every drug known to man and he'd never seen anything like this.

The armed response unit Morrison commanded had been called to Knockout Joe's gym at 7 a.m., just before they were about to go off shift. They'd been sitting around on their arses all night waiting for a raid that didn't come thanks to changing intel. It was the kind of thing you had to get used to in the job. After the clusterfuck out at the farm in Saddleworth a couple of months back, where two of the team had died and another two were signed off with long-term injuries, this was a very different group from the one Morrison had so carefully assembled. It comprised a few holdovers thrown together with new recruits or secondments from elsewhere. Morrison didn't know them and they didn't know each other. The holdovers were all changed in their own ways, too. Despite what people believed, having to shoot somebody was hard on anyone who wasn't a total nutjob, but it was a lot harder to have to watch that thing get back up and keep coming at you. It was the stuff of nightmares. The inevitable cover-up had offered no explanations – at least nothing that held any water. Meth heads high on a bad batch was the official story. Nobody had questioned it.

Morrison had agreed to swallow his moral objections and play along because what was the alternative? Going on YouTube screaming about zombies being real? At best you'd create panic and at worst, almost inevitably, you'd be ridiculed and ignored. The powers that be, whoever the hell they were, were brilliant at making you look like a lunatic if you didn't toe the line. Still, when he'd received the 'bonus' in his pay packet the following month, in very clear terms he'd told them exactly where they could shove it. He was agreeing to give his silence reluctantly – it wasn't being bought.

The prisoner – the one currently eyeballing him – was called Paul Banner. Joe, the eponymous owner of the gym, shellshocked and wearing a tank top covered in someone else's blood, had been used for a pre-engagement briefing. He'd explained that Banner had been coming to his gym for years because it opened earlier than the big boys and was on his route to work. The gym did a mix of boxing and MMA, mostly for enthusiastic amateurs with a few more serious punters thrown in, but Banner had just been there for the weights. A lot of them, judging by the size of him. He was six five and built like the proverbial brick shithouse. Joe said he'd always reckoned Paul had a clear case of body dysmorphia – constantly trying to get bigger and bigger despite being heavily muscled already. For all that, he'd been sweet, Joe had said. A softly spoken guy who was so timid he'd seen him getting kicked off machines by guys half his size. All that changed when he'd come into the gym earlier that morning and climbed into the ring in the middle of a sparring session.

'He just walked in,' Joe had explained. 'Straight into the ring and said some weird shit like, 'Who will challenge me?' Kept referring to himself by a weird name. Jack – Jack Woods, currently the fifth-ranked MMA heavyweight in the country – laughed and then Paul . . . just went off!' Joe had been in tears recalling the scene. 'He . . . Jesus, he tore into Jack and then, when we tried to pull him off, he started ripping into everybody. I never seen nothing like it. I still can't believe it. I mean, Paul – fucking Paul? He's a graphic designer, for Christ's sake. He still lives with his mum.'

Tony had asked about drug use and been told that, as far as Joe knew, Banner was clean. The way he answered the question told Tony enough. No gym owner, even in the most stressful of situations, is going to admit to thinking one of his regular patrons is juicing. Still, steroids, coke, amphetamines – nothing could explain an episode like this.

Eventually, anyone who could got the hell out of the gym, leaving Banner inside with those who couldn't. Given the extreme violence displayed and that, in effect, Banner had hostages, the mission brief had been to subdue. If that didn't do it, lethal force had been authorized. From the get-go, the whole thing had smelled off to Tony and, despite having incapacitated and restrained the target successfully, it still felt wrong. Those eyes. It wasn't as if they were wild and bloodshot, the kind of thing you'd expect. Quite the opposite. Calm, almost mockingly so, like he was watching them all with interest. The guy had killed a man with his bare hands, three more were in hospital in a critical condition, including a police officer with massive internal injuries resulting from a true act of barbarism, and this guy – no record, no history of violence, who'd supposedly done it all in the space of a few minutes – was sitting in the back of the van like he was on a day trip to Butlins. Tony shifted the gun in his grip. The sooner they got this guy into a holding cell and he was no longer their responsibility, the happier he'd be.

He tensed as the prisoner shifted, and he felt his three other team members in the back of the prisoner transport do likewise.

'Who are you?' the prisoner asked in a deep voice.

'None of your business,' shot back Jacobs. She was one of the veterans who'd been at the farm. She had harder edges now. A mean streak. Like she was looking to smash trouble in the mouth before it could start.

'Are you soldiers?'

'No,' said Dylan, one of the newbies. 'We're not the army. You got taken down by the police, ya sick bastard.'

'The police,' he repeated as if trying to understand the word.

'Yeah,' continued Dylan. 'Like that poor bastard you made into a kebab. I imagine everyone at the station will be really happy to see you.'

'Dylan,' snapped Morrison. He didn't like that crap and, unlike Jacobs, Dylan hadn't earned himself any leeway.

'And what magic was it that you used on me?'

Dylan laughed. A harsh sound as it echoed around the van. 'Magic? Fuck me, this guy is as high as a kite.'

Jacobs and Morrison shared a look. They had seen things Dylan hadn't and Morrison had always suspected none of those present had given any details of what happened at the farm to those who weren't there.

'You got Tasered,' said Dylan. 'You should probably get used to the feeling.'

'Everybody shut up,' said Morrison. 'No more chat.'

'Sir,' said Dylan tersely. Not for the first time, Morrison wondered if Dylan was going to work out. In order to replenish their numbers, they'd been forced to recruit a lot more quickly than he would have liked. Dylan had been a transfer from the North East and Morrison had a strong suspicion that if he'd been one of their best and brightest, his old unit would have done more to keep him.

'So,' said the prisoner to Morrison, 'you are the one in command?'

'I said shut up,' repeated Morrison. He locked eyes with Banner again.

Sixty seconds later, he was relieved to feel the van slow and make a sharp left turn before coming to a stop.

'We're here, guv,' announced Jacobs.

'Right,' said Morrison, 'you all know the drill.' He turned back to the prisoner. 'Now, Mr Banner, this can go one of two ways. You behave yourself and it'll go easier for all of us, but you try anything, anything, and we will put you down – hard. Do we understand each other?'

In response, the man tilted his head. 'So, this police – do you rule the people?'

'Jesus H. Christ,' said Morrison, shaking his head. 'I'm regretting not going with the gag.' He turned to his team. 'You know what to do.'

As the back doors opened, Morrison scouted the yard where they'd pulled up. The rest of the squad, having followed behind in the van, had already dispersed around the prisoner transport, as per their training. Satisfied, Morrison returned his attention to the prisoner. His hands and feet were manacled, with a chain between, which meant he couldn't do much beyond shuffle. Still, given his sheer size, Morrison didn't want anyone to have to hold him by the arms, so they were going to be using the poles. They could be connected to the restraints while the prisoner was still in the back of the van and then used to lead him without making physical contact. Morrison watched on as Dylan and Jacobs stowed their weapons then placed the poles through the manacles. In their role as shepherds they would carry no weapons, to remove the possibility of the prisoner going for a snatch.

Banner, under instruction, got to his feet calmly and allowed himself to be led out of the doors, shuffling down the steps and stopping to let the morning sunlight play across his face.

'Enjoy,' said Dylan. 'You won't be seeing that again for a while.'

'Let's go,' said Morrison. After this, he and Dylan would be having words about the standard of professionalism he expected from his team.

Banner started walking again, his entourage maintaining

formation as they moved. They'd made their way halfway across the yard when the prisoner pitched forward, face first. His immense size meant that even with the support of the metal poles, nothing was holding him up once he started going down. The surrounding circle of guards repositioned themselves, with Dylan and Jacobs shifting to maintain their grip on the far end of the bars. Prisoners playing silly buggers was to be expected.

Morrison waved everyone back. 'Get up, Banner.'

The man didn't move.

'Now,' ordered Morrison.

Nothing.

He shifted around to get a good look at the man's face. Banner was face down on the concrete, eyes closed, showing no signs of life.

'Ah, shit,' Morrison muttered, before nodding at Jacobs. She moved forward, bent down and placed two fingers on the prisoner's neck carefully, feeling for a pulse.

She immediately pulled back as Banner jerked suddenly.

'Get up, Banner,' barked Morrison. 'I'm really not in the mood for this nonsense.'

In response, the man shifted back on to his knees and looked around, his eyes suddenly filled with panic. 'W-w-where am I?'

'Get up,' repeated Morrison.

A piercing wail issued from the man and, in a voice entirely different to the one he'd used in the van, he started speaking quickly. 'Oh God, what happened? Was there blood? I remember blood. What did I do?' He stared down at his hands in horror. 'What happened? What did I do?'

Morrison bent down slightly and confirmed that the man was now bawling his eyes out.

'I want my mum,' Banner said in a pathetic whimper.

Morrison swore under his breath.

'Christ, boss,' said Dylan. 'What is this guy on?'

'I don't know, but let's get him up and into a cell, shall we? Jacobs?'

Morrison looked around and was shocked to see the figure of Jacobs walking calmly out the gate.

'What the—Where the hell is she going?'

15

Neil Aiken took a deep breath. The thing he loved most in the world and the thing he hated most were about to collide, and he was trying to prepare himself for the collision.

What he loved most in the world was Christmas. He was aware that was an odd thing for a twenty-eight-year-old man to say but it was true. His childhood had been – well, complicated didn't begin to cover it. He'd accidentally overheard a social worker once describe it as a shitshow, and it was hard to disagree. Neil's abiding memory of his mum's funeral, apart from the scant attendance, was one of her friends, who wore a bright summer dress, smelled of rhubarb and jingled when she moved. She had grabbed his hands and told him that his mother's problem had been that her energy didn't match well with this world's. Never a truer word had been spoken. At the time, people had described his mum as 'kooky', a 'free spirit', a 'character' – these days he suspected words such as 'undiagnosed' would be offered. What hadn't been offered at the time was much in the way of help. Mum hadn't known how to deal with the world, and the world hadn't known how to deal with her. The first twelve years of Neil's life had been spent clasping his mother's hand tightly as they ran away from bad debts, bad ideas and bad boyfriends. One of the first things he'd learned had been how to triage his toys to make sure the one or two he really wanted made it into that battered blue suitcase.

Then there was Christmas. That was the time when his mum's energy had briefly 'matched this world's'. Wherever they'd been and whatever crisis they'd been dealing with recently, his mum had always managed to make it special. People talked about the true spirit of Christmas all the time and whenever they did, Neil wondered if they realized they were referring to his mum. She could make a walk down a street illuminated by Christmas lights a truly wondrous experience, as she told stories, filling the world with wonder. A small plastic Christmas tree with some mismatched baubles became a trip to a fantastical land from which Neil had never wanted to come home. She would take him to see Santa Claus and then, as he'd sat on some befuddled man's lap, his mother would tell them both about Santa's exciting adventures to get there. One time, one of Santa's little helpers had brought in the whole queue and got Neil's mum to tell the whole story again. People had applauded.

Even when there were years when she couldn't afford to take Neil to see Santa, she'd brought Christmas to them. He remembered one night, shivering in the corner of a particularly grim squat in Shaw, when she'd produced a snow globe from her bag, showing Santa Claus and a Rudolph who wobbled precariously on three legs so you had to be careful how you shook it. Still, huddled up in that worn sleeping bag, looking at that snow globe as his mother had woven her spell with her arms wrapped around him, he'd never been happier before or since. If he could, he'd have stayed there for ever.

Then, his mother's arms had fallen away for good and the world she left behind had been that much colder. Stability – how he'd grown to hate that word. It's what social services had told him he needed, over and over again, while being shifted from foster home to foster home. He mostly kept himself to himself. His education had been patchy, but given that his babysitter had often been a book, he read far more and at a higher level than any of his contemporaries. His mother had never cared for subjects such as Maths, and neither did Neil. Still, he was considered well behaved – at least for most of the year.

Every December, he would start to disappear. Skipping school. More often than not, he'd be wandering around, looking at all the lights and decorations. Manchester's Christmas markets were a wonderland all on their own. He'd rarely been able to afford to buy anything, but he'd looked at everything time and time again, while stallholders eyed him suspiciously. The odd food vendor even took pity on him and treated him to the occasional mis-shapen bratwurst. He never understood why people complained about Christmas starting earlier and earlier every year – who wouldn't want more of the most wonderful thing in existence?

He'd tried to keep going to see Santa Claus as he'd grown older. At first, people had laughed, and then they'd stopped and told him firmly that it was no longer for him. He'd made do with sitting in the Arndale Centre, watching from a distance as excited kids queued up with their parents outside the grotto. After a couple of years, the truant officer had known where to find him.

Peter Mambu – nice guy as such fellas went. Rory, one of the lads Neil kept meeting on his trips through the care system, had once given Peter a black eye but he'd been decent enough not to hold it against him. When Neil was fifteen, in exchange for promising to stay in school even if he didn't learn anything, Peter got him a job helping out at the grotto in the Trafford Centre on the weekends. He'd known somebody who'd known somebody and pulled in a favour. Unpaid, Neil had turned up every Saturday and Sunday morning as soon as the place opened, and stayed there right until the end, little elf hat on, doing anything he could. He'd been surprised at the end of that first year when they'd given him an envelope with three hundred quid in it because, as the manager said, it'd be criminal not to pay Santa's best helper. Neil had been considerably less surprised when he'd got home and Rory had taken it all off him. Still, those had been the best three weeks of his life. Even better, the next year, they'd asked him to go back, and now he'd finally left school, he could work there every day. Seeing behind the curtain should have taken away the magic but it didn't.

On into his twenties, he'd flitted from dead-end job to dead-end job for eleven months of the year as he waited for December to roll around. The first time he'd taken on the role of Santa had been because the store's incumbent had been caught by his wife with one of the other little helpers who had been going above and beyond in the 'helpfulness' stakes. Apparently, Santa could not have a broken nose. Oddly, it had never occurred to Neil that he could *be* Santa Claus. He had always assumed there must be some special training course, or possibly a covert organization called something like the Sacred Order of Claus, complete with secret handshake. You couldn't just put on a suit – there had to be some far greater barrier of entry to such a hallowed duty than that. It turned out there was no solemn tap on the shoulder but rather a hassled store manager telling you to just put the bloody thing on and get out there before there was a riot. Still, once Neil had donned the suit, the magic had happened. It had been the greatest day of his life.

Nervous at first, he'd quickly grown into the role. Over the course of the next few years, he'd attempted to also grow into the role literally but, try as he might, he couldn't seem to gain weight. He'd once gone to his GP to ask if there was any way he could pile on the pounds and make his beard grow white. He'd been given a number which, when he rang it, had turned out to be for a drug counselling service. He dyed his hair instead and bought some padding.

Over the years he'd developed a reputation for being the gold-standard Santa Claus. Still, as much as he loved the job, he always found it a bit frustrating. No matter what they said, every shopping centre or big store ultimately was concerned with rattling through as many children as possible as quickly as possible. It was Neil's belief that the experience should be special for every child – he wasn't as good at the stories as his mother had been, but he enjoyed trying. At the very least, he enjoyed listening to the children. It was surprising how many youngsters went through life without anyone really listening to what they had to say. Neil had even been asked to push certain products to the kids or parents, which he'd refused point blank to do, considering it a violation of a sacred code that he couldn't articulate, and which may've existed only for him. Still, when the chance came to be part of a very different experience he'd jumped at it.

Claremont Dibner was an unusual name for an unusual man. He sounded private-school posh but with the kind of rat-a-tat patter to be found in someone running a market stall. He had the kind of wide eyes you normally associated with people who wanted to give you a pamphlet and talk about Jesus. His smile was so big that it seemed to contain more teeth that were commonly found in the human mouth and, as he spoke, he waved his hands about to such an extent that you found yourself expecting him to produce a dove at any minute. When he'd come to Neil with his idea for a grade-A, primo, no-expense-spared 'Christmas experience', with Neil as its centrepiece, he'd jumped at the chance. They were kindred spirits, or at least that's what Claremont had told him. And so it was that Neil had appeared in all the social-media videos inviting families to come visit him at the North West's magical Christmas spectacular – Wonderland. It had been unofficially open for two days ahead of its full launch on Saturday, and it had left people rendered speechless, but not in the way Neil had hoped.

A hard knot of tension formed in his gut as he stood in front of the door to Claremont Dibner's office. Claremont's executive assistant, Clarissa, was absent from behind her desk – presumably, she'd gone on a well-deserved break from scrolling through Instagram while regarding anyone who had the temerity to ask her a question as if they were trouserless and rambling in a foreign language. Christmas might have been the thing Neil loved most in the world, but the thing he'd spent a lifetime avoiding was confrontation. Now, he had no choice. He could have done this before he changed into his costume, but wearing it was like a shield and gave him a confidence he didn't otherwise possess. From the other side of the door, he could hear Claremont on the phone, or at least he assumed that was the case. The man wasn't leaving any gaps for anyone to get a word in edgeways, so it could be called a conversation only in the most nominal sense.

Neil girded his loins and knocked on the door.

'Come in!'

Claremont's smile dipped for just a fraction of a second when he saw who it was before ramping back up to full beam. He was sitting behind a desk festooned with unopened post and empty cans of various energy drinks, a phone propped between his chin and shoulder. 'Neil, great to see you. Sorry, thought you were Clarissa with my breakfast. Is there any chance we could do this later?'

Neil had prepared himself for this. 'You said later on Tuesday, Wednesday and yesterday.'

'Did I? Well, you know how it is. Busy, busy, busy. After all the careful planning, we're almost at the big day, finally. I'm pumped and I know you are, too. Could we put something in the diary for next week?'

'But we'll be closed by then. It's Christmas Eve in two days.'

'Exactly. A debrief.' He threw out his hands towards Neil. 'A post-match interview with the inevitable man of the match.'

Neil steeled himself. 'No, I think we need to do it now.'

The smile didn't dim. 'Absolutely, couldn't agree more.'

Claremont pulled the phone away from his ear and looked at it. 'I think they've hung up on me. Rude.' He set the receiver back in its cradle and raised his voice. 'Clarissa, hold all my calls.'

'She's actually not—'

Claremont waved him into the visitor's chair. 'Sit. Sit. Sit! Or should I come over and sit on your knee?' He laughed uproariously at his own joke. 'Seriously, though, we should take care of your knees.' He shouted at the closed door again. 'Clarissa, find me the best physio in Manchester – we want them on standby. This man is a seasonal athlete of the highest order and we need to keep him in tip-top shape.' He returned to Neil. 'Now, what can I do for you?'

'It's about the experience.'

'Absolutely. Absolutely. Well, we're only in the soft-launch phase ahead of the big day tomorrow, but I can tell you the feedback has already been sensational. The parents love you. The kids love you. We love you.' He stopped and pointed at the ceiling, leaving the slightest of gaps. 'Can you hear that? That excited buzzing noise is love – for you!'

'I think that's from the sewage place next door.' The Wonderland Christmas Experience was located in a warehouse on the edge of town, wedged between a rugby stadium and a sewage plant.

'Not sewage,' said Claremont smoothly. 'It's a water treatment facility.'

When the wind changed, the smell of water treatment was strong enough to leave an unpleasant taste at the back of your throat.

'The point is,' continued Claremont, 'the people love you.'

'That's nice to hear, but I'm afraid the feedback you're getting is different from what I'm hearing.'

'Is this about that kid who got' – Claremont caught himself – '*allegedly* got food poisoning from the Christmas nachos? First off, kids are always licking stuff, eating stuff off the floor, chewing furniture—'

'I think you're confusing kids with dogs?'

'My point is, while accepting absolutely no liability, we are discontinuing that particular concession. What I was assured was guacamole with a festive covering of edible snow may have just been guacamole that had peaked too soon. While an acquired taste, it is considered a luxury in many cultures.'

'Right, no, it's not that. But on the subject of snow—'

Claremont's face lit up. 'Is it snowing?' He looked excitedly at the grimy window despite it being entirely opaque.

'No.'

'Shame. Could have saved us a fortune, that.'

'It'd be a big improvement on the fake snow we have.'

'Not fake,' corrected Claremont. 'Faux. Fake sounds tacky.'

'But it's just ripped-up toilet paper.'

'Recycled toilet paper. Wonderland takes its environmental responsibilities very seriously.'

'OK, but it was a dirty mulch five minutes after we opened.'

'Have you seen real snow? That is a super accurate representation of what happens. But I take your point.' He raised his voice again. 'Clarissa, get Wayne to start ripping up some new bog roll, and will that breakfast burrito be putting in an appearance any time soon?' He turned back to Neil. 'Thanks for bringing this to my attention. My door is always open.'

'It has been locked most of the week.'

'Metaphorically open. Security. You understand, I'm sure. There are some very dodgy characters about.'

'On that subject, are you aware that Wayne—'

'Wayne – vice president of customer relations,' Claremont cut in.

'Yeah. Him. He got out of prison last Tuesday.'

'And we here at Wonderland are committed to being civic-minded employers keen to give those who have strayed from the path of virtue a second chance in life. What could be more Christmassy than that?'

'Yesterday, he told one of the parents he'd slice him open from guts to gullet if he didn't shut up.'

'He has a very dry sense of humour.'

'And a knife.'

'Not a knife,' corrected Claremont. 'A snow facilitation device.'

'He's got the word "Satan" tattooed on his forehead.'

Claremont sat back and held up his hands. 'Whoa, whoa, Neil. I hope you're not suggesting that we here at Wonderland should not be accepting of all faiths and beliefs?'

'But . . .' floundered Neil. 'Satan?'

'You can't spell Santa without Satan,' said Claremont with a cheeky wink that looked as if he'd practised it in the mirror while perfecting his cheeky-chappy persona.

'What does that even mean?'

'I take your point, though.' He raised his voice once more. 'Clarissa, get Wayne a bigger Santa hat.' He turned his attention back to Neil. 'I'm glad we had this confab. Your input is invaluable, now go out there and spread some joy.'

Neil folded his arms, his arse remaining firmly rooted to the chair.

Claremont beat out a drum fill on the table top. 'I'm sensing you have other concerns?'

'The complimentary muffins.'

'What about them?'

'They cost five pounds.'

'Yes, but they've got "love you" written on them in icing, and isn't that the biggest compliment imaginable?'

'They've got other things on them, too.'

'Christmas shapes.'

'They don't look like Christmas shapes. They look very un-Christmassy.' Neil produced one from his pocket and pointed at it. 'What's that?'

Claremont squinted. 'That's a Christmas tree.'

'No, it's not,' said Neil firmly. 'It's a penis.'

Claremont's face became a mask of outrage that was as real as his snow. 'It is not.'

'It's clearly a cock and balls.'

'Those are presents in a sort of big sack waiting under the tree for all the good boys and girls.'

'It's not tree-shaped.'

'A massive problem at this time of year is the waste created because people want a perfectly Christmas-tree-shaped

Christmas tree. We are actively promoting environmentally friendly alternative options.'

'At the top there's a—'

'Shooting star,' finished Claremont. 'That's a shooting star – a big part of the Christmas story.'

'It's not star-shaped.'

'Icing is a limiting creative medium. Look, Neil, nobody is saying everything is perfect. It's why we're having the soft opening before the big day tomorrow. Nothing worked on the first day at Disney World.'

'The only thing we have in common with Disney World is that we also have mice.'

'And car parking. We both have car parking. And, now that I think of it, we're both being sued by the great state of Florida.'

'Why are we being sued?'

'I didn't say sued. I said wooed. The Americans love what we've done here and are very keen to get us over there.' Claremont's body language tensed suddenly. 'There aren't any Americans here, are there?'

'Not that I've seen.'

'Large men in suits?'

'No.'

Claremont relaxed. 'Right. Good. Good. Not that we aren't welcoming of all nationalities here at the Wonderland Christmas Experience. We're for everyone. That's what it says on the flyer.'

Conversation with Claremont was a lot like finding yourself trapped on the central reservation of a busy motorway, desperately hoping for a gap in the traffic to get your point across safely.

'Speaking of the flyer, it has a reindeer on it.'

'Have you not met Rudolph?'

'I have. It's a cow covered in brown paint that's mostly come off already, and the red nose is being held on with a disturbing amount of masking tape.'

'Clarissa, get Wayne to respray the c—' Claremont stopped himself. 'Reindeer.'

'It's a cow. It's not the right species or gender to be Rudolph.'

'I don't want to be hyper-critical here, Neil, but you're coming off a tad sexist and species-ist there.'

'The presents for the children are rubbish.'

'How dare you. We have searched high and low for only the finest bespoke gifts.'

'Half of them are tennis balls.'

'There is an obesity epidemic among the youth of Great Britain. We make no apology for encouraging sporting participation.'

'Then there's the chew toys . . .'

'We're a nation of animal lovers.'

'Yesterday, one of the kids got a block of wood.'

Claremont raised a finger in correction. 'A hand-crafted block of wood.'

'It had a rusty nail in it.'

'A vintage, hand-crafted block of wood.'

Neil held his head in his hands and gave an exasperated howl. A few moments of silence followed before Claremont spoke again in a softer voice.

'Look, Neil, I think you're missing the bigger picture here, fella. What does the sign outside say?'

Neil didn't look up. He didn't want Claremont to see the hot wet tears that were now rolling down his cheeks. 'No refunds.'

'It says . . . What? No. OK, well, when it arrives . . .' As he raised his voice this time he made Neil jump. 'Clarissa, ring the sign people!' He turned back to Neil again. '. . . it will say "Welcome to Wonderland – a world of imagination". We're not some overdone soulless corporate theme park. We're leaving room to allow the kids to let their imaginations run wild.'

'Like the mice.'

'Like the mice. Or, as I like to think of them, Santa's littlest helpers.'

Neil finally looked up at Claremont with his tear-filled eyes. 'I wanted it to be special and it's not. It's a con.'

'No, no, no. Not at all. It's a work in progress. That's all. The magic hasn't happened yet, but you wait, just you wait.'

Claremont moved around the desk and placed a reassuring hand on Neil's shoulder. 'We're a plucky upstart and we'll strive as we go to be all we can be. I just need you to hang on in there. OK?'

'I don't know, it's just . . .'

'And, c'mon. Try not to take it all so seriously. I mean, it's just Christmas.'

The laugh on Claremont's lips died when he saw the look on Neil's face and realized what a terrible mistake he'd made. 'Just . . . Christmas!' Neil breathed.

Claremont backed away quickly as Neil shot to his feet. 'Neil.

You OK, buddy? You've . . . Your eye is sort of twitching a bit there. Maybe we should get you a muffin. Clarissa?'

'She's not there.' Neil's voice came out in a low rumble.

'Wayne?' Claremont was backed up against the wall now, his smile having finally cracked into a wince. 'OK, let's not do anything that would get you put on the naughty list.'

16

As Stella walked along Burnage Lane in Didsbury, she was painfully aware that she didn't know what she was doing. Actually,
no, not what she was doing – the what was simple enough. She'd
set out to find Zoe, the woman who was purportedly Manny's
great-times-about-a-thousand-granddaughter, and she was here
because she had a lead. The why, on the other hand – that was
murkier. Looking for her made sense, but after the alarming confrontation in the printing room, Stella couldn't explain why she
hadn't immediately told any of the others about it. Instead, Zoe
had run off, and when Ox had come asking what all the commo-
tion was, Stella had said it was nothing. Just another loon who
couldn't read the sign on the door outside.

She'd even passed Banecroft in the kitchen, trying to make
himself a cup of tea in the same way he always did – like a man
who'd never seen a kettle before and was personally offended by
having to use one – and she'd said nothing to him either. He
would be apoplectic to discover she hadn't briefed him. Banecroft
was a newspaper editor and, as far as Stella could see, the core
skill required for the job was that forged-in-steel belief that you
should know everything that was going on anywhere at all times,

and it was everyone else on the planet's responsibility to keep you up to date. He'd been livid with Ox last week when he'd discovered that the eight-armed, head-of-a-duck, body-of-a-gorilla, Peruvian goat-stealing demon had reportedly struck again and he hadn't been told about it. She could only imagine what his reaction would be when he discovered Manny's terrifying angel-of-death lodger had damn-near attacked a woman who'd turned up out of the blue claiming to be his descendant. And yet, she'd decided to keep the whole thing to herself.

She'd spent the morning using her by now well-honed digging skills to try to find Zoe. Stella had made a habit of reading any historic books on journalism she could lay her hands on, and she was always struck by how much effort reporters would regularly go to in search of stories – scouring through records, going door to door, spending weeks, months pulling at threads. *All The President's Men* would be much less impressive a story these days. Woodward and Bernstein could probably blow the whole thing open with a few Instagram posts and a couple of Google searches. To be fair, if all Stella had to go on was the name Zoe, it would've been challenging. The girl claimed to be a descendant of Manny, whom she referred to as Emmanuel Devon, but there was nothing to be found about a man with that name, and it was statistically highly unlikely her surname would still be Devon.

Luckily, she'd mentioned that Manny's daughter, Dottie, was ninety-two. Even in Stella's very limited life experience, she'd noticed a weird phenomenon regarding a woman's age. As a child, one's age was counted out in years, often months, then it was still regularly referred to until a woman hit her mid-twenties, after which all mention disappeared into a murky fog where inquiring about or even mentioning it was considered quite the social faux pas. Then, when the woman reached somewhere in her mid-eighties, stating it over and over again any time the lady in question was mentioned suddenly became mandatory. What that meant was that all Stella had needed to do was search for 'Dottie' and 'ninety-two', and what she'd required had popped up instantly. An article in a local paper from last year showing Dottie Clift *née* Devon celebrating her ninety-first birthday surrounded by five generations of her family, including her great-great-great-grandson, three-month-old Jeremiah, sitting on her knee. Dottie was beaming at the camera, full of feisty-old-lady energy. More importantly, while the picture wasn't of the highest quality, to the side of the crowd of fifty-plus people grinning at the camera, Stella was pretty sure she recognized Zoe. It was quite the ensemble. Stella couldn't help but feel a little jealous – when you haven't got any family you know of, not even a history you can call your own, seeing something like that makes you yearn for the life others have.

The article hadn't contained many details but the biggest one had been that Dottie was the founder of Dottie's Delights, a bakery that now boasted seven locations in the North West and was still a family-run business. The first one had been set up on Burnage Lane in 1972 and remained open to that day. Stella had been working on the assumption that someone there might be able to put her in contact with Zoe. In the end, none of that had been necessary – as soon as Stella had reached the large glass-windowed frontage of Dottie's Delights, she'd seen Zoe standing inside, holding a clipboard and briefing a couple of members of staff. Their eyes met over a display of particularly delicious-looking doughnuts and Zoe recovered from her brief moment of shock so quickly that nobody but Stella even noticed it. Zoe held up a couple of fingers to indicate she'd be with her in two minutes and Stella nodded in understanding.

A few minutes later, the two young women were sitting down on either side of a small table in the coffee shop opposite Dottie's Delights. Zoe looked a lot like a woman trying not to be freaked out.

'Sorry about tracking you down,' started Stella. 'But, y'know, I figured . . .'

'Yeah,' offered Zoe. 'That was . . .' She paused. 'What was that?'

Stella found herself totally wrongfooted by the question. 'Ehm . . . complicated.'

Zoe gave a nervous bark of laughter. 'Sorry, but my friend Catherine and her on-again-off-again relationship with this guy she met in Ibiza is complicated. What happened this morning was straight-up insane.'

'Yeah,' agreed Stella. Now that she was here, beginning to explain Manny and his 'situation' seemed like a big ask. 'For the record, I did not know that was going to happen. I was as shocked as you were.'

'Have you ever seen that . . . thing before?' asked Zoe.

'A couple of times.'

'Then, no offence, but you weren't as shocked as me.'

'Good point,' conceded Stella.

'Look, I only got told last week that my great-great-grandfather was not only still alive but incredibly hadn't aged in, like, eighty years. So I think a large part of me was still thinking the whole thing was nonsense but . . .'

'Can I ask,' said Stella, 'how you'd only just found out? I mean, why come searching now?'

A look came across Zoe's face that Stella couldn't decipher. Zoe shifted her coffee cup around without drinking from it. 'You need to understand who Grammy Dottie is. I mean, the woman was . . . is a force of nature.' Zoe pointed her thumb back over her shoulder towards the shop over the road. 'The official story is that she set up Dottie's Delights because she wanted to share her recipes with the world. That's not true, or at least it's not the whole story. She was working in a bakery for years until some racist a-hole of a customer said they didn't like the idea of a Black woman handling their food, and the bakery let her go. Her husband had died in a building-site accident and she found herself with three kids under five and no job. She got money from a glorified loan shark and worked night and day – literally – sleeping for about three hours to, against all odds, make the thing work.' Zoe shook her head in disbelief at her own great-grandmother. 'The second location she set up? It was the bakery that fired her. They went out of business. She even gave the ex-owner a job, which is more than I would've managed. When I asked her about it, she said that none of us want to be judged by our worst days and our biggest mistakes.' She raised her eyebrows, her expression a mixture of sadness and pride. 'I mean, who has that big a heart?'

'Wow,' said Stella.

'And that's only the start of it. Business went from strength to strength and she established her own charity to help young parents who were struggling. She said that everything was set up to help people when they hit rock bottom – she wanted to give them a safety net so they could bounce back sooner.' Zoe brushed a tear away from her eye as she spoke. 'The woman is incredible. She's the matriarch of my whole family. Hell, she's my hero.'

'She sounds amazing. I'd like to meet her.' Stella winced internally as the last bit slipped out before she'd really thought about it. She'd meant it but some part of her sensed the dark cloud hanging over Zoe's story.

'She's . . . she's not what she was. Dementia.'

'Oh, I'm sorry.'

'Have you ever been around it?'

Stella shook her head.

'Brutal disease. Rips a person away piece by piece until there's not much left. The reason my grandma, Grammy Dottie's daughter, told me about, y'know, was that it's very common for someone with dementia to regress further and further in her memories. She doesn't recognize me or any of us now. She just keeps asking for her daddy.' Zoe snatched up a napkin and dabbed at her eyes, as if angry with herself for crying. 'Last night, she got taken into hospital again – heart attack. She's not coming back out this time. She's lying in that bed, right now, an absolute titan of a woman reduced to this frail little thing, and all she wants is her daddy. Hence . . .' She flapped a hand to indicate that Stella knew the rest.

They sat there in silence for a minute or so, Zoe pulling herself back together, Stella trying to think all of this through. Around them, tables of two and three patrons chatted happily as cutlery clattered and staff served the never-ending queue of customers seeking their requisite caffeine hits to get them through their day. Eventually, Stella cleared her throat. 'I should tell you – Manny, Emmanuel, he can't leave the church. The office, our office, it's a former church.'

'Why?'

'That thing inside him. It's tied to the building somehow. Look, I'll be totally honest – I don't really understand it. Manny and the thing that cohabits his body—'

'He's possessed?'

'I don't . . . I don't think you can call it that. The thing, the . . . Well, I know it didn't behave like it, but it looks sort of like an angel with the wings and all that, so we tend to refer to it as that. It's not evil or good or whatever, at least. Look, it was horrible this morning – nobody is saying otherwise – but it's also protected us in the past. Without it, me and several of my cow-orkers would probably be dead by now. It saved us.'

'From what?' asked Zoe.

'No offence, but we should probably not get into that. Trust me, it's not going to make you less freaked out.'

'I doubt it could make me more.'

'Oh, you'd be surprised.' Stella decided to move the conversation on. 'Do you have any idea how Manny ended up where he is?'

Zoe shrugged. 'Only bits and pieces. You saw the picture – he was in the army and then, at some point, soon after he came back, he walked out on them. I know when Dottie grew up it was mostly just her and her mum. That's a big part of her motivation. She knows what it's like to be both the child and parent in a one-parent family. It's why she set up the charity. She never talked directly about her father, just about his absence.'

'And he's been living in that church ever since?' asked Stella.

'I guess.'

'Could I ask your grandmother about—'

'No,' said Zoe firmly. 'She told me all this when we were sitting at Dottie's bedside last week. We're all taking turns. It sort of came out. I tried to talk to her about it again the next day and she got upset. Said to forget all about it. That Dottie had never wanted anyone to go near him and she'd been sworn to secrecy.' Zoe sat back in her chair. 'I don't know, maybe I should have left it alone but . . . sitting there, looking in Dottie's eyes as she pleaded like a little girl who just wants to see her daddy. She keeps asking is he OK. Where's Daddy? Where's Daddy? I just felt . . .'

Stella felt the anger building inside her as Zoe shrugged helplessly, the grief piling up on her shoulders, causing her to slouch in her chair. Stella surprised herself by reaching across and patting her hands. 'I get it. I do. It wouldn't make right what's gone before, but still.' She got to her feet abruptly. 'Thank you for explaining everything. I'm going to fix this.' Even as the words came out of her mouth they surprised her.

'How?' asked Zoe, hope brightening her wet eyes as she looked up at her.

'I have absolutely no idea.'

17

Zalas did not mind this body as much as he had the librarian's. Yes, it was female, but she was strong. Not as strong as the warrior's body had been but that had not gone as he had hoped. It seemed these modern humans did not respect strength in the same way as when he had last walked amongst them. Still, he had enjoyed the experience. It was nice to remember the sensation of squeezing the life out of some worthless fool once again. He was starting to feel more like his old self, and now he was one of these police, so he had power. He just needed to figure out how to wield it in order to start gathering followers.

He stopped and pointed at a man walking down the street towards him. 'On the ground – now.'

The man gave him a quizzical look and continued to walk on by. Zalas noted he had some kind of contraption covering his ears and he could hear an irritating scratching noise coming from it as the man passed.

'Stop,' he shouted at the man's back. 'I am police.'

He didn't

Zalas walked on, clenching and unclenching his fists in annoyance. Impertinent worm, he thought to himself.

The next humans he came across were an elderly couple – a man and woman walking some form of dog that Zalas had never seen before. In truth, he had seen bigger rats so perhaps it was one of those, although it did engage in a form of barking as he approached.

Zalas pointed at the man. 'I am police. Obey me.'

The man glanced at the woman before they both looked back at Zalas and laughed.

'Good luck with that, love,' said his female companion. 'I've been married to him for forty-six years and I've never taught him that trick.'

The man laughed again. 'I've never even got it to work on the dog.'

Zalas looked down and, unsure, pointed at the animal that was now snarling up at him. 'Obey me. I am police.'

At this, the couple stopped laughing. Instead, awkward smiles played across their faces. The man pulled the dog back a little. 'Best be off.'

As they passed, the woman touched Zalas on the arm and spoke softly. 'Are you all right, love? Might you need a lie down or a cup of tea or summat?'

Zalas shook off the woman's hand and walked on.

And on.

The swarm of people around him grew and grew as the day wore on. He wandered amongst them, lost, trying to understand the world in which he found himself. The people rushed by, many of them speaking into small boxes, rarely to each other. There was so much noise. Everywhere he went, hateful tunes about jingling bells or chestnuts roasting on an open fire followed him, taunting him. There were strange trees indoors, adorned with lights and sparkly things. All the while, people laden down with packages bustled around with great purpose. He took to following a few of them at random; they dashed into buildings and joined long queues to buy things before rushing off somewhere else to do the same thing again. None of it seemed to bring them joy. More importantly, Zalas could find no faith in it. No belief.

He wandered on. In many places he saw frames full of moving pictures, portals to other, brighter worlds. More magic he could not understand. At one point he was delighted to find a man standing in the street, shouting about God's vengeance. Finally, something he understood. Then, as he stood there watching him, he realized that those passing by were mostly ignoring him. Some of them were even openly mocking him. Zalas was an old god in need of followers, in a world seemingly devoid of all forms of faith.

He walked on.

Then he saw it . . .

Several of the large moving pictures were arranged to form a wall, all of them showing the same images. In them stood a female figure, hand extended to the sky, glittering among the lights as the horde gathered in front of her screamed with delight. So many people. This. This was what he had been looking for. Finally.

The figure moved and pointed in a new direction, and that simple action sparked a greater frenzy. Zalas stood transfixed before the images – acolytes continued to surround the figure, dancing around for her pleasure. People cried to be in her presence.

Zalas grabbed a member of the throng of passers-by – a

teenage boy. His face, pock-marked with acne, wore a look of shock as he tried to pull away, but Zalas's grip was firm.

'What the fuck?'

Zalas pushed him towards the screen and pointed. 'Who is that?'

'What?'

'Answer me. Who is this goddess?'

'That's Taylor Swift.'

'Take me to her.'

The boy laughed nervously. 'Chance would be a fine thing.'

'Do you mock me?'

'Are you mental? Is this a joke?'

Zalas grabbed the youth by the throat and slammed him against the glass window. 'Do I look like I am joking, you impertinent swine? Take me to her now or I will break your scrawny neck.'

Zalas turned at the sound of voices behind him – a crowd was starting to gather.

'Let him go,' shouted a woman.

'That's police brutality,' said a man. 'Shouldn't be allowed.'

Zalas took in the sea of faces. Many of them were holding up their odd little boxes. He raised his voice. 'I am police. I command you to take me to the one known as Taylor Swift.'

The crowd laughed as one.

Zalas screamed with rage and lunged at them, causing them to scatter.

'I am police,' he roared again, as the people started to run in all directions, mostly away from him. 'Take me to Taylor Swift.'

Someone tried to grab him from behind but he kicked them away. This female form wasn't as strong as the warrior's had been, but these people did not truly know how to fight.

Then there were police. Lots of them. He knew them by the uniforms. They were surrounding him again. With a snarl of frustration, Zalas lunged, but his intention wasn't to flee – at least not in the way they thought. He touched an old man in the crowd who hadn't been fast enough to get away.

As Zalas transferred to his new host, he felt the frail body come under his control. It was incredibly weak. Still, the one he had just left now found itself under a pile of other bodies who were all struggling to pin it down.

Zalas sighed in frustration. Feeling the aching muscles and creaking bones of his new vessel, he started to walk away.

He had found belief. He just needed to figure out how to get to it. He needed to become the one known as Taylor Swift.

Space Monkey Jesus

The theory of evolution is often seen as running contrary to religious belief, but a new cult no longer thinks so. According to chief monk Melinda Spectaculos, 'Human beings came about when space monkeys visited primal Earth millions of years ago and mated with the less evolved locals. Accounts are hazy on the details, but there's a belief that it may have been their version of a stag do. They now feel responsible for how humanity turned out, which is why they keep sending down Space Monkey Jesuses to try to sort us out.'

The group believes the biblical Jesus was just one of many such messianic monkeys, another being the monkey found in the English town of Hartlepool in the early nineteenth century, who was famously hanged as a French spy. When asked why the Bible never mentions that Jesus was, in fact, a monkey, Spectaculos explains, 'Jesus was an incredible guy, and people were naturally far more focused on his words than his physical appearance. Besides, is him being a talking monkey any more far-fetched than the belief, still widely held, that a man born and raised in the Middle East was actually white?'

18

Grace turned off the ignition and sat there in her car, looking around the small car park outside the offices of *The Stranger Times*. She was tired, and not just because she'd been up all hours with the rest of the staff, dealing with that computer-virus nonsense. She didn't really understand such things but she'd been there because, well, everybody else was. She'd hoped that just for once they could do something normal, have a little bit of a Christmas party, but that idea had inevitably fallen victim to circumstance. *Que sera.*

Now she was popping back in to make sure that their editor and the fourteen-year-old delinquent who'd 'attacked' their computer systems had not killed each other. On the upside, she had at least got Vincent to agree to allow Clint to work off his debt to society/the paper/Vincent Banecroft rather than involve the police. The young man's poor grandmother had enough to be dealing with without spending Christmas down at the police station. All it had taken was granting Vincent permission to swear for a day. She felt a tiny bit of pride that she would have let him have a week but she'd outnegotiated him. Considering Clint's charming personality, there was every chance he was already well into his allowance. She offered up a prayer to the good Lord and made her way inside, stopping to pick up and dispose of a KFC box some hoodlum had tossed into their car park.

Given it was a Friday, the bullpen was quite the hive of activity. Brian and Manny were yet again engaged in a game of Connect 4. The two of them seemed to have spent hours playing it over the last couple of weeks. Grace was happy to see Brian partaking in something approaching normal – it wasn't right for anyone to spend their time visiting every grave in Manchester, noble though the sentiment behind the gesture was. Clint, meanwhile, was at the other end of the room, industriously painting the back wall using a paint roller on an extension pole. If Grace were being picky, the colour didn't seem overly consistent, ranging from a whiteish cream to a yellowish cream, but given that the tins of paint he was using had been sitting in a cupboard downstairs for who knew how long, it wasn't the biggest of surprises. Still, seeing Clint working away was heartening, especially as Ox, the person who was supposed to be supervising him, was sitting at his PC and not paying him a blind bit of notice.

'Looking good, Clint,' said Grace, raising her voice. Clint responded by turning around and giving her an excited thumbs-up. This was the healing power of good honest work in action, praise the Lord. Grace moved over to Ox but before she could say anything to him, Brian, always an alarmingly quiet mover, appeared beside her and handed her a piece of paper. She took it and barely glanced at it, knowing already what it was.

'Thank you, Brian,' she said with a smile. 'I will definitely look into it.'

He gave her a big smile in return. With his bulbous eyes, slicked-back hair and yellowish skin, he wasn't someone those annoying experts on breakfast TV would term 'conventionally attractive,' but once you got used to it, there was an endearing childish innocence to Brian and it was hard not to warm to him. With that, he turned around and loped back to his game of Connect 4.

The piece of paper was a flyer for the Wonderland Christmas Experience – for about two weeks now he'd given her one every time he'd seen her.

'He's not forgetting about it, is he?' asked Ox without looking up from his screen.

'No,' said Grace, 'he isn't.'

Grace had been hoping he would. Ever since she had started to put up Christmas decorations, Brian had been charmingly giddy. Given his lack of speech it was hard to know what was going on there, but there was every possibility he hadn't ever experienced Christmas properly. She regularly found him staring at the blinking lights on the Christmas tree. To be fair, she regularly found Manny doing that too, although even Grace understood that he was almost certainly enjoying them on a 'different level'.

The problem with Brian's obsession with Wonderland was that there was a considerable difference between being childlike and actually being a child, particularly at big public events. Parents tended to get judgemental when two lone adults turned up to such a thing and one of them, unfair though it was, could be considered to look 'seriously creepy' (as Ox had helpfully put it). In his own way, Brian was more of a child than Clint. Grace paused for a second as an idea started to form. First things first, though.

'Ox,' she said, 'aren't you supposed to be supervising Clint?'

'I am,' Ox responded, louder than was necessary. 'He's doing fine. I'm just here chillin', y'know, looking at lamps on eBay. You know how much I love lamps.'

'Do I?'

Ox glanced over the top of his monitor at Clint then lowered his voice to a whisper. 'I'm not really looking at lamps. I'm trying to check the system while simultaneously figuring out how to actually do that as quickly as possible.'

'Why?'

'Because Clint keeps telling me that there was only one virus.'

'I see,' said Grace, despite not actually doing so. 'I know this might be a wild idea, but is it possible there was only one virus?'

Ox gave a snort in response. 'Oh yeah, he'd like me to think that.'

'So there is another virus, then?'

'I think he's doing one of two things – he's telling me there isn't because there is, or he's telling me there isn't because he wants me to think there is and there isn't. It's the classic single bluff or double bluff or, possibly, triple bluff. The kid is some kind of evil genius.'

'Or he's telling the truth?'

'Yeah, but he's telling the truth in, like, a brilliantly devious, conniving way.'

'How much sleep did you get, Ox?'

In response, Ox picked up a can of the foul-smelling energy

drink he somehow managed to buy by the crateload and chugged it back before saying, 'Sleep is for the weak. I'm going to destroy this evil bastard.'

He quickly flicked between windows on his screen as Clint began to walk down the office towards them.

'Is it OK if I take a toilet break, please, Mr Ox?'

'Absolutely, little buddy. Take all the time you need. Loving your work.'

'Thank you very much.'

They each gave each other a big thumbs-up as Clint left the room.

'Oh, I'm on to you, ya little psychopath.'

Clint popped his head back in. 'Did you say something?'

'Oh no,' said Ox, the alarmingly wide smile returning to his face, 'just talking to a picture of a lamp. You know me and lamps.'

Grace decided to leave Ox to his breakdown and seek sanity elsewhere. Unfortunately, there were slim pickings in that regard. Before she could even knock, 'Go away,' came the automatic response from the other side of Banecroft's office door.

'It is me,' replied Grace.

'Sorry,' said Banecroft. 'Go away, *please*.'

'I'm coming in.'

'I'm not decent.'

'I am all too aware.'

Banecroft, as she knew he would be, was sitting behind his desk. The office smelled of week-old socks fermented in month-old cigarette butts, with hints of so many other unpleasant aromas that walking into the room was the olfactory equivalent of listening to a grossly underfunded youth orchestra warming up for twenty minutes.

'Can't a man get a moment's peace?'

'Nice to see you are full of the Christmas spirit as always, Vincent.'

'If you must know, I'm currently writing my letter to Santa Claus. Is flamethrower one or two words?'

She looked around the room. 'I would have thought a vacuum cleaner would be a higher priority.'

'And what are you doing here?'

'Checking that the child whose care has temporarily been handed over to this newspaper is still alive and well.' Banecroft gave her a confused look, until she eventually clarified, 'Clint?'

'Oh, right. Him. Yes.' Banecroft took one of the two bottles of wine he currently had open and started to fill the large glass on his desk. 'He's thriving. Well, probably. I'm sure I'd have heard if he wasn't.'

Grace cleared her throat to hide the smile that was in danger of creeping on to her face. As she'd hoped he might, Banecroft was indeed working his way through the stockpile of wine left over from the aborted party, unaware that it was non-alcoholic. Unbeknownst to himself, Vincent Banecroft was sobering up.

'Speaking of Clint,' said Grace, 'I've decided that as a nice surprise, I'm going to take him to see Santa Claus on Sunday at that Christmas Wonderland Experience place.'

'I mean,' said Banecroft, holding up his almost full glass of secretly alcohol-free red wine, 'I'm all for the kid getting punished for his appalling behaviour, but it feels like we might be dipping into the area of cruel and unusual there.'

'It will be fine,' said Grace. 'He will enjoy it.' From her limited experience with Clint, Grace knew there was every chance that wouldn't be the case, but given he was a child, it meant she could fulfil Brian's Christmas wish without running the risk of being followed around by security for the entire visit.

'Anyway, I just—'

'Where the hell is he?'

The shout came from downstairs, the voice was Stella's and the tone was pure rage. Grace and Banecroft looked at each other in surprise.

'What have you done to upset Stella?' asked Grace, instantly annoyed.

'Nothing.' Banecroft furrowed his brow. 'At least, I don't think I have.'

They entered the bullpen just as Stella stomped in through the other door. 'There you are, you worthless piece of crap.'

'Stella!' said Grace, appalled.

Stella point-blank ignored her. It was only when she strode purposefully across the room that Grace realized she had not, in fact, been talking to Banecroft. Nor Ox. Stella stopped in front of Manny, who'd got to his feet and was looking at her warily.

'Turns out under the happy-go-lucky bullshit, you're a dead-beat coward who ran out on his family. I hope you're proud of yourself.'

Grace's mouth hung open in shock as she and Banecroft looked at each other.

'We not what you—' started Manny, before he slumped forward, only to hang in mid-air.

'Oh no,' said Grace.

Sure enough, smoke started to billow out of him and swirl about his limp form.

Banecroft walked forward. 'What is going on?'

Stella raised her chin defiantly. 'Fine,' she roared. 'You want to play the bully again, let's do it.'

Loose papers flapped around the room as the unnatural wind swirled. The distinctive figure of the angel was now forming in the maelstrom above Manny and her face was a terrifying snarl to chill the soul.

'Go ahead,' bellowed Stella, throwing out her hands as blue energy crackled around her fingers. 'You're not the only one round here who can get scary. Let's do this.'

'Enough,' boomed Banecroft as he placed himself between Stella and the angel.

Grace could feel the hairs on the back of her arms stand up as the energy in the room built. She blessed herself.

'I said enough!' roared Banecroft. 'I don't know what this is, but it stops now. I am the boss here and that is final.'

In response, the angel screeched in his face. Anyone else would have turned and run, but Vincent Banecroft, for all his many faults, could never be accused of being a shrinking violet.

'I am in charge,' he said, 'and if you don't like it, you can leave.'

The whole room held its collective breath as, for what felt like an eternity but might have been only a second, the angel locked eyes with Banecroft. Stella remained standing behind him, the blue energy now skittering around her whole body. Then, in an instant, the angel dissolved into thin air and Manny slumped to the ground.

Banecroft spun on his heels to face Stella. 'And you, young lady, have some serious explaining to do.'

She remained stock-still, her eyes filled with intense blue light as she glared at Banecroft.

'Stella,' said Grace, her voice shaking with barely suppressed terror. 'Stella, darling, are you OK?'

This seemed to drag Stella back to reality and the blue light faded. Stella shook her head and folded her arms.

'Now,' said Banecroft, 'what is going on?'

'This . . .' Stella looked down at Manny, seemingly unable to find words. 'He and his not-so-little friend . . . Manny's great-great-granddaughter dropped in this morning and that monster attacked her.'

'What?' asked Grace in disbelief.

'None of that sentence made sense,' said Ox.

'Ask him to explain it,' huffed Stella.

'I would do,' responded Banecroft, 'but he appears to have passed out.'

Ox and Grace bent down to examine Manny. 'I think he's OK,' said Ox, having felt for a pulse. 'I mean, as far as I can tell.'

Manny's eyes opened suddenly and, with a gasp, he reached forward and touched Stella's leg just above the top of her Doc Marten boot. She pulled back as Manny lay supine on the floor in front of her.

'Right,' said Banecroft. 'Someone is going to explain to me what the hell is going on, this instant.'

'Like I said, ask him,' said Stella, turning on her heel and striding away.

'Stella—' started Banecroft, but he broke off at the sight of Clint walking back into the room.

Clint took in all the paper and flotsam lying on the floor. 'What happened?' he asked. 'I only went for a wee.'

'We were all just admiring your artwork,' said Banecroft, his tone shifting immediately to conversational.

'Thanks,' said Clint cheerfully.

'Yes, tremendously creative. You've made wonderful use of light.'

Grace shot Banecroft a perplexed look. In response, he pointed at the wall Clint had been painting. 'I suggest you take about three steps to your right,' he said.

Grace, eyes fixed on the wall, started to move. What she'd mistaken for poor paint consistency rapidly revealed itself to be something rather more deliberate and diabolical. It required the light from the window to catch it just right, but when it did . . .

With a sinking feeling in her stomach, Grace read the message written in three-foot-high letters. 'Ox is a . . . CLINT!'

19

Hannah stamped her feet against the cold. It was a cliché that people from the South banged on about how much colder it felt up north in the winter, but that didn't mean there wasn't any truth to it. Besides, as a tiny voice in the back of her head reminded her on frosty mornings, this time last year she'd been living in Dubai. True, she'd been trapped in a miserable marriage to an inveterate liar with the morals of a dog in heat, but she hadn't owned any thermal underwear. She didn't own any thermal underwear now, wasn't even sure what it looked like, but she kept thinking she really must find out.

She was standing beside a gazebo in the centre of Chinatown. She was sure she'd read somewhere that Manchester's Chinatown was the third biggest in Europe after Paris and London's. Presumably there were bigger ones in America and, come to think of it, China. Still, on any given evening she'd been through here, the place had been a hive of activity and it was doubly so now. It was just after 6 p.m. and the restaurants were doing a roaring trade, as you'd expect on the Friday before Christmas. Between office workers out on the town, boisterous groups in Christmas hats and knowingly terrible jumpers, and people rushing to catch trams, trains and buses in order to travel elsewhere for the festive season, the city was already just shy of manic and only heading in one direction.

She checked her watch again. John Mór had called her two hours ago, from his suddenly working phone, and told her and Sturgess to meet him here at 6 p.m. sharp. Sturgess was late. In Hannah's experience, he was the punctual sort but he'd sounded quite stressed when she'd called him.

Further up the pavement to her right, she noticed the figure of John Mór striding towards her. He was hard to miss in his black overcoat and seemingly ever-present vest. Clearly the cold didn't bother him much. The sea of pedestrians parted before him as he approached. There was something about being a broad-shouldered, six-foot-eight man who looked as if he'd just stepped off a Viking longboat that meant people tended not to stand in front of you when you tried to walk somewhere. He moved aside with a gracious nod for a trio of women clinging to each other as they hurried along. He was entirely oblivious to them check-ing him out as they walked past, and whatever was said between them led to a gale of raucous laughter. If that was how they responded to seeing him just out and about, Hannah could only imagine how they'd react to seeing him dressed as she had that morning. She remembered the tattoo of the rabbit and blushed.

Just as John Mór reached her, Sturgess appeared at her elbow, out of breath.

'Sorry, traffic was insane,' he offered by way of apology.

'You're late,' said John Mór.

'You got here at the same time as me.'

'Yeah, but I'm the one doing you the favour.'

'And we greatly appreciate it,' said Hannah, in her unasked-for and increasingly unappreciated role as peacemaker. 'Although, you didn't specify what the favour was. You just said to be here.'

John Mór tilted his head. 'True enough. I've got you an audience with the lady the inspector met this morning outside the library.'

'Great,' said Sturgess. 'Where is she?' After catching Hannah's pointed look, he added reluctantly, 'And thanks.'

John Mór raised a hand. 'There's a few things we need to go over first.' He looked around then nodded towards the side of the gazebo to which they all moved in order to be a bit further away from the flow of foot traffic. John Mór glanced around then spoke just loud enough for Hannah to be able to make out what he was saying. 'Now, this lady is . . . unusual, but she's also very important.'

'How so?' asked Sturgess.

'She's a Keeper.'

'I presume we're not talking about football,' said Hannah.

'No.'

'What are we talking about, then?' asked Sturgess.

John Mór looked annoyed but not necessarily at the question. He seemed to come to some kind of begrudging conclusion. 'I suppose I'd better explain some things. Before I do, I remind you that it wasn't that long ago that both of you would've dismissed the very idea of magic as nonsense, so I'm asking you to keep an open mind.'

Hannah shared the briefest of looks with Sturgess as they both nodded their agreement.

'Right,' John Mór continued. 'Here's the best way to think of it: imagine an aquarium, like, a big one with lots of different enclosures, only instead of glass partitions between them, there's nets. The nets occasionally allow small things to slip from one enclosure to the next, which isn't great but isn't normally terrible either. Still, if there were any big holes in the net, that'd be really bad as you'd let in a big fishy that'd gobble up all the little fishies, if you get my meaning.'

'Kind of,' offered Hannah.

'Well, a Keeper is in charge of making sure the net is kept in good nick to prevent, y'know, everything going sushi.' John Mór's confidence in his own explanation seemed to be draining away with every word. 'It's one of them, whatchamacallits – metaphors, analogies, whatever. You get the general idea.' The last sentence came out with an air of despairing hope rather than expectation.

Hannah decided to follow up with some questions, as hers were bound to be more tactful than Sturgess's. 'Right, so in this analogy, what exactly are the various fish tanks?'

'Enclosures,' corrected John Mór.

'Right. Yes. Them.'

'One of them is our world – or plane or dimension, I guess you'd say.'

'Ah, right. I get you. And what are the fish?'

'In our enclosure, they're us. In the other ones, they're . . . Well, they could be all manner of things, generally bad, varying from pain in the arse to end of the world.'

'So they're people?'

'No,' said John Mór. 'Well, probably not. I suppose they could be. Could be anything. But more likely something terrible.'

'Clearly, I've met more people than you have,' said Sturgess.

'No, I mean . . . really bad. I'm trying not to use the word "monsters".'

'I see,' said Hannah.

'Don't say it like that,' said John Mór, sounding annoyed.

'I didn't say it like anything,' protested Hannah.

'I'm aware how it sounds. Forget the fish thing. You see, there are places where the thingy . . . ehm, membrane!' He looked genuinely pleased with himself for remembering the word. 'Yeah, membrane,' he repeated. 'There's places where the membrane between here and the other places is much thinner than normal, and here is one of those places.'

'Chinatown?' asked Hannah.

'No. Manchester. The general Greater Manchester area,' clarified John Mór. 'You must've noticed there's a load more weird shit going on here than anywhere else?'

'Now, that,' said Hannah, 'I definitely believe.'

'So, hang on,' began Sturgess. 'This homeless woman I met this morning, who . . . did whatever she did to Wilkerson, myself and several other members of the force—'

'She's not,' interrupted John Mór.

'What?'

'She's not homeless,' he clarified. 'I mean, she doesn't live anywhere as such, but that's by choice.'

'She's still homeless, then,' said Sturgess.

'Nope. It's different,' John Mór said defiantly. 'More like a gypsy.'

'Technically . . .' started Sturgess before he caught Hannah's glare. 'Never mind,' he said.

'So,' said Hannah, keen to move things along, 'this woman is a Keeper, in charge of maintaining the borders between our world and other worlds?'

'Yeah, basically,' said John Mór, looking relieved. 'It's an ancient and sacred role, only most people – and I mean even the Folk – have all but forgotten it exists. Like how you don't give a thought to the little valve on the end of the pipe until the water starts flooding out. Still, those what know, know how important it is. This is my way of saying that this lady, she is deserving of your respect' – he looked pointedly in Sturgess's direction – 'and she will be getting it.'

'Look, I just want to find out what she knows about whatever the hell happened down at the library, that's all.'

John Mór, seemingly satisfied, gave a brusque nod. 'Right, then – follow me.'

Without another word, he turned and strode back up the pavement the way he'd come, so quickly that Hannah and Sturgess had to hurry to keep up with his long strides.

He led them around the square and down a side street, where they came upon a restaurant called the Jolly Luck. In the doorway stood an Asian woman in her early twenties, wearing a traditional cheongsam dress, calmly explaining to a group of four men that there was no room at the inn.

'Fuck's sake,' said one of the men. 'Just let us in.'

'So sorry,' repeated the woman in a thick Chinese accent. 'Reservation only this evening.'

'We'll be quick.'

'No. Apologies. No room.'

'Well now, you're just being an awkward bitch.'

John Mór had walked past the door, but in one fluid movement he spun around to stand beside the group, one hand on the aggressive man's shoulder. 'What was that there, fella?'

The man tried to shake off the hand and turned to face him. One of his friends, who presumably handled his drink a little better, grabbed his mate's arm. 'Nothing. Nothing. We're just leaving. Merry Christmas.'

The mouthy one looked as if he was about to say something else, but having to tilt his head back to look up at John Mór's stern expression must've shaken a little sense free.

As the group walked off, the hostess laughed quietly and said in an accent that was suddenly pure Manc, 'Nice one, Uncle John. Can't help going all Batman, can ya?'

He shrugged. 'You know me, I'm big on manners.'

She angled her head towards the alley at the side of the building. 'The door's open. Let yourself in.'

'Cheers, Mai.'

The trio made their way down the alleyway then John Mór stopped in front of a side gate. 'Right, we're all clear on what we discussed previously?'

Hannah and Sturgess nodded. Just as John turned to knock,

Hannah stopped him. 'Sorry, John. I don't think you said – what's this lady's name?'

'Oh. It's Carol.'

'Carol?' echoed Hannah, failing to keep the surprise from her voice.

'What?'

'It's just, I dunno, from what you said, she's someone who is responsible for maintaining the barrier between this dimension and the next to prevent apocalyptic monsters from getting in . . .'

'More or less.'

'And her name is Carol?'

He looked genuinely confused by the question. 'And?'

'I guess I was just expecting something a bit more, y'know . . . not Carol,' she finished weakly.

'Right,' said John Mór. 'Well, when we go in, it's stuff like that which you definitely shouldn't be bringing up.'

'Understood,' said Hannah, feeling foolish. And with that, John Mór turned and pushed open the gate.

The door led into a narrow passage with high brick walls on either side. Hannah followed as John Mór guided them, his shoulders brushing against both walls. They then had to negotiate their way between two large wheelie bins and a couple of shopping trolleys filled with what could very kindly be described as bric-a-brac.

Hannah was taken aback when they turned the corner and found themselves in a courtyard suffused in a red glow from the rows of Chinese lanterns strung across it. In front of them sat a wide circular table aching under the weight of dozens of fabulous-looking dishes – enough to feed a minibus full of ravenous teenagers. A couple of waiters were moving nimbly around the edges of the table, shifting plates to try to fit yet more on.

Across from where Hannah was standing, an older woman in several layers of clothing was sitting on a large wooden chair with ornate carvings on it, sucking industriously on a chicken leg while ignoring her visitors entirely. Now that they were in her presence, Hannah realized that she'd seen the woman around Manchester before, her two shopping trolleys tied to her as she trundled along, with a raven sitting proudly on the front of one of them. An odd feeling came over Hannah. Surely such a striking sight would have stayed in her memory, not to mention drawing other people's attention? And yet earlier on, when she'd heard Sturgess describe the woman to John Mór, nothing had rung a bell. It was as if her mind had somehow chosen to delete the image from her mental photo album. The aforementioned raven was now perched on the back of the wooden chair, his black eyes shining with a haughty belligerence.

John Mór stopped in front of the table and stood with his hands clasped respectfully in front of him. Sturgess and Hannah fell in beside him. Hannah was beginning to understand why John Mór had used the word 'audience' earlier on – that was certainly what this felt like. As they waited, Hannah was able to get a better look at the woman. With her anorak pulled tight over the layers of clothing, her hands in fingerless gloves and the bobble hat on her head, she did fulfil the cliché of what a homeless person might look like. And yet, the closer you looked, the less the image held up. The woman herself was scrupulously clean, her fingernails immaculate, and while her clothes were patched in places, they were done so with loving care and flawless precision.

The two waiters, having managed to find the very last available space to set down the latest dishes, bowed so low they risked headbutting the ground, then backed away obsequiously. The woman, having finally sucked the marrow from the chicken leg, casually tossed the bone over her shoulder where the raven caught it and crushed it in his beak, chewing it to splinters before swallowing it.

She favoured her visitors with a smile. 'I hope you found that impressive. Me and Frank have been practising it.'

The raven cawed.

'Oh, hush, Frank. If I actually cared about impressing these people, we both know there's a whole lot more than that I could do.' She reached across and picked up a dumpling. 'How've you been, John?' she asked as she inspected her catch.

'Fine, thank you, Carol.'

'Friday before Christmas – not the best time to be dragging a landlord out from the back of his bar.'

'We'll be all right for a bit, thank you. Speaking of which.' He drew a bottle out of his coat pocket and, bowing his head, held it out before him like an offering.

Carol inspected it before nodding approvingly. 'Much obliged. Leave it in one of the trollies on your way out.'

'Of course.'

'You'd best introduce me to your friends, then,' she said before shoving the entire dumpling in her mouth and chewing it expansively.

'Right you are. This is Hannah – she is the assistant editor of *The Stranger Times*.' Hannah nodded. 'This is Tom Sturgess – he's police.' There was a distinct difference in tone between the two introductions that didn't go unnoticed.

They waited as Carol swallowed then took a large gulp of wine before issuing an unapologetic and forceful belch. 'I've been wanting to have a word with you.'

'Likewise,' said Sturgess.

Carol waved the DI away dismissively. 'Not you – you'll wait.' She picked up a spring roll and pointed it at Hannah. 'Why did you change stock?'

'I'm sorry?' responded Hannah, entirely lost.

'Stock,' Carol repeated. 'You used to print on a different type of paper. Then a couple of years ago you changed to this thinner stuff.'

'I'm afraid I don't know. I've only worked there nine months.'

'Tell whoever is in charge over there to change it back,' she said firmly. 'It used to be useful but now I wouldn't wipe my arse with it, and that's not a euphemism.'

'Right,' said Hannah. 'I will definitely bring it up.' She'd save this particular nugget for the next time Banecroft was being particularly annoying. Him finding out their paper was formerly considered a good source of improvised toilet roll would undoubtedly go down well.

Carol nodded, seemingly satisfied, then turned her attention to Sturgess. 'Which brings me to you. Am I still under arrest?'

From her position between the two men, Hannah could feel John Mór's eyes burning into the side of Sturgess's face, daring him to say something out of place.

Sturgess cleared his throat. 'I apologize. We got off on the wrong foot.'

'Yes,' said Carol, munching the spring roll in half before talking around it, 'you can say that again.'

'I did ask who you were.'

Carol narrowed her eyes. 'And it's my job to explain myself to the likes of you, is it?'

Hannah felt John Mór tense.

'John has explained the vital role you play, keeping the world safe. In our own way, that's what the police try to do, too. I was just attempting to do my job the best I could in demanding circumstances.'

Carol considered Sturgess for a long moment. Behind her, Frank the raven cawed.

'Yes, Frank, I think you're right.' No explanation was offered as to what Frank was right about, but Carol seemed to have reached some kind of decision. 'Ask your questions but be quick. It's too cold to be sitting around too long.'

'If you would like,' said Hannah, 'we could go inside once you've finished or . . .'

Carol shook her head firmly. 'I don't do inside. I live under the sky. I've got to be able to smell the air or else how am I supposed to do my job?'

Hannah had no answer to that. After an awkward moment, Sturgess cleared his throat and said, 'If you could, can you tell me what you were doing down at the library this morning?'

'My job,' replied Carol.

'So, there was a . . . I don't know the correct term but—'

Carol waved the remaining half of the spring roll to cut him off. 'Something had ripped a great big hole in the world and it was my job to close it up again, pronto. Right big one, too. Not seen the like since . . .' She turned to look at John Mór. 'Was it nineteen ninety-eight the thing happened?'

Hannah noticed John Mór's face register surprise. 'Really?'

'Yeah.' Carol licked her lips and considered a large bowl of noodles. 'Really big hole.'

'And something came through this hole?' asked Sturgess.

'I assume so.'

'Do you know who or what?'

'Nope. Not my job.'

'I'm sorry?'

'Not my job,' repeated Carol.

'I thought it was your job to watch the border or' – Sturgess hesitated – 'barrier between the worlds?'

She looked at John Mór again. 'Did you explain things?'

'I tried,' he said apologetically.

'You didn't use that aquarium spiel, did you?'

'Sorry.'

Carol shook her head. 'No wonder he's confused.' Only then did she turn her attention back to Sturgess. 'I'll save you some time here, copper, as my food is getting cold. I'm not border patrol. It is not my job to know what's over there or what came through, or who might or might not be responsible for doing that.'

Frank cawed.

'Yes,' she agreed. 'Although we wouldn't mind having a word with that last person or persons. They left one hell of a mess behind them. But still, my job is maintenance. I spend most of my time tending to the defences, otherwise they wear down. That's not what happened here. Here, some silly sausage punched a hole. It's my job to fix the hole. End of.'

'And you've no idea how we can find out who did it?'

Carol tsked. 'Didn't I already say that?'

'And how can we find whatever came through?'

She threw John Mór a look of exasperation. 'Am I not making myself clear?' She picked up a fork, wielded it like a conductor's baton and warbled in a falsetto, 'All together now. One . . . two . . . three . . . Not. My. Job.'

'Whose job is it, then?' asked Sturgess, sounding rather irritated himself now.

'Seeing as you're here,' said Carol, grabbing an empty plate and forking a copious amount of noodles on to it. 'I'm guessing yours.'

'But I don't know how to—'

'Best of luck with that.'

'Right,' said John Mór firmly. 'I think we've taken up more than enough of the lady's time.'

Sturgess looked frustrated. 'But . . .'

'But nothing,' said John Mór tightly, waving them back the way they'd come.

Sturgess looked as if he was about to say something else but thought better of it. Instead, he cleared his throat again and said, 'Thank you for your time.'

With that they began to make their exit.

'Oh, Inspector . . .'

They turned back to see Carol having already formed a pyramid of myriad samples of different dishes. 'Don't worry too much about how to find it. Something that big – it's only a matter of time before it finds you.'

20

Neil was not the greatest of drinkers and he'd spent the day attempting a great deal of drinking. He had still been wearing his Santa Claus suit when psycho, Satan-loving Wayne had kicked him out of Wonderland, and he hadn't exactly been offered the chance to change first. It had happened in front of the kids queueing to get in, too. The horrified looks on their little faces as they'd watched Santa being physically ejected were burned into his soul. Neil had ruined Christmas. Christmas was dead. Long live Christmas.

In the last bar he'd visited, giggling groups of twenty-somethings had bought him drinks and took pictures, girls draping themselves over him or sitting on his knee while he'd sat there numbly. Then he'd started crying and people had stopped taking pictures. The bouncer had politely suggested it was time Santa went home. Neil had then vomited on the guy's shoes and he'd been considerably less polite after that.

It had taken three attempts, but he'd finally found a shop that would let him in for long enough to buy a bottle. He wasn't even sure what was in the bottle. He'd just pointed and paid for it. It tasted like cough mixture. With his free hand Neil attempted, not for the first time, to wipe away the streaks of vomit splattered down the front of his suit.

'Have to the keep the suit clean,' he muttered as he stumbled then righted himself against a wall. "S important'.'

He walked on.

Zalas was tired. He'd been walking for hours and the body he'd jumped into when the policewoman had become unpopular was not a good one. It was old and had not been taken care of when it was young. Its knees ached, the left hip throbbed with a dull pain, and it was regularly shaken by phlegm-filled, hacking coughs. Ideally, Zalas would have found himself a better vessel but, after jumping three times already, his power was waning. He needed to conserve what he had left. What he really needed was belief, but it was proving infuriatingly difficult to find.

He looked around at the passers-by with disgust. They had no faith. They didn't believe in gods. They didn't trust their leaders. They didn't respect authority. Even his show of strength in the gym had not won people over as it once would have. Instead, they'd scurried away like vermin and waited for someone to come and protect them. Pathetic, mewing creatures. They may have advanced with all these mighty, shiny buildings and wonders they took for granted, but they had become unforgivably soft.

Zalas's day was going so badly that he had been forced to take a new tack, and he'd actually attempted to ask people politely where he could find the one among them who still had believers. This had elicited a range of responses, from mockery to pity, none of which was of any use to him. This Taylor Swift seemed impossible to find.

He walked on.

Blurry though his vision was, Neil had managed to find a relatively quiet corner to one side of an office building where he could answer the call of nature. He sighed with blessed relief as the growing pressure on his bladder was finally alleviated. Having to maintain a tight grip on the bottle had left him with only one hand free, though, so the front of his trousers had caught more than its fair share of friendly fire. He began to tuck himself back in to the best of his inebriated ability.

As he turned around, the first thing he saw was the shocked face of the little girl looking up at him. Her wide, sorrowful eyes struck the very core of his soul, and his heart broke as she stared at him with the conflicting emotions of love and repulsion. Her mother shared no such conflict. She glared at Neil and hurried her daughter along the pavement as quickly as possible, hissing the word 'disgraceful' at him as they moved away. Neil raised the bottle and gave a plaintive 'Merry Christmas' in their wake.

The mother's voice carried back to him as he slumped against the low wall. 'Ignore the horrible man, sweetheart. That's not the real Santa.'

Neil stumbled, then fell to the ground ungraciously. As he lay there, he couldn't think of one earthly reason to get back up. Well, there was one. He watched the cars go by. They weren't moving anywhere near fast enough.

A bridge.

Yeah, he'd need to find a bridge.

Maybe after he'd closed his eyes and had a little rest first. It wasn't as if he was in a hurry.

Zalas felt it. Across the street from him. That giddy tingle. Belief. Actual belief. It was faint, but in a world that had so far seemed devoid of it, it rang out like a bell.

He strode across the road immediately, as fast as this feeble vessel could move. A large vehicle screeched to a halt and blared its horn as he passed in front of it. He continued walking, his eyes focused on his target.

Neil came to and noticed a pair of legs standing in front of him. He looked up to see an old man staring down at him.

'What are you?' the man asked in a gruff voice.

''Scuse me?' Neil replied as he struggled into an upright position.

'What are you?' repeated the man.

Neil patted his beard as he spoke forlornly. 'I'm Santa Claus. Merry Christmas.'

The old man reached down and touched his hand.

Zalas stood up and inspected himself. The body wasn't much. Puny and unfit. In truth, it wasn't a great improvement on the old man's. Speaking of which, his former vessel was now standing in front of him, gawping at him in confusion.

'Go away, old man,' Zalas growled.

In response, the elderly man turned and shuffled back up the street as fast as his decrepit body could carry him.

Zalas looked down at the red suit, soiled and dishevelled as it was. He needed to understand what this was. Instead of relegating the host into the background, on this occasion Zalas chose to let him in. He closed his eyes and searched for answers from the pathetic creature he had just superseded.

Interesting. Very interesting. There was something here. Not the Taylor-Swift-goddess level of power he'd been looking for, and not something he understood, but it was something nonetheless. What's more, his unwilling host craved belief as much as Zalas did, albeit it for very different reasons. He could use that. He didn't need to understand this world if he had someone who was willing to act as an unwitting guide.

That being said, after yet another jump into a new host, he was now dangerously weak. This was his last chance or he would fade away from this world, reduced to a nothing once again. He would not let that happen.

He glanced around and noticed a crowd spilling out of a building a few metres down the street. The part of the mind that was not his informed him in its little voice that it was the Palace Theatre and the big sign above the entrance proclaimed it contained something called *Cinderella*. Zalas's mind swirled as it filled with new information. The little voice whispered, 'Please, don't upset the children.' Zalas closed his eyes again and spent a little of the power he had left. When he opened them, the front of the red suit was once again clean. In fact, it sparkled. The little voice was pleased.

Zalas laughed.

He looked up to see the crowd heading towards him. He let the little voice in once again. Let it guide him. He could feel it filling him, telling him what he needed to do, who he needed to be.

Zalas watched the people streaming towards him and took in the faces of the little children, which lit up when they saw him. He threw out his hands expansively in greeting. 'Merry Christmas!' he boomed.

An ecstatic little boy broke away from his parent's grasp and rushed towards him, arms outstretched. 'Santa!' He threw himself around Zalas's legs, hugging him for all he was worth.

And Zalas felt it. Belief. Behind him, another child was running towards him, her face animated with delight.

The power surged through his body. For the first time in a long time, he felt alive.

And he laughed along with the children, his joy matching theirs. As if all their dreams, and his, had just come true.

21

Stella typed and then deleted the opening three words of her essay for the four thousandth time before tossing her laptop down on to the bed. After her confrontation with Manny – if you could call it that, given that the man himself had bailed out and his literal guardian angel had taken over – she'd retreated to her room. Inevitably, Grace had 'just popped in', doing a terrible job of trying to appear casual as she enquired about what was going on and whether Stella was OK. Stella had given a brief summary of what she'd found out from Zoe. Grace had looked exactly as confused and perplexed as Stella had felt when she'd first heard the story herself.

The whole thing was hard to get your head round. First, there was the sheer impossibility of the number – that Manny was over a century old. Then there was the emotional wrench of realizing that the seemingly kind-hearted, happy-go-lucky Manny was in fact some arsehole who had walked out on his family. Stella had sensed that Grace had wanted to talk about it more, but Stella had excused herself, citing her suddenly pressing need to get her essay done.

In truth, it pissed her off that as soon as the confrontation was over, she knew they would have all been in the bullpen, huddled together, talking about her behind her back. 'Did you see? She threatened to use her power. Wanted to fight the angel. What are we going to do? She's unstable.'

She knew that she was deliberately casting people being concerned for her in a bad light, but at that precise moment she didn't care. She was sick of being 'managed'. Meanwhile, Manny the deadbeat was no doubt being left alone to drift away on a cloud of pot smoke, leaving all his responsibilities behind. Nobody seemed to care about that, but she bet they would have been out there engaging in amateur pop psychology about her. Was she taking this all so personally because she didn't have any family of her own? Was this her own abandonment issues coming to the fore? She assumed they were thinking it because *she'd* been thinking it. She'd also decided it was all nonsense; she was pissed at Manny because Zoe's revelation had cast him in an entirely different light. Worse still, she'd witnessed his enabling angel ward off Zoe when all she'd asked was for him to step up and be a father while he still could.

Stella spent the rest of her day sitting in her room, seething and getting nothing done. Before she knew it, it was past midnight and she was wide awake. She absent-mindedly scratched at the small red mark on her leg. It didn't look like much, but it itched like a bugger. Her annoyance creeped up a further notch as she realized it was from where Manny had reached out and touched her. Great. Between that and her simmering anger, she was never going to get to sleep . . .

★

When is a dream not a dream?

Stella was laying brick – actually laying brick – on an actual building site. She was looking out of her eyes, watching herself doing it. More than that, she could feel the weariness in her muscles from a long day's toil.

It was a dream but she knew it was a dream. Shouldn't that mean she should wake up? Come to that, who finds themselves in a dream wondering why knowing it is a dream hasn't caused them to snap out of it?

Stella stopped and looked down at her hands. They were black, a darker shade than hers and obviously male. Callused from hard physical labour.

A man walked by, carrying a hod of bricks over his shoulder and smiled. 'Oi, Devon, you lazy prick – pull the lead out!'

'You're one to talk, Quinnie!' The voice was hers – only not hers.

And then she was simultaneously still inside the bricklayer's body while also observing it from outside. She was Manny. Not quite the Manny from the picture she'd seen earlier but far closer to that than to the one who lived downstairs. A young, fresh-faced version of Manny, not much more than a teenager.

Somewhere a whistle blew and she was back inside Manny's head. She was now standing in a sparsely furnished bedroom, looking in the mirror. Manny was wearing a simple suit and, without being told, Stella knew it was second-hand. Worn in places but mended with excruciating care. He turned this way and that, a man determined to look his best.

And then another jump. He's walking down the street, part of a larger crowd of men, laughing and talking loudly. Quinnie, the man from the building site, is walking in front of him, beaming back at him. Then he moves out of the way and, with a shock of recognition, Stella realized that she knows where they are going. The Ritz on Whitworth Street West. She passed it several times a week. Stella was in Manny's memory and yet she could turn around and look up and down the street. The cars, the people, everything looked different, but the Ritz looked remarkably similar to the one she knew, save for the absence of the ubiquitous corporate branding. She could feel the excitement running through Manny. He'd been saving up for this, his one night out in a couple of months.

Another jump and he was standing beside a dance floor, surrounded by the same crowd, but now they're only one small group in a massive swathe of revellers. The dance floor is huge but it was still early enough in the night that it was not yet heaving. Manny held a pint of ale in his hand. He needed to make it last. He could only afford a couple. Some of the lads would be drinking all night, but not him. His feet were already tapping restlessly to the sound of the big band on the stage. Manny was more of a dancer than a drinker, and not just because dancing comes included in the price of admission.

The crowd parts and, through Manny's eyes, Stella sees her. A girl in a yellow dress, like sunlight breaking through clouds. She felt the moment the exquisite ache hit, as the girl catches him staring and shoots back a shy smile that breaks his heart into a thousand pieces and reassembles it in her image. Stella has heard of the idea of love at first sight, but her generation are far too worldly-wise to believe in such fairy tales. And yet here she is. The rest of the room – no, the rest of the world – fades away and the only thing before Manny is the girl in the yellow dress. Stella, seeing what he saw and feeling what he felt, is swept along yet also just far enough removed to notice the scowling face of the heavyset friend behind the girl, eyeing Manny warily like a mama bear assessing a danger to her cub.

And then they're dancing. Manny and the girl in the yellow dress. Not just one dance either. But all night. Rosa. Her name is Rosa. Manny has his eyes fixed on her constantly but is aware that they're drawing admiring and jealous glances in equal measure. They're a good-looking couple but, more than that, they can dance. Really dance. It was as if they were born to dance together.

Now they're walking home, Rosa's arm locked through his, while his free hand carries a trophy proudly. In the background, the scowling friend walks behind, looking none too happy with this state of affairs. Manny is so filled with joy as he and Rosa talk and laugh, walking the long road home having missed the last bus, that it is almost painful. Stella has never felt anything like that.

★

The joy remains but the scenes shifts, and Rosa, radiant in white, is walking down the aisle towards him. Behind her, the bridesmaid is still scowling while dabbing her eyes with a handkerchief.

★

And then Manny is carrying Rosa over the threshold into their new home. A terraced house. It isn't much but it is a palace to them. They work every hour, Manny forever scrabbling for work wherever he can get it, no matter what it is, and, together with Rosa's job as a typist for the council, they get by.

★

The scene shifts again and Rosa is giving Manny exciting news. While Stella cannot make out what is being said, she feels the joy fill Manny's heart once again as he lifts Rosa off her feet and spins her around. Then he remembers himself and carefully places her down on the sofa, as if she is a China doll that might break. She laughs at him and pulls him close to place a kiss on his lips.

★

Fast forward to Manny sitting in a waiting room, in the company of three men he doesn't know. One is asleep, leaning against the wall. Another is reading the newspaper while smoking. The third one wants to talk but Manny is struggling. He can't concentrate. His knee is jigging up and down. He notices the paper reader shoot a pointed look at it and, with an effort, he stills it, before it starts again not a minute later. His whole body is one anxious ball of energy – terrified, excited, fit to burst. How long has it been? Does it normally take this long? What if something has gone wrong? His whole body tenses as if trying to physically reject the idea.

A nearby door swings open and a doctor in a white coat emerges. He looks at Manny and, smiling, tells him something. Losing the run of himself, Manny hugs the doctor then attempts to do the same thing to the other three men. The sleeping man falls off his chair in shock and the reader wields his paper with intent to fend off this entirely inappropriate outpouring of emotion.

★

And then, beaming, Rosa is carefully transferring the tiniest, most precious thing he's ever seen into his trembling arms. And Manny's heart breaks into a million pieces yet again and reforms itself into an image of this incredible woman and the daughter she has blessed him with. He looks down into that tiny, precious little face and can find no words. Unseeing, unknowing of the world she has just entered, the baby reaches out and her tiny fingers wrap around one of his. Unapologetic tears are streaming down Manny's face.

★

Manny and Rosa bring little Dottie home, and Manny berates a teenager who passes within ten feet of the pram, walking at a speed that Manny considers to be excessive. Rosa waves at the perplexed boy and laughs at her husband, who is too busy monitoring a world filled with potential dangers to feel embarrassed.

★

Manny is up in the middle of the night, tired beyond belief, rocking Dottie in his arms as she cries. He sings to her softly and, as always, she stops, seemingly mesmerized by her father's voice. 'Hush, little baby, don't say a word . . .'

★

Then Dottie is taking faltering steps, Manny and Rosa following closely behind her, in case there is any hint of a fall.

★

And they're reading a book together, all three of them. Dottie laughs, and Manny and Rosa share a look, unable to believe how lucky they are.

★

They're standing in a friend's front room, because they don't have a wireless of their own. Dottie sits on the floor with two other children, piling blocks on blocks, oblivious to the serious looks on the faces of the adults. Manny tries to smile reassuringly as

Rosa bites the knuckles of her right hand nervously, listening to the man tell them that the world has changed for ever.

★

Manny is looking into the same mirror as earlier, only this time he is in his uniform – the one from the picture that Zoe showed Stella. Stella knows now that he is back home briefly, having completed basic training. He is shipping out in the morning. Rosa, a bundle of nervous energy, as if desperate to wring every last drop out of their time together, has borrowed some money from her mother and booked them in with a photographer. Dottie is excited. This is her first picture and she is peppering the photographer with questions. Only six, she has a relentless determination to find out how the world works, which is already driving her teachers to distraction. The photographer will take a picture of the whole family too, but first, Rosa wants one of just daddy and daughter.

Manny smiles at her, then turns directly to the camera, trying to look like he thinks a soldier should. Calm. Brave. His little daughter stands in front of him, smiling into the lens, in her world where the only danger is that she might fall and mess up her lovely dress. Stella realizes it's the image from the photograph.

The camera flashes and, suddenly, Stella is awake. Her mouth is dry, her head throbbing, the early dawn light coming in through the high windows the only proof that time has passed.

When is a dream not a dream? When it is a memory.

22

Crowds made Claremont Dibner nervous.

It wasn't that he wasn't a people person, far from it – people, after all, were customers, and Claremont Dibner loved nothing more than a customer. It was just that on Saturday morning, as he pulled up outside his Wonderland Christmas Experience in the rented Audi, he hadn't been expecting to see a crowd of people standing outside, an hour before they were due to open. His fear of crowds was rooted in his experience of their propensity to turn into mobs. He used to say he was his own worst critic, but there's only so many times you can be forced to climb out of a bathroom window before having to admit that may not be the case.

The problem– at least as far as he was concerned – was that people expected too much from life, frankly. Like, if they turned up at an event in Blackpool expecting to see the comedian Peter Kay, and instead got the magical duo of Peter and Kay. Was it his fault if they couldn't read a flyer properly? Whatever happened to the great British ability to make the best of a bad lot? Or to see the funny side of life? Admittedly, the word 'and' had been in a significantly smaller typeface than the words 'Peter' and 'Kay', but you had to allow graphic designers their typographical liberties.

The entertainment industry was challenging to break into, sewn up as it was by the big companies with their venues, acts and refunds. Claremont was forced to work on the peripheries. He considered himself a guerrilla promoter, in the Che Guevara sense, as opposed to King Kong-style gorillas.

That being said, he had once organized an event in Pontardawe, where the locals had been disappointed to discover the gorilla was Wayne in a suit. He hadn't even got as far as the bit where he mimed along to the drums on 'In The Air Tonight' when the patrons of the miners' club had started to demand their money back. Claremont had thrown the kit in the van while Wayne fought off four locals in the car park, half the town cheering them on. To be fair, they'd all enjoyed it and CD Promotions had even been offered a repeat booking for that one – a very rare occurrence indeed.

Wayne, Claremont's current head of security, had featured in many of his previous endeavours. Claremont said this was because he was keen to give Wayne a fresh start in life, something he was in regular need of after his latest stint in prison. Besides, despite Wayne's faults, he also had two big pluses. Namely, he was ferociously loyal while being incredibly bad at remembering how much money he'd been promised. He was a simple man of simple pleasures, and the fact that the greatest of those pleasures was to indulge in acts of violence was a tragic, if useful, character flaw.

Claremont had hit on the idea of a Christmas wonderland

while seeking refuge in a shopping centre in Hull during an unscheduled game of hide-and-seek with a crowd of angry Jehovah's Witnesses. While nobody owned the rights to God legally, it turned out a lot of people felt they did in some other way, and when you advertised washing away sins for much less than anyone else was offering, you ran into all kinds of problems of a theological and bloodthirsty nature.

Nobody owned Santa Claus, though. People thought the Coca-Cola Company did, but they didn't – this time around, Claremont had the foresight to do a quick Google before getting posters printed. The whole of Christmas was wide open, in fact. This was his big chance and when faced with a true big chance there's only one thing you can do – go big. The downside of doing so was needing investment, and he'd found the traditional banking institutions to be alarmingly unimaginative. This was why he'd been forced to seek 'alternative financing' from another source, aka Ivan the Mad Russian.

The 'mad' part of Ivan's name could be proved in many ways, the most significant of which was the fact that he was not Russian. He was by all accounts a bloke called Darren who'd been born and raised in Salford. At some point during his teens, possibly influenced by a Guy Ritchie movie, he'd decided to rebrand himself and had stayed one hundred per cent committed to the role ever since. So much so that he'd never broken character, although he had broken anyone who'd pointed out he was playing one. One of the earliest stories Claremont had heard about Ivan – and one that he very definitely believed – was that he'd found out which of his former associates had fingered him for a particular crime and had then bitten off all the poor bastard's fingers. Word about something like that gets around, and suddenly people start forgetting what you look like and what you may or may not have done real quick.

Someone like Wayne was violent because he had problems with impulse control, but Ivan was violent because he had a calling. In another age, he'd have led armies; in this one, he ran criminal enterprises while talking in a hammy accent that any actual Russian would laugh at, albeit very briefly. Ivan had originally been Claremont's backer and then, at some point, he'd taken it upon himself to become his partner. Controlling partner, in fact, because Ivan was a take-control kind of guy. Ivan had even assisted Claremont in acquiring a short-term lease on the former warehouse they were using for this venture. It was a decent size and a good deal, so long as you ignored the large stain in the centre of the floor which was one hundred per cent definitely not blood.

Still, ticket sales had been strong and it looked like the Wonderland Christmas Experience would make money. True, he'd inevitably need to navigate a few teething problems where customer expectations may exceed reality, but he was well used to that. On the upside, Wonderland would only be properly open for this weekend, Claremont being a big believer in the 'leave 'em wanting more' adage. If there had been one consistency in his career, it had been that he'd always left people wanting a whole lot more. He just needed to get through the next two days and he'd be home free, and still in possession of all of his limbs and digits. Ivan had the rather unnerving habit of asking you to use your fingers while explaining numbers to him, and would then stare intently at them as you did so.

Wayne rushed over to Claremont before he'd even managed to get out of the car. Clarissa, Claremont's assistant, followed behind him, not looking up from her phone even once. Claremont had never managed to achieve eye contact with her, but she had come highly recommended by Ivan. He assumed she was keeping an eye on him on his partner's behalf, or at least she would be if she ever took them off her phone.

'There's people here,' said Wayne.

'Yes, well, there're supposed to be,' replied Claremont. 'We're running an experience, after all. No refunds.'

'That's just it, though – they don't want refunds. They want to buy tickets.'

Claremont stopped and took in the queue of nearly one hundred people. 'Really?'

'Yeah. They got here early in the hope we aren't sold out.'

'They did?'

Claremont was finding this new development perplexing, but he was nothing if not adaptable. 'Right, Clarissa, start selling them tickets.' She nodded, turned around and headed back towards the queue. 'Add a fifty per cent mark-up for buying on the door . . . and a ten per cent discount for cash!' he called after her.

Clarissa gave no indication of having heard any of that last bit, but he decided to assume she had. He turned his attention back to Wayne. 'And why aren't you in your Santa Claus outfit?'

'That's the other thing,' said Wayne. 'He's back.'

'He's— Do you mean Neil? Neil is back?' Claremont reflexively ran his hands over the bruising on his neck from where the psycho had tried to strangle him. Being attacked by Santa Claus – it was the kind of thing that'd leave a man traumatized for life. He'd have tried to sue somebody if he himself wasn't the employer of the aforementioned Father Christmas. 'Well, if he's here looking for his pay, he can whistle for it. In fact, you can throw him out again, and this time you have my permission to not be polite about it.'

'No, he's in the grotty.'

'Grotto,' corrected Claremont. 'It's grotto.'

'Right. He's in there, ready to go. I thought I should wait for you rather than, y'know, using my initiative.'

There had been previous discussions about Wayne's use of his initiative. It rarely ended well for anyone involved.

'Hmmmm,' said Claremont. On one hand, Neil had proved to be rather flaky. On the other hand, Wayne was not natural Santa Claus material. 'I'll go talk to him.'

Claremont, through sheer force of habit, walked everywhere at high speed. It was how you avoided people stopping you to ask awkward questions. It was also how he ran into the enormous slab of humanity that was standing at the entrance to the Wonderland Christmas Experience.

'Jesus!' said Claremont.

'Oh yeah,' said Wayne. 'This is my cousin, Wayne.'

Claremont took a couple of steps back in order to drink in the full picture. There was indeed a family resemblance, in the sense that this new Wayne looked like the old one, if you'd asked a not terribly gifted child to do a drawing of Wayne and then somehow that Wayne had come to life. True, Cousin Wayne didn't have the word 'Satan' tattooed across his forehead, although there was certainly room for it. The man's forehead was so large he could actively consider renting it out as a billboard.

'How many Waynes are in your family?'

'It's funny you should ask that—'

'Actually,' said Claremont, quickly remembering how long and tedious Wayne's stories could be, 'never mind. Why is Wayne here?'

'Because you said I had to be Santa and I said what about security and then you said just get someone else to handle it and why did you have to do everything around here.' You couldn't fault Wayne's remarkable faculty to recall conversations word for word.

'Right,' said Claremont. 'Well, as you said, it seems we're no longer down a Santa' – he paused as, behind the new Wayne, the old Wayne put himself in Claremont's eyeline and emphatically started to shake his head in a downright pleading manner –'but I'm sure we can find a job for you, Wayne. I'm always on the look-out for a likely lad.'

Claremont tried to tap Wayne on the shoulder playfully. It felt like rock.

'Right, then.'

'Hello, my name is Wayne,' said the new Wayne, as if some kind of programming had kicked in belatedly.

'Yes,' said Claremont. 'Yes, it is. Welcome on board. Now, if you'll excuse me, I've got to go to the grotty— grotto. Wayne.'

The old Wayne fell into step beside him. 'Thanks for that, boss. Wayne is a good lad, but he's got a bit of a temper on him.'

Claremont resisted the urge to ask further questions. If Wayne described someone as having a bit of a temper on them, that was really quite something. A tiny part of Claremont's brain that he rarely ever listened to piped up with a point about the advisability of having such an individual near children, but he shouted it down quickly when the image of Ivan looking hungrily at his fingers popped up.

Claremont stopped inside the door, his attention drawn to the floor. 'The snow.'

'Yeah,' said Wayne.

'It's more snowy.'

'Yeah.'

'What did you do to it?'

'Nuffink. I thought it was you.'

'Oh,' said Claremont. 'Right.'

He looked up to see Mrs Pierce, one of the vendors in the 'Christmas village' area and their self-elected spokeswoman, glaring at him. What she lacked in height she made up for in sheer stubbornness. 'Mr Dibner, I'd like a word.'

'I would love to but—'

His attempts to bypass her were halted by her bosom being shoved in his path. The woman wielded it like a weapon. 'I'm not happy, Mr Dibner.'

'None of us are, Mrs Pierce. It's the curse of the modern age. I blame social media.'

'I don't. I blame you. Mr Princaka's shop is inappropriate.'

'Excuse me? This is a fantasy land of wonder and he's selling fantasy.'

'Filth is what he's selling. Pure filth.'

'We've been through this. He's put the items in question in the curtained-off area with the "Daddy's special pressies for Mummy" sign, as agreed.'

The Christmas village was always going to be overpriced and underwhelming, because, well, they always were, but Ivan had also decided to use it to force people who owed him money to sell stuff he had in lock-ups that he'd been unable to get rid of. It was sort of like a pyramid scheme, in that anything you didn't sell you'd end up being buried with. Mrs Pierce was one of their few genuine vendors, a woman intent on selling the world porcelain models of cats whether it wanted them or not.

'It's not good enough. I'm not having my pussies associated with this smut.'

Claremont smiled and ignored Wayne's ill-hidden guffaw. 'Mrs Pierce, I assure you that nobody takes the reputation of the Wonderland Christmas Experience more seriously than I do, but we are advertised as fun for all the family and, whether you like it or not, I'm afraid mummies like to have fun, too. I'm sure you're not judging your fellow women for their choices? That would be most unfortunate and a real kick in the teeth for feminism.'

'What? No, I . . .'

That wrongfooted her enough to give Claremont the moment of hesitation he needed to get away before she could rally her outrage for a counter charge.

'Bloody hell,' he said to Wayne in a hissed whisper. 'Why did I ever let that woman in?'

'She paid upfront.'

They were now approaching the back of the warehouse where the grotto was located. Claremont took in the sight before him. 'Did you . . .'

'I thought you did,' said Wayne.

It looked . . . nicer. It was weird. It was adorned with the same tinsel and decorations but they seemed, well, nicer. There was a glow to the whole place.

Claremont pushed open the entrance flaps and the impression of the grotto's significant upgrade became all the more pronounced. He and Wayne stopped across the threshold. Over the years, Claremont had used the word 'ambiance' many times. It was a great word, a real multitool that could cover all manner of sins because nobody really knew what it meant. Even Claremont hadn't, until right that instant. The grotto was positively awash in the stuff. It hit you in the face like a delightful mince pie. The massive pile of presents in the corner positively shimmered. Candlelight suffused the place and, somewhere in the distance, Claremont swore he could hear sleigh bells.

'Is it me,' said Wayne quietly, 'or does Santa's throne look a lot more . . .'

'Throne-y,' finished Claremont. 'Yeah.'

As he stepped forward, Neil looked up at the pair. There was something different about him but Claremont couldn't put his finger on exactly what it was.

'Ah, Neil,' he said, as he tried to refocus his thoughts. 'I see that you've come to your senses and decided to come back. Well, just this once I'm willing to let bygones be bygones, as long as there is . . .'

Claremont trailed off. He'd reached the throne and was now looking Neil directly in the eyes. His mouth went dry, his mind went blank, his knees went weak and his bladder went seriously in danger of doing something that shouldn't happen to a man his age. He kept trying to talk but all that came out was 'Wabba abba nah Christmas.'

Santa Claus smiled at him and those eyes shone ever more brightly. 'Bring me the children.'

Ten seconds later, Claremont and Wayne were standing outside the grotto, both looking at the ground.

'That was . . .' started Wayne.

'Yep, it certainly was.'

'Should we . . .' They looked at one another, neither having the slightest idea what the rest of that sentence should be.

Just then, the cow walked by.

'Oh,' said Claremont. 'How'd you get the red nose to stay on without tape?'

'I d—'

'Don't say it,' said Claremont. 'Forget I asked.'

'What are we going to do?'

'Do?' echoed Claremont, striving for a level of confidence he wasn't really feeling. 'Why, we're going to open, of course. Let the wonder commence!'

Always Look on the Slide Side of Life

A playground in the Chorlton area of Manchester has become the focus of international attention after a series of unsettling incidents involving its slide. The slide in question – one of the fancy, swervy ones with an enclosed plastic tube – has begun exhibiting inexplicable characteristics. Local parent Toby Hadoke, who wished to remain anonymous but also spelled out his name three times, commented, 'Toddlers have been going in one end and coming out the other as teenagers. It's incredible. We've asked them what the hell happened in there, but they just shrug and don't answer – because they're bloody teenagers.'

Scientists have speculated that the slide may now contain a wormhole or temporal anomaly that accelerates the ageing process. Police have since closed off the area after several parents got into a violent altercation while attempting to climb up the slide the wrong way, in the hope it might have the opposite effect.

23

Over a day after stepping in there for the first time, DS Andrea Wilkerson was back at the scene of what the medical examiner had at least confirmed was a triple murder at MMU's library. She would have very happily gone through the rest of her life never seeing it again, but one of the academics specializing in linguistics and semiotics with whom she'd been in contact had sent some questions on the positioning of the various symbols in relation to each other. Something about which ones were directly facing one another on opposite walls. The email had sounded like someone clutching at straws, but seeing as they were currently strawless, Wilkerson felt compelled to indulge him.

She'd just come from the morning briefing for DI Clarke's taskforce. Neither she nor Sturgess had been invited but she'd known it was happening and had made it her job to turn up anyway. Nobody was going to push her out of the room once she got there. Clarke's normal brashness had been noticeable by its absence. It seemed that being in the unenviable position of leading a massive manhunt which despite the plethora of resources dedicated to it for over twenty-four hours had somehow been unsuccessful in its attempts to locate a blood-soaked librarian with no criminal record of any kind – could take the wind out of even his sails. She'd have felt sorry for him if she wasn't so convinced that at that very moment he'd be looking for some way to shift the blame on to DI Sturgess and, by association, her. Sturgess often expressed his utter lack of interest in 'playing politics', as he called it. Unfortunately, not wanting to play the game didn't mean you weren't playing, it just meant you were doing so badly. In truth, she resented the hell out of having to constantly try to protect her boss's arse, even more so given that he'd never asked her to.

The police presence around the library, while still significant, had been scaled back. Keeping this shitshow under wraps had been an impossible task from the very beginning – after all, the library was metres away from the Department of Journalism. However, it being the Saturday before Christmas had played in their favour somewhat. The incident had still made the papers, but the ongoing nature of the investigation and whatever pressure was being applied by the powers that be meant the reporting had been remarkably restrained. So far, all the more salacious details had been omitted.

Working with Sturgess in their team with no name and, officially, no remit meant Wilkerson saw all manner of weird and wondrous crap, but when you sat back and thought about it, one of the most unnerving things about it all was how little of it was picked up by the media. By all rights, some of it should be on the front pages, headlines full of exclamation marks and utter disbelief, yet it passed mostly without comment. Somebody somewhere was stopping that from happening – whoever they were, they had an almost unimaginable level of power. She'd long suspected Sturgess knew more on that front than she did, but for whatever reason, whenever it came up he'd always change the subject.

Wilkerson nodded at the officer on station and signed in on the log. She didn't recognize him. Fresh-faced lad. Not a surprise – the day before Christmas Eve, anyone with a bit of seniority would have made sure to be off the rotas. She pushed through the plastic sheeting that hung over the door. Thankfully, the bodies had long since been catalogued and removed. Only numbered pieces of card indicated where what could euphemistically be described as 'elements' were found. This also meant that she didn't have to suit up, as it was no longer designated an active crime scene. The symbols were still on the walls. However, they were not the most arresting sight as Wilkerson entered.

'Who the fuck are you?' she said, with her usual lack of tact that came with being caught off guard.

The man, who had been standing in the centre of the room, hands outstretched and looking up at the ceiling, turned to offer her a tight smile. She didn't recognize him, and he wasn't the kind of bloke you'd forget in a hurry – starkly bald, he must've been near seven feet tall and was wearing a black three-piece suit. The unnerving image of a vulture sprang into her head. He took a few steps towards her.

'Good morning,' he said in an accentless voice. 'I did not mean to startle you.'

'Well, you did. Can I see some ID right now?'

'Of course.'

The man reached into his pocket and pulled out something that was not a wallet. Wilkerson noticed the golden object, which caught the light as it danced between the man's freakishly long fingers, before she could say anything. She felt a lurching sensation, followed by a wave of nausea.

'What in the hell?' she said, fighting back the urge to throw up.

The man tilted his head and regarded her curiously. 'Oh dear,' he said with the air of somebody who'd failed to secure his preferred parking space, 'that is inconvenient. It appears you have been glamoured recently, which is in itself interesting, is it not?'

The question didn't appear to be directed at her.

Wilkerson blinked rapidly several times in an effort to clear her head then took a step forward. 'I am arresting you for—' was as far as she got before the man made a brief series of movements with his left hand. Suddenly she found herself unable to move.

'No,' he continued, 'I don't think we shall be doing that. It appears we shall have to do this the' – he made a noise that sounded like a cough but might have been his version of a laugh – 'old-fashioned way. I do apologize. It is not the cleanest of approaches.'

Wilkerson desperately wanted to scream as every fibre of her being strained against whatever force was holding her in place. Seemingly unconcerned, the man ran his long fingers over the waistcoat of his suit. Some small part of Wilkerson's brain, the tiniest part that wasn't overwhelmed with blind panic, noted the unusual stitching on his outfit, the patent leather of his shoes. She was helpless, utterly helpless. She had felt this way once before in her life and had sworn then that whatever happened, it would never happen again. Yet here she was.

She couldn't even breathe.

'Try to remain calm, officer,' continued the man. 'I mean you no harm. I am here seeking a book.' He paused. 'I appreciate the irony, given our location, but it is a very particular book. It is, let us say, "leather bound", and it has a symbol on the front.' He swirled the index finger of his right hand in the air and a strange marking appeared, sketched out in purple light. It was an ouroboros, only in this version the snake was eating its own tail right in front of her. 'It is very important to my employer,' continued the man, his tone infuriatingly calm, 'and we wish to have it back.'

He looked at her quizzically then raised his eyebrows.

'Ah, apologies.'

He clicked his fingers and, suddenly, Wilkerson could breathe again. As the fresh air entered her lungs it felt like the greatest thing she had ever experienced. She still couldn't move her mouth, never mind the rest of her body, but at least she was no longer drowning while standing up. She refocused her attention on the patent leather of his shoes so that her mind would not give in to the fear.

'Now,' continued the man, 'I shall give you the opportunity to speak in a moment. When I do so, you will respond to my questions calmly and truthfully. Let us not make this any more unpleasant than it has to be.'

After a second, Wilkerson's jaw unlocked and her mouth flew open. She inhaled another deep breath, ready to scream for all her worth, but the man raised his hand and, suddenly, she was frozen again.

'Did I not make myself clear?' For the first time a flash of irritation passed across his face. 'Please do not take my civil tone as a sign of weakness. You people do seem to so deride manners. I do not wish to harm you, but my time is valuable and you are not.'

He used the same finger to make a slashing motion through the air this time, and Wilkerson felt an intense pain slice across her chest. Her face immobilized, she was just able to shift her eyes downwards and catch sight of the small bloom of blood spreading across her blouse just above her left breast. She winced. She hadn't imagined it. Her skin had been cut.

'So,' said the man, 'we shall try this again.'

His fingers danced through the air as before and Wilkerson's jaw was once again free to move. She didn't try to scream this time.

'Fuck you,' she hissed.

All this earned her was an eye roll, as if the man was a frustrated teacher with a particularly dim student.

'I see you are determined to make this difficult. Very well.'

His finger slashed through the air again and Wilkerson felt another line burn across her skin above her right breast. Deeper this time. Even without looking, she could feel the wet, sticky blood against her skin.

The man leaned in very close. Close enough that she could feel his oddly cold breath play across her skin. 'Rest assured, officer, I will run out of patience a long time before you run out of skin.'

24

Since Stella had woken from her dream that was not a dream, she hadn't been able to get back to sleep. The small red spot on her leg from where Manny had touched her still itched like a bugger, too.

She had gone over what she'd seen, again and again. Another way in which it didn't feel like a dream was that she was able to recall every part of it in crystal-clear detail. Even though she already knew what the answer would be, she still went ahead and Googled whether the O2 Ritz on Whitworth Street had indeed been a dancehall back in the 1930s. It had. She was forced to admit the obvious to herself: what she'd seen hadn't been a dream, it had been Manny's memories. It was his life flashing before her eyes.

She didn't get why Manny, or his not so little friend, would want her to see it, but there it was. The whole experience had been draining. It hadn't even been memories really, in the sense that while being an observer, she was also experiencing the emotions right along with Manny. She also had some form of agency – she'd been able to get him to turn around and take in his surroundings. It was like she was controlling a character in a game, but it wasn't open world, she was obliged to follow the story.

She thought about talking to someone about it. Not to Manny – she was still very pissed at him – but maybe Hannah? Where would she even start, though? 'Hey, don't want to worry you, but I appear to have our Rastafarian printer's life flashing before my eyes. How's your week going?'

She was shaken from her thoughts by the sound of someone banging loudly on the front door downstairs. She leaped to her feet, her first thought being that it might be Zoe returning to try to have it out with her great-great-granddaddy again.

As she exited her room, Ox was already crossing reception and heading towards the staircase.

'I'll get it,' said Stella.

Ox didn't break his stride. 'Get what?' he snapped.

'The door.'

'Oh, fine,' he said, reaching the top of the stairs. 'Whatever.'

As he turned to walk down in front of her, Stella saw that most of the right side of his head and body were covered in cream paint.

'I need to get into the shower because' – he raised his voice to an angry holler – 'I have been attacked by an irredeemable delinquent.'

'You said you were holding the ladder,' came Clint's response as he emerged from the bullpen, failing to suppress a grin. As he noticed Stella, his grin changed from gleeful to creepy. 'Hey, babes, how's it hanging?'

'Ugh,' said Stella. 'He is absolutely the worst.'

'You have no idea,' hollered Ox without looking back, as he trotted down the stairs towards the bathroom.

'Don't get paint on the—'

She was cut off by the bathroom door slamming shut.

'Some of us have to live here, y'know,' she shouted.

Clint appeared beside her. 'If you're getting lonely, give your boy Clint a holler, sweet cheeks.'

'Yeah,' said Stella, as she stomped downstairs, 'if I ever want to find out which is the best Tellytubby, you'll be the first person I call.'

'Whatever, babes. For the record, Tinky-Winky is clearly the best one.'

Stella shook her head as she reached the ground floor. 'Damn it, he's right,' she muttered under her breath. 'He's clearly the best one. Got the bag and everything.'

It was not Zoe at the door. Instead, it was a truly massive human being, standing there in the steadily pouring rain. The man must've weighed at least four hundred pounds and was wearing a bright orange poncho that covered his entire body save for his flushed face. It was like being addressed by a low-flying hot-air balloon.

'Hello,' he started in an unexpectedly high-pitched voice, 'I wish to . . . ehm . . . speak to the . . . man in charge, please and thank you.'

'I—' started Stella.

'It's Banecroft, Alejandro – his name is Vincent Banecroft. We've been over this.' The second voice was coming from beneath the poncho. Stella looked down to see a bulldog poke out his head and glare up at them. 'It's one name. How can you not remember one name?'

'Sorry, Zeke,' said the big man, sounding genuinely upset.

'Don't worry about it, big guy – I'm just in a mood. Besides, this one we know.'

'Zeke?' said Stella, studying the dog's jowly little face.

'How many other talking bulldogs are you acquainted with?'

'Just one, which is honestly more than I'm entirely comfortable with. No offence.'

'Taking some anyway.'

'What are you doing here?'

'Well, primarily, I'm being cold and miserable, but I'm also here to see your boss – I'd have thought that was obvious.'

'But why?'

'It's not for the good of my health, I'll tell you that. Bad enough we've had to walk all the way up here, some fluffy-faced bastard then decides to come up and sniff my arse. I mean, the indignity of it. Everyone's always banging on about the bullies and the staffies but meanwhile they're letting those permed rodents run amok because, "Oh, don't worry, my dog is friendly." First off, there's such a thing as too friendly, and secondly, little dogs are way more bitey, but everyone turns a blind eye to those cute little psychopaths, don't they?' Zeke stopped. 'Where was I?'

'Psychopaths,' offered Alejandro.

'Before that. That's literally where I just stopped.'

'Banecroft?' ventured Stella.

'What about him? Oh, right, yeah – I'm here to see him.'

'And you were about to explain why.'

'I don't think I was. To be honest, I'm rather surprised that you haven't invited us in by this point in the conversation.'

'Oh,' said Stella. 'Sorry, come on in.'

'No, thank you, but it's nice to be asked. Now, get Banecroft down here – the boss wants to see him.'

'The boss? Cogs?'

The suggestion earned a laugh from both Zeke and Alejandro. 'Cogs? Ha, good one. No, not him. Tell Banecroft he needs to get his arse down here, the clock is ticking and, no offence, Alejandro, but while it is dry under this here poncho it is not all one could hope for in the olfactory stakes.'

'What's an oil factory?' asked Alejandro.

'I'll explain on the way back. So, what's going on? Why's Banecroft not down here already?'

'Because I haven't spoken to him yet,' responded Stella, folding her arms.

'Well, you should definitely do that, and so help me, Alejandro, we're having a serious discussion about your diet when we get back. I can tell which takeaway you ordered last night. That ain't healthy, my man.'

'Fair warning,' said Stella, 'Banecroft doesn't respond well to ultimatums.'

'Oh, it's not an ultimatum,' clarified Zeke, 'it's an invitation. Gods help him if it was an ultimatum. Trust me, he doesn't want to find out what happens if you turn down an invite.'

'I do. What will happen if he turns down this mysterious invite?' asked Stella.

'Well, let me put it this way' said Zeke. 'The last person to do so ended up being forced to live on a boat and cursed to only tell the truth for all eternity.'

'You mean Cogs, so . . .' Stella's eyebrows shot up. 'So, when you refer to "the boss", you mean . . .'

'A certain River Goddess, yes. So I suggest you get grumpy boy down here pronto as, believe me, if you don't, it will get a whole lot wetter around here really fast.'

25

Things were going well.

Very well.

If anything, too well.

Claremont Dibner wasn't used to this. The Wonderland Christmas Experience had been open for half a day now and so far there hadn't been even one complaint. The customers seemed happy. The vendors seemed happy. Even Mrs Pierce seemed happy. He'd been steeling himself to have to deal with all manner of problems, but none had cropped up.

In fact, with the flow of customers far greater than expected, he'd been on the verge of opening up a second grotto with the two Waynes on Santa duty when he noticed something peculiar. No matter how busy it got, the queue for the grotto seemed to stay the same length. Kids and their parents would go in and then come out the other side after what seemed like only a few seconds, and yet when you asked them, they all said how great it was that Santa Claus had taken so much time to talk to them. And the stories, he told such wonderful stories. The parents all had a slightly dazed air to them that wore off after a couple of minutes, but the children left with eyes shining brightly, full of the magic of Christmas.

Claremont had then taken himself off to sit in his office. He'd been in there all morning, doing everything in his power not to think about anything. Not to question anything. Clarissa kept bringing in bags of cash and on his laptop screen he could see the account total getting bigger and bigger from credit card sales. People kept buying tickets online or just showing up. So many people. He should have imposed a limit, and yet something inside him told him with a sickening level of certainty that no matter how many tickets they sold, the place would never reach capacity.

A knock sounded on the door. Claremont found himself oddly reassured. A problem. Finally, a problem that needed dealing with.

The door opened and Original Flavour Wayne looked in, a worried expression on his face. 'Boss . . .'

'We got a problem?' asked Claremont hopefully.

'We got a problem,' confirmed Wayne.

Two minutes later, Claremont was at the back door of the warehouse that housed Wonderland, staring at a problem that was not the kind of problem he'd been hoping for. 'When did it turn up?'

'A few minutes ago,' said Wayne.

'I don't suppose anyone saw anyone drop it off in a van or anything?'

'Nah,' said Wayne. 'I even asked Wayne. I mean the other,

other Wayne. Oh, yeah, meant to say – I had to call in my other cousin Wayne to help with the car parking. It's getting pretty full out there.'

'Right,' said Claremont, who was quickly realizing that there were bigger problems in the world than an excess of Waynes.

'I mean, it's not ours, is it?' asked Claremont.

'No.'

'But we've not stolen it or anything?'

'Definitely not,' confirmed Wayne.

'Could it have escaped from somewhere?'

'Possibly.'

'It's not like they're just roaming around the place, willy-nilly.'

'Not in my experience. No, boss.'

Claremont swallowed and looked the beast up and down. It returned his gaze with unnervingly intelligent eyes. As if it were patiently waiting for some form of answer, and it'd be fine so long as it was the answer it was looking for.

'Did . . .' started Claremont, his voice catching in his throat for a second, 'did you realize reindeers were this big?'

'I did not.'

'And the nose . . .'

'Surprisingly red,' confirmed Wayne. 'But again, I'm no expert. Been inside for the last few Christmases.'

Claremont thought that an odd clarification. It wasn't as if there'd been a recent influx of reindeers in the country. Like grey squirrels displacing the red squirrel population only to find themselves displaced in turn by hordes of seven-foot reindeer with red noses.

'What should we do?' asked Wayne.

'I think we should let it in.'

'Why?'

'Because I think it wants to come in.'

Claremont and Wayne stepped back and opened the large double doors to the warehouse. Sure enough, the reindeer clopped inside calmly.

They closed the doors behind it then stood there in silence for a very long time.

It was Wayne who eventually spoke again. 'What should we do?'

Claremont's mouth worked as if on autopilot. 'Tell Wayne – the other, other Wayne – to start charging double for car parking, twenty per cent discount for cash.'

Meanwhile, in his grotto, Santa took a brief pause and stretched out his back. This was going well. All so very well.

Neil was the happiest he'd ever been. Child after child came in to the grotto and left full to the brim with the magic of Christmas. It was all a dream come true, and the trick with dreams was not to question them or you'd wake up and ruin it all.

Behind his broad smile lay another. Zalas was happy too.

He could feel the power surging through him. And this was only the start. For the first time ever, he'd permitted the host of the body he was occupying to stay. They were working together, in a manner of speaking. He was sitting back and allowing his host to do all the talking, and it was working. This one wanted to believe even more than the children did.

He leaned back and let out a roar of delight, which morphed into a laugh like he had never heard before. It sounded a great deal like 'ho, ho, ho'.

26

Banecroft had engaged in quite a few unusual conversations in his time, but this particular one was right up there in the weirdness stakes.

As the rain pelted down around them, he addressed the beponchoed individual known as Alejandro, who was walking ahead of him, panting away heavily. 'Is it going to be much further?' Banecroft asked.

Alejandro, as expected, did not answer.

'We get there when we get there,' came the voice from somewhere underneath the big man's poncho. Zeke had been mostly out of view for the duration of the journey, sheltering himself somewhere under Alejandro's considerable circumference. It had meant that the limited conversation they'd engaged in as they walked had felt as if Banecroft was chatting with a large man's nether regions that had quite the attitude.

Zeke, as per legal requirements, was on a lead. Technically. In fact, it was an unusual double-lead affair, with Alejandro holding an end in each hand. After watching for a while, Banecroft realized that the dog was using the set-up to direct his associate, as a sort of reins to guide the big man left or right. The dog was walking the man rather than the other way around.

Their journey had brought them near Castlefield. Given it was the wrong end of town for last-minute Christmas shoppers, at least it meant the pedestrian traffic was relatively light. And anybody who didn't need to be out in this weather wasn't.

'Far be it from me to complain,' said Banecroft, 'but the coverage of this umbrella is exceedingly limited, given the deluge.'

'Oh, I'm so sorry to hear that,' came Zeke's response. 'I'm down here, inches from the ground, with no umbrella, no overcoat, no shoes, dodging the footfalls – no offence, Alejandro – of a man who could crush me without realizing, but please, continue to tell me how hard your life is.'

Alejandro's facial expression indicated the 'no offence' had not provided the blanket coverage Zeke had anticipated.

Banecroft decided to bite back his response, for no other reason than arguing with what was ostensibly a dog felt like a situation in which there were no winners. This whole undertaking was annoying him, representing as it did a clash of two of his driving principles – on one hand, he prided himself on not being the kind of man who could be summoned by anyone, but on the other, he was a news man, and whatever this was, it smelled very definitely newsy. Admittedly, the threshold for what Banecroft considered newsy had been skewed drastically in the last few months. Previously, 'talking dog walks man' would have comfortably cleared that bar on its own. Still, being summoned by something that considered itself a River Goddess was, if nothing else, at least an interesting wrinkle in his Saturday.

Admittedly, if he'd have known he was going to get soaked in the process, he might have been less inclined to accept the invitation that had not been an invitation. He would have offered to drive them wherever they were going but Alejandro didn't look like he could fit into a car. Or if he could, he didn't look like he would be able to get out again. Banecroft's Jag was a classic, and while it had many fine attributes, it wasn't built to carry such a heavy load. Banecroft would not like the truth to get out, but despite appearances, he did not go out of his way to offend the undeserving. The problem was that there were just so few people in existence who were undeserving of being offended. Annoyingly, given the circumstances, Alejandro had so far proved himself to be one of those people.

The trio were afforded a brief respite from the rain as they walked through a covered lane between buildings. However, if anything, it served to emphasize just how drenched Banecroft was. His left shoe made a squelching sound on every other step. When they reemerged into the open, a canal lay to their right.

A rivulet of water running off a gutter somehow managed to angle itself around the umbrella and down Banecroft's neck. 'Christ almighty!' he roared, throwing the umbrella down. 'That's it. That is it. That is it!' He stomped on the jettisoned brolly in case his point needed any more emphasis.

Banecroft turned to see Alejandro regarding him with one of the blank expressions he did so well while, from the ground below, Zeke was giving him a very judgy look.

'Screw this,' he said, stepping back into the lane. 'I'm not moving another inch. If anyone wants to talk to me, they can come and do so here.'

'Believe me, that's a terrible idea,' replied Zeke.

Banecroft folded his arms. 'Not. One. More. Step.'

He then watched a bulldog sit down and give an exasperated shake of his head before shouting, 'Alejandro, point.'

Nothing happened for several seconds. Banecroft saw a thought occurring to Alejandro in real time. It looked as if it was coming from a long way off. Eventually, Alejandro started to speak. 'Where—'

'Where we're going. Point to where we're going!'

'Oh.'

Alejandro turned and pointed past the bridge where a canal-boat was moored.

'Hang on,' said Banecroft. 'That's your boat? *The Nail in the Wall*?'

'Well,' said Zeke, 'not technically mine, but—'

'It's moored in exactly the same spot it was the first time I was on it.'

'And?'

'And,' snarled Banecroft, 'you could've just told me that, and I could have met you there.'

'Yeah, but then we wouldn't have had the pleasure of your company.' Zeke grabbed one of the leads in his mouth and tugged on it before shouting, 'Mush!'

Alejandro duly turned and started walking.

Banecroft looked down at the mangled remains of his umbrella. 'That may not have been my wisest decision ever.' He turned up the collar of his overcoat and followed Zeke and Alejandro towards the boat.

As he stood on the bank of the Bridgewater Canal, Banecroft didn't consider it possible for anyone to look as miserable as he felt, but the individual known as Cogs was giving it a good go. Sitting hunched under a golf umbrella on the deck of his canalboat, he was wearing jeans and a leather waistcoat over a bare chest, his ever-present bandana tied around his head and seemingly as much a part of him as the distinctive Van Dyke beard. Before him was a camping stove on which he was forlornly cooking sausages with all the enthusiasm of a McDonald's worker who was never going to make Employee of the Week.

The boat, seemingly of its own volition, moved across to the bank where it came to a halt. Zeke broke for cover from under Alejandro and jumped aboard, stopping only when he'd reached the safety of Cogs and his umbrella.

As Banecroft stepped on to the deck, Zeke turned to address his associate, who remained on dry land, now holding two dog leads that were missing a dog. 'Good lad, Alejandro. Appreciate your help.'

Alejandro nodded, then turned wordlessly and began to walk away.

'And remember what we talked about,' Zeke shouted after him. 'Vegetables. Try some vegetables.'

'He's a good kid,' said Cogs.

'Yeah,' agreed Zeke, who then shook himself violently, sending droplets of water flying in all directions.

'Oi, oi, oi!' exclaimed Cogs. 'Go easy.'

'Don't even start with me. I've had a hell of a morning.'

'You and me both, brother. You and me both.'

'What are you doing out here? The cooker isn't broken again, is it?'

'Nah. It's the smell of sausages.'

Zeke nodded. 'Oh, right.'

'I know. I mean, I'm all for assisting the poor thing but this ain't the most practical of arrangements, is it? We only got the one bed and we ain't vegetarians.' As if in response, the boat jolted, causing Banecroft to almost lose his footing. Cogs raised his voice. 'Not that I mind in the least – happy to be of help.'

'Not to break up this scene of domestic bliss,' said Banecroft, 'but I'm getting drenched here.'

'Oh, hark at poor Cinderella. Getting a bit wet, is it?'

'He's been moaning all the way here,' confirmed Zeke.

'D'ye know what,' said Banecroft, 'I've had just about enough of this. I'm leaving.' He looked around and was greeted by the realization that the boat had silently eased its way back into position in the middle of the canal.

'Best of luck with that,' said Cogs with a smirk.

'You—' The rest of Banecroft's riposte was lost as the downpour came to an abrupt halt. Actually, it didn't. In every direction he looked, it was still teeming with rain, it just no longer appeared to be raining on them.

Cogs and Zeke looked at one another. 'Blimey,' said Cogs, 'did you know she could do that?' He closed the golf umbrella and held out a hand to confirm they were indeed now an island of dry weather in a sea of deluge. 'Can't help thinking that'd have been useful on laundry day.' The boat lurched again. 'Right,' said Cogs quickly, 'best get a move on. Take a seat, Mr Editor.'

Banecroft perched on a small wooden barrel. It was wet but then so was he.

'You may be wondering why I called you here,' said Cogs before turning to Zeke. 'I've always wanted to say that.'

'I've heard you say it about a dozen times in the last year alone.'

'Well, excuse me, I'm sure.' Cogs turned his attention back to Banecroft. 'First off, to confirm, this whole conversation is covered by that hypocritical oaf thing.'

Banecroft considered this for a moment. 'If you mean the Hippocratic oath, then no, it isn't. That's the one doctors take.'

'Oh. What's the one journalists have, then?'

'There isn't one. We try to resist the urge to end almost all government-related articles with the phrase 'don't blame me, I didn't vote for these arseholes', but that's more of a guideline than an actual oath.'

'What about the one about protecting your sources?'

Banecroft raised an eyebrow. 'You're my source now, are you? Given that you went AWOL for the last few months, that is surprising to hear.'

'And whose fault is that?' countered Cogs.

'Excuse me?'

'He doesn't know,' chided Zeke.

'What?' said Cogs, taken aback. 'What you on about?'

'He doesn't know why we went q-u-i-e-t on them.'

'Why are you spelling it out?' asked Cogs. 'He's not a toddler.'

Zeke scratched at his ear with a paw. 'It's been a very long day.'

'Moving on . . .' said Cogs.

'No,' said Banecroft. 'I don't think we'll be doing that. Why did you go q-u-i-e-t on us?'

'Ah, crap,' said Cogs, a pained expression on his face. It looked as if he was trying to hold his breath for a few seconds, then he blurted out, 'Hannah showed up here with that DI Sturgess fella looking for information.'

Zeke tsked, which caused Cogs to throw out his arms in exasperation and almost knock over his frying pan full of sausages. 'I am literally unable to not tell the truth. It's your job to redirect the conversation before this kind of thing happens.'

'I am not my brother's keeper,' offered the dog.

'Here we go. Now he's being all sombre and whacking out Bible quotes, whereas yesterday I had to pull a grassy poo out of—'

'You swore you weren't going to mention that!'

'I can only tell the truth,' roared Cogs. 'If you don't understand that, then gods help us all.'

'Telling the truth doesn't mean you've got to bring everything up.'

The boat jolted so dramatically that Banecroft threw out a hand to steady himself while a dog squealed in anguish as a frying pan of sausages tipped over and on to the deck.

'Five-second rule,' shouted Cogs before yelping several times as he picked up and then dropped several hot sausages.

Eventually, he gave up and looked thoroughly miserable as he sucked his burned fingers.

'I think we annoyed her,' said Zeke as he mournfully regarded the fallen sausages.

'Ya think?'

'Can't you just eat them off the floor?' asked Banecroft. 'I mean, you're a dog.'

Bulldogs' facial expressions are limited but Zeke still managed to treat Banecroft to a withering scowl. 'A dog, am I? You know many talking dogs, do you?'

'Yeah,' said Cogs supportively. 'You tell 'im.'

'And just because you're ostensibly a guest here,' continued the canine-adjacent (but crucially not equivalent), 'doesn't mean I can't bite you.'

'Excellent use of the word "ostensibly",' said Cogs.

'Thanks,' said Zeke. 'So, we should get on with . . .'

'Right. So, where were we? Oh, yeah, the whole protecting your sources thing . . .'

'Actually,' said Banecroft, 'you were explaining how my assistant editor brought a relatively high-ranking law enforcement official with her to meet a source.'

'In her defence,' said Zeke, 'I think it's safe to say she realized it was a bad idea fairly quickly.'

'Well, that's reassuring.'

'What are the odds you might not bring that up with her?' asked Cogs.

'Less than stellar.'

'It's not covered by the whole protecting your sources thing?'

'I'm afraid it falls into the category of important teaching moment. I say moment – in the spirit of total honesty, I will confess it may come up more than once.'

Cogs sighed. 'I figured. I hate being a snitch.'

'It's not like you've got a lot of choice,' offered Zeke.

'Ain't that the truth.'

'Meanwhile,' said Banecroft, 'to get to the crux of the question you posed somewhere in there, I can assure you that in the twenty-four years I've been a journalist I have never revealed a source, an achievement in which I appear to have bested my assistant editor by about twenty-four years.'

'Even to the police?' asked Cogs.

'Especially to the police. It's not my job to do their job. In fact, it is my job to make sure that they are doing their job, among many other things.'

'Right,' said Cogs, nodding his head. 'Not that we don't take your word for that, but you should know that this particular source is protected.'

Banecroft looked around distractedly. From out of nowhere on a very wet but otherwise still day, a thick fog had descended and was now enveloping the boat.

'I'm not going to reveal you – either of you,' said Banecroft, trying hard not to appear disconcerted as the world around them disappeared from view, cloaked in the densest mist he'd ever seen.

'We're not the source,' said Zeke.

Cogs turned to the hatch that led below deck. 'All right,' he said, 'you can come out now.'

A thin, red-headed woman wrapped in an oversized woollen

blanket emerged nervously. Her skin was pale and she was visibly shaking.

'Ah,' said Banecroft, putting two and two together. 'And I'm guessing you would be a certain librarian.'

She nodded.

27

Fifteen minutes after receiving the phone call from Sturgess, Hannah was walking through the main entrance to Manchester Royal Infirmary. An orderly directed her to the third floor. The call had been brief, and the only information provided before the not-quite-an-order to get here now had been that DS Wilkerson had been attacked while visiting the crime scene at the MMU Library.

Hannah had been meant to be casually dropping into the office, in the hope of accidentally bumping into Stella for a chat. Grace had been in a state when she'd rung Hannah the night before, explaining how Stella and Manny's angel had almost got into a fight. Hannah assumed Grace was overreacting a teeny bit there, but seeing as it was all to do with Manny being over a century old, apparently, even if mediation wasn't required she wanted to find out what the hell was going on. All that would have to wait, though.

She found Sturgess sitting in the middle seat of a row of three plastic chairs, looking like a man doing his best not to rip the Diet Coke can he was holding into pieces, followed by anything and anyone who bothered him after that. He looked up with a start when Hannah appeared in front of him, having been lost in his own thoughts.

'How is she?'

'I don't know,' he replied. 'I mean, stable and all that, I guess. Not in any danger. Probably.'

'What happened?' asked Hannah as she sat down beside him.

'I don't know. She went to visit the scene – her message said something about double-checking some things. Something about questions one of the academics had about the relative position-ing of symbols. Next thing I know, a PC guarding the scene is reporting that she's been found in the library, having lost a great deal of blood and rambling incoherently.'

'Who else was—'

'Nobody, supposedly,' said Sturgess. 'But I'm heading there right after I'm done here. I'm going to put the mother of all rock-ets up whoever dropped the ball. You can believe that.'

'Where is she?'

'A private room up the hall there. The doctor's in with her now. I've been sent down here to wait. Bloody doctors,' he rum-bled. 'Always throwing their weight around.'

'I'm sure she'll be OK,' said Hannah.

'What are you basing that on exactly?' snapped Sturgess, before catching himself. 'Sorry. Sorry. I'm . . .'

'It's OK.'

'No, it isn't. None of this is OK. An officer under my com-mand has been attacked in broad daylight at an actual bloody crime scene. That is so far from OK. That OK is nowhere within sight.'

Hannah tried to think of something to say in response but nothing came to mind.

Ten minutes later, a doctor sauntered down the hallway towards them. He could have been classed as distinguished – a word that implied old without out and out saying it. He was wearing a suit that'd seen better days and a hangdog expression that indicated he mostly expected life to be terrible and so far it hadn't disappointed. Hannah wasn't aware of there being a mandatory retirement age for doctors but if there was, this man must be rubbing up against it. He also smelled strongly of cigarettes, which in this day and age was increasingly rare for anyone, quadruply so for a medical professional. The man's demeanour gave the definite impression that he couldn't give a rat's arse about your feelings on this or any other matter.

'DI Sturgess?' he said in a Scottish accent that was more Sauchiehall Street than University of Edinburgh.

Sturgess leaped to his feet. 'Yes. Can I see her?'

'In a moment,' said the doctor. 'First, arse back in the chair, please.'

'Excuse me?'

'Sit,' said the doctor, making remarkably little effort not to make it sound like a command given to a dog.

Sturgess looked as if he was considering saying something in response to this but he managed to contain himself. Instead, he plonked himself back down.

'Now,' continued the doctor, 'seeing as you were kind enough to ask – Dr Black. I'll be Andrea's physician. Virgo. Favourite colour is blue, ironically. Quite partial to a whisky, stereotypical though that is.'

'How is she?'

'Ah, I see we're done with the small talk already. Fine – she is stable. Shook up. Pissed off. Uncooperative. Terrified. Take your pick.'

'You don't speak like a normal doctor,' said Sturgess.

'It's too late to try and win me around with flattery, Detective Inspector. What was Andrea doing when she sustained her injuries?'

'I don't know. I just know she was in the MMU Library.'

'Really? Well, now, I can only assume libraries have changed a lot since my student days.'

'What exactly are her injuries?'

'No comment.'

'Excuse me?' said Sturgess, surprised.

'I said no comment, as in I'm not telling you that.'

'Is there someone else I can talk to?'

'There's all manner of people you can talk to, but none of them are going to give you confidential medical information regarding my patient. Not if they don't want to end up in a bed beside her.'

Sturgess got to his feet again. 'I am her commanding officer.'

'And I'm her doctor. Want to see what carries more weight around here?'

'Will it be possible for us to see her?' asked Hannah, keen to take the unexpected heat out of the situation before things got truly stupid.

'As it happens,' said Dr Black, 'it will be. She has requested to see him.' He nodded at Sturgess before turning back to Hannah. 'You'll just have to tag along and try your luck. So there is nothing either of you can tell me about the nature of her injuries?'

'No,' said Sturgess.

'I don't believe that,' said Dr Black, 'but seeing as they're no longer allowing me to pull a scalpel on people, I'm going to be forced to take your word for it. On you go.'

Dr Black stepped around Sturgess and headed down the hallway. He nodded at Hannah as he passed. 'Ms Willis.'

'Doctor.'

Sturgess took off down the hall. Hannah started to follow but then faltered. 'Hang on, how'd he know my name?'

Thirty seconds later they were face to face with a uniformed PC standing guard at the door to Wilkerson's room.

'I requested two PCs around the clock,' said Sturgess.

'Yes, sir. I'm afraid Sergeant Burden said to tell you that we could only provide one due to staffing constraints.'

Sturgess leaned in. 'I appreciate this isn't your fault' – he looked down at the man's badge – 'PC Walthrope, but please do pass this message along. An officer under my command has been attacked by person or persons unknown while executing her duty. When I say I want two PCs on protection duty on her room, around the clock, I wasn't making a suggestion. Inform Sergeant Burden that if you don't have company by the time I come back out of this door, I'm heading straight down there and he will need considerably more than two PCs to protect himself from me. Clear?'

The PC swallowed and nodded. 'Sir.'

With that, Sturgess pushed past, and Hannah, with an apologetic smile, followed him into the room.

Wilkerson was sitting up in the bed, bandages around her neck, arms and torso visible under her hospital gown.

'Jesus!' exclaimed Sturgess, rushing to her side and taking a seat in the visitor's chair.

'Oh, thanks, guv,' she replied. 'You really know how to make a girl feel special. I'm fine.'

'The fuck you are.'

Wilkerson raised her eyebrows. 'Y'know, I think that's the first time I've ever heard you swear. About damn time. It's not natural to be a copper in this town and not let rip with the effing and jeffing.'

Hannah couldn't help but think there was a false shine to Wilkerson's bravado, like she was trying way too hard to put on a brave face.

She looked at Hannah. 'What's she doing here? I'm not ready for a press conference, thanks very much.'

'Whatever this is,' said Sturgess, 'I'm assuming it isn't some scrote with a knife. Like it or not, she's got access to people to ask about this that we don't.'

Hannah could see Wilkerson wanting to object, but the logic in the statement was hard to refute. 'All right, but all of this is off the record.'

'Of course,' said Hannah, offended by the implication but allowing it to slide given the circumstances.

'So, what happened?' asked Sturgess.

Wilkerson flinched slightly but tried to hide her change in

demeanour. She reached over and took a sip of water from the cup on her bedside table. 'All right, I'll give you the play-by-play. Please hold all questions and applause until the end.'

Hannah and Sturgess listened in silence as she took them through the incident in the library, making every effort to keep the emotion out of her voice. Out of respect for that, Hannah did her best to dampen her own reaction as much as she could. It was horrifying, listening to Wilkerson recount what happened in an almost monotone, devoid of emotion. She explained calmly that the tall man had attempted to do something to her that had failed, presumably something similar to whatever Carol had done the previous day. A glamour. Wilkerson's speculation that the same trick can't work on the same person twice within a certain amount of time certainly seemed plausible. She had then gone on to explain how she'd been held in a near paralysed state as the man had asked her questions and, for every answer he didn't like, he opened a wound on her skin by merely flicking his finger in the air.

He'd asked her a lot of questions, primarily about a book. She'd had no answers and even if she had, Wilkerson had been animated in expressing that she wouldn't have given them to him. It seemed extremely important to her that they know that. Sturgess just nodded and eventually she finished.

Sturgess cleared his throat then spoke quietly. 'How many?'

Hannah didn't know what he meant at first. Wilkerson clearly did but she tried to brush the question off.

'Ah, who's counting?'

'I am, and I'm guessing that Dr Black did too. How many?'

Wilkerson gave him an unreadable look then turned to look out the window before answering. 'Seventy-eight. Give or take.'

'I'm so sorry,' said Sturgess softly.

Wilkerson turned back, her face filled with fury now. 'What the hell are you sorry for?'

'You're—'

'You didn't do it,' said Wilkerson. 'That prick did it. You know what I can't figure out, though? I don't know why I'm alive. I don't think that was the plan. He got a text at one point and he tutted at it. As far as I can tell, I'm alive because he got a text.' She slapped angrily at her face as tears finally started to flow. 'How fucked up is that?'

'I'm—'

'I swear to God, Tom – you dare try and tell me you're sorry again and I will happily get out of this bed and beat you to death with my bedpan. My used bedpan. You want to do something for me, tell them to let me out of here so we can go find this bastard, or else you go out and do it for me.'

'You're not going anywhere,' said Sturgess. 'Sorry. Doctor's orders.'

'Bloody doctors, always throwing their weight around.'

'That's what I said.'

'And the guy stinks of ciggies,' continued Wilkerson. 'I mean – what's that about?'

'Doesn't exactly inspire confidence,' said Sturgess. 'Does it?'

'And he's, like, one hundred and eight.' Those words caused a slight pang of guilt to pass through Hannah. She might have all the good reason in the world not to keep her promise to Grace that she would talk to Stella, but she hated letting her down again.

'Can we get a sketch artist in to sit with you?' asked Sturgess.

'Fuck's sake, Tom – he's a seven-foot-tall baldy psycho who dresses like an undertaker. How hard can such a guy be to find?'

'She's right,' said Hannah, speaking for the first time since Wilkerson had started her explanation.

The two police officers turned to look at her.

'Do you know where to find him?' asked Wilkerson.

'No,' said Hannah, 'but I think I've met him previously.'

'Where?'

'Best not get into that. The point is, I'm fairly sure I know someone who would like a word with the guy almost as much as you would.'

'Let me guess,' said Sturgess.

'Yes.' said Hannah. 'Him.'

Sturgess got to his feet and patted Wilkerson on the hand. 'I'll keep you in the loop.'

She nodded. 'Be careful.'

He nodded and turned to Hannah. 'Let's go.'

They'd reached the door when Wilkerson called out, 'Tom. I'm bloody serious. Be. Careful. You don't know what this bastard can do.'

'No,' agreed Sturgess, glancing at Hannah, 'but I'm guessing we might know someone who does.'

28

Banecroft had met a few murderers in his time, enough to know that the librarian Debra Brimson didn't look like someone capable of slaughtering three friends in a spectacularly brutal fashion. He of all people was very aware that the capacity of human beings to prove themselves both surprising and disappointing was infinite, but still, seeing her in person made the already hard to fathom, official version of events smell even fishier than they had initially.

Debra sat down on a small wooden crate at the far end of the deck from Banecroft, hugging the blanket wrapped around her shoulders to herself. She had a haunted look to her, more survivor than perpetrator.

When she'd settled, and once Cogs had availed himself of the opportunity provided by the break in the conversation to corral the errant sausages into a bucket, he spoke again in a noticeably lower register. The kind of voice people automatically adopted when dealing with someone fragile.

'So,' said Cogs, 'I take it you know who Debra here is?'

Banecroft nodded, not requiring the blank to be filled in.

'A murderer,' said the woman quietly while numbly regarding the fog surrounding them.

'We – by whom I mean our boss ' – Cogs nodded pointedly towards the water in case the entity he was referring to wasn't blindingly obvious – 'became aware of Debra here when she ended up in the canal over near Albion Street Bridge.'

'Ended up?' asked Banecroft because, whether he liked it or not, it was hardwired into his nature to ask follow-up questions.

'She was thrown in,' said Cogs.

'By who?'

'That's a surprisingly complicated question. We'll get to that. She was unconscious, and I think it's fair to assume that the individual responsible assumed she was either dead or soon would be.'

'I see,' said Banecroft, then he stopped himself. 'Actually, I'm not sure I do. I only know the figures, as there's that ridiculous urban myth about there being some serial killer going around pushing people into the canals of Manchester, but nevertheless, lots of people drown in the waterways of this city every year. How come nobody intervenes in those cases?'

Cogs didn't answer. Instead, he looked down as Zeke nudged his leg pointedly. The duo locked eyes and Cogs looked around, suddenly on edge. 'Ohhhh.'

Zeke ambled over to Banecroft and sat down in front of him. 'A word to the wise, Mr Banecroft. I appreciate you've got this whole irascible thing going on, but you might want to seriously resist the urge to play up to it or this is going to go really badly.'

'I have spoken to a vulnerable person before,' he said, glancing at Debra.

'You're not understanding me,' said Zeke. 'There are some

situations where minding your manner is a matter of life or death. This is very definitely one of those times.'

Before Banecroft could respond, Zeke rose on to his hind legs and lowered himself into a bow. Banecroft looked at Cogs, who was bowing in a similar fashion, while Debra Brimson was gawping in his direction in disbelief. After a moment, Banecroft realized they weren't looking at him, but just to the right of him.

Banecroft glanced over his shoulder and gave an involuntary yelp as he leaped off his seat. Behind him, standing on the water, was a figure, if you could even say that, given that the figure itself was made entirely of water.

'Your Majesty,' said Cogs and Zeke in unison.

As Banecroft's eyes adjusted to the concept, he could see that the figure in question was indeed that of a woman. She was standing with her arms folded in front of her, looking at him calmly. Distractingly, a small fish appeared to be circulating inside her body.

Banecroft felt a hand on his trouser leg and turned to see Cogs pulling him down, a pointed look on his face. Banecroft swallowed every instinct he had and knelt on one knee.

The figure offered no introduction. When she spoke, her lips didn't move but the surface of her liquid form rippled. Her voice was surprisingly deep and melodious. 'In answer to your question, I do not normally interfere when people end up within my domain. That is the affairs of man, and they do not concern me. Other humans are not even the worst things you people discard. I could list the abominations to which my domain is regularly subjected, but we do not have that kind of time.'

She paused before continuing. 'The reason I intervened in this case is that this was not an affair of man. This involved the touch of an old god. Zalas walks the earth again. This is bad news for everyone and everything. He cares only for chaos. He brings only death. He was barely contained the last time and those who stopped him before are now long lost to us.'

Banecroft tried to look at where the figure's eyes would more or less be and focused on not giving away quite how freaked out he was by her presence. 'Who exactly is this Zalas?'

'He is of the darkness. Someone brought him back into this world.'

'Who would want to unleash something like that?'

'Someone who is also of the darkness. Who sees some advantage in chaos. I have no wish to understand the motives of man. Zalas, like all his kind, needs belief. He will try to gather believers to him, as that is from where his power truly comes.'

'I don't . . .' started Banecroft.

'You have been told what you have been told. Cogs and Debra will add what information they can, but it will then be up to you to deal with this matter.'

'How am I supposed to do that?'

'Quickly,' she said. 'For all our sakes.'

'But—'

'Silence!' The figure turned to the librarian. 'Debra, you may trust this man. Tell him all you can. I have spoken.' She seemed to hesitate and then turned to Cogs. 'You are looking well,' she added in a surprisingly awkward voice.

Cogs cleared his throat. 'Thank you, m'lady. I . . .'

Before he could say anything more, with a soft splash the figure was gone.

Cogs eased himself to his feet, as did Banecroft, and Zeke sprang back up, too.

'Well,' said Banecroft, retaking his perch on the barrel, 'there's a thing you don't see every day.'

'I've not seen that since . . .' started Zeke.

'A very, very long time,' finished Cogs. 'You need to understand, Vincent – if she's putting in an appearance then this is . . . serious. Very, very serious.'

Banecroft nodded. 'Is she . . . scared?'

The boat rocked violently.

'I wouldn't say that,' said Cogs. 'I definitely would not say that.' As the boat stopped its forceful movement, Banecroft couldn't help but notice 'wouldn't say that' was considerably different than 'no', especially when coming from a man who couldn't lie.

'Debra,' said Cogs, clearly trying to move things along, 'perhaps you could fill in Vincent here on what happened to you.'

Debra, who still retained the haunted look of someone trapped in their own personal hell, nodded. 'I . . . We . . . I . . . We summoned this Zalas . . . thing.'

'You summoned it?' repeated Banecroft.

'We didn't know that's what we were doing,' she clarified, her irritation giving her some focus. 'We thought we were . . .' She paused and, for a second, Banecroft thought she might burst into tears, but she gathered herself and continued. 'We thought we were casting a healing spell, naive as that may sound. We . . . I was tricked. It was the book.'

'The book?'

'I was given a book. I . . . We needed objects – magical objects to do our spells – and . . . I was given this book.'

'By who?'

'I don't know.'

'You don't know?' repeated Banecroft, which elicited a flash of defiance in the woman's eyes.

'I've been trying to remember and I can't. Believe me, I've been thinking of little else. Someone . . . something was done to me. I wasn't in control – there was a voice in my head. It was guiding me, instructing me. We did the thing and then' – she gulped and held her hand to her mouth – 'he was in me. I was a passenger in my own body. I can't explain how that felt. How violated . . . And then he . . . I couldn't stop him. I couldn't . . .' This time she couldn't stop the tears and she stared at her own hands in horror. 'The blood. Oh God, so much blood.'

Cogs went to comfort her but stopped as she pulled away. Instead, Zeke padded over and lay his head upon her knee. She stroked him and it appeared to help.

'I know this is difficult,' said Banecroft, 'but anything else you can tell me might prove really useful.'

She nodded, sniffling. 'I don't know how much I can. At a certain point, after he'd been in control for a while, I don't remember anything. I don't remember leaving the library. But ask your questions and I'll try.'

'OK, good,' he said softly. 'Thank you. You don't remember anything about how you got this book?'

'No. And I've been trying. It's – I can't explain it. I used to go to Paulo's Emporium at Afflecks but it's not from there. I'm sure of that. Someone gave it to me but . . . I can't remember who or how or . . .' She trailed off, looking like someone lost within her own mind, terrified by the areas of darkness it suddenly contained.

'OK,' said Banecroft, 'what did this book look like?'

'Leather,' she said, clearly comforted by being able to give an answer. 'It was bound in leather and had one of those ouroboros symbols on the front. Y'know, a snake eating its tail. Just that, nothing else.'

'Can you remember what was in it?'

Debra squinted in thought and then, after a few seconds, gave a frustrated shake of her head.

'All right,' said Banecroft, deciding on a different tack. 'Do you know who threw you in the canal?'

'It was him. Zalas.'

'Right,' said Banecroft. 'So he, while he was in control of you, jumped into the canal?'

'No.' She stopped again, trying to corral her thoughts into a coherent formation. 'I . . . When he had control of me, like I said, I only remember bits. Flashes. The blood, and then the next thing I know, I'm standing on the street somewhere and he's there in front of me. I mean, not him. He's . . . I guess he's controlling this really big guy – muscles. Like a body builder or something. He's in an orange gilet. But I know it's Zalas, even though . . . Well, I know. Then he hits me and the next thing I know' – she looked at Cogs – 'I'm being dragged out of the water. I'm sorry,' she added weakly, 'I know that's not much use.'

'No, it is,' said Banecroft. 'We need to figure all this out and anything could be of use. Do you recall what happened to this book?'

'No, I . . . Sorry,' she said again, placing a trembling hand over her mouth. 'Bleeding. I remember the book bleeding. I mean, blood coming out of it – around the symbol.'

'Right,' managed Banecroft, having no earthly idea what else to say to that.

'I've said I should hand myself into the police.' Debra's voice was suddenly urgent. 'Try to explain.'

'No,' said Cogs. 'That's not a good idea.'

'But—'

'The boss said no.' He looked at Banecroft.

'And she was right,' he said. 'You spending your life behind bars isn't going to help anyone. Quite the opposite, in fact. It would only give the authorities the chance to create the illusion of resolution. Nothing to see here. Everyone go back to buying Nutribullets and watching home improvement shows – we are in control.'

'But,' protested Debra, 'I killed . . . I killed people.'

'No,' said Banecroft, getting to his feet, 'you didn't. You were just used as an unwitting weapon.'

'What are you going to do?' asked Cogs.

'I have no idea,' conceded Banecroft. 'I mean, how do you hunt down something or someone that can apparently jump from person to person?'

Cogs shrugged. 'That's a good one all right.'

'I know a guy in London who deals in rare books,' said

Banecroft. 'I guess I can ask him' – he glanced at Debra and decided to avoid repeating what she'd just described – 'if that rings any bells.'

'Actually,' said Zeke, looking pointedly at Cogs, 'we might be able to help you a bit on that score.'

Cogs returned his gaze, bewildered. 'Do you . . . do you want to, like, try and sniff out the book?'

'No, you donkey. An expert in books. Someone who reads a lot of books.'

Still lost, Cogs pointed warily at Debra.

'Bloody Nora,' said the not-a-dog. 'How are you this bad at picking up on clues?'

'Maybe you're rubbish at giving them.'

'Maybe,' said Banecroft, 'just maybe, you could simply say what you mean and I can go about my day?'

'Haçienda,' said Zeke, ignoring Banecroft.

'Haçienda!' exclaimed Cogs, finally getting it.

'Haçienda.'

'Haçienda.'

Cogs and Zeke smiled at each other broadly then said in unison, 'Haçienda!'

Banecroft rubbed his temples. 'Christ on a bike, it's like I'm trapped in a shit Marx Brothers skit.'

Cogs hurried below deck, being careful to give the jittery Debra as much room as he could. 'I've got that ticket here some-where,' he shouted up.

Banecroft turned to Zeke. 'How is whatever you two are on about supposed to help me?'

'Might help, might not,' conceded Zeke. 'You got any nice clothes you can get dressed up in?'

'These are my nice clothes.'

'Wow!' said the not-a-dog. 'Well, look on the bright side, at least you won't have any fluffy bastards coming up trying to sniff your arse.'

'I Had Twitter's Baby'

A woman from Bolton is claiming that her two-year-old son, Retweet, was fathered by Twitter. Rose Marshall, forty-two, further asserts that she was in a romantic relationship with the social media platform for five years, and that its rebrand to X was a deliberate attempt to avoid paying paternal support. When *The Stranger Times* posed the quite reasonable question of how such a thing was biologically possible, Ms Marshall provided a full and graphic description of the process. In an editorial first for this publication, we have decided not to share these details with you. Let's just say two members of our staff are now refusing to own mobile phones and it's going to be a cold day in hell before any of us touches a turkey baster again.

29

Dr Carter sat looking at the bobbleheads laid out on the table in front of her.

Her hand hovered over Fozzie Bear. 'Perhaps if I could . . .' She pulled her hand away. 'No, that won't work.' She picked up Gonzo and Dr Teeth from the Electric Mayhem. 'Perhaps if we . . .' She swapped them over, tutted then swapped them back.

She looked up with a start and realized Tamsin Baladin was standing beside her desk.

'Christ. Sorry, Tamsin, I didn't hear you come in.'

'You certainly appeared lost in thought.'

'That's one way of putting it,' said Dr Carter.

'Is everything all right?'

'Well, now, that depends how you define "all right". Ahead of the traditional Christmas Day feast to follow the Council meeting, I have already had to change an entire menu twice, I have had to find alternative accommodation for three of our guests, whose main problem with their previous accommodations was that they were within half a mile of each other, I've had to negotiate a situation where at one point after Miss Piggy over there insisted his food taster must sit at his right hand, everyone else insisted that their food tasters must be similarly located, requiring a table the size of which literally does not exist, so I've now, after more shuttle diplomacy than was required to avert the Cuban Missile crisis, managed to secure an agreement for a kiddies table full of food tasters.

'Then there's the fact that some of these individuals have feuds that go back centuries, but it turns out a few of them fell out last week over a game of golf and now there are a whole new set of parameters within which I have to work in order to manage the Sisyphean task that is a seating chart. In other words,' she finished with a smile, 'things are going exactly as anticipated.'

The irony of that statement was that it was largely true. By this time next year, Dr Carter would be hard at work establishing her own set of feuds to run for millennia that some other poor bastard would have to deal with.

'I see,' said Tamsin Baladin. 'That really is quite something. Can I ask, what are all these little figurines?'

'My little joke to myself,' confessed Dr Carter. 'I needed some way to depict fifty-one different individuals and only the Muppets provided a cast broad enough to accommodate.'

'The Muppets?' echoed Tamsin Baladin.

Dr Carter leaned back in her chair. 'You have heard of the Muppets, haven't you?'

'It doesn't ring any bells.'

'The Muppets?' repeated Dr Carter, failing to keep the outrage from her voice. 'Kermit? Miss Piggy? *Sesame Street*?'

'I think I may have heard of that *Sesame Street* thing. Was it a television show?'

'Was it a . . . It's *Sesame Street*! How've you never seen it?'

'Our parents didn't actually allow us to watch television when we were growing up.'

'Good god.'

It was now Tamsin's turn to look offended. Still, thought Dr Carter, this did explain a great deal.

'Well,' Dr Carter continued, trying to soften the tone of the conversation, 'you must check them out. They're a delight. In fact, you should start with *The Muppets Christmas Carol*. Wonderfully seasonal.'

'Ah,' said Tamsin, striking out for familiar land, '*A Christmas Carol*. Yes, the Charles Dickens book. I have of course read that.'

'Right,' said Dr Carter. 'Well, that's the book of the film.'

'I don't . . .' Tamsin Baladin gave that smile of hers. 'You are, of course, joking.'

'I am. So, how are things outside the world of the Muppets and Michelin-starred chefs I've flown in at obscene expense?'

Tamsin consulted her ever-present tablet. 'That matter in Chester has been dealt with.'

'The . . . Oh yes,' said Dr Carter, remembering. 'Good, good.' Her eye was caught by the Scooter bobblehead. Now that she thought of it, there were a couple of people down the far end whom he hadn't yet offended. She could move him that way and that'd allow Big Bird to flap his wings in what she was already thinking of as the truly toxic section.

'The investigation about the thing in the Manchester Met Library is ongoing. I have a report from that Detective Inspector Clarke fellow – heavy on film-flam, light on detail. They haven't found this Debra Brimson woman but they seem confident she's their perpetrator and that they'll apprehend her soon. DI Sturgess has been called in as well, I believe, so we might need to . . .'

Baladin really was like a dog with a bone when she decided she wanted something, with Sturgess being the bone in this analogy. 'Yes.' Dr Carter said with a nod, then eyed the section where Dr Teeth and the Electric Mayhem were seated. Could they accommodate a three-hundred-year-old Scandinavian Elmo who was obsessive about the widely disproven pseudoscience of phrenology, not to mention some other considerably less socially acceptable fascinations. 'I'll check in on the inspector later. If I recall, he spent last Christmas Day in the office catching up on paperwork.'

'And finally,' continued Tamsin, 'a disused warehouse in Tameside caught fire.'

Dr Carter looked up. 'I assume you're telling me this because . . .'

'Yes.'

Dr Carter slammed her hand down on the tabletop. 'Did I not make it clear to everyone that there was not to be a hint of any kind of trouble over this sensitive period?'

'You did.'

'Very well. Dispatch Alpha team. Mr Malagan shall be spending his Christmas in one of our most comfortable cells.'

'As you wish,' said Tamsin. 'Unless there's anything else?'

'Not unless you've found a way to go back in time two hundred and six years and not have a certain Dutchman's carriage run over a Scot's most beloved hunting dog, because if you did, that would make my life a lot easier.'

'I'm afraid not.'

'Then yes,' said Dr Carter, focusing her attention on the table again, 'that will be all.'

Her hand hovered over Statler before she withdrew it. 'He slept with the Swedish chef's wife, randy sod.'

30

As soon as Hannah walked into the Kanky's Rest pub, the tension was obvious, but it did not come as a shock. She had not been popular there in the past, and that was before she'd worn out her welcome with the landlord by ruining his lie-in yesterday. She had even steeled herself for the very real possibility of being shouted at as soon as she opened the door. That did not happen either, and what made it all the more surprising was that her unpopularity had been brought about by the establishment's clientele getting wind of the fact she had been assisting the police with their inquiries.

The Folk did not like the police. Hannah didn't know the history behind that clearly widely held sentiment, but it had seemed remarkably heartfelt and universal. Mention had been made of the police being nothing but a tool of the Founders, the immortal leeches who literally sucked the life out of the Folk, which, admittedly, would probably do it. Given all that, the fact that a detective inspector in the Greater Manchester Police, who wasn't wearing a uniform but might as well have been given how much he stuck out, had followed her through the doors of the pub was less than ideal. She'd tried to talk him out of accompanying her but

Sturgess was having none of it. They'd just come from visiting poor DS Wilkerson in the hospital and it was fair to say his mood was dark, with more than a hint of looking for a fight, any fight. And so it was that Hannah had walked in fully prepared to duck in case considerably more than dirty looks were thrown their way.

It turned out she need not have worried. Their arrival drew zero attention. The reason for this was that each and every patron of the packed pub was gathered in a semicircle, in the centre of which, with his back to the door, stood John Mór. You didn't need to see his face to know it was him. In fact, Hannah guessed a room did not exist on this planet where John Mór wouldn't be instantly recognizable. In this particular room, tatty Christmas decorations were dotted around the place, with threadbare tinsel and strings of half-working lights that gave off an air of obligation rather than celebration.

The big man raised his arms and quietened the hullabaloo of voices. 'Right,' he said firmly, 'everybody settle down. I've been asked to give a ruling and, as the lord of this here establishment, I will be. Everyone had best remember, under the law of the house, what I say goes.'

There was a general mumble of unenthusiastic assent.

'And,' continued John Mór, 'if any of you decided to ignore the law of the house, rest assured, I won't lift a finger against you. I got Margo for that.'

A flicker of nervous laughter passed through the room. The kind that indicated that while the statement had been dressed in a colourful glove of humour, it contained a very real fist of hard fact.

'Now, then,' he continued. 'Larkin, step forward and be heard.'

A squat man with thick glasses did as he was asked and smiled nervously at the crowd. If looks could kill, he would have been atomized instantly. As it was, a swirl of invectives went up as soon as he made himself known.

'Don't make me go over the rules again,' growled John Mór, sounding a lot like a man running short on patience. 'Now, Mr Larkin here started a turkey saving club some six months ago, where anyone who signed up could put a little away once a month and get themselves a fine bird come Christmas.'

Larkin gave a nod, as if keen to acknowledge that there were facts they all agreed upon.

John Mór held up a piece of paper. 'I have here a list of the members of said club. Would it be churlish of me to remind them all, every last one of them, that I warned them collectively and several times individually, that this was not a good idea?'

'What's "churlish" mean?' shouted an older female voice.

Several people laughed.

'And you lot can shut up and all,' snapped the voice. 'There's people here laughing who are forgetting who makes the ointments for certain issues they've had.'

'Never you mind, Leonora,' said John Mór quickly, 'never you mind. Anyhow, we have now come to the day of reckoning . . .'

One man let out a boisterous roar of excitement.

'In terms of turkey delivery,' clarified John Mór. 'Any more from you, J. P., and I'm cutting you off.'

'It's Christmas,' said the man in a pleading tone. 'A man is entitled to a drink.'

'That wasn't the cutting off I was referring to. Margo still remembers that stunt you pulled with the watermelon.'

A smattering of sniggers passed through the pub.

'On to the matter at hand,' resumed John Mór. 'I am led to believe there has been some issue with what could be loosely termed quality control.'

'I'm known for providing nothing but the finest of merchandise,' protested Larkin.

'Firstly,' said John Mór, 'you'll speak when spoken to in this here court, and secondly, even your own dear gran ain't buying that line, Larkin.'

'He'd not know,' shouted a voice at the back. 'He sold her when he was a lad.'

This received an appreciative ripple of laughter, and even Larkin appeared in on the joke as he smiled along half-heartedly.

'Bring forth Exhibit A,' ordered John Mór.

Margo, who hadn't been anywhere to be seen, was now standing in front of him, holding what looked like a turkey in one hand and a set of scales in the other. Hannah was slightly gratified to see that even members of the Kanky's Rest's clientele shifted uneasily at her sudden appearance.

'Now,' said John Mór, placing the scales on a nearby table before taking the bird, 'this specimen is meant for Fionnuala, have I got that right?'

Larkin, among others, nodded.

'Right,' he continued, referring to his list. 'Says here, you're down for a seven-kilo bird. That's an awful big one, Fionnuala. How many are you and Pete cooking for this year?'

'Eighteen,' said a small woman at the front of the crowd. 'Our Siobhan has triplets.'

'Has she now? Congrats to her. Let's see what you got.'

John Mór dropped the bird on the scales. 'Says here, seven point one kilos.'

'That's—' started Fionnuala, jabbing a finger in Larkin's direction, but she was stilled by John Mór's raised hand.

'Mr Larkin?'

'As you can clearly see, 'tis only the finest of birds, and I didn't even charge extra for the additional hundred grams.'

'Admirable,' said John Mór. 'Margo?'

With a blur of movement, Margo's hand – long, wickedly sharp nails and all – sliced through the turkey and emerged from it holding a large rock.

The crowd erupted, swearing and hissing in Larkin's direction.

'Mr Larkin?' said John Mór, raising his voice above the noise.

Larkin, his face a picture of innocence, spread his arms in protest. 'Am I to be held at fault for this bird having made some unhealthy dietary decisions in life that have reverberated in death?'

'To be clear,' said John Mór, raising a hand for quiet once again, 'you're claiming this is somehow the bird's fault?'

'It's unusual, I grant you,' conceded Larkin, 'but of all people, I'd have thought the patrons of this here establishment would be willing to keep an open mind about unexplained phenomena in the natural world.'

'Call the paper,' shouted the joker who'd made the grandmother remark earlier.

Hannah felt a weird flush of pride. When the Folk referred to 'the paper', they meant *The Stranger Times*.

'Right,' said John Mór. 'We shall set that aside for the moment.'

Fionnuala went to say something but John Mór silenced her with a look.

'For the moment,' he repeated. 'Now, I believe there is an Exhibit B?'

A rotund man with a large sun symbol tattooed on his bald pate and several metal bolts through each ear stepped forward. He handed John Mór a large sack, a pair of bird's feet clearly poking out the top of it.

'Ah, yes,' said John Mór. 'Eusébio Jones. Says here you went for one of the unplucked options – an eight-kilogram unprepped bird – is that right, Eusébio?'

The man merely glowered at Larkin and nodded.

'Right, then.' John Mór opened the bag and slammed the bird down on the scales. More than a few gasps passed through the room.

Larkin pointed at the scales triumphantly. 'Nine point two kilograms. Where else do you get that kind of value?' he proclaimed. 'Case dismissed.'

'Whoa, whoa, whoa, Larkin,' said John Mór. 'I think we need to address the elephant in the room. Or, rather, the non-turkey.'

'Excuse me? Non-turkey? I've never been so insulted in all my life.'

This earned him a raised eyebrow from John Mór. 'The night is young, Larkin. I'd imagine the bar on how insulted you've been in your life is going to be raised considerably. Now, would you like to take this opportunity to perhaps issue any clarifications or apologies?'

I'm sorry, you've lost me.'

'Have I?' said John Mór. 'Well, let me clarify.' He held the bird up by its feet. 'This here supposed turkey is a vulture.'

'Agree to disagree,' said Larkin.

'Excuse me?'

'That, to me, is a turkey.'

'Right,' said John Mór. 'Well, it's not a matter of opinion.'

'That, in itself, is a matter of opinion.'

'Is it now? Well, as I'd like to think anyone here would vouch, I'm not one to blow my own trumpet, but back in my day, I was a bit of a hunter—'

'Finest in the land,' shouted a man standing near Hannah, which elicited a number of cheers.

'If it can be tracked,' called another female voice from the other side of the room, 'John Mór is the man who'll find it.'

'My grandad says he's the best he's ever seen,' chimed a third voice.

John Mór, slightly embarrassed, raised his hand for silence. 'Much obliged. Although, your grandad, Stevie? Way to make a fella feel old.'

This earned him a laugh.

'And now,' said John Mór, 'my credentials somewhat established, I feel obliged to repeat, this here is a vulture.'

'I see what's happened here,' said Larkin. 'Not for the first time, it's the mainstream media that is to blame.'

'I was wondering when they'd put in an appearance. How're you figuring that?'

'It's a well-known fact that vultures are very temperamental birds, not to mention all manner of bad luck. That's why, most of the time, when you see one on the TV or in the films, it's actually being played by a turkey, which, as we all know, is a bird of a much more thespian bent.'

John Mór nodded. 'So, this here is a turkey with a Meryl Streep-like range. Is that your final answer?'

'I would also like to remind the court that there is such a thing as a turkey vulture.'

'Indeed there is,' conceded John Mór. 'Also known as the *Cathartes aura*. This here' – he held up the bird for the whole room to see – 'is your *Vultur gryphus*, also known as the Andean condor. Now, I'm not sure where to start, but seeing as it is only found living wild in the mountains of South America, I for one would like to know how you got hold of it. By the by, as well as being the largest bird of prey in the world, it's also an endangered species.'

'Yes!' said Larkin with a sudden air of excitement, like a drowning man who is convinced he can see a lifeboat nobody else can. 'It is indeed an endangered species, and if we all become so close-minded as to be unwilling to sit down and eat one with our beloved families on that most sacred of holidays, then what hope is there for the poor vulture farmers of Peru, who do such noble work in preserving the stocks?'

A peculiar moment of near silence fell in the pub, as an entire room tried to get its head around a lie so big that even an Andean condor would have trouble digesting it in one sitting.

John Mór nodded. 'Not for nothing, Larkin, that's one of your more impressive servings of bullshit. And not unlike this poor thing, it ain't flying. Have you any more evidence you'd like to enter into the record?'

Larkin looked as if he was about to say something, but then he scanned the increasingly irate-looking faces in the crowd and shook his head.

'Very well, then. By law of the house, I shall make my ruling. Cornelius Larkin has twenty-four hours to make what he has wronged right, and if he fails to do so, he is exiled for no less than one year from that date.'

John Mór's words were met with shocked gasps.

'Exiled?' said Larkin.

'You were warned, Larkin. Actions have consequences.'

'How am I supposed to find that number of turkeys not two days before Christmas?'

'I've no idea,' conceded John Mór, 'which is why I don't spend my time swindling my friends out of their hard-earned coin, promising them birds I ain't got.'

Larkin went to pick up the vulture but John Mór laid a firm hand on it to stop him. 'No, you don't.'

'But it's mine.'

'No, it isn't. It belongs nowhere near here or near you, and count yourself lucky that I'm in the Christmas spirit and not of a mind to go looking into how you managed to end up with it. Now, time is pressing so I suggest you get moving.'

Larkin pulled a face and turned towards the door.

'Oh,' said John Mór, raising his voice once more for attention, 'and just to be clear – I hear anything about some poor charity having their birds stolen or anything like that, and exile will be the very least of your worries.'

Larkin hissed something under his breath as the crowd started to disperse. 'And a Merry Christmas to you, too,' finished John Mór.

Now that the show was over, people had started to notice the presence of Hannah and Sturgess, and the pair were not being received favourably.

'Speaking of vultures . . .' said John Mór, as he looked pointedly in their direction then nodded towards the door that led out to the alleyway.

Two minutes later, Hannah was back outside the door to John Mór's flat with DI Sturgess in tow. It flew open to reveal the man himself for the second time in as many days. This time he was wearing his more usual attire, although his normal good humour was absent.

'I appreciate, Hannah, that it's the season of goodwill to all men,' he said throwing a meaningful look at her companion, 'but that has limits. By the way, everything you heard in there is inadmissible in court.'

'No, it isn't,' said Sturgess, 'but rest assured, I don't care.'

'We wouldn't be here if it wasn't serious, John,' said Hannah.

'So you say.'

'Just give me sixty seconds of your time,' she continued.

'Then, if you want, you can tell me to go to hell and I promise I'll never darken your door again.'

He considered her offer and made a show of looking like he wasn't going to accept it, but Hannah knew he would. John Mór was a good man, and he was also only human, as far as Hannah knew, which meant he couldn't help but be just a little curious.

As quickly and efficiently as she could, she explained what had happened to Wilkerson, including the extent of her injuries.

As she finished, John Mór leaned against the wall in contemplative silence. 'As you probably guessed,' he said eventually, 'he tried to do what practitioners of magic call a glamour on her. Ain't nothing glamorous about it. It's sort of, like, what you know as hypnosis. The reason it mustn't have worked is that Carol would've done something similar to the sergeant and Mr Sturgess here the day before. Don't know why, but there's normally a period where only them of incredible power can re-glamour someone.'

'So,' said Sturgess, 'is this individual who attacked Wilkerson something like Carol?'

'No,' John Mór said firmly. 'This ain't that. Couldn't be further. People like Carol follow a strict code.'

Hannah moved on to the part of the story she'd deliberately left out until now. 'Are you wondering what this person looked like?'

John Mór raised an eyebrow. 'Not as much as I'm wondering why you haven't told me yet.'

'My guess,' she began, 'going from the very distinctive description, is that you and I have met this man before.'

John Mór scrunched his brow.

'On a certain golf course.' Hannah didn't want to go into the exact details of what happened, to avoid both explaining it to Sturgess and having to relive it.

John Mór gave a firm shake of his head. 'He's dead. All kinds of dead.'

'Not him,' clarified Hannah. 'The man who attacked Wilkerson was described as around seven feet tall, bald with—'

'Xander,' exclaimed John Mór.

'You know him?' asked Sturgess.

'I know what he is. After' – he glanced at Sturgess – 'whatever happened on the golf course happened . . . I made it my business to ask around, trying to find him. His kind – Standers, we call them, at least when we're feeling polite – let's just say back in another life, I had reasons to clash with them more than a few times. Enablers, they'd call 'em these days. The sort that follow orders and take pride in it, no matter what those orders might be. All the worst things I've ever seen, there'd be a Stander there somewhere, making sure the whole thing runs smoothly and doing whatever their master asks of them. They're powerful in their own right, sure enough, but they're also their own particular kind of evil. The kind that'll do anything, and the worse the ask, the more they seem to like it.'

The dark look that came over John Mór's face sent a chill down Hannah's spine – as if he was trying to push away memories he didn't want to be confronted with.

'Still,' he continued, 'this Xander character. I checked, and he got the hell out of here right after his employer' – he looked at Sturgess again – 'had their little accident. He's long gone.'

'Well,' said Hannah, 'I'm afraid he's not. Or if he was, he's back. And seeing as we just heard that you're quite the hunter, I was wondering if you would like to help us find him?'

John Mór pulled a face like a foul stench had just reached him. 'The question you need to be asking is who is this Stander working for and why. Whoever it is, they'll have some serious heft to 'em. Standers don't come cheap and they don't work part-time either. If someone has got one, then they've got 'em for life – or, to be more exact, until death. Long as you keep paying them, they're the most loyal beasts you could ever have, but let's just say if you miss a payday they won't be taking you to no tribunal. A Stander is going to be the worst and last break-up you ever have. '

'How do I find this Stander?' asked Sturgess.

'You don't.'

'With respect to your status as the world's greatest hunter, the Greater Manchester Police might not have your skills or knowledge but we have found the odd person before this, especially if they've hurt one of our own.'

'You might find him,' conceded John Mór. 'Won't be easy, but it'll be a cakewalk compared to taking him down.'

'We have people for that, too.'

'Not for this you don't. You have rules and a Stander doesn't.' John Mór scratched his beard. 'You want this done, you walk away now and leave it to us.'

'No,' said Sturgess firmly.

'See?' said John Mór to Hannah. 'No trust.'

'It's not a matter of trust,' snapped Sturgess. 'He hurt one of mine. Someone hurts one of yours, you hurt them.'

John Mór gave Sturgess a surprised look. 'Your law isn't going to be much use to you here.'

'Yes, it is. If he doesn't come quietly, it justifies using lethal force, and nobody's going to be crying about it when we do.'

John Mór rubbed his hands up and down his beard absent-mindedly, thinking things through. Eventually, he sighed and said, 'Give him the list.'

'What I—' Hannah jumped as Margo appeared inches behind her and Sturgess, holding out a rolled-up piece of paper. As she took it, Hannah tried to ignore the shredded remains of raw turkey carcass still visible under Margo's long fingernails. She handed it to Sturgess, who opened it up and read it.

His head flew up. 'Is this a joke?'

'No,' said John Mór. 'You want to track a Stander, that's how you do it.'

Sturgess looked between John Mór and the list again, still clearly unsure about whether or not this was a wind-up.

'Look,' said John Mór, leaning against the wall again. 'This fella, Xander – did you catch him on CCTV at the crime scene?'

'No,' admitted Sturgess reluctantly. He'd received a call on their way down here explaining as much. Hannah had shifted awkwardly in the passenger seat as the normally reserved and unfailingly polite DI had lost it with the poor unfortunate tech who'd delivered the news.

'That's what I thought,' continued John Mór. 'He can deal with all your technology nonsense with a click of his fingers. Standers leave no trace. What's more, you can interview as many witnesses as you like and not one of them will remember him. You'd think such a strange creature would be remembered by everyone who sees him, but it's the exact opposite. For such an odd-looking man, he can walk through this city like a ghost. It's not that Standers are invisible, it's just . . . Easiest way to think of it is they can make it so your mind just prefers not to see them. They leave no trace, they leave no scent. It'd be like trying to trap fog.'

'So?' said Hannah.

'So,' said John Mór. 'Standers, they like the finer things in life. At least, the things they see as that. That list – that's how you find him.'

Sturgess read its contents aloud. 'Caviar, foie gras, *casu marzu* . . . What the hell is *casu marzu*?'

Despite knowing full well she was there, Hannah still jumped when Margo explained in her distinctive West Country accent, 'A traditional Sardinian cheese, made from sheep's milk, known for containing live insect larvae.'

'Gross,' said Hannah.

'Yeah,' agreed Margo. 'Nice on toast, though.'

'I haven't heard of half these foods,' said Sturgess, holding up the piece of paper.

'That's exactly the point,' said John Mór. 'You find the shop that stocks them, you'll find your Stander.'

'Thank you for your help, John,' said Hannah.

'Don't thank me yet,' he said. 'Finding him isn't the hard part. That's just the start of your troubles. Now, if you'll excuse me, I've got a pub to run.'

31

Claremont Dibner spent the rest of his day in his office, in a weird state of exultant panic. He'd heard people talk about not being able to cope with success, but he didn't think that was what this was. That sort of thing was meant for people who didn't know what to do when the little game they'd developed turned out to be the new Tetris, or their diabetes drug turned out to be the accidental cure for obesity. It didn't cover setting up a shonky Christmas experience for it to become some kind of fever dream come true.

It was near closing time now, but he could hear the brass band playing outside still. They'd turned up a couple of hours ago. He didn't know where they'd come from, and when he'd informed them he wasn't paying them, they'd seemed confused by the very idea. Meanwhile, what seemed like every kid in England had come to sit on Santa's knee and yet the queue, impossibly, had remained exactly the same length for the entire day. Queues didn't work like that. Nothing worked like that.

A knock sounded on the office door. 'Yes?'

It opened to reveal Original Flavour Wayne standing there. 'It's, ehm, it's almost closing time.'

'Is it, though?' said Claremont. 'I mean, do we know that?' He could hear the agitation in his own voice and made a conscious effort to calm himself.

'It's all going . . . well,' offered Wayne.

'Yes,' said Claremont. In fact, he already had enough money to clear his debt to Ivan. He'd considered doing so earlier in the day but had decided against it. If he paid early, Ivan would smell a successful rat and come looking for where all the cheese was coming from.

Claremont briefly considered what would happen if Ivan met the thing he was still insisting on calling Neil. It *was* Neil. It was just Neil. He was a department-store Santa Claus. A good one? Sure. But that didn't make him anything more than a guy in a suit. Claremont told himself to keep it together – the success was going to his head.

'Right, then,' he said. 'Well, if it is closing time, we should close.'

'Yes,' said Wayne. 'Also, there's something you should see.'

'Do I have to?' asked Claremont.

Wayne didn't answer, he just stood there.

With a sigh, Claremont got up and headed to the door. 'So, what exactly do I need to . . .'

He trailed off because what he needed to see was immediately apparent.

It was snowing.

Snow at this time of year in the North West of England was unusual but not without precedent. He'd heard someone on the radio saying the odds of a white Christmas in Manchester were about five to one. But snow inside an old meatpacking warehouse that still had a roof was a different matter. It was coming down quite heavily, too. Claremont looked at the tumbling flakes, then looked at the giddy families walking by as if they'd just stepped out of a supermarket Christmas TV advert. Big smiles, wide eyes, laughing joyously at seemingly nothing – like they were all off their faces.

Then, Claremont – not wanting to but not being able to resist – looked up at the roof and couldn't see it. Come to that, he couldn't see the walls either. They must be back there somewhere, it was just . . . Well, it was like Wonderland had become its own world, which was of course nonsense.

He cleared his throat and made himself speak. 'If I was to ask you if it was snowing outside . . .'

'I'd rather you didn't,' said Wayne.

'Right.'

'Is this . . .' Wayne paused, searching for the right words. 'Is this all right, do you reckon?'

'As in?'

Wayne waved a hand at the mob of delirious people walking past. One of them was eating a massive gingerbread man. Claremont knew for a fact that none of their vendors was selling such an item. 'All these people. They seem happy.'

'They do,' agreed Claremont.

'So this can't be bad, can it?'

'I guess not.'

'Right,' said Wayne, who seemed determined to take Claremont's word for it. 'There's something else, too.'

'Let me guess,' said Claremont, staring up into the dark void where he was fairly sure a warehouse roof used to be. 'Another eleven reindeer just showed up.'

'No.'

'Thank God for that.'

'There's only eight of them.'

Claremont turned to look at his head of security. 'Really?'

'Yeah. Santa only has nine reindeer.'

'I thought it was twelve?'

'I think you're thinking of Jesus and the apostles.'

'Right,' said Claremont, returning to staring up at the sky. 'You don't think he's going to show up, do you?'

Beside him, Wayne shrugged. 'Dunno, boss. The night is young. So, what do you want us to do?'

Claremont stood there, taking in the thing he had somehow created. A thing of beauty but something more than that, too. He couldn't put his finger on what it was exactly, but he thought back to the look in the bloodshot eyes of their Santa Claus and a shiver went down his spine that had nothing to do with the snow falling all around him. Their Santa Claus, the one who'd been seeing children all day without a break and whose grotto appeared to exist somewhere outside of space and time.

Claremont made a decision. 'Wayne, there's only one thing we can do at a time like this.'

'What's that, boss?'

'Double the price of car parking.'

32

Despite having worked with the man for almost a couple of years now, Reggie realized this might have been the first time he'd ever been alone with Vincent Banecroft for an extended period. They were standing in a small car park on Whitworth Street West, to the rear of which lay an opening on to the canal. A steady stream of people were using it as a handy cut-through to the lock with the pedestrian bridge. A conga line of a half-dozen office workers in ugly Christmas jumpers had just passed through, seemingly unaware that they were singing two entirely different Cliff Richard songs as they danced along drunkenly. It was a Saturday night, and tomorrow was Christmas Eve to boot, so the entire city was positively bubbling over with exuberance, none of which was carrying over to Reggie or his boss.

'Are you sure—' started Reggie.

'Yes,' snapped Banecroft. 'For the third time, he said to wait here.'

'Exactly here?'

'Exactly here.'

'OK,' said Reggie.

Several seconds of silence followed and then Reggie, much to his own horror, found that he'd started talking again.

'Would it be possible—'

'No.'

'You don't even know what I was going to ask.'

'Yes,' said Banecroft, 'I do.'

'Right,' said Reggie. 'Good.'

He pulled his moleskin coat tightly around himself. It was a cold night made all the colder if you were standing still, and they'd been doing so for well over an hour now. Banecroft was even less well kitted out for this than he was, given his green overcoat that had lost whatever lining it once had and his brown suit that was clearly a pair of trousers from one and a jacket from another, hence the disconcerting difference in their shades. Ox had once joked that Banecroft's brown suit was a walking representation of the Bristol chart – the medical tool used to classify stools – and now Reggie couldn't help thinking of it every time he saw it. He was also regretting not wearing his beloved deerstalker hat to fend off the biting night air, but he'd felt sure that Banecroft would've made some witheringly memorable comment that would have sucked all the joy out of ever wearing it again in the future.

'Can I ask a question?' said Reggie.

'Is your question, by any chance, the question I thought you were about to ask when I cut you off?'

'As it happens, yes, it is.'

'Well, there you go, then. I've just proved my ability to antici-pate the questions you are going to ask me and deal with them in an efficient manner.'

'Right, then.'

'Right.'

'Good,' said Reggie.

'Excellent.'

They stood there in yet more silence – in the loosest sense of the word. It was 11 p.m. on a Saturday, and between passing traffic, inebriated people full of the joys of Christmas stumbling in front of said traffic, strangers arguing, couples arguing, couples very definitely not arguing, strangers coupling and more than a couple of people acting strangely, the silence was almost deafening. Not for the first time, Reggie found himself wondering how anyone could live in the apartments right in the heart of a city. There was only so much work double glazing could do.

A drunk bloke walking by in a parka decided he'd had enough of his box of fried chicken and dumped it over the short wall that separated the car park from the street. Wordlessly, Banecroft stepped forward, picked up the box and, with an unexpected nimbleness, scurried the few feet to catch up with the man and placed it in his hood. The litterer wandered off into the night, entirely unaware of what had just happened until it inevitably started raining later on. Reggie guessed there wasn't much he and his boss agreed on, but he had a grudging respect for that particular piece of vigilantism.

Banecroft returned to his position without casting so much as a look in Reggie's direction.

Reggie stood there for as long as he could before drawing a deep breath and releasing his words in a flood. 'Are you sure this isn't a piss-take? There, I said it. I know you know what I was going to say but I said it anyway because it is my right to say things, so I did. Is this a piss-take? I think it might be a piss-take. I think someone is taking the piss out of you and, by extension, me. You can't stop me saying it, I have a right to say it and now it has been said.'

'Feel better for getting that out, do you?'

'As it happens,' said Reggie defiantly, 'I do.'

'Good. So, to recap, if I may: your question, which, by the way, was exactly the one I knew you were going to ask was "Am I sure Cogs isn't doing this as some kind of wind-up?"'

'Yes,' said Reggie marginally less defiantly as, in the back of his mind, the horrible feeling that the ground he was making his stand on might not be as solid as it seemed to be a second ago.

'Is the man who we know is cursed to literally – and please note I'm using that word in its appropriate context – the man cursed to literally be able to only tell the truth, is he trying to take the piss by sending me on a wild-goose chase?'

'Oh.'

'Yes. Oh, indeed,' said Banecroft. 'As someone who employs you for your deductive reasoning, may I comment on how reassuring this line of questioning you are so insistent in pursuing is.'

'It's eleven o'clock on a Saturday night and, frankly, I get enough of your abuse five days a week. It'll shock you to know that this isn't my dream way to spend my weekend. In fact, screw it – I'm leaving!'

'OK,' said Banecroft.

'OK?'

'OK.'

'That's all you have to say?'

'Were you expecting some heartfelt speech begging you to stay?'

'No,' said Reggie. 'I was very definitely not expecting that.'

'You can head home. I just thought you might want to . . .' Banecroft trailed off.

'What?'

'I'm sorry?'

Reggie resisted the urge to stamp his foot. 'You just thought I might want to what exactly?'

'Oh, right. Meet a ghost.'

'I'm sorry, what?'

'I mean, it's silly, I know,' said Banecroft, making a show of examining his nails nonchalantly. 'What with you being our supernatural correspondent, you've probably met hundreds, if not thousands of them by now.'

'A ghost,' said Reggie, attempting to remain calm. 'We're going to meet a real live ghost?'

'Well—'

'Don't,' snapped Reggie. 'I heard it as soon as I said it. We're going to meet an actual ghost?'

'Well, assuming the man who is cursed to tell only the truth wasn't lying to me, which I know is a very real concern.'

'Oh my God,' said Reggie. 'It's going to happen. It's actually going to happen.' He started to adjust his cravat. 'Why didn't you tell me this was going to happen?'

'Why else do you think I asked you to come?'

'Because Hannah is off with that DI Sturgess doing God knows

what, Stella is working on her essay, Grace would have made tut-
ting noises every time you took a sip from your little flask there,
and you find me marginally less annoying than Ox.'

'Who told you that?'

'You did. I mean, you told Ox that. Obviously, you wouldn't deliberately pay anyone even the most backhanded of compliments.'

'I have a robust management style.'

'Those are all certainly words.'

'All I was saying was . . .' The reason for Banecroft's distraction was a man who'd just turned to the wall in front of him and
unzipped his fly. 'No, no, no, no, no,' said Banecroft, going over
and reaching up to tap the man on the shoulder. 'We will not be
having that.'

'D'ya mind, mate,' came the outraged response. 'I'm trying to
take a piss here.'

'Actually,' said Banecroft, 'I do.'

'Who the fuck are you? The piss police?'

'No, I'm another human being with whom you share the
planet. One who doesn't want to watch you take a piss, one who
doesn't want to hear you take a piss, and one who most certainly
doesn't want to have to stand here both seeing and smelling said
piss after you've gone on your way. So, no, we're not having that.'

The bloke re-holstered his unfired weapon of choice and
turned around. Reggie noted he was even less appropriately
dressed for the weather than Banecroft was, but perhaps the
combination of the sheer mass of muscle he'd built up over a
considerable amount of time and the state of inebriation he'd
built up over a considerable amount of drinking would be

enough to keep him warm. Failing that, the rage that appeared to be building at that present moment might do the trick. He towered over Banecroft.

'Who the hell are you, going around telling people what they can and can't do?'

'To be fair, I think anyone will tell you urinating in public is something of a social faux pas. I'm surprised they didn't mention it at whatever finishing school you attended.'

Reggie could feel a headache coming on. It was bad enough standing here, freezing to death, but he was also going to have to extricate Banecroft from the fight he was rapidly talking his way into. Then, with a depressing sense of inevitability, things worsened in the form of three lads walking around the corner.

'Here, fellas,' said the man in need of spending a penny, 'this bloke's got a problem.'

'Has he now?' responded the one whose tattoos made up for in size what they lacked in accurate spelling.

'We got a problem,' added the second.

'This fella's taking the piss,' chimed the third.

'No,' said Banecroft, not backing down an inch. 'Quite the opposite, in fact.'

Reggie shifted his hands in his pockets, making sure he had the things he didn't want to have and was not going to use, but would begrudgingly wave around if he had to.

'Not so clever now, are you?' offered the first of the foursome.

'False proposition,' said Banecroft. 'I am, in fact, exactly as intelligent as I was at the beginning of this exchange, but I will admit the average IQ in this postcode has probably taken quite a hit.'

Banecroft's words were met with a couple of furrowed brows as two of the four tried to figure out if they'd been insulted and, if so, exactly how.

'You wanna watch yourself, pal,' said the first of the foursome, untroubled by any thought at all. 'Out here, only your boyfriend there for back-up, throwing your weight around. Who the hell do you think you are?'

Reggie shifted his hands again while keeping them firmly in his pockets, reflexively checking his switchblades were in full working order.

'Ah,' said Banecroft, 'now we've reached the nub of the question, haven't we? Who am I? What kind of a person, standing out here, giving up twenty years and several stone to any of you, never mind all four of you, would be so confidently making a stand? That person would be one of two things: one, stone-cold crazy, or two, someone you don't know you should know. Someone that if you were in the know, you would be apologizing to and moving quickly away from. Someone with connections. Someone with friends. A lot of friends. The kind of friends you wouldn't want to meet. The kind of friends that, should the need arise, can be downright unfriendly. So, you need to be asking yourself, lads, how badly do you want that piss? How badly do you want to take out your frustrated machismo and issues with authority on a middle-age man you've got heavily out-gunned and outnumbered. How badly do you want to make this night into one you'll remember for the rest of your lives, however brief they may be. You'll want to think really carefully about that.'

Reggie stood stock-still as Banecroft, with an absolute confidence, smiled up in turn at each of the four men surrounding him.

It was the second one who broke first. 'We should head on, Dan.'

'Yeah,' echoed the third and fourth.

Dan, aka number one and the man with the need, gave his friends an annoyed look.

'C'mon, Dan,' said number three. 'Leave it. We've got places to be.'

Dan's confidence seemed to desert him finally and he stepped back, mumbling something as his friends guided him away.

Banecroft moved to stand beside Reggie, who returned his nasty little surprises to their hiding places then drew his hands out of his coat pockets and blew on them. 'Does that normally work?' he asked.

'Yes and no,' said Banecroft. 'I don't want to worry you, but there's a better than even chance that they'll walk on for a bit and come to the conclusion they've just been had. Best not to be here when they get back.'

'So, we're leaving?'

'No,' said Banecroft. 'Cogs said to wait here, so we wait here.'

'OK, well, given the recent change in our circumstances, I must now insist you tell me exactly what he said or I really am leaving.'

'Him and what's-his-face . . .'

'What's-his-face?'

'Yeah. Talking dog.'

'Right,' said Reggie. 'I believe the name is Zeke.'

'Whatever. They kept talking about the Haçienda then they gave me this ticket.'

'Right, not to worry you, but the legendary Haçienda club was indeed just up the road from here, but it closed in about nineteen ninety-seven. It's now this rather bland apartment building.'

'Shockingly,' said Banecroft, 'I knew that already.'

'Oh, good. So what does this ticket say?'

'It's a cloakroom stub.'

'For a club that closed down almost thirty years ago?'

Banecroft shrugged at this.

'And you have this ticket?'

'Yes.'

'Can I see it?'

Banecroft considered this, rolled his eyes then reached into his pocket begrudgingly.

He stopped dead.

'Please don't tell me you forgot it.'

'No,' said Banecroft, taking out the ticket and holding it before him while looking all around like a man waking up from a dream. 'I've got it. I just . . .'

Reggie stood there considering Banecroft's bewildered expression for quite some time. 'You stopped talking.'

'Did I?'

'Yes.'

Banecroft handed Reggie the ticket. 'Here you go.'

'OK, well . . .'

Reggie fell silent.

'So,' said Banecroft, 'you can see it too?'

'Yes.'

Suddenly, where the pair were standing had another world lay-ered on top of it. Everything that was there was still there but the concrete wall in front of them – the one that hadn't been peed on thanks to Banecroft's intervention – now featured a large door with stairs leading to a basement. The sign above the door read 'The Haçienda Spirit' and there was a queue off to one side made up of bored-looking youths that Reggie could both see and see through at the same time.

'Yes,' said Reggie again.

'Yes what?' asked Banecroft.

'I have no idea.'

'Me neither.'

'What should we do?' asked Reggie.

'We're going to do the thing that made this country great.'

'Invade another country?'

'The other thing,' clarified Banecroft.

'Oh, right,' said Reggie. And without another word, they both moved across to join the queue.

Cat Flap

A team of bioveterinary scientists at the University of Chester has revealed that your cat is almost but not entirely sick of you. According to head researcher Dominic Flanders, 'Five years ago, we undertook some research involving two hundred domestic cats, which confirmed the hypothesis that in 93.5 per cent of cases, your cat really doesn't like you that much. They mostly regard you as a necessary evil: someone who provides food, shelter and will worship them when they feel like it. Since that initial study, we've continued monitoring and, using a complex suite of behavioural and biological indicators we've developed, it's become clear that cats are growing steadily more sick of us. It feels like only a matter of time before they reach a tipping point and, well, we shudder to think what they'll do then.' Foreboding as this revelation may be, the team's research does hold some good news for certain pet owners: it confirms that your dog still thinks you're brilliant.

33

Banecroft took a step forward as the line of people moved along slowly. 'Bloody hell, if this is one in, one out, we could be here all night!'

Beside him, Reggie was vibrating with a level of excitement that meant the possibility of him out-and-out fainting couldn't be discounted. 'Oh my God, do you think all of these people are ghosts?'

At this, the female standing in front of them with a mohawk hairstyle, her arm slung proprietorially around a shorter female, turned and shot Reggie a dirty look. 'Rude!' she said before turning away again.

Banecroft meanwhile could see through the couple, and indeed the rest of the queue, while at the same time also being able to see them all individually.

'I'm so sorry,' said Reggie, looking mortified. He then whispered to Banecroft, 'Oh no, I might have just met my first ghost and offended them, or they might not be a ghost at all. I may have mis-somethinged them.'

'I'm going with mis-mortalized,' said Banecroft. 'The act of getting someone's state of existence incorrect.' This earned him a snotty look from the couple in front but Banecroft smiled broadly in response. 'Feel free to use that, but I would like credit for it. Vincent Banecroft.'

The pair turned away again and proceeded to make an effort to ignore Reggie and Banecroft whereas before they'd just been doing it incidentally.

The queue shuffled forward another step. Banecroft stood on his tiptoes to look down along it. 'Bloody hell, this is gonna take a while.'

'I don't think you're appreciating the magnitude of this,' said Reggie. 'It's like we're somehow both in and not in another plane of existence. We can see our world but since touching that ticket we can now see this world, too.'

'Yeah,' said Banecroft, 'I get it. It's a bit like being in one of those tedious magic eye posters. I think I'm getting a migraine.'

'Well, don't look now,' said Reggie, 'but it looks like your friends are back.'

Banecroft craned his neck to where Reggie was pointing and clocked the quartet of knuckle-draggers he'd only recently ran off. 'Ha. I bet they're wondering where the hell we are.'

On cue, one of them pointed at Banecroft. 'There he is.'

'Or not.'

'Oh God,' said Reggie. 'Please don't get into a fight and embarrass me in front of what may or may not be g-h-o-s-t-s.'

The mohawk turned around at this. 'Do you seriously think we can't spell?'

She shook her head and turned away, just as the man in need of a pee reconnected with Banecroft via the medium of slapping him in an unplayful manner on the shoulder.

'I want a word with you.'

'Excellent,' said Banecroft. 'Well, I'm a little busy right now but if you'd like to make an appointment and drop by the office . . .'

'I'm going to smash your stupid face in.'

'Or we could go with that.'

Out of nowhere a figure appeared in front of them – not in a puff of smoke but more in a she'd-been-standing-there-all-the-time sort of way. She was ethereal like the members of the queue, but also seemed more solid. The handset of a walkie-talkie was strapped to her chest and she somehow managed to pull off a high-visibility jacket with 'security' written on it that was still also see-through.

'These men bothering you?' she asked in a bored tone.

'Have him, Dan!' shouted one of the quartet, as Dan duly drew back his fist and prepared to let fly. Weirdly, it seemed as if the world was slowing down.

'Yes,' said Banecroft in answer to the bouncer's question.

'Right,' she said, and clicked a queue counter in her hand.

Banecroft then experienced the odd sensation of watching a very solid-looking fist heading straight for his face before passing through him harmlessly, sending its owner sprawling to the ground at Banecroft's feet.

'Where the fuck did he go?' yelled one of the guy's mates, before spinning around in a circle like a dog trying to catch its own tail. He then stopped before gawping open-mouthed at the wall once again then running off. Banecroft's erstwhile attacker staggered back to his feet and, with one last disbelieving shake of his head, stumbled away in the same general direction.

'Thanks for that,' said Banecroft to the security woman.

'You're welcome. Never gets old. Enjoyed your line earlier about the average IQ in the postcode going down when they showed up.'

Banecroft gave Reggie a pointed look. 'Thank you. At least someone appreciates my work.'

'What the hell were you doing standing there like a couple of spare pricks for an hour when you had a ticket?'

'Ehm . . .' said Banecroft.

'Can I just ask—' said Reggie.

'No,' said the bouncer firmly, before disappearing again.

'That was a bit rude,' said Reggie haughtily.

'She did just save our arses.'

'Yours, you mean,' said Reggie. 'I'd have been absolutely fine.'

After that, the pair stood in silence save for the occasional shuffle of their feet moving forward. Finally, the punk plus one were granted entry and Reggie and Banecroft found themselves at the head of the queue. The bouncer was back. 'Ticket?'

Banecroft held out the raffle ticket that Cogs had given him along with his instructions.

'Just picking up, is it?' asked the bouncer.

'I guess,' said Banecroft.

She moved the rope aside. 'In on the left.'

Banecroft and Reggie moved through the door that was also a solid brick wall. Banecroft decided not to think about it as it struck him that convincing your brain something was impossible was a good way of encouraging it not to accept it, and he was here with a purpose.

To their right, stairs led down into a smoky darkness punctuated by occasional flashes of multicoloured light that offered nothing in the way of illumination. A throbbing back beat vibrated through the floor. To their left, next to the cloakroom area, was a man wearing nothing but a pair of shorts and holding some glow sticks. Sweat was pouring off him and he was throwing dance moves while grinding his teeth.

Banecroft looked him up and down with an expression of consternation. 'Are you the attendant?'

The enquiry received nothing by way of response as the man continued to gurn and dance, in a world of his own.

Banecroft held up the ticket and raised his voice. 'Cogs sent me. Are you the attendant?'

'No,' came a voice. Banecroft turned around to find a girl standing at the cloakroom window. 'That would be me.'

The second most noticeable thing about the girl was her fluorescent orange glasses. They really paled into insignificance once you noticed her arms. Individually, they were unremarkable, but it was their quantity that drew the eye. At a rough count, Banecroft could see eight. Two of the hands were holding books, with a further two holding electronic tablets of some kind, while the remaining four were running fingers along the various pages of the books at remarkable speed before flipping them. The girl was also wearing two sets of headphones – one atop the other.

'Oh, sorry,' he said. 'I was . . . I just thought that when he said "the attendant", I didn't think he just meant the cloakroom attendant.'

'Wow, way to make a girl feel special,' she replied with a smile.

'Just the cloakroom attendant. Know lots of chicks who can read five books at a time, with an additional two audiobooks on the go, while also doing their job, do you?'

'No, I . . .'

'The name is Trixy, by the way, unless you insist on calling everyone by their job title.'

'No, I just—'

'Baz!' Trixy shouted at the guy dancing furiously. There was no response. 'Baz!' she tried again, this time attracting the man's attention long enough for him to dance around in her direction. Yet another pair of arms appeared and tossed him a leather jacket. 'There you go, and for heaven's sake, hydrate, would you?'

He gave her a big thumbs-up before dancing his way out of the door.

'How long has he been dancing for?' asked Reggie.

Yet another arm appeared and Trixy consulted the watch on it. 'Let's see. It's eleven thirty now, so . . . thirty-eight years, seven months, two weeks, three days, six hours and fourteen or so minutes, give or take.'

'Right,' said Reggie, as he'd no idea what other answer to give to that.

'So, you got a ticket?' Trixy asked.

'Yes,' said Banecroft, holding it up triumphantly.

'Coat, is it?'

'Actually,' said Banecroft, 'we're looking for a book. Cogs said you might be able to help.'

'Don't know where he got that idea. See, I can read five

books simultaneously and do sarcasm, but I'm feeling rather under-appreciated. Most people are impressed if not by the simi-reading, then by the sheer number of arms. Hey!' She looked pointedly over Banecroft's shoulder to where Reggie was starting to walk down the stairs. 'You can't go down there.'

The bouncer came in as Reggie quickly retraced his steps while holding his hands up in the air. 'Sorry, sorry, sorry.'

The bouncer pointed a finger at him. 'You're on a warning.'

Reggie turned back to Trixy. 'Sorry, but why can't we go down there? Is it the afterlife? Hell? Heaven?'

'No, no and no,' said the girl. 'It's a nightclub and, no offence, but you two are well old.'

'Ouch,' said Reggie.

'This book,' said Banecroft, giving Reggie a pointedly annoyed look. 'Cogs said you could help us with it?'

'What's it called?'

'I don't actually know.'

'Super. What's it look like? And before you answer, can I say on behalf of bookshop workers everywhere, "it's got a blue cover" is not an acceptable answer.'

'No, it's got a leather cover and one of those ouroboros symbols on the front.'

'Right.' She gave him a wary look. 'Is there anything else you can tell me about it?'

'Well, I believe on occasion it has been known to bleed.'

The girl nodded solemnly. 'That's what I thought.'

'You know what it is?'

'Might do,' she said, holding out her hand. 'Ticket first.'

Banecroft duly handed over the ticket and Trixy examined it carefully. 'Ohhhh, we've had this one for quite a while.'

'You've got the book?' asked Banecroft.

'No,' said Trixy, waving the ticket about, 'the coat. This is a cloakroom, you know. Central Library is thataway,' she added with a wave of her hand.

'So, what is it?'

'What it is,' began Trixy, 'is very, very bad news. It's called the *Black Grimoire* and not because it's that colour. I believe it's brown. Oh, and, spoiler alert, that isn't leather it's bound with. It's an example of anthropodermic bibliopegy, which is . . .'

Yet another hand appeared out of the mêlée of arms surrounding Trixy and pointed at Banecroft.

'A book bound in human skin,' he responded.

'Ding, ding, ding, ding, ding, ding!' responded Trixy with an appreciative grin. 'Give the esteemed editor a prize.' Then she added, 'Yeah, I know who you are. Like I said, I read a lot. Glad you've finally sorted the crossword out.'

'Sorry,' interjected Reggie, 'this book is bound in human skin?'

'That's right,' confirmed Trixy.

'That's disgusting.'

'Well, duh! That ain't even close to the worst thing about it, though. Sometimes the only place you can keep evil is bound by evil, so that book contains all manner of heinous shit, and you do not want to let it come out to play.'

'Where is it now?' asked Banecroft.

'That's not the question you asked.'

'Wait, we only get one question?' asked Banecroft.

'No,' said Trixy. 'But it doesn't mean I have to tell you everything you want.'

'This is really important, though.'

'Where did anyone last see it?' asked Trixy.

'The last place it was seen was a library.'

'So ask a librarian, then.'

'I did,' said Banecroft. 'She didn't know.'

'Maybe you asked the wrong one.'

'Please, I—'

'Seriously,' said Trixy. 'That's all your questions.'

'What about him?' asked Banecroft, pointing at Reggie.

Trixy puffed out her cheeks. 'All right, be quick.'

'Of course,' said Reggie. 'I have to know, is everyone here a ghost?'

The next thing Banecroft knew he was being lifted off his feet. The bouncer had both him and Reggie by the scruff of the neck. The last thing he heard before they were flying through the air was, 'You were warned!'

Banecroft landed heavily back in the car park and turned to the wall, which was once again just a wall. He pulled himself back to his feet as, beside him, a rather sheepish-looking Reggie was doing the same.

'Well, congratulations,' said Banecroft. 'You are now officially no longer less annoying than Ox.'

34

Stella was sitting on her bed. Through sheer force of will, she had written the first paragraph of her essay. It somehow took the opposite position to the one she'd intended to take and was possibly a hate crime against her own generation, but on the upside, it was a good eighty-six words towards the two thousand she needed – so that was progress.

She put the laptop down. She'd stayed in her room for most of the day, telling Ox she'd finally caught the cold that had been going around the office, so nobody had questioned her absence. What's more, it was Saturday night and, nominally, they weren't even supposed to be working.

While she didn't have a cold, she certainly didn't feel right. The red mark on her leg was itching more and more, and she had a strong sense that whatever the dream/vision/unwelcome intrusion into her mental space had been, she hadn't seen the last of it. Maybe she should talk to somebody or even confront Manny and the damned angel, but she didn't want to. She also didn't want to go to sleep. If she stayed awake, it meant she wouldn't let in whatever this was. She had plenty of caffeinated fizz at her disposal – maybe she'd just stay up all night not working on her essay while bingeing that new animé series that Netflix had just dropped? It can't get in if—

The pain felt like an icy spike being rammed into her skull. She gave a pathetic yelp of anguish and then . . .

She was on a boat. Only she wasn't herself any more. She knew what this was now. She was Manny and he was the one on a boat, surrounded by fellow soldiers. They were passing a cigarette around, chatting away happily. Quinnie, Manny's best mate, was there too, laughing and joking as always. They all looked quite dapper in their uniforms – clean-shaven heroes, off to show Hitler what's what.

★

They are marching into a French village where the locals are standing out by the side of the road. The children are cheering, the adults' expressions are a mix of appreciative and worried. The boys wave back. Spirits are high.

★

They're marching along a country road, enjoying the early spring morning. Manny spots a rabbit in the hedgerow, its bright eyes shining as it stares out at this new thing. Manny smiles and waves back. He thinks he might put this into his letter to Rosa and Dottie. Mail services are patchy at best, and they can't say anything about where they are – the army is paranoid about everything to a ridiculous degree – but he reckons he can mention the rabbit all right. Dottie's favourite book has one in it, and he's always promised to take her to see a real one someday. She's been a city girl so far, with Rosa choosing to keep her with her rather than let her be part of the evacuation. Her mum is able to watch her while Rosa is at the factory and Dottie provides some much-needed help and company for her nana. They'd agonized over that, but Manny had been sure it would be for the best. He couldn't stand the idea of his little princess being surrounded by strangers.

Manny nudges Quinnie, who is marching beside him, and points at the rabbit. Quinnie jokingly pretends he's going to shoot it and Manny fends him off. Sergeant Richards – their dour-faced NCO and a manager at the council back in the real world – barks something at them and they stop, smirking like admonished schoolboys. Quinnie, grinning, is about to say something when he hesitates.

When the first shell hits, the men dive in all directions. Manny ends up in the hedgerow he's just been looking at. Hands over his head, hanging on to his helmet, he spots the flash of fur as the rabbit bolts away across the field. He can't believe how loud the attack is. All he can do is lie there, waiting for it to end. After perhaps a minute it does.

Quinnie helps him up and everyone looks around. One of the lads, Baker, sits on the road, a surprised look on his face as he clutches at the wound on his neck, blood pumping out across his nice clean uniform. They try to staunch the flow but he bleeds out in front of them, wordlessly, his lips mouthing something nobody can make out. They dig him a grave in the field and

Richards says a few words. He keeps calling him Barker and one of the lads, Marshall, loses his temper about it. The rest calm him down and then they fill in the grave, marking it with a rough wooden cross. Baker never even got to see the enemy.

★

It's nighttime now and Manny is taking cover behind a loose stone wall. Bullets are singing through the air. They can't see who is shooting but, seeing as they are shooting, Manny's unit shoots back. He hopes that whoever their unseen attackers are, they're the damned enemy at least. Wilson, the little tubby fella from Bolton, is to one side of him. He ships a shot straight to the chest. He goes pretty quickly, asking for his mum.

Quinnie finds some tarpaulin and places it over Wilson's body. It's all they can do for him now, bar taking his weapon and ammunition.

★

They're marching again. They're going one way, and a steady stream of civilians and wounded is going the other. There's less talking now, and what there is happens in low voices.

★

And they're in battle, under a bright sun. They charge forward as artillery shells land all around them, raining down dirt and God knows what else. Something hits Manny and he finds himself thrown to the side, dazed. Quinnie hauls him back to his feet. Manny catches a glimpse of what struck him – a severed arm – before he starts running again. His own blood from a cut on his forehead flows down his face, stinging his eyes as Quinnie drags him forward.

★

Another village, where half the buildings are rubble. Manny's unit is positioned around it. He has a bandage on his head. Behind him, one of the lads has got a fire on the go, out of sight amid the rubble. Another of them has caught a rabbit and there's an excited buzz. It isn't near enough to feed them, but rations are running out and anything not from a tin is very welcome.

★

They're under fire. All sides. Too much. Retreat. They're trying to retreat. Manny sees a tank advancing through the smoke at the end of the street. They don't have anything that can fight that. Nothing.

He ducks as a shell hits the wall of the building beside them, sending rubble crashing down around them.

★

Heart pounding, he's running along a street. Quinnie and another man beside him.

Quinnie falls.

The other lad keeps running but Manny turns back. Quinnie has taken one in the upper leg. Manny drags him back to his feet. He's talking, Quinnie – even now, always bloody talking – but Manny can't make it out.

He looks into his face.

He doesn't hear the shot. Can't even tell which way it's come from – their side or the enemy's. Doesn't matter. Hits Quinnie right in the head and takes half of it off.

Manny feels the wet viscera splatter across his face. It's in his mouth. All over him.

Quinnie falls and, despite knowing his friend is dead, Manny still tries to pick him up. Drag him away. Then, hands are on him and Manny is the one being dragged away, fighting to try to get back. They have to help Quinnie.

★

They're slogging across a field through the rain now. It's pelting down, the mud sucking at their boots. You can't call it marching. Their unit is half what it was, plus a couple of stragglers. Two of the boys are limping. The others take turns helping. A low whine comes from overhead and, suddenly, they're all running, throwing themselves to the ground as the plane flies by low. Manny's heart is pounding in his chest and he has that taste in his mouth again. Bullets riddle the ground around them, tearing chunks out of it. The aircraft makes a second pass as the soldiers scatter further.

When it's gone, two more are dead and they have to pull Marshall off Richards. Says he doesn't know what he's doing, leading them across wide open spaces. Richards is shouting back. He's their commanding officer and this is mutiny. Says he'll have Marshall up on charges.

Manny calms Marshall down as best he can, then tells Richards to forget it. From then on, they do what they all think is sensible and Richards watches on sullenly, saying nothing and only offering the odd haughty stare.

Clark points at a tree numbly and swears he recognizes it. Baker's grave is around here somewhere but the ground is so chewed up, they couldn't find it if they wanted to.

★

They're back in the first village they passed through. Gone are the waving children. Everyone is flowing in the same direction now. Back to the beaches.

They take cover as, yet again, the air is filled with artillery shells. After that, planes – so many planes – swooping low. Nothing to stop them. It's like shooting fish in a barrel, and they're the fish. Where the hell are the RAF? Nowhere to be seen. The Nazis own the bloody sky. The unit fires back occasionally but they've so little ammo and are so outmatched, it's more an act of defiance than defence.

Just as the aeroplanes are finally leaving, Manny stands up, his ears ringing so much that he doesn't hear the latest barrage of artillery until it's too late. A shell lands right in front of him and he's thrown backwards. He's flying. Then he lands and the world is silent.

He comes to, finds his feet. He can't hear anything save for the pound, pound, pounding of his own heartbeat in his ears. That taste again. A lot of stuff is on fire. An acrid smoke hangs in the air like pea soup fog. He's walking. Doesn't know where. Just walking.

He turns a corner and there is a young boy there. A toddler. He's crying as he attempts to pull a body behind him. A body is a generous description – there's not enough of it left to call it that. Manny sees that amid all the mess there is a sliver of a yellow dress. The boy's mother, most probably. Or sister. Aunt. Grandmother. Impossible to tell. Still deaf, Manny looks into the crying boy's face then picks him up, holds him in his arms and keeps walking.

Next thing he knows, Richards is there, shouting something at Manny that he can't hear while wrestling the boy out of his arms. Manny resists. He won't let the boy go. Richards is getting irate now. Manny still won't let go. Quinnie. He won't. Then there are more hands on him and he's being held down. The boy is prised out of his grip. Manny is on his feet and being pushed away. He looks back one last time and sees the boy, a numb expression on his young face as he stands there, watching them leave.

★

A beach. He's standing on a beach. He can hear again but his heart is still pounding in his ears. He can't keep control of himself. His limbs are twitching, shaking. Around him, weary faces, some of which he recognizes, most of which he doesn't, are trying to calm him down.

★

He's on a boat, still shaking. Can't stop. He's shouting now, too. Someone is angry. Screaming at him to shut up while Marshall stands over him defensively. His fists are cocked above him as he lies hunched in a ball on the deck. His heartbeat thunders in his ears and that damned taste is back in his mouth again.

Stella found herself lying on the floor of her bedroom, awash with sweat, struggling to breathe. And she had that damned taste in her mouth.

She pulled herself upright and rubbed at her face, which was covered in tears. She managed to take a few steps forward before the icy spike of pain rammed into her skull again and she tumbled on to the bed.

★

She's on a boat. That same boat. The soldiers are passing a cigarette around. Laughing and joking. Quinnie smiles at him. They all look dapper in their uniforms . . .

35

DI Tom Sturgess had a mental image of the quintessential sniper. He guessed it was the same one most people had: a cold-blooded, preternaturally patient individual who could sit statue-still for hours, even days at a time, calmly waiting for the perfect moment to strike. A *Day of the Jackal*-style sphinx with the precision of a surgeon.

Whoever came up with that archetype had clearly never met Dave Dinsdale. Sturgess had met the guy only thirty minutes ago and already Dave's never-ending monologue had so far taken them through his relationship with his dad; his dad's relationship with online poker; his mum's relationship with their former neighbour, which had led to the admittedly unusual situation of his divorced parents living next door to each other; the fact Dave was ping-ponging starter, main course, dessert between the two houses on Christmas Day to keep everyone happy; and they'd now moved on to Dave's relationship with his girlfriend, Amanda. Sturgess wasn't quite sure how they'd got there – he might have blacked out for a minute or two.

'And I'll just say this,' said Dave, which was the biggest lie Sturgess had ever heard in his law enforcement career, 'no matter what someone says, no matter how many times they say it and no matter how much they swear they mean it, never ever, ever, ever get them a Dyson as a Christmas present.'

Dave Dinsdale was a member of the GMP armed response unit and, honestly, Sturgess was amazed he'd enjoyed a career lasting nearly a decade, working with people who carried arms for a living, and hadn't come under friendly fire even once.

The fact that it was 7.38 a.m. on Christmas Eve wasn't helping matters. The two men were on the fourteenth floor of an eighteen-storey apartment block called Skyline Central 2. The reason for that was the raid about to take place on the building about fifty yards away – the imaginatively titled Skyline Central 1 – and Sturgess was being allowed to watch from the sniper support and command position.

The apartment block was described as high-end city living, complete with twenty-metre rooftop swimming pool and gym. Brochures for the place were fanned out on the nearby coffee table and, in an unsuccessful attempt to stop Dave talking, Sturgess had picked up one and flicked through it. While the words 'rooftop pool' conjured the image of an open-air affair, Sturgess saw that thankfully wasn't the case. High-altitude open-air swimming in Manchester could be described as dangerously close to self-harm for about half the year. A large glass structure enclosed the pool and there was a sauna and steam room, too. Maybe it was just him, but Sturgess didn't like the idea of sitting around seminaked, surrounded by your neighbours. Mind you, he'd recently had to have words with his own neighbour about their propensity to walk around the garden stark-naked. The neighbour in question had turned the encounter into an argument about why Sturgess didn't mow his lawn more regularly.

Sturgess and Dave the stream-of-consciousness sniper were sitting just inside the glass double doors that led to the apartment's balcony. Through a pair of binoculars they were watching apartment 1007 of the building opposite where, at that moment in time, absolutely nothing was happening. Sturgess checked his watch. That would all change in about five minutes.

The target of the raid was the man they were provisionally referring to as Xander, pending identification confirmation. The lease paperwork for 1007 listed him as, honest to God, Mr Smith. Sturgess hated to admit it but they'd found Xander by following the plan laid out by John Mór. After Sturgess had briefed DI Clarke's team – which had been made available to him owing to the complete blank they were drawing playing hunt-the-librarian and Clarke's subsequent desire to produce anything his bosses might see as a result – they'd headed off to hit up every high-end delicatessen they could find. Then, a junior detective called Grimes had rather sheepishly come up to him with an idea. Through a robbery case she'd worked in her first year on the job, she'd come across a chef who ran a lucrative sideline in sourcing banned foods for a select clientele of thrill-seeking foodies. Protected species, poisonous if incorrectly prepared fish, all manner of illegal cheeses – essentially, must-have delicacies for the idiot with more money than sense who wanted to impress their friends with the very real possibilities of food poisoning or death.

At the time, the officers working the case had been instructed not to do anything other than tell the chef to cease all such operations. Grimes had guessed he'd probably ignored the warning and she'd been right. They hadn't even had to arrest him to get him to cooperate. As it turned out, the Saturday before Christmas was a busy night in a high-end restaurant and a sous-chef will give you any information you need as fast as humanly possible to get you out of the way. He'd provided them with the address for 'the weird guy' before they'd even finished describing this Xander character. In truth, the chef seemed positively relieved at the prospect of losing him as a customer.

From there, it had been a matter of proof by absence. The apartment complex was manned by a twenty-four-hour concierge and access was by encoded key fob only. Sturgess was granted the entry and exit footage only to discover that any time the tenant of apartment 1007 entered or left the building, the camera feed became an unusable squall of distortion. The embarrassed manager apologized and explained they'd had engineers in repeatedly, trying to sort the issue. Sturgess didn't bother to explain the reason for the malfunction, or the fact that he'd seen the exact same thing on the CCTV feeds at the university and surrounding areas from around the time Wilkerson was attacked. They'd found their man all right, and the entry log showed that, as of 8.30 p.m. the previous night, Xander had been in his apartment.

DI Clarke was given approval for armed response, and for the overtime required to carry out the swoop on Christmas Eve. He'd then met privately with Sturgess and DS Tony Morrison from armed response, a meeting during which Clarke had displayed enough sense to allow the other two men to discuss the 'unique wrinkles' of the situation, as Morrison had diplomatically put it, without interruption. The last time they'd worked together had been the disastrous raid on the farm in Saddleworth, and nobody needed reminding of that. Given they didn't know what this Xander fella was capable of, they'd decided on an early morning raid, full tactical with flash bangs, and then 'maximum restraint', involving manacles and a gag.

An hour ago, they'd started clearing floors ten and twelve of Skyline Central 1. Morrison had insisted on the evacuation as, given the unknowns, they didn't want any weapons being discharged around innocent bystanders. Over the radio, Sturgess heard that the armed response team was now in place at the door to apartment 1007, and that the residents on that floor were being woken up very carefully and moved to safety. It was the most dangerous moment aside from the raid itself. They couldn't move the neighbours from the same floor until the breach team were in location, in case the target bolted, and it also put a lot of civilians far too close to live weapons and whatever the team might face on the other side of that apartment door. From the chatter on the radio, it appeared one of the neighbours was a French man who had been enjoying the company of a lady of negotiable virtue. They'd had some difficulty explaining to him that no, he wasn't being arrested, but if he didn't get dressed and out of there fast, then yes, somebody might call his wife.

DI Clarke was down on the street, organizing the cordon they'd thrown around the perimeter of the entire two-building complex. They'd had to wait until the last minute on that too, in case the target happened to glance out the window. In the earlier briefing, it had been suggested that the cordon was excessive, given that they were raiding an apartment on the tenth floor of an eleven-storey building. Morrison had shut down the objection by stating that the subject was considered armed and highly dangerous, and that the operation needed what the operation needed. It was vague enough not to have to spell out to all and sundry that the idea that someone couldn't jump out a window on the tenth floor was based on the assumption that the individual in question was entirely human.

Sturgess had been allowed to sit in apartment 1405 of the building opposite, safely out of the way. It was possible he'd just been sent up there to keep Dave company, although he had the distinct impression the sniper would've been talking regardless of whether anyone else was there or not.

'. . . and I know what you're going to say, Dave – why not just get her some jewellery, mate? I'll tell you why – it's tricky, that's why. You produce one of those little cases and, if you're not careful, she's saying yes to a question you haven't asked and you're having to pay for a wedding you didn't want because, take it from me, some guns you cannot unfire. You always hear about people getting engaged on Christmas Day – what they don't tell you is how so many of them engagements come as a surprise to everybody involved . . .'

Morrison's calm voice came over the radio. 'Positions.'

Dave immediately ceased his chatter and, with military efficiency, moved out on to the balcony, his sniper rifle trained on the balcony of 1007 opposite. He pressed the radio transmitter on his collar. 'Alpha Three in position. All quiet.'

Sturgess moved behind him, careful not to get in the way as he looked on. He craned his neck and saw the cordon being silently put in place down on the street below.

A few tense moments of silence followed before the radio burst into life.

'Armed police. Armed police. Breach. Go. Go. Go.' Crashes. Explosions. From their vantage point the flashes of the stun grenades were visible. 'Armed police. Armed po—' General sounds of mayhem followed, and then, 'Man down. Man down. Hostile. Balcony. Balcony!'

The balcony door to 1007 was hurled open and, in the darkness, Sturgess could just about make out a tall figure rushing outside.

'Subject on balcony. I have a shot,' reported Dave. 'Orders?'

Nothing came back over the radio except a hubbub of confusion.

'Repeat. I have a shot. Over. I—Fucking hell!' The last words from Dave came out as a near scream.

Morrison again. 'Report?'

'He jumped,' said the sniper, trying to regain his composure. 'He fucking jumped.'

'Negative.' This was DI Clarke. 'No sign of that down here.'

'No, I mean he's on the roof. He jumped on to the roof.'

'How the hell—' started Clarke, but he was cut off by Morrison.

'Strike team, subject on roof. I repeat, on the roof. Secure.'

Sturgess, already running towards the apartment's front door, grabbed his walkie-talkie out of his pocket. 'Negative. He's not on the roof of that building. He's on the roof of this one.'

'What?'

Sturgess gave no answer. He had no explanation for how some-one had leaped eight storeys up and on to the roof of a nearby building without so much as a run-up, but he was determined to make sure the bastard didn't get a chance to do it again.

36

It was only after Sturgess had come crashing through the doors to the eighteenth floor of Skyline Central 2 that it occurred to him quite how stupid an idea his foolhardy entrance had been. His assessment was confirmed a second later when Dave Dinsdale popped his head through the doors once, then again, before stepping through quietly in Sturgess's wake. The detective inspector perceived the slightest hint of a glance of admonition thrown in his direction from the sniper.

Thankfully, all that greeted them was an empty corridor with glass doors leading to a gym at one end, and wooden doors bearing a sign that read 'swimming pool' at the other. The only sound was Sturgess's panting after running up four flights of stairs – Dinsdale appeared to be unaffected by the exertion. The gym was dark, save for the slightest touch of morning light starting to creep in. Any question about which way to head was removed by a loud bang that came from the direction of the pool, followed instantly by the shattering of glass.

Sturgess pressed the button on his walkie talkie and spoke as quietly as he could. 'DI Sturgess with Dinsdale from armed response. We are on the eighteenth floor of Skyline Two, attempting to locate and engage the subject. Dinsdale is armed. Going silent.'

He then shut off the radio and removed his earpiece before he could hear Clarke utter anything more than 'Do not—' Sturgess knew what he would inevitably say, but while waiting for back-up was a good idea in theory, in practice, what was going to stop this Xander character from pulling another jumping trick on to one of the adjacent buildings and being long gone by the time Morrison and his team got up here? Not that Sturgess wasn't keen to see them again soon.

'Be ready for anything,' he whispered to Dinsdale, aware of how pointless a statement it was even as he said it. They'd both just witnessed a – for want of a better word – man leaping from one high-rise building to another. Nothing human could do that.

Dinsdale had stowed his rifle on his back and was now hold-ing his sidearm out in front of him. Sturgess wouldn't have minded one too, but armed response had rules about who was permitted to carry a weapon when undertaking an assault. With a jerk of his head, Dinsdale indicated that Sturgess should get behind him. Remembering his firearms training, Sturgess placed his right hand on the other man's shoulder and kept in step as the duo crouched down and advanced down the hall towards the pool.

When they reached the wooden doors, Dinsdale bobbed his head up quickly to peer through the porthole-style window. After a second, slightly more lingering look, he shook his head and looked over his shoulder at Sturgess. The two men stayed that way for a few seconds until, feeling like a prize idiot, Sturgess realized that Dinsdale was waiting for him to do something. He quickly withdrew the plastic keycard the concierge had given him and held it against the reader. The thunk of the lock disengaging, a sound barely perceptible in normal circumstances, was deafening in the hushed silence.

Dinsdale pointed at himself, held up three fingers, then pointed at Sturgess and held up three fingers again. Sturgess nodded his understanding and took a step back. He watched as the other man bobbed his head three times and then, crouching low, pushed through the door. In one fluid motion, Dinsdale spun one way and then the other, taking in as much of the room as he could. After three seconds, he took a step to the side and Sturgess followed him through.

The room was about thirty metres long, with the pool taking up most of it. Floor-to-ceiling glass made up two of the external walls, with a tiled walkway a couple of feet in width wrapping around it on two sides. Sturgess and Dinsdale stood on a five-foot-wide walkway on the near side, which led to a mezzanine area at the far end of the room. Sturgess could make out a couple of sun loungers, a small coffee table and a jacuzzi. The blue underlighting given off by LED lights in the water washed the area with an ethereal glow, mixed with the first touches of light from the morning sky through the windows.

What Sturgess couldn't see was any sign of Xander. The strong scent of chlorine caught in the back of his throat, requiring him to stifle a cough. Along with the soft lapping of the water was a persistent rattle, and a gust of cold wind drew his attention to the far corner of the mezzanine. As his eyes adjusted to the dim lighting, he realized where the noise was coming from. There was a door that he'd missed on first inspection, a glass one that led out to a balcony. It had been forced open, and the faint sparkle of shattered glass could be seen on the ground. There were only two other doors leading off from the pool area, both to his and Dinsdale's right. Sturgess assumed that one would be the steam room and the other the sauna. This place offered very limited options for hide-and-seek.

Based on what had gone before, he considered the situation and decided that attempting to surprise their quarry might be a bad idea indeed. 'Armed police,' he shouted. 'Come out with your hands up.'

Despite being the one to have shouted it, he was a surprised as anyone when a tall figure limped through the second doorway, hands held aloft. Bizarrely, the individual was wearing pyjamas. Not just ordinary ones either, but ones with little ducks on them. The reason for the limp was the man's right leg dragging behind his left, looking all but useless.

'On the ground,' ordered Sturgess.

'You are not armed,' said the man in an unnervingly calm voice.

'I'm not, but he is,' Sturgess said, gesturing behind him. Dinsdale shifted slightly to emphasize the point.

The man nodded. 'True.' Then, with an almost casual wave of his hand, some unseen force lifted Dinsdale into the air and tossed him into the pool where he landed with a loud splash.

Sturgess took a step backwards, looking between where Dinsdale was thrashing around and where Xander was standing watching him. 'This place is going to be swarming with armed police in a second.'

'Yes,' said Xander, his voice still infuriatingly even and quiet. 'Hence why I will need a hostage. Please come over here.'

'Stay where you are.'

'Your friend is drowning.'

Sturgess glanced at Dinsdale struggling in the water.

'He can swim.'

'Not at the moment he can't, I assure you. Tick-tock.'

Sturgess pointed in the water. 'Stop whatever you're doing to him – now.'

'It will be over soon. But not in the way you hope. You can stand there and watch him die or come over here.'

Sturgess considered his options quickly, before realizing he didn't have any. He raised his arms and started walking forward slowly.

'That's enough – turn around,' said Xander when Sturgess was a few feet away.

Sturgess did as instructed as Dinsdale's thrashing grew increasingly desperate. 'Now, let him go.'

He could hear Xander shuffling towards him from behind. A bony hand came to rest on his shoulder.

'I will do that when . . .' The splashing in the swimming pool stopped suddenly. 'Oh dear, too late.'

Sturgess's eyes widened in horror. 'You—'

Before he could say anything else, he felt his entire body freeze. He couldn't move a damn muscle – exactly as Wilkerson had described what happened to her in the library. A terrifying helplessness that felt more like a nightmare than anything a logical mind could believe was really happening. All Sturgess could move was his eyes, just enough to see the sickening sight of Dinsdale floating face down in the pool. His unhelpful mind replayed Dinsdale nattering on about his mother, father and girlfriend.

A succession of sniffs sounded close to Sturgess's ear then Xander's voice came from behind him. 'Ah, yes, it is you. We have met before. You and your little friend. How interesting.'

Sturgess had no idea what he meant by that. He wanted to scream at him, turn around and unleash his fury, but all he could do was stand there, unable to move or speak. He could feel the man's breath on the back of his neck. While he couldn't move any parts of his body, apparently they had enough agency for the hairs on his skin to stand up, as a shiver that had little to do with the cold draught passed through him.

'This is all rather foolish, officer,' said Xander, his voice now a sibilant whisper in Sturgess's ear. 'Believe me, you and your associates do not have the advantage here that you think you do. You are merely an inconvenience, and how many people must die to prove that will be entirely your choice.'

'Let him go,' came another voice, the source of which Sturgess couldn't see.

Xander's hand slipped off Sturgess's shoulder and Sturgess sensed his captor spin around behind him.

'You,' Xander hissed.

''Fraid so,' said the voice, which Sturgess now realized he recognized.

John Mór.

Sturgess had no idea how it was possible, but right at that moment he didn't care. He felt himself being shoved and as he pitched forward, his rigid body turned slightly, meaning his left side slammed on to the cold wet floor. The temple of his unprotected head whacked against the tile, sending sickening amoebas of light scattering across his vision.

Dazed, he lay there, his position allowing him a skewed view of the stand-off taking place behind him. The blow to his head had left his eyes blurry with tears, which was made worse by his inability to even blink. He could just about make out the figure of Xander facing away from him. At the far end of the pool, having entered through the same balcony door used by Xander, it seemed, stood the equally imposing figure of John Mór.

'I know what you are,' said Xander.

'As I do you,' said John Mór, slipping off his coat calmly and draping it over the back of one of the chairs. 'Nice jimmy-jams, by the way.'

'You work for the police?' Even in Sturgess's weakened state, he caught the disparaging way in which Xander uttered the word 'police'.

'Christ, no. I just couldn't turn down the chance to kill one of you bastards,' said John Mór, not quite pulling off the cheery tone he was going for.

'Your people can only usually manage that when hunting in packs. What chance do you think you stand when alone?'

'Ah, well,' said John Mór casually, 'I never was great at the sums.' As he raised himself to his full height, a few of the tattoos that covered his body suddenly started glowing with a gold light.

'You are the one known as—'

'That'd be me, all right. Not been that fella for a while, mind. I'm hoping it'll come back to me.'

'It will be an honour to kill you.'

'Y'know,' said John Mór, 'if I had fifty pence for every time someone said that to me, I'd have . . . two pounds seventy-five.'

Xander tilted his head. 'Two—'

'One of them was dead before he finished. A Stander, in fact – you might've known him.'

In answer to this, Xander threw out his arms, sending John Mór hurtling backwards through the air and crashing into the wall. Sturgess could just make out the shattered plaster left behind by the big man's impact.

With a jolt, Sturgess realized that he was back in control of his body. He rolled over and dropped into the pool, the shock of the cold water helping to clear his head. After a moment's disorientation, his feet found the bottom and he righted himself before heading straight for the still, floating body of Dinsdale.

In his peripheral vision he caught a no doubt expensive sun lounger bursting into flames as John Mór ducked behind it. Focusing on his task, Sturgess lunged forward, grabbed the sniper's body and turned him over. Cinching him around the shoulders, he hauled Dinsdale's limp form towards the side of the pool. As he did so, he managed another quick glance up. John Mór was leaping over the jacuzzi, now holding long curved blades in each hand, only to be greeted by a flash of green light from Xander's direction that sent him hurtling backwards once again. A triumphant snarl escaped the Stander's lips.

Sturgess couldn't worry about that now – the lifeless man in his arms had to be his priority. As he dragged Dinsdale backwards, Sturgess thought he heard the doors behind him open, but when he looked up nobody was there. When he finally felt the pool edge thump into his back, Sturgess hauled himself out of the water while keeping a firm grip on Dinsdale. Then, summoning all the strength he could, he dragged the sniper's dead weight out after him. In the background, he could hear the battle raging on. He glanced across to see John Mór toss a chair in Xander's direction, which the Stander sent skittering away with a dismissive wave of his hand.

All police officers complete a first-aid course as part of basic training. Sturgess had come top of the class, resulting in Terry Pritchard having people calling him 'dummy fucker' for six months based on the idea that he'd 'slipped the dummy the tongue'. Hopefully, everything he'd learned would all come back to him in this moment. He locked his hands together and began chest compressions. 'One . . . two . . .' Thirty. He was pretty sure it needed to be thirty.

Another brief glance over his shoulder confirmed Sturgess's fear – namely, that John Mór was losing. He was lying on the tiled floor, his face bloodied, with Xander standing a few yards away from him, a victor looking down upon his vanquished foe.

'You are weak,' hissed the Stander. 'Disappointing.'

'I'm not going to lie,' said John Mór through gritted teeth, 'I'm a bit upset about that myself. Still, death comes to us all.'

Whatever Xander was about to say next was lost as John Mór propelled himself into a combat roll before coming up and launching both of his knives at his opponent. Xander dodged the first, but the second hit around his abdomen, causing him to expel a hissed snarl.

Blue lighting shot out of the Stander's hand and caught John Mór in the chest, leaving him spasming on the ground.

The part of Sturgess's brain that had been counting nudged him to realize he'd reached thirty. He turned his attention back to Dinsdale and blew two rescue breaths into his mouth.

Nothing yet.

He resumed the chest compressions.

A quick scan of his surroundings confirmed that Dinsdale's sniper rifle must have come free when he was tossed into the water. It was most likely resting at the bottom of the pool along with his sidearm.

Xander was now standing over the crumpled and smoking form of John Mór. He seemed even taller than before, while the formerly imposing John Mór looked utterly diminished. The golden glow of his tattoos had faded away to almost nothing.

'What was the point of this, Hunter?' said Xander.

John Mór spoke around short, tight breaths. 'I'll be honest with ye – it was either this or Christmas shopping.'

'How unsatisfactory.'

'You weren't on my list, anyway.'

Xander raised his hands above his head, preparing for the *coup de grâce*.

'Do you want to know how I killed all them people back in the day?' asked John Mór, causing the Stander to pause for a half-second. Before Xander could say anything in response, a hand was at his throat. Sturgess must have blinked. One moment there was nobody there, and then the next, Margo, the woman Sturgess had met earlier, was poised behind the Stander, her razor-sharp nails shining in the dim light.

'A little help from my friends,' finished John Mór. 'Any last words?'

'We need him alive,' shouted Sturgess.

'No,' said John Mór, 'you don't. He'll not give you anything. I guarantee it.'

'He would know,' said Xander, sounding remarkably calm. 'He has tortured enough people in his time.'

Sturgess flinched as, in a glorious moment of relief, Dinsdale threw up a lungful water in his face before crumpling into a coughing fit.

'Nobody is dying today,' said Sturgess, wiping the water from his face.

John Mór and Margo's eyes met. He gave the smallest of nods and her free hand became a blur of movement, after which, Xander's wrists were bound with thick manacles.

John Mór dragged himself to his feet unsteadily then planted a firm headbutt into Xander's face, sending him flying to the ground, blood spouting from his shattered nose.

He looked at Margo. 'Not a criticism, but you took your time. Are you slowing down?'

The doors behind Sturgess flew open and armed police poured in.

★

A couple of chaotic minutes later, Sturgess was standing with John Mór and Margo, having convinced Morrison and his boys that the duo were 'innocent bystanders'. Morrison clearly didn't believe him but had enough sense not to query the assertion. He also had enough sense to simply nod and not ask questions when John Mór pulled him aside and said, 'The prisoner will be meek as a lamb so long as you keep him in those manacles. Those particular manacles.'

The prisoner himself was being covered by half a dozen armed individuals with itchy trigger fingers while a paramedic tended to his bloodied nose. Meanwhile, at the other end of the pool, Dinsdale was being checked out by another paramedic. In the surest sign of making a full recovery, he was maintaining a stream-of-consciousness monologue while she did so.

'Well,' said Sturgess, 'this is going to take some explaining.' He turned to John Mór. 'Speaking of which, I thought you said you couldn't track him?'

'I couldn't. I tracked you.'

'What?' said Sturgess, appalled.

Before he could lodge any further objections, they all had to step back as Xander, surrounded by armed police, was led away. He carried himself with the air of a man who had been mildly inconvenienced at best.

'John Mór,' the Stander said, 'I hope we will meet again.'

'Unlikely,' replied the big man.

'And, officer, I know I will see you again. You and your little friend.'

Sturgess caught John Mór shoot a look at Margo.

'Why does he keep—'

'Don't worry about it. Standers are always trying their hard-est to be creepy buggers. Speaking of which, I wouldn't normally snitch but do you know that your next-door neighbour comes out naked in the middle of the night and pisses over your wall?'

37

Claremont Dibner, walking on unsteady legs, exited through the main doors of Wonderland and shook the snow from his hair. It had been falling inside the building constantly, only settling in just the right picturesque locations that didn't interfere with foot traffic. He found Original Flavour Wayne standing outside, surveying the logjam of cars waiting to get in that stretched all the way back out to the motorway. They didn't open until 9.30 a.m. on Sunday – Christmas Eve – still thirty minutes to go and already there was a queue of people standing outside too. A close-up magician was working his way up and down the line, performing tricks for their amusement.

'Did you hire a magician?' asked Claremont.

'Nah,' said Wayne. 'I think if you have enough people, they just turn up.'

'Yeah.' The part of Claremont's brain that processed things rationally had long since put up a sign that said 'closed for the holidays' and buggered off.

'I did hire a few more of my cousins to help with parking, though.'

'Right. How many Waynes are we up to now?'

'What?'

'Never mind.'

'We're not going to be able to fit all these people in,' said Wayne, nodding towards the queue.

They would, though. Claremont knew it. Even Wayne knew it – he'd just felt obliged to state the obvious. By all rights, there should be no way that many people could fit into the building behind them. By all logic, they should find themselves policing a riot of angry parents and bawling kids, but they knew they wouldn't. Everybody would get in and have a bloody lovely time.

'I've just been in to see Neil,' said Claremont.

Wayne threw him a quizzical look.

'Our Santa Claus.'

'Oh, right. Yeah. Yeah. Yeah.'

They both shifted awkwardly. Claremont was still determinedly thinking of him as Neil because, well, what was the alternative? *Hey, you know that frightening entity that's making Christmas dreams come true and yet is somehow the most terrifying thing you've ever seen? Yeah, that guy.*

'He wants a bell,' said Claremont, trying to clear his head of all the unpleasant thoughts that kept pushing their way in.

'What?'

'A bell,' repeated Claremont. 'He wants us to get him a bell. A big bell. Biggest one we can find.'

'Why does he want that?'

'I don't know.'

Claremont had gone ahead and agreed to the request immediately. The reindeer had a way of staring at you.

'Are reindeers supposed to be scary?' asked Claremont.

'I know what you mean,' said Wayne quietly. 'They're as big as horses, with those massive bloody stick things on their heads.'

'Antlers,' said Claremont.

'Yeah,' said Wayne. 'Them.'

'What ever happened to the cow?'

'You don't want to know.'

'Oh God,' said Claremont. 'They didn't eat it, did they?'

'Worse.'

'What's worse than that?' Wayne was right, he really didn't want to know, but he felt compelled to ask.

'It's wandering about the place mooing note-perfect renditions of a medley of Christmas hits.'

A groan escaped Claremont's lips before he could stop it. He felt like he might cry.

'This is all . . . all right, isn't it?' asked Wayne.

'It must be,' said Claremont. 'I mean, we're making people happy.'

'Yeah.'

'It's just because we've never done that before, and so it feels weird.'

'Right,' said Wayne. 'That does make sense. Yeah. Yeah.'

The pair stood there in silence as they watched a close-up magician produce a plastic bunch of flowers for a terminally unimpressed six-year-old girl.

'What do you want to do about this bell thing?' asked Wayne.

'I dunno. Just have a look on Facebook Marketplace or something.'

Wayne pulled his phone out and started typing. 'Facebook Marketplace? Nobody's going to be selling a big ol' bell on Facebook Marketp— I take it back.' He held up his phone. 'There's one. Warrington.'

'Right. How much do they want for it?'

'Well, initially they had it up for ten grand.'

'And now?'

'Hundred quid.'

'Right,' said Claremont. 'Offer them fifty and send one of the other Waynes to go get it.'

'Will do,' said Wayne. 'Anything else you want done?'

Claremont considered this. 'Yeah.'

'Don't tell me . . .'

They said it together. 'Double the price of parking.'

38

'Hello, little boy. What's your name?'

The child's face lit up with excitement, but he did not speak.

His mother leaned in. 'Tell Santa your name.'

'I'm George.'

'Well, now, George, have you been to see me before?'

He shook his head.

'I didn't think so. I'm sure I would recognize such a distinguished young man. Would you like to come and sit on Santa's knee and tell me what you want for Christmas?'

The child looked at his mother, who nodded, then the boy was picked up.

Zalas was not used to sitting back and waiting. He had never done so before, but he was adapting to this new world. Still, he could feel the power growing and growing, swelling inside him. He had discovered that if he just let this vessel, this Neil, have some free will, he would do exactly what was needed. Zalas could wait a little longer. Soon, everything he required would be in place and he could dispense with this charade. He would finally be able to exact his vengeance on a world that had dared to forget his name.

They will burn.

They will all burn.

And as they do, they will scream his name.

And he will laugh.

And laugh.

And laugh.

Zalas realized he had momentarily lost control and his laugh was echoing around the walls of his grotto as the reindeer pawed at the ground excitedly with their hooves. The child's mother gawped at him in terror as she tried to prise her crying child from his hands.

He expended a fraction of his energy and soon she was smiling again while the boy sat on his lap, docile, staring up at him in wonder. The child would leave overflowing with belief, just like all the others had.

Believing, but not yet a true believer.

But soon.

Soon.

Mad Hatters?

Stockport County Football Club has made history by becoming the first professional sports team to be officially reclassified as a religion. Former chairman – and now newly minted bishop – Pete Wild explained the thinking behind the move: 'We were saying how we've got a devoted fanbase that turns up religiously every week, and the missus said it was a shame the club wasn't tax-exempt, like a religion. And I just thought, hello? I mean, what's the difference? We ask our supporters to believe that somehow we're going to end up in the Premier League one day. That's no more absurd than all the stuff about getting into heaven.

'Plus, our supporters – sorry, believers – are arguably more devout. They turn up and stand in the pissing rain, whereas most so-called religious people won't show up to church if the central heating's busted. All we did was change the chants to prayers, ask fans to stop singing the one about the randy duck, and job's a good 'un.'

Stockport County – colloquially known as the Hatters as a nod to the town's former status as a global centre of hat-making – has already seen a sharp rise in season ticket sales, thanks to them now being classed as a charitable contribution and hence tax-deductible. Striker Davey Dickins has also officially been declared 'the Messiah', who will lead them to the promised land. However, believers' faith was immediately tested when Dickins injured his knee twenty-seven minutes into the first match of the season. He is not expected to rise again until Easter.

39

This time, when Hannah entered the Kanky's Rest pub on Christmas Eve morning, she found herself under attack immediately. The attacker in question was a large white aquatic bird, which came charging towards her, wings outstretched, hissing furiously. Hannah screamed before John Mór stepped in front of her, arms extended, and her assailant thought better of it.

'G'wan, ye bastard!' he roared as the bird veered away. 'The bird, not you,' he clarified in a quieter voice.

Hannah tried to gather herself now that death, while not off the table entirely, at least didn't seem imminent. 'Is that a swan?'

'Depends on who's asking,' said the man in thick, jam-jar glasses she'd seen the previous day – Larkin, if she recalled correctly. He was standing at the far side of the pub, in front of a large wire cage, holding out a broom in front of him. The swan was now eyeing him with a look of pure hatred.

'No, it doesn't,' said John Mór wearily. 'It's a bloody swan.'

'You say that,' said Larkin. 'Swans are supposed to be serene and shit. This bastard is anything but.'

'I wonder why that could be,' muttered John Mór, slowly

moving away from the front door and inching his way towards the bar.

'Why've you got a swan in your pub?' asked Hannah.

'I don't,' he replied. 'This idiot does.'

'I just brought it here to show him that compared to a rubbish turkey,' began Larkin, 'there's loads more good eating in a swan. I just opened the cage and, all of a sudden, the sleepy bastard was very awake and very bloomin' angry.'

'Doesn't the King own all the swans in Britain?' asked Hannah, who vaguely remembered reading that somewhere.

'Great,' said John Mór. 'He's welcome to pop around and take this one away.'

'Can't you just kill it?' pleaded Larkin.

'No,' said John Mór firmly. 'I cannot.'

'But isn't that what you do?'

Larkin's question may well have earned itself a unique place in human history by being the only one to elicit a burning glare of sheer hatred from both a large man and a large swan.

'I mean . . . Sorry,' said Larkin weakly.

'Maybe,' said John Mór through gritted teeth, 'you should call whoever sold you the vicious sod and get them to come take it back.'

'I can't do that,' said Larkin. 'He only sold it to me on the condition I didn't tell y— I didn't tell anyone who I got it from.'

The swan leaped on to the bar, flapping its massive wings, and instantly knocked a bottle of whiskey off the shelf.

'You're paying for that.'

'Too right he is,' added Larkin.

'You,' snapped John Mór. 'Not the bird.'

Hannah watched as Larkin considered protesting then wisely opted to shut his mouth instead.

'And as for your agreement with the seller, I would point out two things. One – you should consider long and hard who you're more frightened of, me or him, and two – if you really think I wouldn't guess the him in question isn't Dropper Drake, then you think I'm almost as big a fool as you are.'

'I never said that,' said Larkin.

'Me and Drake are overdue a chat,' said John Mór, 'and it ain't going to be friendly. Now, stop standing in front of the cage. It ain't getting back in there if you're blocking the way.'

'I don't think it wants to go back in anyway,' said Larkin.

'Your inability to understand animals is second only to your inability to understand people, Larkin. Now, shift over and hopefully, if I'm one side and you're the other, it'll run towards it.'

'It didn't the last two times.'

'You're saying that like it's something I don't know,' growled John Mór. 'Either come up with a better idea or shift your arse.'

Larkin duly moved.

'Right' said John Mór, spreading his arms to make himself appear even bigger than he already was. 'We both move in on the count of three. One . . . two . . .'

In a blur of indignant feathers, the swan went from being on the bar to being in the cage.

'. . . three,' finished John Mór weakly as he stood up and looked sheepishly at Margo, who was standing beside the cage, glaring at him. Her face was covered in what looked like a yoghurt face mask and she wore a blue, puffy dressing gown.

'Sorry, Margo,' said John Mór, suddenly seeming a lot more like a schoolboy who'd been caught acting the fool than the imposing figure he normally was. 'It's this bloody idiot's fault.' He pointed at Larkin. 'Don't worry, I'll take care of it. You can head back to bed and you won't be disturbed again, I swear . . .'

And then Margo was gone again.

'How does she do that?' asked Hannah, genuinely gobsmacked.

'None of your business,' said John Mór, but she saw him look guilty for his abruptness almost instantly. 'By which I mean, it's one of life's great mysteries.' He turned back to Larkin. 'Along with how this blithering idiot is still alive.'

'I'm just trying to earn a crust,' whined Larkin.

'I'm going to make Ms Willis a cup of tea, and when I get back, that swan is out of here and back in your van.'

Larkin sighed and nodded.

'And,' said John Mór, glancing at his watch, 'by, let's say ten thirty, you will have sent me a picture of this swan swimming around in a pond, free as the bird it is.'

'But—'

'No buts,' snapped John Mór. 'Take it up with the twat who sold it to you, because he didn't own it in the first place. Or are you going to tell me that you got it directly from the King?' he added with a nod back in Hannah's direction.

Larkin stared at his feet sullenly. 'Like the bloody royals would miss a bird or two.'

'Picture,' said John Mór firmly. 'And don't you dare send a

photo of another swan, because I'll know. I'll be seeing this bastard in my nightmares for weeks. Are we clear?'

Larkin looked like a man attempting to construct a counterargument.

'Are we clear?' repeated John Mór with the kind of emphatic delivery that turned a question into a threat.

Larkin nodded.

'Excellent.' John Mór turned back to Hannah and tilted his head towards the door behind the bar. 'Cup of tea?'

Steering as clear as possible of the cage that now contained the remarkably serene swan, Hannah headed in the direction suggested.

John Mór gave Larkin one last look then pushed through the door. 'God save the King.'

Two minutes later, Hannah was sitting at the table in John Mór's kitchen as he placed a mug of builder's tea in front of her.

'Sorry,' he said, 'we're out of sugar.'

'No worries,' said Hannah. 'You've had an eventful Sunday morning.'

'Yeah,' he said ruefully. 'With the gods as my witnesses, if Larkin put half the effort he puts into barely making a dishonest living into making an honest one, he'd be a millionaire by now. Fancies himself some kind of wheeler-dealer wide boy, only he's really a sheep in wolf's clothing.'

'I was actually referring to earlier on.'

'Oh, that,' said John Mór.

'Sturgess rang me. He did his best not to say it, but am I right in thinking you might've saved his life?'

'Gods,' said John Mór, 'I think I speak for the inspector when

I say that neither of us want that getting out, thank you very much.'

'Still, though – you did. So, thank you. And they've got that Xander guy in custody.' Hannah paused. 'Wait a sec, Xander the Stander – is that rhyme deliberate, do you think?'

'I know you've had limited contact with their kind,' said John Mór, 'but let me assure you, they're not known for their whimsy.'

As he sat down, he rubbed a hand against his ribs and winced slightly.

'Are you OK?'

'I'll live. Speaking of which, is there anything about your Detective Inspector Sturgess that you're not telling me?'

'Well,' said Hannah, shifting her mug around awkwardly. 'It's complicated.'

'How so?'

'We were sort of an item, kind of, and then I disappeared because of a work thing and I sort of broke up with him over text. Only not really – I just had to as part of my story because I was going undercover, but he didn't know that and, well, then I came back and tried to explain it but it's kind of like one of those vacuum-packed mattresses that once you open it, the whole thing goes "poof" and then you can't unpoof it if you've realized you've bought the wrong size. Sturgess isn't the mat-tress in that analogy, he's the – well, the mattress is the break-up that wasn't a break-up, only then I suppose it was a break-up and . . .' Hannah clocked John Mór's expression and trailed off.

'Right,' he said diplomatically. 'This'll shock you, but that wasn't what I was getting at.'

'Oh.'

'I meant more . . .' John Mór shifted in his chair. 'When Xander was being led away, he made some remark about looking forward to chatting to Sturgess and his little friend again, and just . . . the way he said it. Like I said, Standers ain't known for their whimsy.'

'Oh,' said Hannah, her mind racing to a point it really didn't want to get to. 'Ohhhh.' Then she remembered that when she'd first seen Sturgess's little secret, she hadn't been the only one present. Banecroft had also been there, as well as Moretti, the lunatic they'd foiled in his attempt to do some terrible, terrible things and . . . 'Ohhhh, shit.'

'That,' said John Mór, pointing a finger at her from across the table. 'I'm guessing what I'm referring to is whatever that is.'

'Yeah.' Hannah bit her lip. 'If I tell you something, can we agree it is in the strictest confidence?'

John Mór simply raised an eyebrow.

'Sorry,' she said. 'Course it is. You've been nothing but brilliant and discreet and super helpful and a fantastic friend to us and—'

'Hannah,' he said, not unkindly trying to get her to bring her point in for a landing.

'Sorry. Yes. I just . . . Sturgess has . . . There's this eyeball-on-a-stalk thing living in his head, and it's like a spy that the Founders – as in that bloody Dr Carter woman – have, where it can see what he sees. Only, he doesn't know about it and can't, because from what I've been told, if he knows then it knows, and in order to protect itself, whatever the hell it is will kill its host immediately.'

'Right,' said John Mór.

'I know it sounds insane but—'

'No,' he said. 'I mean, it does sound insane, but it is also believable. I've seen them before.'

'Really?'

He nodded. 'You forget, I fought a war against the Founders. Those things were the stuff of our nightmares. They're known as Eye Spies."

'You're kidding,' said Hannah.

The big man shrugged. 'I'm not in charge of nicknames. I'm sure the Founders have a proper name for them – probably something in Latin. Daft name aside, those things meant you had a hard time trusting everyone and anyone, because some-one could be a spy and not even realize. Bad as they are, the paranoia they bring is worse.' As he spoke, Hannah noticed a distant look appear in his eyes, as if visiting some very unpleasant memories. 'They're nasty little bastards and no mistake.'

'Thing is,' began Hannah, 'now that you mention it, Xander knows.'

'But how?'

'He was there,' said Hannah. 'That day in the warehouse when that Moretti monster discovered it. It literally popped out right in front of him.'

'Oh,' said John Mór. 'That's bad. Really bad.'

Hannah bit her lip. 'That's what I was afraid of. Do you know how to get rid of one of those things?'

'Yes.'

'That doesn't involve the host dying?'

'Then, no,' said John Mór. 'Sorry.'

'Terrific,' said Hannah, sitting back in her chair.

'I don't think you're getting this, Hannah,' he said, leaning forward and jabbing the tabletop with his finger. 'Xander knows. He knows what's in Sturgess's head. The man who is presumably going to be interrogating him. Those monstrous things are programmed to destroy themselves, and their host, if discovered.'

Hannah stood up suddenly, sending her chair tumbling to the floor behind her. 'Oh God. If he says anything—' How could she have been so stupid? 'What am I going to do?'

'I don't know,' said John Mór, 'but no matter what, you can't let Sturgess speak to Xander.'

'And I can't tell him why he can't.' Hannah heard her own voice, on the verge of screaming. 'How do I . . .'

She looked at John Mór, who only offered an apologetic shrug. 'Not my area, I'm afraid.'

Hannah's hand dived into her pocket and came out with her phone. She fumbled with it briefly then jabbed at the screen.

'It's ringing,' she said.

Every trill of the dial tone grated against her every nerve. What if they were too late? What if he'd already . . .

'Hello.'

'Tom!' She almost yelled the DI's name as the wave of relief passed through her.

'Are you OK?'

'I'm . . . What are you up to?'

Sturgess's voice lowered slightly. 'DI Clarke and I are about to go in and have a chat with—'

'Don't!'

'What? Why?'

'I need to see you right now,' she said, her mouth running ahead of her brain.

'OK. Can it wait until—'

'No, it's really urgent. There's been a massive development in the case. Like, huge. Really, really big. Can you meet me at our offices straight away?'

'What's—'

'I can't say over the phone. Just get there as soon as you can. Promise you'll leave straight away.'

'I'll try but—'

'Promise!'

'OK.'

'Straight away.'

'Yes,' said Sturgess. 'Straight away.'

'Good.' Then she hung up immediately because she couldn't think of anything else to say and didn't want to have to field any more questions.

'Well done,' said John Mór.

'What am I going to do? I don't have anything to tell him to keep him out of that interview room.'

'Hmmmm,' said John Mór. 'You could always talk about your relationship. That sounds like it'd take up quite a lot of time.'

'Shut up!' snapped Hannah, before remembering herself. 'By which I mean, thank you, but also, shut up.'

John Mór picked up his mug of tea. 'I really enjoy our little chats.'

40

Stella couldn't move.

No matter how hard she tried, she couldn't bring herself back to full wakefulness. Manny's memories played through her mind again and again. It didn't matter how many times she'd seen them, whenever they replayed, she experienced the same fresh shock as the first time. In some ways it was worse, knowing what was coming. The thundering of her rapidly pounding heartbeat, that taste in her mouth – again and again and again.

Occasionally, the running order changed – the boy first, then Quinnie; the rabbit running, roasting; the smoke, the explosion – but it was all still there. It played through, she fell into a brief, fitful sleep, and then it started over.

The odd time, the timeline would move forward a little further and something new came into the mix.

Manny wakes up in a hospital with doctors examining him. Then he's in the corner of the room, his pulse thundering in his ears. That cursed taste filling his mouth again, and a nurse looking down at him. Her look is filled with pity as she tries to speak, her words soothing, while an older man in an orderly's uniform stands behind her, regarding Manny suspiciously.

Then Stella would be back on the boat and they'd be sharing that cigarette again. She'd tried to break the narrative, screaming and shouting, trying to make the soldiers listen to her. Quinnie just kept on laughing and joking, and she realized that the impression of having agency was just an illusion. With effort, she could alter the perspective slightly, but not the order of events. It was that horrible quagmire of knowing that whatever you do, nothing can be changed.

The sequence runs through yet again. Only, at the end of it, Manny is standing in a field and a man in uniform with a thick moustache and an almost comical scowl thrusts a rifle into his hands and starts shouting. Then comes the taste, the thundering of his heartbeat and he cannot move. He just stands there, shaking. Memories within memories as the boy, the rabbit, Quinnie – they all come back to him as he stands in that field, shaking. The sergeant says something and Manny looks down in horror to realize he has lost control of his bladder.

Then the sequence goes back to the start and they're on that boat again.

Another time Manny has returned home. He's walking down the street – Rosa holds one of his hands and Dottie the other. She/he should be happy – this is all they wanted – but they're not. They're walking down Market Street and, as they do, people give them dirty looks. Not them – him. They're looking at him. Rosa holds her head up high, defiant, proud. Dottie, mercifully unaware, swings from her daddy's hand, singing a happy song to herself. But the eyes – all Manny can feel are those eyes boring into him.

His heartbeat thunders, the taste in his mouth returns, and now he's in a park, sitting on a bench, alone. He has a bottle of something, foul-tasting. He takes a drink but, try as he might, he can't wash that taste away.

And, with a terrifying inevitability, the whole thing starts again.

41

Hannah rushed up the stairs and into the reception of *The Stranger Times* offices, out of breath, out of ideas and fast running out of time. As she stood there, panting, with her hands on her knees, she was surprised to see Grace and Ox standing at the reception desk, mugs of tea in hand.

'What're you two doing here?' asked Hannah when she regained the power of speech.

'We're just back from taking the kids to see Santa,' said Grace.

'It was really nice,' said Ox, before they both smiled contentedly at each other.

'The kids?' asked Hannah, confused.

'Clint and Brian,' said Grace.

'The kids?' Hannah repeated.

Ox laughed. 'I suppose Brian is only really a kid at heart, but he loved it. They even let him visit Santa.'

'It was really nice,' said Grace.

Both she and Ox smiled at each other again. There was an unnerving, morning-TV-presenters-on-Mogadon vibe going on with them.

'Yes,' said Ox. 'We had a really nice time.'

Hannah glanced at the corner of the room where Brian was on his knees, bowing down before a large fibreglass statue of Santa Claus. 'Right, I can definitely see that,' she said. Then she remembered why she was there. 'Is Banecroft here? Vincent!' she shouted at the top of her lungs.

Reggie emerged from the bullpen, wearing the same three-piece tartan suit he'd been wearing the day before. 'What's all the shouting about?'

'What are you doing here?' asked Hannah.

'And a happy Christmas Eve to you, too, I'm sure. I could ask you the same thing. I'm here because I'm being punished.'

'Why are you being pun—'

'He knows why,' said Banecroft, emerging from the door that led to his office at the other end of reception.

'OK,' said Hannah. 'Well, I asked because I wanted to know why.'

'If you must know, he got us thrown out of a nightclub we hadn't even got into yet.'

'You two went clubbing?'

'No, we didn't. We didn't get past the cloakroom.'

'Of a nightclub that may or may not have been entirely populated by ghosts,' added Reggie.

'We just came back from visiting Wonderland,' said Grace.

'It was really nice,' said Ox.

Banecroft gave the pair a withering look. 'Have you two been hanging out with the Rastafarian? Ox I expect it from, but you, Grace? And Brian! What the hell are you doing over there? If the staff of this paper are going to worship anyone as a god, it had damn well better be me.'

'Brian is staff now?' asked Reggie.

'Well, he's either that or some freeloader who occasionally shits in the corner.'

'Language,' said Grace, but in a singsong voice far removed from the schoolmarmish tone she normally used when dishing out admonishments.

'Speaking of little shits, where's that hoodlum, Clint? He's supposed to be—' Banecroft screamed and jumped away instinctively as he realized Clint was standing beside him, holding a tray of mugs.

'Would you like some tea, Mr Banecroft?'

'Where the hell did you come from? I'm going to tie a bell around you. Can't have you sneaking up on people like that.'

'Apologies, Mr Banecroft.'

Hannah and Banecroft both took a step towards Clint, bent down and looked at him. He was smiling up at them brightly, and his hair looked funny, too. With a jolt, Hannah realized it had been combed. His T-shirt was neatly tucked into his jeans, which were pulled up well above the butt-crack line.

'Are you feeling OK, Clint?'

'I'm fine, thank you, Ms Willis.' He proffered the tray. 'Would you like a cup of tea?'

'Right,' said Banecroft, pointing at the tea. 'What's in it, ye little so-and-so?'

'Currently? Only milk, but I do have a bowl of sugar here, too.'

'What's it laced with?'

Clint looked honestly confused. 'Laced with?'

'Clint is being a very good boy,' said Grace.

'Yes,' agreed Ox. 'He's on the nice list.'

They both laughed at this.

Banecroft looked back at the inanely grinning duo and then at Clint. 'All right, forget the tea – what have you given them?'

'We haven't got time for this,' said Hannah, belatedly finding some focus amid the weirdness. 'Sturgess is on his way here and I've told him there's been a big break in the case.'

'Oh,' said Reggie. 'Has there?'

'No. Unless . . .' She looked back and forth between Reggie and Banecroft. 'Did you two come up with anything?'

'*He* came up with absolutely nothing,' said Banecroft. 'I, on the other hand, had a reasonably productive day until he ruined it.'

Reggie rubbed a hand across his forehead then stepped forward to where Clint was still holding the tray of mugs. 'Do any of these have in them what those two are on?' he said, nodding towards Ox and Grace. 'Because if so, sign me up.'

'I think they're just full of the joy of Christmas,' said Clint brightly.

'Good Lord,' said Reggie, taking one of the mugs. 'I have got to find myself somewhere else to work.'

'What did you find out?' said Hannah to Banecroft. 'And tell me quickly.'

Banecroft raised his eyebrows. 'Excuse me, do I work for you?'

'Sturgess will be here any minute.'

'Do I work for him?'

'If you want your legs to keep working, Vincent, you'll shut up and tell me what you found out, right now!'

'OK. Well, seeing as you asked so nicely, I met a certain librarian.'

'You found her?'

'Technically, she found me. Well, Zeke and Ox did.'

'This is brilliant,' said Hannah. 'We can tell Sturgess this.'

'We most certainly cannot,' said Banecroft, outraged. 'We're not in the business of turning innocent victims over to the police so they can be thrown in prison for the rest of their lives. Which brings me rather neatly on to a little lecture I'd like to give, entitled 'Why we don't bring our policeman boyfriends with us to meet sources'. There's also a PowerPoint presentation – it's seventy-eight slides of the word 'no' in different fonts, with a great deal of underlining and exclamation marks.'

'Shut up,' said Hannah. 'You can be horrible to me later. Right now, I need something to tell Sturgess.'

'I think I speak for all of us when I say I'd rather not be dragged in to be used as a prop in your tawdry love life.'

'It's not . . . There's . . . Arghhh! It'll take too long to explain. What else did you find out?'

'If you must know, our poor librarian did those terrible things while temporarily possessed by some ancient so-called god called Zalas that she caught from a book. Like some cosmic STD, this Zalas character can apparently hop from person to person.'

'Yes!' exclaimed Hannah, pointing excitedly at Banecroft with both hands. 'Excellent.'

'Rather odd response to that sentence,' commented Reggie.

'That must be the book that Xander the Stander was looking for,' said Hannah, pacing up and down.

'Who?'

'No time. Tell me more stuff about this book.'

'It's called the *Black Grimoire*,' said Banecroft.

'And it's bound in human skin,' said Reggie. 'Which is unspeakably horrid.'

'Right, and where is it now?'

Reggie groaned at the question.

'We don't know,' said Banecroft. 'I was trying to find that out when Rupert the Bear here annoyed all of the people who may or may not have been ghosts, and got us thrown out of the nightclub.'

'There's an awful lot to unpack in that sentence,' said Hannah.

'They were all see-through, but also not,' said Reggie, 'and I was just trying to figure out if they were ghosts or something else. If they were ghosts, I have to say they were disappointingly rude.'

'Although,' said Banecroft, 'one of them did stop me from getting punched in the head.'

'That is true,' conceded Reggie. 'More's the pity.'

'Crap,' said Hannah, looking around. 'I think I heard a car pulling up. That'll be Sturgess. I need to give him more than this.'

'Would he like a cup of tea?'

'Not now, Clint. The book,' said Hannah, grabbing Banecroft by the arm. 'That's got to be the big thing. What did they tell you?'

'Trixy,' said Banecroft.

'Nice girl, eight arms,' added Reggie.

'I thought at least ten.'

'Really? Because—'

'Focus!' barked Hannah. 'What did she say about the book?'

'Nothing much,' said Banecroft. 'She said if a book goes missing in a library, ask a librarian, but, as I said previously, I'd already spoken to the librarian.'

'You spoke to the librarian?'

At this, Hannah spun around to see DI Sturgess standing at the top of the stairs.

'Well,' said Hannah, 'look who it is.'

Sturgess gave her a funny look. 'Yes. You called me to come here straight away, remember?'

'Yes. Yes, I did,' said Hannah.

'Would you like a cup of tea?' asked Clint.

'No, thanks.'

'Are you sure?' said Hannah. 'There's nothing in them.'

'Right.' Sturgess gave her a wary look. 'Well, as tempting as that is, I'm still going to pass. Sorry,' he said, turning his attention to Banecroft, 'did I hear you say you've talked to the librarian?'

'*A* librarian,' clarified Banecroft. 'I met her last night, in the queue to a nightclub Reginald and I were in.'

'OK,' said Sturgess. 'Nothing you just said sounds in the least bit believable.'

'Would I lie to you?'

'Yes. Yes, you would.'

Banecroft nodded. 'Fair point. I would. D'ye know, Clint, I think I will have one of those cups of tea.'

Clint beamed up at him. 'Absolutely. And thank you once again for believing in me, Mr Banecroft. I appreciate this opportunity to turn my life around.'

Banecroft considered him for a long moment then glared at Ox. 'All right, seriously. Whatever about corrupting Grace – I cannot believe you took the kid with you.'

'I don't know what you're talking about,' said Ox.

'We went to see Santa Claus,' said Grace.

'It was wonderful,' said Clint.

Banecroft scanned the room. 'Is it possible we have some kind of gas leak?'

'Excuse me,' said Sturgess, sounding irritated now. 'I don't mean to interrupt whatever the hell all of this is and . . . Sorry again, but do you know there's a guy in the corner, worshipping an effigy of Santa Claus?'

'Brian!' barked Banecroft. 'I will not tell you again. Grace, we need to get a statue made of me.'

'I left an important interrogation for this,' said Sturgess, 'and probably did my career yet more damage, so could someone tell me is there any reason why I need to be here?' He threw Hannah a very pointed look.

'Yes,' she said. 'Absolutely yes. The . . . the book . . .'

'The one Xander was looking for?'

'Yes, it's called the *Black Grimoire*.'

'OK. And how do you know that?'

'Someone told us.'

'We do not reveal our sources,' said Banecroft. 'Y'know, journalism, et cetera, et cetera.'

'OK,' said Sturgess, starting to turn back towards the stairs. 'To be honest, you probably could've told me this over text.'

'Ah, but there's more,' said Hannah, trying not to sound as desperate as she felt.

'Which is?'

'The . . . the source said . . . if a book goes missing in a library, ask a librarian.'

'Right,' said Sturgess, his confusion having transformed mostly into anger by this point. 'Well, if we ever find her, I'll make sure to do that.'

'She doesn't have it,' said Banecroft.

'And how could you possibly know that?' asked Sturgess accusatorially.

He then glanced at Hannah, who cringed internally. Bereft of other ideas, she smiled back at him like an idiot.

'Didn't someone tell me that you have CCTV footage of her leaving the scene?' asked Banecroft.

Sturgess considered this. 'As it happens, we do.'

'And did she have a large book about her person that may or may not be bound in human skin?'

'No,' said Sturgess, 'she didn't. Again, is there anything you'd like to tell me?'

'No.'

'Just to remind you, you are aware that withholding evidence in a murder investigation is still very much a criminal offence?'

'Is it?' said Banecroft. 'What will they think of next? I'll tell you what you brave boys and girls in blue should be dealing with – public urination. It has reached epidemic levels.'

'We'll get right on that,' said Sturgess. 'Well, if there's nothing else?'

Hannah's mind was working feverishly, trying to think of something – anything – to keep him out of that interrogation room. She'd already run through the options as she'd rushed back to the offices. She couldn't simply ask him not to go in there and tell him he could never ask her why – he'd never go for that. Could she faint? Just collapse? No. In fifteen minutes she'd be on her way to the hospital and he'd be heading back to work. Think. She had to think. *Ask a librarian.* What was that supposed to mean?

Sturgess gave a curt wave, turned and started to head back down the stairs.

'LIBRARIAN!' screamed Hannah at such a volume that Clint dropped the tray of teas.

'Oh, botheration,' exclaimed Clint.

'Botheration?' echoed Banecroft, bewildered. 'Oh no, Grace – you didn't get him into Jesus, did you? I'd have preferred drugs.'

'Shut up, Vincent,' said Hannah excitedly.

'Excuse me?'

Sturgess, who'd come back up the stairs, looked at her.

'Librarian,' repeated Hannah at a more normal volume. 'Ask a librarian. There's more than one.'

'Yes,' said Sturgess, 'I imagine there're lots.'

'But you said a librarian came in early and found the scene.'

'I did,' said Sturgess, seeming very interested all of a sudden. 'A Richard Duff.'

'He's got it,' said Hannah. 'The book.'

'And you know that how exactly?'

'Think about it. It's not in the library. This other librarian . . .'

'Debra Brimson?'

'The suspect, right. You said yourself she didn't have it. We know Xander went there to try and find it and he couldn't. So, who else could have it? Ask a librarian!' she repeated triumphantly. 'It was a clue! A bona fide clue!'

Hannah scanned the faces looking at her. She kept expecting someone to point out how she was wrong, only the more she thought about it, the more she realized she was right.

'We need to go and find this Richard Duff character,' said Banecroft.

'We do,' said Sturgess. 'I mean, *I* do.'

'Be fair,' said Hannah. 'You wouldn't have thought of this without us, and this could get hairy. You might need back-up.'

'I don't mean to brag but I do have access to the Greater Manchester Police force.'

'And how much use were they this morning?' asked Hannah pointedly. 'They're not exactly built to cope with weird stuff.'

'Whereas that is all we do,' said Reggie.

Sturgess considered this, his top teeth lightly grazing against his bottom lip as he did so. 'All right, then,' he concluded.

'Excellent,' said Banecroft. 'I'll drive.'

'No, you won't.'

'We can all go in your car, Tom,' said Hannah.

'OK,' the DI agreed reluctantly.

'I'm coming, too,' said Reggie. 'Without me, you'd never have got the clue.'

'Fine,' said Sturgess. 'But that's it.' He looked at the rest of the room pointedly.

'We're OK,' said Grace.

'Yes, thank you,' said Ox. 'We've already had a very exciting day. We went to see Santa Claus.'

Banecroft rolled his eyes towards the ceiling. 'Right, that's it. We're bringing in mandatory drug testing.'

42

Sturgess pulled the car up in front of the address he'd been given for Richard Duff. A new-build end-of-terrace in Ardwick. If you asked him to describe the archetypal domicile for a single librarian, this would be it. 'Right, then.'

'So,' said Banecroft from the passenger seat, 'do you want us to wait here while you kick the door in?'

'I thought I'd try ringing the doorbell.'

'Really? My, my, this really is the new police force we're always hearing about.'

'Could we please get out of the car?' asked Reggie from the back seat.

'Nobody's stopping you,' said Sturgess.

'Actually, you sort of are. I think you've got the child locks on.'

'Oh, right,' said Sturgess, poking at the various perplexing buttons scattered across the centre console. 'I'm not used to having people in the back.'

'Imprisoning people against their will,' said Banecroft as he stepped out of the vehicle. 'Now that's the GMP I've come to know and love.'

Eventually, Sturgess managed to liberate Reggie and Hannah

from the back seat. Hannah had been very quiet, not saying a word since they'd left the offices of *The Stranger Times*. Admittedly, there hadn't been a lot of room to get a word in edgeways around Banecroft's monologue on public urination being an inevitable sign of a forthcoming apocalypse, but even so.

'Are you OK?' Sturgess asked quietly.

'Yes. Fine, fine,' said Hannah, treating him to an overly bright smile. 'In fact, I think I'm going to leave you boys to it – I've got stuff to do.'

'What?'

'Yes, I . . . I need to do my Christmas shopping.'

'But it's Christmas Eve,' said Reggie.

'Exactly. I'd better get cracking.' She turned and started to walk determinedly down the footpath before spinning around briefly. 'Ring me as soon as you're done. Let me know how it goes.'

'OK,' said Sturgess, watching her hurry away. 'Is it me or is she acting weird?'

'Compared to what?' said Banecroft. 'Now, do you want to establish a code word for if you want us to leave the room, so you can rough up the suspect, or will we just go with the flow?'

Sturgess sighed. 'Just shut up and come on.'

Ringing the doorbell and knocking on the door produced nothing in the way of results.

Reggie pressed his face up against the glass. 'I can't see much through the lace curtains, but there's definitely a lamp on. And I can hear music. In fact . . . Ahhhh, no!'

'What?' said Banecroft.

'Nothing.'

'What?' said Sturgess.

Reggie looked at his feet, embarrassed. 'Well, if you must know, I've just been Whamageddoned.'

Sturgess shook his head.

'Whamageddoned?' repeated Banecroft.

'It's a thing people do,' said Sturgess. 'See how long they can go without hearing the Wham! song "Last Christmas" in December.'

Banecroft gave Reggie a look that could strip paint. 'I've a good mind to make you go and wait by the car.'

'I just . . .'

'Not another word.'

Sturgess led them down a side passage which emerged into a small, neatly maintained garden. A rockery with a few jovial-looking gnomes took up around half the available space. Peering through the rear windows didn't reveal a great deal more. The glass-panelled back door and kitchen window showed a remarkably ordinary-looking kitchen, with some pots sitting in the sink. The other window had lace curtains drawn across it but a flickering light gave the hint that somewhere behind it a TV was on.

'What do we do now?' asked Reggie, after hammering on the back door yielded nothing more than doing so on the front door had.

'Well,' said Sturgess, 'we can try ringing him again, and I can talk to the higher-ups about possibly seeing if we can get a—' He was interrupted by the sound of shattering glass. 'What the hell?'

'Sorry,' said Banecroft. 'I was picking up one of those delightful gnomes to examine it when it slipped out of my hand and went crashing through the top pane of this glass door.'

'I should arrest you right now,' said Sturgess.

'I agree.' Banecroft nodded towards the door. 'Perhaps you should step inside and see if the homeowner is here and would like to give a statement.'

'Anything we find is completely inadmissible now.'

'Right. So, to clarify, if we happen to find this *Black Grimoire* that possessed the soul of a librarian with some god from the dark ages, you're saying we won't be able to rely on that in court?'

Sturgess gave Banecroft a long look before going over to examine the door. 'I really don't like you.'

'You're hiding it well.'

'It might be a bad time to point this out,' said Reggie, holding up a key, 'but this was underneath the gnome you just chucked through that window.'

'Well,' said Banecroft, 'the important thing is we're in.'

'I'm in,' said Sturgess. 'You two idiots are staying outside.'

'Hello,' called Sturgess, while stepping carefully through the shattered remnants of glass and gnome. 'Is anyone here?'

'If they were, they'd have heard that and come running . . .' said Banecroft from outside.

'I swear,' snapped Sturgess, 'you take one foot inside this house and I will arrest you.'

'For a man who's entered a dwelling illegally, you're very judgy.'

Sturgess endeavoured to ignore him. From the inside the kitchen looked as remarkably bland as it had from the outside. It led to a hallway where nothing seemed unusual apart from the smell. It was hard to identify but not something someone would have deliberately cultivated – sort of sickly-sweet, with the emphasis on the sickly.

Sturgess gave a quiet knock on the door leading to the back room before entering – on the other side of it, he found a small sitting room with a TV showing a gardening programme. The walls were lined with bookshelves. The front room was remarkably similar – minus the TV but with even more bookshelves. Sturgess didn't know what this *Black Grimoire* was supposed to look like exactly, but he still didn't think it was any of the books he saw on any of the shelves.

As he reached the bottom of the staircase, the smell grew stronger, as he'd somehow known it would.

'Hello,' he said, not expecting an answer as he began to climb the creaky stairs.

At the top sat a simple bathroom, with a spare room to the right of it that contained a fold-up bed and yet more shelves of books. That left one closed door on the landing. As Sturgess approached, the smell crossed the line into full-on stench. He pulled his sleeve over his fist and held it up to his nose before pushing the door open and stepping slowly inside.

The room was surprisingly bright, with the low winter sun hitting the window and bathing everything in painfully intense sunlight. Sturgess shielded his eyes with his other hand, giving them time to adjust. Then he saw the figure in the bed. It was small. Impossibly small. All he could see was its shrunken head on the pillow, facing the window. He'd only ever seen the man briefly, and there was so little left of him to make him look human, let alone like any one in particular, but Sturgess assumed this poor husk had been Richard Duff. The duvet hung over his body in a peculiar way.

Sturgess was reaching for his phone in his pocket to call it in when the head unexpectedly turned in his direction. He screamed, stumbling backwards into the wall. The emaciated face and sunken cheeks had left the man's skin looking sickly translucent. His dried, chapped lips were moving, trying to say something that Sturgess couldn't make out. Sturgess steadied himself and walked around the bed to reach him.

The eyes in the head followed him across the room, the lips mouthing the same words over and over in a breathy whisper. Sturgess, now standing in front of the window, tried to calm himself and leaned in to listen. It took him a second before he realized what the voice was saying. In a fast, never-ending sequence like an offered-up prayer, Duff intoned, 'Protect the book, protect the book, protect the book, protect the book, protect the book, protect the book, protect the book, protect the book . . .'

Sturgess stood back up and looked into the man's face again. There was little in the way of recognizable humanity there. He looked at the oddly positioned duvet, a terrible certainty grabbing hold of him. He had the presence of mind to grab the corner of the duvet with his sleeve-covered hand, preserving the scene, then closed his eyes for a moment to gather himself before tossing it back.

The man's left leg was completely missing, as was half of his right arm. Amid the dried bloodstains on the bedding lay a book. As Sturgess had known it would, there was an ouroboros on its cover.

Like a bolt of ice-cold lightning, a voice sounded in his head without having gone through his ears. *Help me, you must help me. Please, help me!*

And then Sturgess passed out.

43

Not long ago, Zalas had been trapped in the void for what felt like eternity, powerless and tortured by his own impotence, having been bested by lowly mortal ingrates. Now, his strength was swelling to previously unimagined levels and all he had to do was sit back and allow it to happen. It was hard to conceive that he might find himself bored, and yet that was exactly how he felt. He watched on through the eyes of the host and fought off the urge to scream.

The child sitting on his lap had been talking for at least a month by this point, its monologue prompted by the question 'And what would you like for Christmas?'

'. . . and Madeline says that Barbies are so last year, but Samantha says that she's just a hater and you shouldn't pay attention to haters, and I think that Barbie is kinda cool still but I'm not sure if . . .'

It didn't seem to need to draw breath at any point. It just went on and on and on, speaking without any input from anyone else. Its father stood idly by, dividing his attention between looking at what Zalas now knew to be something called a phone, and glancing nervously at the reindeers. For their part, the beasts were growing increasingly restless, waiting for it to begin, and then . . .

The moment.

Finally, the moment had arrived.

Zalas could feel it. He was ready. At long last, he was ready. The reindeer all stepped forward, forming a semicircle around him, because they knew it too.

He took control of the host and spoke to them. 'Yes, my loyal disciples. It is our time. Time to turn belief into the true faith with which to set this putrid world aflame.' He stretched his arms wide and looked towards an unseen sky, as if letting the light of this new dawn wash across his face. It would not be a dawn of light, though – it would be darkness. The deepest darkness this world had ever seen. The time of man would soon be over. The time of Zalas was at hand.

He let out an exultant roar as nine bolts of blue light shot forth from his hands, connecting with the antlers of each of the reindeers before dividing again into innumerable tendrils, shooting off into the world, seeking out the seeds of belief from which true believers could be grown.

The reindeer howled their hoarse calls, a cacophony of elation as the room filled with the blinding light. Zalas clapped his hands with delight. 'For truly,' he shouted, 'it is better to give than to receive!'

The air itself burned with the friction of so much power being sent out into the world, but it would be nothing compared to what would be returning. He would be unstoppable. By the time this was done, he would be able to summon those who had defeated him back from death itself, so that he could spend his days coming up with new ways to torture them.

He looked down to see the father of the child curled up into a ball on the floor, having soiled himself in sheer terror.

Meanwhile, on his lap, the child continued, unaffected. '. . . Monica didn't invite Tracy to her birthday party because she wasn't invited to hers, but that was because it was tickets to go see *Wicked* the musical, and she says there's only so many people you could fit in a box, but Gemma said her mum said her auntie worked there and you can definitely fit twelve people in, so now they're feuding and Ciara is, like . . .'

Zalas looked at her in awe, fascinated. He had just conceived a new method of torture.

E. T. Phone Poll

In what is being seen as a damning indictment of politicians every-where, one of the largest opinion polls ever undertaken – surveying 100,000 people from across the globe – has revealed that a whopping seventy-three per cent of respondents would prefer aliens to take over the running of the planet.

It seems that mankind has lost faith in its ability to self-govern. Professor Philomena Truckstop of Manchester Metropolitan University's Faculty of Arts and Humanities explains, 'It's like when your parents go away when you're a teenager. For the first few days, it's all parties and pizza. Then you wake up one morning and the hamster is dead, some guy named Barry is living in your basement, and the dishwasher has the steering wheel from a Ford Cortina jammed in it. You're way out of your depth and you just think, "I wasn't ready for this." '

While respondents acknowledged the high possibility that aliens could turn out to be flesh-eating monsters with megalomaniacal tendencies, the general feeling was that we'd at least be no worse off than we currently are.

44

Ox was standing by the reception desk, drumming his fingers on the counter while Grace typed away.

She coughed politely, and then more pointedly when politely didn't get the job done.

'Sorry,' said Ox stilling his hands.

'That's quite all right, dear.'

He looked around. 'Where's Stella hiding?"

'She is working on her essay. Don't disturb her.'

'Right. Right. Essay.' Ox paused, trying to find the right words. 'Did you . . .'

'What?' asked Grace.

'Did you feel a bit weird earlier?'

'How so?'

'Like, you and I kept saying how nice that Wonderland place had been.'

'Well, it was nice,' said Grace.

'Yeah, but – I felt a bit, sort of stoned.'

'I am a respectable lady,' said Grace firmly. 'I would not know about such a thing.'

'Right. Course. But did you feel a bit . . . peculiar, perhaps?'

Grace stopped typing. 'Now that you mention it, I did a little, yes.'

'Yeah, what do you think was going on there?'

'Hmmmm.' Grace pursed her lips. 'I would like to think that we were full of the Christmas spirit.'

'I guess,' said Ox, far from convinced. 'How do you feel now?'

'Absolutely fine,' said Grace.

'I do too. I guess whatever it was sort of wore off?'

'Well, all good things must come to an end.'

Clint emerged from the bullpen. 'Hello, just to let you know I've completed painting the back wall, properly, and I'm now going to get on with scrubbing the floors until they're as bright as a new penny.'

'What's up with you?' asked Ox.

'What do you mean, Mr Ox?'

'Why're you talking like you're a Victorian kid who's just appeared out of a closet in a horror movie?'

'I'm afraid I don't know what you mean.'

Clint stood there, beaming a smile at them and seemingly happy to do so until hell froze over.

'Thank you, Clint,' said Grace. 'You're doing an excellent job.'

They both watched him trot happily back into the bullpen.

Ox turned around sharply and spoke in a lower register. 'And that is definitely weird.'

'What? The young lad is responding very well to being given some responsibility and your fine mentorship.'

'He's gone from Hellboy to Ned Flanders in a day, Grace – a day.'

'Children are so adaptable.'

Brian exited the bullpen, hugging his large Santa, and, with a nod, headed down the stairs.

'And as for him . . .' said Ox.

'Brian has always been a little odd,' said Grace.

'Yeah, fair point on that one,' he conceded.

The phone started ringing and Grace tutted as she picked it up. 'Hello, *The Stranger Times*.' She listened for a few seconds then rolled her eyes. 'Yes . . . Is that right? How fascinating. Honestly, you are a grown man, and it is Christmas Eve. Surely you have something better to do with your time? If not, you should volunteer at a soup kitchen or help an elderly neighbour with their shopping.' With that, Grace slammed down the receiver.

'What's going on there?' asked Ox.

'Prank call. Not a new occurrence but we've been getting an awful lot of them in the last hour or so.'

'What are they saying?'

'Well, let me see,' said Grace, counting on her fingers. 'A unicorn was spotted in Levenshulme, a robot in Altrincham, forty-eight rabbits roaming across Gorton – that was a good one – someone's child in Leigh suddenly inflated and started floating away . . .'

The phone started to ring again.

Grace scowled at it. 'I may have to pull it out of the wall if this keeps continuing.'

Then another phone started ringing in the bullpen.

And another.

And another.

Soon, a cacophony of ringing echoed through the office.

Ox and Grace looked at each other. 'I know you can't say it, Grace,' said Ox. 'So I will. Oh shit.'

45

Sturgess came around to the disconcerting sight of Vincent Banecroft staring directly into his face at close range.

'What the hell happened?' asked Sturgess as he felt a bump on the back of his head that hadn't been there previously.

'You passed out,' said Banecroft. 'C'mon.' He hooked a hand under Sturgess's armpit and started to lift him up off the carpet.

'Why did I . . .' Sturgess stopped when he saw what remained of the figure of Richard Duff, lying on the bed, still mouthing the same three words.

'Yes,' said Banecroft sombrely. 'That. Poor bastard.'

Reggie was standing against the far wall, his face frozen in a horrified expression as he stared intently at the book.

Banecroft propped Sturgess against the windowsill. 'Right, we need to call an ambulance for this wretched soul and—'

He darted across the room to where Reggie had stepped forward and was reaching for the book. He slammed him back into the wall but Reggie tried to push him away.

'Reggie,' shouted Banecroft, right into his face. 'Reginald.'

When Reggie tried to push past him again, Banecroft slapped him in the face – hard. It seemed to do the trick.

Reggie blinked a few times and put his hand to his face. 'Why did you do that?'

Banecroft gave him an assessing look then released his grip on his arm. 'What did you think you were doing?'

'I was . . .' Reggie looked at the carpet in confusion for a second. 'I was going to pick up the book. I need to protect it. There was a voice telling me to.'

'Take a look,' said Banecroft, waving in the direction of the bed. 'Does it look like the book is the thing in need of protection around here?'

Reggie threw a hand over his mouth as if expecting to throw up.

'The voice,' said Sturgess. 'I heard it too, just before I passed out. Telling me I had to help it.'

Reggie dropped his hand. 'I recognized it. I think it was my sister.'

Sturgess thought for a second. 'My late mother.'

'Right,' said Banecroft, looking at Sturgess. 'You need to get this fella an ambulance and I need to find something to put this book in so I can get it the hell out of here.'

'Hang on a second. How come it isn't affecting you?'

'Well,' said Banecroft, 'while I'd like to put it down to my mental strength, hardy constitution and high-fibre diet' – he pulled an old-fashioned key out of his pocket – 'I imagine it's because I'm carrying this. It's a key to the office and, apparently, it protects the bearer from being affected by certain types of magic.' He turned to Reggie. 'I'm assuming you don't have one with you?'

Reggie shook his head.

'All right,' said Sturgess, 'but you can't touch the book. It's evidence.'

'Of what exactly, Detective Inspector? Are you going to charge it with GBH? You might want to accept that we're now a little outside the scope of the law.'

'But . . .'

'If you keep this book,' said Banecroft, 'what's going to happen? It'll end up in an evidence locker, where it'll start whispering to somebody new. Then we'll find that unfortunate soul in the same state, or worse, than this poor fool, and where will that get us?'

'So what are you going to do with it?'

'Well,' said Banecroft, 'first, I'm going to get it the hell out of here, and then I'm going to try very hard indeed to destroy the thing.'

'How?'

'I have not got the first idea, but I reckon a bonfire would be a good start. Failing that, I know a couple of people I can ask, who know a lot of other people they can ask, and none of them are going to talk to the GMP.'

Sturgess considered this for a long second before pulling his car keys out of his pocket and tossing them across to Banecroft. 'Take my car, and be careful.'

'I won't leave a scratch.'

'I didn't mean the car,' said Sturgess, now tapping away at his phone. 'Although do be careful with the car. And hurry – I'm putting in a priority call, so this place will be crawling with ambulance and police in about five minutes.'

46

It never ends.

Again and again, Stella found herself back on that boat, sharing that cigarette. Watching that rabbit run across the field. Burying the first body, walking by the last. This time he has the boy and, no matter what, he will not let go. He is staying with him. He can't save Quinnie or any of the others, but if he can save the boy, then it won't have been for nothing. If he can save the boy, then he is not nothing.

Finally, Stella wakes. Only to realize that she hasn't. She is still Manny and he has woken up from another nightmare, cowering in the corner, his knuckles bloodied for some reason. His Rosa, his sweet Rosa, is looking down at him, speaking to him softly. Her eyes are full of love, concern for him, and he finds himself hating her for it.

Then he's in a pub, drinking. He doesn't dance any more but he does drink now. Somebody says something and before Manny knows it, he's hit the man. He's on top of him, raining down punches. His heartbeat thunders in his ears, and that taste. People are dragging him away. Some of them look like they want to tear him apart.

He wakes in a cell, shaking. A policeman is standing there; Rosa, embarrassed, by his side. They are walking home, arguing now.

Manny leaves. Finds a different pub. A different fight. He is woken up on a bench by an elderly park warden poking him with a stick.

He goes home. More fights. He goes to work. They make him do a succession of jobs – there's still a war on, even if he refuses to fight it. He works. He drinks. He and Rosa fight. He leaves. He drinks. And there are women, too. All he wants is sweet oblivion but, try as he might, he can't find it.

Then he's back on that boat again.

He and Rosa argue again – a bad one this time. He sleeps on the chair in the front room, only to wake and find himself cowering in the corner once more, screaming, howling, knuckles bloodied. The boy. The smoke. He's there, holding out his hands, begging him just to take him.

Rosa stands at the far side of the room and, behind her, Manny sees Dottie – his Dottie. His angel. She is clinging to her mother's nightie, hiding behind her legs because she is terrified. Terrified of him. And his heart breaks into a billion jagged pieces.

And then he's walking.

Let it end.

Please, let it end.

Stella doesn't know if that's her thought or Manny's.

Please let it end.

There is a way. There is one way. There is only one way.

47

Ox stood there, notepad in hand, and for the life of him, he couldn't think what to write down. Luckily, a resident of the pleasant-looking terraced house he was standing outside opened the front door, hopefully to offer him some much-needed context.

The man glanced up and down the street, where many of his neighbours were gathered, talking excitedly. 'What are you lot looking at?'

'The weird horse,' said a little boy, who was not yet familiar with the concept of rhetorical questions.

'It's not a horse.'

'What is it, then?'

'It's none of your business, fella. That's what it is. None of your business.'

'It's a unicorn,' came a shout from somewhere.

The man looked up at this. 'Those don't exist, ya daft bugger. Can my family and I please get a little bit of privacy?'

The woman who lived opposite, and who was filming it with her phone, said, 'Screw that, Joel. You've got a unicorn's head sticking out your front-room window.'

'And you do not have my permission to film it,' he barked in reply.

'It's a free country,' the woman said defiantly.

'And who are you?' snapped the man, this time in Ox's direction.

'I'm the . . . I'm from *The Stranger Times*. You rang us.'

'I did,' he confirmed. 'And what the hell am I supposed to do about this?'

'Well,' said Ox, looking at the blank page of his notebook again, 'first things first. What's your name?'

'Joel Tigner.'

'Are you the homeowner?'

'I am.'

'And are you the owner of the . . .' Ox left his question hanging, seeing how Mr Tigner had reacted to the previous mention of the U word.

'Unicorn,' Mr Tigner whispered. 'No. We just came home and there it was. Standing in the front room, having attacked the Christmas tree and smashed the fuck out of the presents.'

'I see. Do you have any idea how it got there?'

'Well, I didn't leave a key out for it. Nobody broke in. All I know is my daughter, like every other six-year-old girl, wants a unicorn and now we've got a bloody unicorn.'

Ox leaned a little closer and studied the animal that was currently poking its head out of the open window of the front room. It looked back at him with an air of indifference and a hint of a snarl. 'I presume it's a horse that someone has stuck a horn on.'

'That's what I thought too, but look at it. Does that look stuck on to you?'

'No,' admitted Ox.

'And then there's the other thing.'

'What other thing?'

Mr Tigner shifted nervously and lowered his voice. 'It shat out a rainbow.'

'Excuse me?'

'I know how it sounds but I'm telling ya, me and the missus were standing there, arguing about what to do, when it lifts its tail, shits out a rainbow.'

'Right. Did you get a picture of that?'

'A picture?' echoed Mr Tigner, sounding affronted. 'What kind of a pervert do you think I am?'

'Right. Sorry. Is it still in there?'

'The rainbow? No. Shot out through the back of the house. Broke the kitchen window and all. Who's going to pay to fix that, I ask you?'

Ox looked up from scribbling notes and realized that the man was expecting an answer. 'Ehm, have you got insurance?'

'That's what the wife said,' said Mr Tigner. 'Not sure what this'll come under, though. More importantly, what the hell am I supposed to do with a unicorn? The dog is absolutely terrified.'

'Right. RSPCA?'

'I've tried them and the council.'

'Nothing?'

'You try explaining to someone that there's a unicorn in your front room and see how long it is before they hang up. The bloke from the council said something very unprofessional. I'll be lodging a complaint. I pay my taxes.'

'Right, I—' Ox's phone had begun to ring. 'Sorry, I'm going to have to take this.' He stepped away.

'Ox.'

'You're not going to believe this, Grace—'

'Before you get into that, I've got a lot more calls. The phones are still ringing off the hook. I don't know what to do with them all.'

'Aren't any of the others about?'

'Reggie and Hannah are off with Vincent and that nice DI Sturgess, and Stella is doing her essay, remember, so I'm leaving her be.'

'So it's just me?'

'For the moment. Don't go to that thing in Ancoats – I'll try to get Reggie to head there when he's back. I need you to go to Chorlton. There's a very irate woman who wants us around straight away.'

'Right,' said Ox, as he turned to see a young girl, presumably Mr Tigner's daughter, standing outside their house, happily feeding a ham sandwich to the unicorn while her parents tried to encourage her to come away from it.

'Something very strange is going on, Ox,' said Grace.

'Yeah,' he replied. 'I think you might be right.'

48

'Baladin!' Dr Carter screamed at the top of her lungs.

She was watching the map of Manchester on the big screen in her office. It allowed her, on behalf of the Founders, to monitor for any 'magical incidents' in real time and coordinate a response so that the great unwashed remained blissfully unaware of the true nature of the world. The problem was the damned thing was lighting up like someone had just turned on the Christmas lights. It wasn't just that every couple of seconds a new alert flashed up, or that the smaller screens to either side of it were scrolling through social-media posts so fast that it was impossible to track them. The most worrying element of this shit stew was that the alerts had a three-colour grading system – yellow, orange and red – and some of the dots appeared to be escalating from one level to the next at impossible speed.

'This cannot be right,' she said. 'This cannot be right. Bala—'

'Yes?' said Tamsin, rushing through the door.

'What the hell is going on?'

'I don't know.'

'What do you mean, you don't know? How can you not know? I came out of an emergency meeting about bloody desserts and suddenly there are alerts all over the place.' She jabbed a finger at the screen. 'Chorlton just went from yellow to red without even hitting orange. This AI monitoring system you put such stock in is having some sort of massive breakdown on the worst day imaginable.'

'No, it isn't,' said Tamsin. 'There really are this many alerts happening.'

'How?'

'I don't know.'

'I don't know,' snarled Dr Carter, 'is not an acceptable answer from the person in charge of damage control for this city.'

'I—'

'Shut up.' Dr Carter didn't need to hear it. Tamsin Baladin wasn't in charge of that – not yet. It was still very much her job for one more day.

She looked again at the map, where the situation was worsening by the second.

'Right, get every single resource we have up and running. Prioritize the reds.'

'There isn't enough—'

'I know that, just do it. We need to find the source.'

'The source?' asked Tamsin.

'A massive outpouring of magic like this doesn't just happen,' Dr Carter said, waving a hand at the screen. 'This is all coming from somewhere. We need to find out from where and shut it down, fast.'

Before the bloody Council finds out and my world comes tumbling down, she added to herself.

49

Hannah looked around her apartment. The place needed a good, deep clean and she'd promised herself that over the Christmas break that was exactly what she was going to give it. She was aware that when people asked if you had big plans for Christmas, that was not generally what they meant. Still, although this apartment was the smallest place she'd ever lived, having gone from her parents' house to the various frankly unnecessarily big pads she and her ex-husband, Karl, had shared, she took a weird pride in this cramped, ground-floor flat. For the first time it was hers, just hers, and that made it special in a way nowhere else had been.

To say the Christmas break hadn't gone to plan so far was the mother of all understatements. Reggie had rung with an update on the horror show they'd found at the poor librarian's house and, since then, she'd called Sturgess every five minutes until he'd finally picked up. She'd badgered him until he'd promised that he'd drop around to her flat as soon as he was able to leave the crime scene that the librarian's house was being treated as, even though there was no crime on the books that could begin to describe what had happened there.

She'd known better than to try the 'there's something really important I need to tell you' trick again, so she'd gone with the logical approach that so much had happened and they needed to go over everything to make sure they weren't missing anything important. While it was a ruse to get him there, it did strike her that it was also a good idea. Some bloodthirsty old god had broken through to their world and was currently on a rampage around Manchester doing who knows what, having been summoned through the use of some awful book of pure evil. Even by the standard of recent events, it felt like something very bad was afoot and they had no idea who or what was behind it.

A knock sounded on her front door. She shifted the can of Diet Coke on the counter in front of her nervously.

'Right,' she said out loud. 'Here we go.'

As she opened the door, she couldn't help but notice that Sturgess looked even paler and more stressed than usual. 'Thanks for coming,' she said, letting him in.

'Sure. Nice place.' It was the first time he'd been there.

'Thanks. Reggie told me all about the . . .'

'Yeah, it was something, all right. Poor Richard Duff's been taken to hospital. Ambulance crew had to knock him out. Once Banecroft took the book away, he – well, it wasn't pleasant.'

'How awful,' said Hannah, moving across the room. 'Can I get you a drink?'

'I'm OK, thanks,' said Sturgess. 'Mind if I sit down?'

'Sorry, yes, of course. Can I take your coat?'

He plonked himself down on the sofa. 'I should probably get

going pretty soon. I've got to get back to the station. DI Clarke shouldn't be interrogating that Xander guy on his own – he's no idea what he's dealing with. Plus, the creepy bastard seems to be the only person who might have some answers.'

'Do you mean . . .'

'Xander,' clarified Sturgess. 'Clarke might be a creepy bastard in his own way, but he's clueless when it comes to answers that aren't about who else to blame.'

'I imagine whatever's going on is well beyond him.'

Sturgess sighed loudly and rubbed at his eyes. 'Well, it's beyond me, so I wouldn't hold out much hope of Clarke making some kind of breakthrough. He can't even find one blood-soaked librarian.'

'Even if he did,' said Hannah, 'she'd probably be useless to us. According to Banecroft, this Zalas character seems to be able to jump from person to person. Are you sure you won't have a drink? I'm having one.'

'I just had one, thanks. Are you positive Banecroft won't share his source with me?'

'I mean, I could ask, but you know what he's like.'

'Yes,' said Sturgess. 'A deliberately obstructive pain in my arse.'

'That's certainly one way of putting it. Do you think this poor librarian – I mean the other librarian, the guy . . .'

'Duff,' offered Sturgess.

'Yeah, him. Do you think he'll be able to tell us anything?'

'My guess is not much, and not for a while. They'll have to operate on him to save whatever they can and . . .' Sturgess visibly shuddered, the memory of the man's injuries sending a wave of revulsion through him.

'Do we know why he took the book away?'

'It . . . seemed to be able to control people. It tried it on me but I passed out.'

'Really?'

'Yeah. Banecroft was able to cope with it because, apparently, the keys to your office protect whoever's holding them from being attacked through the medium of magic.'

'Oh,' said Hannah, 'he told you about that?'

'Yes, but only because he had to. Banecroft, not unlike everyone else around here, only tells me things when there's no other option.'

'Ouch,' said Hannah.

'Sorry, it's just . . . It's been a hell of a couple of days and, in a personal career low point, I've just given Banecroft of all people the book – aka a key piece of evidence – to destroy.'

'How's he going to do that?'

'I don't know, but I assume he's going to ask another one of those sources he refuses to share with me.' He eased himself to his feet. 'You know what, I should get going. I'm nowhere near understanding what's happening and Xander is the only person I can think of who might provide answers.'

'All right,' said Hannah, 'but before you do, I'm going to ring Banecroft. I'll tell him he has to share his sources with you or . . . or . . . I'll resign.'

'I don't want you to—'

'No,' said Hannah firmly. 'I insist. Let me just grab my phone.'

She turned to the counter and picked up the can of Diet Coke. 'And drink this thing, would you, please? I've already opened it.'

He took it. 'OK.'

Hannah scooped up her phone and tapped at the screen.

'It's ringing.'

He stood there watching her.

Hannah grabbed the glass of squash she'd poured herself earlier. 'My throat is killing me. Think I'm coming down with something.'

As she took a long drink, Sturgess did too.

'Yes,' said Hannah. 'Vincent, it's me. I need to talk to you, and you need to listen to me. I want you to stop being so bloody awkward and start sharing your sources with Sturgess.'

Sturgess blinked once, twice.

'This investigation is important,' she continued, 'and . . .'

She trailed off as Sturgess slumped to the ground.

'Tom?'

He didn't stir.

She hung up the phone call she hadn't actually made.

'He's out.'

John Mór emerged from her bedroom. 'Bloody hell, took you long enough.'

'Are you sure we should be doing this?'

He stopped. 'You rang me, remember?'

'I know.'

'Begged me for my help, in fact.'

'I know.'

'Pleaded.'

'All right, I know, I know. It's just . . . drugging him?'

'What other option did you have?' asked John Mór, heaving Sturgess up and on to the sofa.

'None.'

'Well, there you go, then.'

'So what do we do now?' asked Hannah.

'Before we get to that,' said John Mór, 'some kind of Pavlovian response, I guess, but any chance I could get a drink?'

50

Grace was sitting behind her desk, the phone receiver held to her right ear while she pressed her left hand against her other ear, trying to block out the sound of all of the phones in the office ringing at once. 'I'm sorry, can you say that again? Could you perhaps—'

She pulled the receiver away from her ear and stared at it in disbelief. 'They hung up? How rude.'

Movement at the other end of the room attracted her attention and she looked up to see Banecroft wearily climbing the stairs, with Reggie following a few steps behind.

'Thank the Lord you are back,' she said.

Banecroft looked pointedly at the box he was carrying. 'I'm not sure the Lord is with us today.'

'He is always with you,' responded Grace automatically.

'And yet he never splits a bill. Why are the phones going mental?' asked Banecroft.

'We are having an emergency,' said Grace. 'Crazy things are happening all over the city.'

Banecroft sighed. 'Why am I not surprised?'

'Ox is out trying to cover them, but we are getting swamped by calls.'

'Right,' said Banecroft. 'Where are Hannah and Stella?'

'I thought Hannah was with you?'

'No,' said Reggie. 'She ran off. Said something about Christmas shopping, which I'm assuming was a lie.'

'And Stella?' asked Banecroft, raising his voice to be heard over the din.

'I haven't seen her. She's working on her big essay and the door is locked.'

'OK. Not to spoil the illusion but you know the lock on her door is actually just a sign she flips over?'

'We all agreed to respect it,' said Reggie.

I think she is in a mood,' offered Grace.

'Is she?' said Banecroft. 'Well, we must be sensitive to that, of course. STELLA, GET YOUR MOODY ARSE OUT HERE NOW OR YOU'RE FIRED!'

'Congratulations on your sensitivity,' said Reggie.

'It's a gift. If she's not here in thirty seconds, God help me!'

'I doubt he will,' said Reggie, 'so I suppose I'll have to.'

As Reggie headed off towards Stella's room, Banecroft made his way towards Grace, carrying a Carcassonne box held out in front of him.

'Why do you have a board game with you?' asked Grace, indicating Banecroft's cargo.

'I don't – the box was just a handy size.'

'For what?'

'You know how I sometimes say "you don't want to know" and then you proceed to needle me because me saying that only makes you want to know more?'

'Yes.'

'This one time, please believe me, you seriously do not want to know. By the way, have you still got a key to the office?'

'Yes.'

'Good.' He placed the box down on the desk and stretched out his back. 'Is there anything we could do about all the phones ringing?'

'You could answer them?'

He gave her a look.

'Or I could turn the ringers off.'

'There we go. That sounds more like—'

They both turned at the sound of Reggie screaming.

Banecroft reached Stella's room just before Grace did. They were greeted by the sight of Reggie standing over Stella, who was lying on the floor, shaking violently, her eyes closed as she rambled feverishly.

'What the hell?' said Banecroft.

'I just found her like this,' said Reggie, placing his hand on her forehead. 'She's burning up.'

'Oh my God!' wailed Grace, blessing herself.

'Get her up. We're taking her to the hospital. Now. Grace, go start your car.'

Grace remained rooted to the spot, transfixed in horror, looking down at Stella.

'Grace!' shouted Banecroft, which snapped her out of it and sent her scurrying towards the stairs.

A minute later, Reggie and Banecroft had carried Stella downstairs and out the front door to where Grace's car was waiting. They eased her on to the back seat as carefully as they could.

'OK,' said Reggie. 'Let's go.'

Banecroft looked back towards the office, where he'd left a certain box sitting on the reception desk. 'Damn it. You go. I'd better stay here and . . .'

Reggie nodded and rushed around to the front passenger seat.

'Ring me as soon as—'

The car had already sped off before Banecroft could finish his thought, with Grace driving in a very un-Grace-like manner.

He turned around to find Manny standing at the front door, looking sombre. Banecroft went to walk past him but stopped and looked him square in the eye. 'I don't pretend to know what is going on, but I do know this – if she is hurt in any way and it turns out you're responsible, you'll need a lot more than that damned angel to help you.'

51

Ox got off his bike and doubled-checked this was indeed the address Grace had texted him. A semi-detached house in Chorlton. Satisfied it was, he locked his bike to a tree and walked up the garden path. He didn't get a chance to ring the bell before the front door flew open.

'Are you from the Co-op?' asked the blonde woman with the pinched face who was looking at him like a tax bill.

'No, I'm . . . ehm, from *The Stranger Times*.'

'Oh. And do you know who we're supposed to talk to about this?'

'I . . . I . . . To be honest, I just received a text with this address. I don't even know what this is about.'

Before the woman could respond, a man appeared behind her, holding a phone. 'I've been on to them again. Even when I finally convinced someone it wasn't a joke, they said it wasn't their problem.'

'Clearly it is, Derek' said the woman. 'I mean, we paid for a service and . . .' She gestured to the door leading to their front room with her hand.

'You don't need to convince me of that, Veronica. I've asked to speak to a manager.' Her husband stopped and eyed Ox suspiciously. 'Who's this guy?'

'He's from that *Stranger Times* newspaper.'

Derek's face darkened. 'Go on, get out of here, you vulture.'

'Stop it,' said Veronica. 'I rang them.'

'Why?'

'Why?' she repeated. 'Because we don't know what to do, the police aren't interested, and you said yourself the Co-op aren't going to help.'

'Well, who does he think we should ring?'

'I've no idea,' said Ox, growing annoyed at being spoken over, 'because you still haven't told me what the problem is?'

In response, the woman motioned for him to step inside. She looked up and down the street before shutting the front door behind them, then started speaking in a stage whisper. 'I'll tell you what the problem is. My daughter is mad about my old uncle Bertie. Always loved him.'

'He was mad about her, too,' chimed the husband. 'Never had any kids of his own.'

'He was always very kind to us growing up,' continued Veronica, retaking control of the narrative. 'A lovely, sweet man. So, he naturally became a sort of surrogate grandfather to Maisie.'

'Right,' said Ox, still not seeing the point of any of this.

The woman opened the door to their lounge where Ox took in the wholesome sight of an elderly gentleman in an armchair by the fire, reading a storybook to a little girl sitting cross-legged in front of him, clearly entranced.

The woman closed the door again.

'All seems very nice,' said Ox.

'Yes,' said Derek, 'only Bertie died six months ago.'

'What?'

'Yes,' confirmed his wife. 'I nipped out to pick up some whipped cream, came back and there he is, sitting there by the fire, asking for a cup of tea.'

'How did he—' started Ox.

'If we knew that,' snapped the man, 'we'd know what to do with him, not to mention the answer to some of life's bigger theological questions. All we do know is that the police aren't interested in people being found alive and well, the church doesn't have an emergency number you can ring and, despite us having paid Co-op Funeral Services a pretty penny to bury him, they've got what I can only call an appalling attitude to customer aftercare. Now, what can we do about this?'

Ox knew neither the answer to that question nor why anyone would reasonably expect him to have it. He never got the chance to express this, however, as, from outside the house, came the sound of screaming.

52

Hannah watched nervously as John Mór settled the unconscious Sturgess on her sofa.

'And you're sure this will work?' she asked.

'I am no more or less sure than the last three times you asked me that,' he responded.

Hannah was well aware she had long since worn out John Mór's goodwill, but she couldn't stop herself from fretting. 'I mean, we don't have any other options. We have to do this. It was either this or we let him interrogate Xander, and we all know what could happen there.'

'I agree with everything you just said, other than your continued use of the word "we",' said John Mór. 'This is all you – I'm not even here.'

'Right. Sorry. And thank you.'

'What are you thanking me for?'

'Your help with—'

'I'm—'

'Not here,' finished Hannah. 'Right. I've got that.'

Seemingly satisfied with DI Sturgess's position, John Mór moved around to behind the back of the sofa and pulled what looked a lot like a divining rod out of the small rucksack he'd brought with him.

'Seriously?'

He shot her a dirty look.

'Sorry, again. Sorry. I talk when I'm nervous.'

'Margo is like that, too.'

'Really?'

'Well, if you substitute spectacular acts of violence for talking.'

'What's the deal with you and her?'

He folded his arms and his look of exasperation made Hannah wince.

'Wow,' she said. 'I have no idea where that came from. It was so inappropriate. I don't even know where to begin.'

'Shutting up strikes me as a really good starting point.'

Hannah mimed locking her lips and throwing away the key.

John Mór took a little, carved wooden statue of a goat's head and placed it in Sturgess's right hand. Then he held the divining rod in both hands above the unconscious police officer's head and started to hum. This carried on for quite some time.

Nothing seemed to be happening.

Hannah noticed John Mór open his left eye slightly and take a sneaky peak to confirm that nothing was happening.

Eventually, he stopped humming and stood there looking rather embarrassed. Hannah resisted the urge to say anything as he scratched at his beard contemplatively.

'Wait a sec,' he said to himself as much as to anyone else. He looked at his hands and then at Sturgess, seemingly figuring something out. Finally, he reached forward and transferred the statue into Sturgess's left hand. 'Been a while since I done one of these,' he mumbled, before raising the divining rod again and resuming the humming.

After a minute or so, Hannah was starting to wonder if this was going to work at all when she noticed the rather sickly sight of the flesh on Sturgess's scalp beginning to undulate. After a few more seconds, an eyeball on a stalk popped out, causing Hannah to jump. It was precisely what she wanted, and indeed, hoped to happen, but some things you just never get used to.

The eyeball scanned the room and John Mór dived behind the sofa for cover, seemingly keen to limit his involvement. After a second, the eyeball focused on Hannah.

She stood up. 'Hello, my name is Hannah Willis and I am the assistant editor of *The Stranger Times*.'

In response, Sturgess's eyes flew open and his mouth started to move, although the voice that came out wasn't his. It sounded like a peculiar amalgamation of his and that of a female. 'Good Lord, are you giving a talk to a school assembly?'

'I needed to speak to you,' said Hannah.

'I'm glad to hear it,' said the voice. 'I was worried I'd been called accidentally as part of one of your kinky sex games.'

'What? No, I . . .'

The eyeball started looking around the room more urgently. 'There's no way you could have done this on your own. Who did you have to . . . Aha!' said the voice triumphantly, as the eyeball peered down behind the couch.

John Mór straightened himself up, looking embarrassed and holding one of Hannah's slippers. 'I found it. There it is.'

'Gods save us,' said whatever you could call Sturgess at this point.

Hannah had never seen an eyeball on a stalk roll its entire self, and she wouldn't have thought it was possible, but the thing certainly gave it a good shot. 'I'm rather busy at the moment, so if you don't mind . . .'

'I do,' said Hannah firmly. 'Xander knows about you, and so we need to make sure that DI Sturgess doesn't attempt to interrogate him or else – well, you know what will happen.'

Hannah added a double-take to the things she didn't think it was possible for an eyeball on a stalk to do.

'I'm sorry,' said the voice, 'the one known as Xander is not only in Manchester but also in police custody?'

'Yes,' said Hannah, taken aback. 'Wait, don't you see everything Sturgess sees?'

'I can . . .' said the voice slowly, 'but it doesn't mean I do. I have other matters to attend to at times. Why did . . . When did . . .'

Hannah realized that the voice at the other end, which she guessed belonged to the woman known as Dr Carter, was wrongfooted. 'How did the police capture a Stander?'

'Ehm . . .' faltered Hannah, who was now wondering if she should perhaps not be telling this thing stuff it didn't already know.

'Never mind. I've a good idea.' The eyeball swivelled around to look at John Mór. 'How's retirement treating you, Mr Mór?'

'It's not Mr Mór,' he said petulantly. 'It's John Mór, as you bloody well know. Let's not pretend we don't know who is on the other end of this.'

'Pardon me.' The eyeball turned back to Hannah. 'What has he done?'

'Do you mean John or—'

'Xander!' snapped the voice. 'I assume he has been arrested for a very good reason.'

'I . . .'

'And rest assured, if you don't tell me, I can and will get the information out of the good inspector. It'll just take a little longer and be incredibly painful for him.'

Out of the corner of her eye, Hannah noticed John Mór give a small, begrudging nod of confirmation.

'We believe he was responsible for giving a book called the *Black Grimoire* to Debra Brimson, a librarian who—'

'The murder at the library? Good gods. The *Black Grimoire*. That explains a lot. I . . .'

Without another word, Sturgess's eyes closed and his head slumped to the side. The eyeball took a final look around and then, with a truly unpleasant sucking noise, disappeared back to where it'd come from.

'She's gone,' said John Mór.

'But . . .' said Hannah. 'She didn't confirm she wouldn't . . .'

'Forget that,' snapped John Mór. His whole demeanour had changed. 'When were you going to tell me about the *Black Grimoire*?'

'What?' said Hannah. 'Sorry. I didn't not mention it, I just . . .'

'Do you know what that is?' he asked angrily. 'Do you have the first idea?'

'No.'

'No,' he repeated. 'No, you don't. Most people don't even think it's real. A book of pure evil used to bind ancient evils, because that's the only way you can contain 'em. Something that dangerous is knocking about Manchester and you've got me pissing about helping you keep your boyfriend out of trouble.'

'What? No, I . . .'

She was denied the chance to say anything else as John Mór opened the front door and stormed out. Or at least he tried to. The effect was ruined when he forgot to duck and slammed his head into the lintel. He swore furiously before slamming the door behind him.

Hannah considered going after him, but her phone, which was on the counter, started to ring.

She answered it. 'Reggie, now isn't . . .' And then, for the second time in two days, Hannah was told she had to get to the hospital immediately. 'I'll be right there.'

She hung up and spun around in a panic, trying to find her coat, before stopping at the sight of the unconscious detective inspector she still had on her sofa.

53

'Tamsin!' This time the word came out as a screech.

Her mind having quite literally just been elsewhere, Dr Carter was experiencing that familiar moment of discombobulation as she got used to being in her own body again, which, on this occasion, was sitting in her office. She glanced up at the large screen on the wall, where multiple red lights were now flashing in all areas.

Tamsin Baladin came rushing into the room. 'I was just attempting to—'

'Xander.'

Baladin stopped and looked surprised. 'I'm sorry?'

Dr Carter got to her feet and started to walk around her desk towards her subordinate. 'You remember Xander? He was that damned fool Dominic Johnson's assistant. You were tasked with helping him with his stupid plan that blew up in his face so spectacularly and led to his untimely but unmourned death.'

'Yes, but . . .'

'You met him. You knew him. You worked with him.'

'Hardly. I—'

'When were you going to tell me he's still in Manchester?'

Tamsin Baladin gave looking shocked another go. 'He is? But you asked me to check at the time. If you remember, we had visual confirmation of him getting on a flight to—'

'Well, he's back. If indeed he ever left, and he has apparently unleashed the bloody *Black Grimoire* on us.'

'Is that bad?'

'That,' said Dr Carter, glaring at her butter-wouldn't-melt underling, before waving a hand at the screen, 'explains not only all this but also the worse that is undoubtedly about to come. The world is crumbling down around our ears, and rest assured it is because of Xander and whoever is pulling his strings.'

'Who would—'

'Oh, I don't know,' said Dr Carter, a cold rage filling her belly as she looked at the person her gut told her was responsible. 'But I do know that Standers are never the organ grinder, only the monkey. Someone is behind him and believe me, when I find out who it is – and I will – my vengeance shall be swift and terrible.'

'As it should be,' said Tamsin. 'How can we find out who it is?'

Dr Carter narrowed her eyes. 'Don't you worry your pretty little head about it, Tamsin, dear. I'm heading over to talk to him right now. As you know, I hold a substantial amount of sway with our friends in the GMP. Standers, of course, are famously loyal to their employers, and people say they will never betray a confidence.'

'Is that so?'

'But don't worry,' said Dr Carter with a cold smile, 'the people who started that little rumour did not have access to the methods I have to squeeze the truthy goodness out of someone.'

'That is good news,' replied Tamsin.

Dr Carter had no doubt that if the woman had a mind to, she would be a magnificent poker player.

'Yes, rest assured I will get the truth of this. Every last drop of it.'

54

Hannah narrowly avoided stumbling as she staggered up the remaining flight of stairs to the third floor of the Manchester Royal Infirmary building where she'd been directed. She was fully aware that she was a hot sweaty mess but right then, she couldn't have cared less. After spending a futile few minutes in an attempt to find a taxi amid the chaos of last-minute Christmas Eve shoppers, she'd abandoned the idea and just run to the hospital. It was almost two miles from her flat to where she was now standing, but sheer terror and adrenalin had carried her most of the way there.

From the little she had gleaned from Reggie's phone call, Stella had been found in her room in some kind of feverish state they couldn't wake her up from. Hannah's mind had been a whirl of emotions as she'd dodged dawdling pedestrians and made her way up Oxford Road. She felt terrible because she'd said she was going to talk to Stella and then hadn't. She'd let other things get in the way and now, along with fear, her guilt over that gnawed at her.

She started to run down the hall and would've missed Grace and Reggie entirely if Reggie hadn't shouted after her. The pair were sitting alone in a room that was bare apart from a couple of sofas, and Reggie was comforting Grace as she tearfully worked her way through a box of tissues. As soon as Hannah sat down beside them, Grace dragged her into a hug.

'What do we know?' Hannah asked, still struggling to catch her breath.

'Not a lot more than I told you over the phone,' said Reggie. 'They put her in a room up the hall. We haven't seen her since. The doctor's in with her now.'

'That poor child,' said Grace. 'She was suffering alone in her room for the good Lord only knows how long, and we had no idea.'

'That's not important now, Grace,' said Hannah in as calm a voice as she could muster. 'What matters is that she's in the best place possible.' She looked over at Reggie. 'Do we know what's wrong with her?'

He shook his head.

'The doctor in A and E kept asking us if she had taken any-thing,' said Grace. 'Stella does not do drugs. I told him. She does not.'

'Now, now, Grace, dear,' soothed Reggie. 'We talked about this. They were just going through the questions they have to ask.'

'Stella does not do drugs,' repeated Grace, clutching a ragged tissue between her fingers tightly.

'Ah, Ms Willis.'

Hannah looked up with a sinking heart to confirm that the Scottish brogue did indeed belong to the self-same Dr Black she had met previously.

'We have to stop meeting like this,' the doctor continued. 'People will start to talk.'

'How is she?' asked Hannah.

'Just for once, it'd be nice if someone asked about me.'

'Has anyone ever told you that you've got the most appalling bedside manner?' snapped Hannah.

'Yes, actually. Several times.'

'I can believe it.'

The doctor looked at the clipboard he was holding, although not in a way that suggested he was consulting it. 'What can I tell you? You want customer service, go private. I mainly do medicine. You are all members of staff at *The Stranger Times*, correct?'

'Yes,' confirmed Reggie, exchanging a look with Hannah. 'How is that relevant?'

'Maybe it isn't,' he said. 'Who can say? Follow me, please.'

He turned and walked out of the room. They all got up and hurried to follow him.

'In the name of the good Lord, man, tell me how Stella is?' shouted Grace after him.

'Oh, did I not mention?' replied the doctor. 'Mostly stable.'

'Mostly?' said Grace. 'What does "mostly" mean?'

In lieu of a response, Dr Black pushed open the door to a room. Stella was lying on a bed inside, unconscious, with a drip hooked up to her arm and various machines taking readings. The trio all rushed to her side.

'Stella,' murmured Grace, brushing the hair from the young girl's forehead tearfully. 'It's Grace. I am here. So are Hannah and Reginald.'

'She is unconscious,' clarified Dr Black, 'which is mostly a good thing. Well, I say that – it's a mixed bag.'

'I do not like you,' said Grace, turning around angrily. 'I would like a better doctor.'

'None are available,' replied Dr Black.

'Well, one that doesn't stink of filthy cigarettes, then.'

'Those are available, but trust me, you don't want them, you want me.'

'I don't think we do,' said Hannah.

'What is Stella?' he asked.

'Excuse me?' said Reggie.

'What is she?'

'What the hell kind of question is that?' asked Hannah.

Dr Black sighed and then, still looking at his clipboard, gave a twirl of his finger. The door to the room slammed shut behind him and the venetian blinds on the window closed themselves with a thrumming noise. 'Very well,' he began. 'To clarify my credentials' – the contents of the fruit bowl sitting on the drawers next to the door proceeded to float up into the air where they spun and circled above their heads – 'I am not what you would term an ordinary doctor.'

'Oh,' said Hannah.

'Indeed,' continued Dr Black. 'I am somewhat of an unofficial specialist. So much so that virtually nobody here knows I am one. You see, other doctors just understand human physiology – or at least they're supposed to. I have that knowledge plus that of the many variations that exist among the Folk, not to mention the entirely different species living among us that most people assume are human because, well, they've been conditioned to believe everybody else is human. And that's not even factoring in the numerous and dramatic effects magic and related powers can have upon a subject, all of which I'm the only person within many a mile who has the first idea how to treat. So, believe me when I say you definitely do want me as Stella's doctor. You want me because of all that and because I can say, with no humility whatsoever, that I am a genius, which I think we can all agree is handy.'

He finally looked up from his clipboard at the three people gawping at him in stupefied silence. 'Oh, and to go back to your remark about the smell of cigarettes. I am, as mentioned, a genius, and in an overworked and understaffed NHS I have to keep my workload manageable so that I can be available to intercept all Folk-related medical matters before the normies start trying to deal with them and lose their tiny minds. Through exhaustive deductive testing I've found that the smell of cigarettes is the best way to do that. Not even smokers want a doctor who smells of cigarettes. I, in fact, don't smoke. Never have. I do, however, enjoy a good single malt, if you're looking to do any last-minute gift purchasing. I'm also quite partial to a chocolate-covered Brazil nut – can't get enough of them. Now we've cleared all that up, let's return to my original question – what is Stella?'

Hannah patted Grace on the arm because she looked as if she was finding all this a bit much. She couldn't blame her – she was too. 'We don't know.'

'OK,' said Dr Black. 'Thank you for the clarification, Ms Willis.'

'How do you know my name?'

'Really?' said Dr Black, raising one of his magnificently bushy eyebrows. 'I go through all that, and me knowing your name is the surprising bit, is it?' He glanced up and noticed the apples, pears, mandarins and oranges that were still circling overhead. With a casual wave of his hand, he sent them back to their fruit bowl. 'By the way, that was a magnificently accurate rendering of the orbital cycle of our solar system I'd created. Just thought I'd point it out as nobody seemed to notice.'

'For the love of God, man,' said Reggie, 'will you tell us what the hell is wrong with Stella?'

'Oh, you really don't know?'

'No,' they all answered in perfect unison.

'Interesting. I assumed, given what you do for a living . . . OK, well, she has been infected with someone else's life.'

'Excuse me?' said Hannah.

'Someone else's memories have been put into her, and that's the kind of thing a mind doesn't like. There's currently a battle going on inside her as . . . Well, think of it like an organ transplant, and she's rejecting the organ.'

Grace gave a small whimper.

'That's actually a good thing. If she accepted them – well, then she'd cease to be her. And you say you really don't know what she is?'

'No,' said Hannah. 'To put it in the rather cold terms you seem keen to use, not even she knows what she is.'

'That is genuinely fascinating, as you could argue the next most likely person to know is me, and I haven't got a scooby.'

'So you're not as clever as you think?' said Reggie.

'Oh no,' Dr Black said mildly, 'I definitely am. It's more that she is quite possibly one of one, and believe me, that is truly something.'

'Forget all that. Will she be OK?' asked Grace, looking like she'd moved on to the stage where she would happily throttle the doctor.

'I don't know.'

'You don't know?' she repeated icily.

'None of us knowing what she is makes an already tricky diagnosis damn near impossible from a clinical standpoint.'

Hannah tried to place a calming hand on Grace's arm. 'OK. Well, whose memories is she infected with?'

'Ah,' said Dr Black, 'now that is an excellent question.'

There followed a long moment during which nobody said anything.

'Well?' said Hannah, when it became clear Dr Black wasn't going to fill the silence.

'Oh, I've no idea. How would I know that?'

'I would like a second opinion,' said Grace.

'Really?' said Dr Black. 'Would you like me to get one of the comparative dumb-dumbs in here, who can look at her in utter confusion and then freak out when . . .'

In the bed beside them, Stella's hands started to glow with a soft variation of the blue light they'd all seen come off them before.

'Look at that,' said Dr Black, sounding cheerful for the first time. 'Happened right on cue. By the way' – he pointed at the various machines around the bed – 'her vital signs are nowhere close to an ordinary human's. I'm making most of this machinery do what it's doing just so the nurses don't lose their shit. Would you still like that second opinion?'

'Can I ask . . .' began Hannah. 'Your general demeanour? Is it like the smell of cigarettes, in that you use it as a way to put people off, so that you and your genius are available to deal with what they're needed for?'

'No,' he said. 'This is just me.'

'So,' said Hannah, through gritted teeth, 'what *can* you tell us?'

'Well,' he said, 'Stella's mind must fight off the infection itself. There's nothing any of us can do about that. All I can do is keep her stable and protected while she battles her way through what-ever's going on in there.'

'In summary,' said Reggie, 'your genius is entirely useless to us?'

'At the moment, yes,' conceded Dr Black. 'Unless you'd like me to do the thing with the fruit again?'

55

Detective Inspector Clarke, with DS Robertson beside him, stared across the desk as he had thousands of times before. He often found the best thing was to use silence as a weapon, make the suspect feel compelled to fill it. He had the definite impression they could wait until the cows not only came home but also learned to milk themselves and this fella would still be sitting there staring back at them. The guy didn't blink. Clarke wasn't being hyperbolic – he'd tried not to pay attention to it once he'd noticed it, but it was impossible not to – the man literally didn't blink. He had to force himself to still think of him as a man, but he didn't want to start considering other possibilities. Regardless of all that, a suspect was a suspect was a suspect. Clarke glanced down at the manacles on their prisoner's wrists and took reassurance from their presence. Whatever party tricks this freak might be capable of, it seemed like he couldn't do them now.

'You're in big trouble, Mr Xander.'

The man leaned back from his hunched position and stretched his back out straight for the first time since Clarke had laid eyes on him.

'I do not doubt that,' came the response.

'Yeah,' continued Clarke. 'You're going to prison for a very long time.'

'Am I?' said Xander, genuinely curious. 'On what charge, I wonder?'

'Let's start with assaulting a police officer.'

'And who would that be?'

'DS Wilkerson, as you well know, you sick fuck.'

'Hmmmm,' he said. 'I did not lay a finger on the detective sergeant, a fact to which I assume she would testify. Not that it would come to that.'

Robertson leaned forward. 'Did I just hear you threaten a police officer?'

'No,' said Xander, 'I do not believe you did.'

'And then, of course,' continued Clarke, 'there's resisting arrest. Or are you going to claim you didn't run from us this morning?'

Xander pursed his lips as if considering this. 'No, I suppose you do have a point there. I will concede that.'

'Yeah,' said Robertson. 'Not so clever there, were you? We caught you.'

Xander narrowed his eyes, their tiny pupils pitch black. 'Did you "catch" me, Detective? Or did you have help with that?'

'All that matters is we caught you,' said Clarke.

'That is true,' conceded Xander, 'and it is terribly inconvenient, I grant you. However, as I said previously, I will not answer any more of your questions until I can speak with your DI Sturgess.'

'You'll talk to us,' said Clarke.

'No, I won't.'

'You're in no position to make demands,' said Robertson.

'It is not a demand. Consider it a last request.'

All three looked up as the lights above their heads began to flicker. 'Never mind. It is already too late.'

'Go see what's happening,' said Clarke to Robertson, who gave a nod and left the room.

Just as the door closed behind him, the lights failed completely, to be replaced by the red emergency light in the corner.

Clarke gave an involuntary yelp and moved back in his chair, his swagger having deserted him entirely. He kept his attention trained on Xander. 'If this is you pulling some kind of bullshit . . .'

'Oh, I assure you it is not.'

Under the red light, Xander's pupils seemed to glow an unsettling yellow. Clarke got to his feet and looked at the tape recorder that had already cut out with the power outage. 'I'll be back in a minute,' he said. 'Don't you try anything.'

In response, Xander held up his manacled hands. 'Would that I could, Detective, but I am as helpless as a little lamb.'

Clarke turned and headed for the door, his hurried movement unable to hide how unsettled he was. He kept a wary eye on Xander as he banged on the door to be let out. After a couple of seconds, it opened and he completed his hasty exit.

Alone, Xander rolled his head around his shoulders, his neck cracking as he did so. Then, after a couple of seconds, he spoke. 'My compliments, sire. That was very well done.'

A figure dressed in black stepped out of the shadows behind him. 'Thank you.'

'Your powers are continuing to develop at an impressive rate.'

A set of white teeth flashed in the darkness. 'I believe they are.'

'I wish to apologize for letting you down. It seems there were some variables I did not anticipate.'

'Most unfortunate,' agreed the figure.

'And I assure you, in accordance with the code of my people, I will never betray you.'

'I know you believe that.'

'It is a rock-solid principle for which we are known.'

'Yes, but there is a rule I live by: everyone, but everyone, has a breaking point.'

Xander nodded as if conceding defeat. After a long moment, he ventured, 'Of course, you could free me.'

'True,' said the figure. 'You have been, and no doubt would continue to be, an invaluable asset in my work. And yet, to do so would feel like I was in some way rewarding failure.'

Xander bobbed his head. 'Yes, there is that.'

56

Despite the diminutive Dr Carter reaching barely five foot in heels, Detective Inspector Clarke found himself hurrying along the hall behind her, trying to keep up. 'I'm afraid I don't understand,' he said.

'Really?' she responded in a cheerfulish tone. 'You're a senior office in the GMP and you don't understand a detainee's right to legal representation? That is disturbing.'

'But he hasn't requested it.'

'How do you know that?'

'He hasn't made any calls since he's been here.'

'Interesting,' said Dr Carter as she turned a corner. DI Clarke didn't understand how the woman knew where she was going, but it appeared she did. 'The right to a phone call can only be withheld in exceptional circumstances. Can you detail to me what they were?'

'He was offered one,' clarified DI Clarke, 'and he declined.'

'So you say. I shall, of course, verify that with my client.'

'But what makes him your client?'

Dr Carter stopped abruptly and Clarke nearly ran into her, barely managing to halt himself in time.

'Do you think I am in the habit of turning up at police stations on Christmas Eve, trawling for work, Detective Inspector?'

'Well, no, but . . .'

'Would you like a phone call from the superintendent, clarifying my right to speak to my client?'

'As it happens,' said Clarke, 'I know for a fact that he's on a holiday with the wife and kids in Mauritius.'

'To be clear, I'm not expecting him to be in a good mood when he gets you on the phone.' She started walking again. 'And why are the staff downstairs running about like headless chickens?'

'We had a minor power outage a few minutes ago.'

She stopped again and looked up at him. 'Did you indeed?'

'It's all sorted now.'

'I'm so glad. Will you be opening this door?'

With a start, DI Clarke realized they were outside Interview Room 4, the one he'd left just a couple of minutes previously.

'I . . . I . . . I . . .'

'Unless you're going to break into your no doubt mesmerizing rendition of the sadly departed Whitney Houston's cover of a Dolly Parton classic, I'm going to need you to start using more words.'

'I will let you in,' said DI Clarke, 'but I will also insist that the individual verifies you are in fact his legal counsel.'

'Of course,' said Dr Carter, offering him the kind of sweet smile that contained cold, hard steel.

'Right, then.' In an attempt to compose himself, Clarke took a deep breath before pressing his pass against the card reader. After a moment, there was a buzzing sound and the light on the door turned from red to green. 'If you'd like to follow me please, Dr Carter, I will . . . FUCKING HELL!'

The pair stood in the doorway, struck dumb by the lifeless form of Xander lying slumped over the desk, still in manacles. The lifeless part seemed like a fair supposition, given the sheer volume of blood that was pooling on the floor beneath him.

Dr Carter bit her lip in irritation. 'I think we had better ring the superintendent after all, don't you?'

57

Claremont Dibner studied the screen of his laptop. He'd just converted a very large sum of money into bitcoin because, as much as he understood these things, that was as close as you could get to cold hard cash. Bank accounts could be frozen, transactions could be reversed but bitcoin was the entrepreneur-on-the go's best friend. Well, second best. His best friend was the massive bag of cash sitting beside the desk. It was literally a Santa's sack full of used notes – the greatest gift of all. That and the Wonderland location's shocking lack of parking alternatives.

He'd done it. He'd finally done it. He was a success. He now had enough money to pay off Mad Ivan and clear most of the other debts he'd built up over the years. He wasn't going to settle the latter, of course, but still, the fact that, in theory, he could do so was really quite something. He would definitely be paying Wayne, and not just because the man had a phenomenal capacity for violence. He'd stepped up admirably, into much more of a management role, and it turned out the army of Waynes and Wayne-adjacent individuals that made up his family were an invaluable resource.

All in all, Claremont felt like he should be ecstatically happy, and yet he wasn't. He couldn't shake the feeling that he was the bloke having an incredible run of luck on the roulette wheel at casino night on the *Titanic*. Even now, having cashed in most of his chips, he didn't feel any less uneasy. It felt as if, somewhere over his head, an almighty shoe was waiting to drop, and when it did, it'd turn out Godzilla had been wearing it.

A knock sounded on his office door. This would be it.

'Come.'

It was Wayne.

'Problem?' asked Claremont.

'Problem,' confirmed Wayne.

A minute later, they were standing outside the main entrance to Wonderland where, incredibly, punters were still flowing in. In front of them, on the ground, was a massive bell, with a Wayne standing either side of it, looking as if breathing in and out in the right order was taking up a huge amount of mental effort.

Claremont was no campanologist – in fact, his knowledge of bells extended only to knowing the word 'campanologist' – but the thing looked pretty damn big to him.

'Looks pretty big to me,' he said, because he felt it was good management to acknowledge when people had followed the brief.

'Oh, yeah,' said Original Flavour Wayne. 'It's a good size. That's not the problem.'

'So what is?'

'It's not got a doo-dah,' said Wayne.

'A doo-dah?'

'A thingy.'

'A thingy?'

'A whatchamacallit.'

'A whatchamacallit?'

'Yeah.'

'I'll be honest with you, Wayne,' said Claremont. 'I think this conversation is crying out for a recognizable noun.'

'He means a clapper,' said one of the other Waynes, much to everyone else's surprise.

'Oh,' said Claremont, waggling his fingers about. 'You mean it's got no wotsit inside it to do the actual ringing.'

'That's what I've been saying,' said Original Flavour Wayne.

'I see,' said Claremont, who, if nothing else, at least now knew two different things about bells. 'He didn't specify it needed to have a . . .'

'Clapper,' supplied Campanologist Wayne.

'Yeah,' said Claremont. 'He never said that.'

'I appreciate that,' said Original Flavour, 'but does ehm . . .'

'Neil?'

'Yeah. Him. Does he strike you as the kind of bloke who would be happy with something that is *technically* what he asked for, as opposed to, y'know, what he *actually* asked for.'

'Well . . .'

'By the way, have you noticed his size?'

Claremont knew what he was referring to. Not that it was the most unusual thing happening around the place, but Neil was no longer wearing padding under his Santa outfit. In fact, he'd gone from a bloke who looked like he could be used as a human pipe cleaner to a man of a good four hundred pounds in weight. Most people packed on a little during the Christmas period, but this was something else.

'All right,' he said, 'we need to see if we can find a—'

The rest of the sentence was rendered moot as, more loudly than Claremont could have imagined, the clapperless bell began to toll. The ground beneath their feet shook as each sonorous peal rang out.

After a couple of seconds, a couple of bells in the distance started to chime. As they all stood there listening, more and more bells joined in the chorus.

'Do we think that's a good thing?' shouted Original Flavour Wayne.

'Probably not,' conceded Claremont.

'Yeah. That's what I thought.'

58

Stella finds herself back on the boat again. The memories flash by. The rabbit. Baker's grave. Quinnie. The tank. The boy. The planes. The beach. Walking down Market Street. The pub. *The shame. The shame. The shame.*

Manny's walking down the road on a sunny day, hand in hand with Dottie, when he recognizes someone coming the other way. It's Quinnie's girl. She and Quinnie are engaged – *were* engaged. She doesn't say a word. She just walks up to him and spits in his face before rushing off, crying. Manny stands there, not knowing what to do. His daughter is confused, peppering him with questions that he does not answer – *cannot* answer.

Then he's home again. Cowering in the corner. And the look in his little Dottie's eyes as she clings to the hem of her mother's nightdress. Terrified of her daddy.

Let it be over. Just let it be over.

As he walks through the Manchester night, rain pelting down, that same thought rings in his head: *let it be over.* He doesn't have a coat, so the cold rain seeps through his shirt, making it cling to his skin. It's dark everywhere – they have to keep the lights out in case Hitler realizes they're here and comes looking.

He has a bottle with him. He tries to drink from it but finds it empty. He smashes it against a wall in frustration. The glass cuts his hand.

He watches the blood as it flows across his palm before being washed away by the rain.

He's still holding the end of the broken bottle in his hand.

Somewhere quiet. He needs to find somewhere quiet. All he wants is peace. What he wouldn't give for just a moment's peace.

The clouds part to offer a full moon's worth of illumination and, there in the distance before him, he sees a church. Sanctuary. Peace.

By the time he makes his way over, the moon has ducked behind the clouds once more. Manny walks around the church, eventually finding himself a sheltered spot in its lee.

All he wants is peace.

He sees his little Dottie. Rosa. Then he sees Quinnie. Quinnie's girl spitting in his face. The rabbit. The boy. Quinnie. Rosa. The rabbit. The boy. The boy.

He says a prayer to the God that on a good day he no longer believes in, and on a bad day he believes is hellbent on punishing him.

Let it be over.

He's bleeding now, blood pouring from his wrists.

Let it be over.

And then a hand touches his face. He looks into the eyes of an angel and she speaks to him. Not with words. As the light fades in his eyes, they come to an arrangement and she takes it all away.

The pain. Everything. He can have peace and a purpose. It won't hurt any more.

Tears roll down his cheeks now.

Peace.

All he ever wanted was blessed peace.

Stella woke up. Actually woke up. She knew it was for real this time because Grace's tear-stained face was looking down at her, with a smile like a sunrise. Stella found herself buried in a hug that left her in serious danger of suffocation.

Reggie and Hannah were there, too. After a few moments, they stepped back and an older man who stank of cigarettes shone a light in her eyes.

'How do you feel?' he asked.

'Better,' said Stella. 'I'm better now. I think I understand.'

He didn't ask what she understood, but simply nodded.

'And can we get you anything?'

'No,' she said. 'I would like to go home.'

He nodded again. 'I'm not going to stop you, but—'

Before he could get to what the but was, their attention was drawn towards the window. Outside, bells were ringing.

59

Dr Carter was standing in the car park of the police station, her phone pressed to her ear while she rested a hand on the roof of her car. 'Believe me, Your Lordship, nobody takes this matter more seriously than I, and rest assured I will be getting to the bottom of it . . .' She winced. 'I appreciate the timing could not be worse. In fact, it is suspiciously so but, first and foremost, I need to get on with containing . . . Yes, of course I understand that but . . .'

She pulled the phone away from her ear, and not just to seek some respite from the man screaming at the very top of his lungs. She could hear something. Feel something. A disturbance in the air.

Ox was running down the street, as were many other people. Quite a lot of them were screaming. He narrowly avoided colliding with a man who, for reasons that weren't clear, wasn't wearing any trousers and screaming 'Godzilla' over and over again, which was also wrong but more understandable at least. The only people not running were those unable to override their instinct to take out their phones and film what was behind them. It was like watching the Darwin Awards play out in real time.

Ox reached a junction, paused to catch his breath and turned to risk a look back. The Godzilla guy was an idiot. The thing stomping down the otherwise ordinary-looking suburban street behind him was not Godzilla but your ordinary, garden-variety Tyrannosaurus Rex. It was about thirty feet in height and a living, breathing, just-put-its-foot-through-a-Tesla dinosaur. Ox had no explanation for its existence or, indeed, why a community police officer appeared to be trying to arrest it, but there it was, breaching the peace.

Ox looked to his left. There were two other people who weren't screaming – a man and boy in the garden of the house he was standing in front of. They were calmly kicking a football back and forth between themselves. The little boy was about ten and the man was—

'Holy shit!' exclaimed Ox.

'Hello,' said the man. 'My name is Ronaldo, and I am Darren's best friend.'

'Right,' said Ox.

He then looked down as something brushed past his foot.

Storm troopers. Imperial storm troopers. From *Star Wars*. About a dozen of them. They appeared to be heading towards the dinosaur. Given that they were ten centimetres tall, Ox didn't fancy their chances, even if they had finally learned how to shoot straight.

It all felt like a dream but it wasn't. Ox was definitely awake.

It was just that reality had jumped the shark. Numbly, he noticed that everyone was running away from the T-Rex aside from the community support officer with a death wish and the storm troopers, and one young boy, who was following behind it excitedly, whooping and cheering the beast on. Ox fumbled for his phone, thinking he should probably grab a picture of this demonic child when he heard the sound. Initially, it was far off in the distance, but then it built up like a wave, washing across the entire city. A clanging, chiming cacophony like nothing he'd ever heard before. Even the T-Rex paused its rampage, as if it too were listening. All around them, bells were ringing.

Back in his office, bottle of wine in hand, Banecroft sat and considered the innocuous box on the desk in front of him.

'What the hell am I going to do with you?'

In response, the box rattled like a caged animal.

'Down, boy.'

He'd finally managed to get hold of Grace at the hospital. Stella was stable and her doctor was an arse, apparently. She hadn't phrased it quite like that, of course, but he could read between the lines. More than anything, Banecroft wanted to be there, but he couldn't be, because he had this to deal with. How had Trixy of the multitude of arms described it? 'That book contains all manner of heinous shit, and you do not want to let it come out to play.' He didn't doubt it for a second. This accursed thing could not be left alone — that he was certain of. Unfortunately, it was one of the only things he was certain of.

'Y'know,' he said, 'normally, I'm not a fan of burning books.

It's typically the kind of thing small-minded buffoons do because they don't like the outfit a teddy bear is wearing, or similar, but you might be the exception.' He took a swig of wine. 'There's been evil books before, of course – that Hitler prick's whiny little self-justification, essentially the same search for someone to blame for his own inadequacies, which a million other impotent little arses have made before or since. There is the all-but-forgotten *Malleus Maleficarum*, or *Hammer of Witches* – the book that set off the witch-hunting craze of the Middle Ages, very much the Pokémon of its day. And, of course, there's anything by Russell Brand. Either from before, or after him finding Jesus, for whom he only went looking in the first place in the hope he might know a really good lawyer. Still, you wretched, blood-drenched, carnivorous bastard, you might be the worst. Well, at least on a par with *Booky Wook 2: This Time It's Personal.*'

He leaned forward. 'And I would burn you, but why do I get the feeling that wouldn't work? Or that, worse still, you might enjoy it? And then there's the small matter of this Zalas bastard that you were used to unleash on to the world. I'm going to assume that we haven't heard the last of that megalomaniacal, power-hungry monster and, seeing as we've not got an election any time soon, he's going to have to find a less obvious route to express those urges. So now it becomes a question of . . .'

Banecroft trailed off as, in the distance, he became aware of the sound of bells ringing.

Claremont Dibner didn't bother to put on his seatbelt as he threw the Audi into gear, amid the deafening sound of clanging bells coming from all directions. He made it all of twenty feet before having to slam on the brakes. Three reindeer were blocking his path. Theoretically, he could try to drive through them but something about their demeanour made it very clear that they would be more than happy to see him try. Instead, he threw the car into reverse, making it all of six feet before another of the reindeer appeared behind him, causing him to slam on the brakes again. Before he could come up with a plan C, a fifth reindeer charged into the side of the car, flipping it over with a terrifying ease. The world became a washing machine and Claremont its forgotten sock.

After a few seconds, he opened his eyes. So many things hurt that he wasn't able to distinguish one pain from another immediately. Groggy and disorientated, he blinked a few times in an attempt to regain some form of focus. He found himself upside down, covered in shards of shattered safety glass. The car rotated on its roof slowly, affording him a view of ominous hooves in all directions. He retched, only in part because of the car's pine-scented air fresher that had somehow ended up in his mouth. After a moment spent scrabbling around, Claremont managed to locate both the bag of money and his laptop, and crawled out of the smashed window. Clutching the sack containing his nest egg to his chest, he eased himself to standing, his legs wobbly. Everywhere he looked he was confronted by demented reindeer, the breath from their flared nostrils steaming the air.

'OK,' he shouted over the clanging of the bells, 'everybody just relax. I am more than happy to make a deal.'

A violent tremor shook the world and sent him tumbling on to his backside. He glanced up to see the ground in front of him crack open like the crust of a crème brûlée. A giant pyramid began to rise out of the earth.

Nobody else was there to hear it, but he said it anyway. 'That's probably not a good thing.'

A minute later, Banecroft was standing in the car park of the Church of Old Souls aka the offices of *The Stranger Times*. Not only were bells ringing from every direction but bells that weren't there were also ringing. The church's steeple wasn't home to a bell and, as far as he was aware, it hadn't been for a very long time. Still, he could make out the clanging of just such a thing coming from it, rising to join the cacophony sweeping across the city.

'Well, this is unlikely to be good news.'

He turned in the direction of the noise and found himself facing a red glow in the sky to the west. 'Nor that,' he mused. 'What is it they say? Red sky at night – apocalypse brought about by some demonic entity summoned by a well-meaning librarian.'

Just then, Brian walked by.

'Where are you off to?'

Brian didn't turn around.

'Brian? Don't ignore me, Brian. Where are you . . .'

Then Banecroft noticed that Brian wasn't alone. A small figure was leading him by the hand.

'Oh no, you don't. Hey, Santa Claus!'

The figure didn't turn around.

'Santa Claus, you chimney-bothering, cake-stealing, kid-watching weirdo.'

That did it.

Brian and the now-somehow-alive Santa Claus plushie turned to look at Banecroft. Both had glowing red eyes.

'Ho, ho, ho,' Santa Claus boomed cheerily, in a surprisingly deep voice for such a small figure. 'And who do we have here?'

'Get your hands off my employee, ye jolly little prick.'

Santa Claus's eyes narrowed. 'Brian, go and get your bicycle, there's a good boy.'

Brian happily gambolled off to do as instructed, leaving Banecroft and Santa Claus to square off like two gunfighters, neither of whom had a gun and one of whom was only three feet tall.

'Ho, ho, ho, you've been a very bad boy,' said Santa Claus.

'I always thought you were a judgy little shit,' said Banecroft. 'Especially considering you work one day a year, and all those little helpers of yours are pretty much slave labour.'

'You're on my naughty list.'

'Is that right? You want a piece of me?' Banecroft tilted his head first one way and then the other to stretch his neck out. 'Let's dance, fat man.' He cracked his knuckles. 'And, seeing as I won't get this chance again, let's say this is also for not getting me that Sinclair ZX Spectrum I wanted as a kid. The one with the built-in tape deck.'

Santa Claus took a step and rushed towards Banecroft, his eyes still glowing red as he screamed, 'Merry Christmas!'

60

Banecroft, in one of his many monologues on what it means to be a journalist, once said that in order to find the real story it came down to being willing to go against the crowd. In this case, however, Ox had done the exact opposite. He'd hopped on his bike and followed the throng, realized where they were all heading, then proceeded to try to get there as fast as his pedalling little legs could carry him.

Another axiom in the never-ending series of Banecroftian rules of journalism was that no journalist worth their salt should ever use the phrase 'there are two types of people in the world' and expect to remain employed beyond the end of the day. However, once again, everywhere Ox looked, that's exactly what he saw. Type one had glowing red eyes and were determinedly travelling in one direction, whether on foot, in a car, on a bike, or on one of those annoying e-scooter things. The second type of person didn't have the glowing red eyes, and most of them were attempting to stop the first group of individuals from achieving their objective. The problem, as Ox had quickly realized after watching some well-meaning attempts, was that as soon as you touched a member of the first group, the rest of them turned on you. He'd seen a father try to stop his possessed wife and two daughters from following the crowd of similarly red-eyed zombies, and watched in horror as the dad and whoever tried to help him were set upon by a remorseless crowd of attackers, with his own family members front and centre.

Ox resisted the urge to try to help as he knew it wouldn't do any good. Instead, he pedalled for all he was worth, following the crowd towards the glowing red dome of light, the location of which he was increasingly certain he knew, while avoiding coming into contact with any of the zombies. On his way, he circumnavigated various similarly distressing rolling battles, where people tried in vain to stop their suddenly single-minded loved ones in their march towards God knows what.

As he grew closer, his suspicions were confirmed. The immense dome was indeed covering the area where the Wonderland Christmas Experience had been. Ox strongly believed that the only thing preventing him from being one of the thickening throng of people marching towards it determinedly was the key for *The Stranger Times* offices that he could feel in his jeans pocket. God bless Grace for insisting that anyone who went out on a story took it with them. Even so, the hairs on the back of his arms were standing on end and there was a weird acrid taste to the air. The massive car park was already full to capacity and lines of haphazardly abandoned vehicles could be seen along the nearby motorway, too. Everywhere he looked, crowds of children and adults, now on foot, were marching along the roads, trying to get to the same place.

A crash behind him caught his attention. He turned to see

a car he recognized, tearing across the adjoining field. Even here, the two-types-of-people-in-the-world axiom was holding strong – the pitiful, possessed, red-eyed souls marching to their doom while more or less obeying the rules of the road, and Vincent Banecroft, who seemed to be driving like the devil himself.

61

Having run out of road and opted for field instead, Vincent Banecroft skidded to a halt when he eventually ran out of both. The sea of cars in front of him meant that he'd have to abandon his Jag and walk the rest of the way. As he got out of the car, the infernal bell-ringing finally stopped. While it was a most welcome development in itself, as he was starting to get one hell of a headache, he doubted it was good news in the grand scheme of things. He moved around to the boot of the car to retrieve the board-game box containing the second-most-evil book in existence. The thing was vibrating as he picked it up.

'That'll be forty-eight quid.'

Banecroft spun around to see that the source of the request was a massive human in a high-vis tabard.

'What?'

'You've got to pay for parking.'

Banecroft, exasperated, waved a hand in the direction of the dome of energy. 'Have you noticed that something is a tad off? There's an enormous glowing bubble of ominous red light behind you, which now seems to contain a pyramid? Bells, some of which no longer exist, have been ringing out across the city? Mobs of literally thousands of possessed people are marching here from all over the place?'

The man folded his arms. 'None of that is my job. My job is parking, and it's forty-eight quid.'

Banecroft, mouth open, stared at the man for a long moment, unable to find words. Eventually, another part of his brain kicked in. 'Hang on, forty-eight quid for parking? Are you insane? That's a ludicrous amount.'

The man shrugged. 'It was six quid when I started working here yesterday. Cost-of-living crisis, apparently.'

'I'm not—'

The man unfolded his arms and clenched his massive fists. 'What?'

Banecroft looked at the apocalyptic dome of throbbing ominous energy and decided that he probably shouldn't let himself get distracted. 'Fine,' he said, shifting his grip on the box and resentfully reaching down to his sock, where he kept a fifty-pound note for emergencies. 'Have you got change from a fifty?'

'No.'

'Why am I not surprised?'

62

Banecroft was making his way across the Wonderland car park when he heard a familiar voice calling his name. He turned to see Ox running towards him.

'What the hell happened to you?' Ox asked, panting heavily when he finally reached his boss.

'In what regard?' asked Banecroft.

'You've got a black eye, a bloodied lip, your coat has been ripped and . . . ehm, is that the remains of your underpants dangling around your belt?'

'If you must know, I was set upon by a pint-sized psychotic Kris Kringle that brutally assaulted me and attempted to administer what I believe the kids would call a nuclear wedgie, which would have caused me irreparable damage had my underwear not thankfully lost its structural integrity mid-process.'

'Oh,' said Ox. 'Kinda sorry I asked now. What are you doing here?'

'Paying forty-eight quid for parking,' said Banecroft. 'And worse still, I ended up having to give a tip. Where the hell are we?'

'That is . . . was Wonderland.'

'The Christmas experience place you and Grace went to?'

'Yeah.'

'Hmmmm,' said Banecroft. 'That does explain a couple of things. So, do we reckon all these people are happy returning customers, then?'

'I guess.'

'By any chance do you happen to have one of the office keys upon you?'

Ox took the key out of his pocket. 'Standard procedure – we take it if we're called out to a story. I've seen a whole lot of weird shit on my way here. An actual T-Rex, a unicorn, a grandad who came back from the dead, quite a lot of SpongeBob SquarePantses and Blueys . . .'

'And a three-foot-tall Santa Claus?'

'No, actually,' said Ox. 'I haven't seen one of those.'

'Oh,' said Banecroft, tugging distractedly at the seat of his pants, 'you will. We'll be seeing him again. I guarantee it.'

'Have you got a plan?'

'Not as such.'

'Why've you brought a board game?'

'I've not. This box contains a demonic book of terrifying power that's bound in human skin.'

Ox nodded towards the dome in the near distance. 'And you thought you'd bring it here?'

'To be honest, I wasn't sure, but when in doubt . . .'

'Yeah,' said Ox uncertainly, 'better to have a whatchamacallit bound in human skin and not need it than to need it and not have it. What's in the petrol can?'

'That . . . is petrol. Come on, we need to get moving.'

The pair began to weave their way through the parked cars.

'I just had a thought,' said Ox. 'We're OK because each of us has got one of the office keys, but what about the others?'

'Brian is here somewhere,' said Banecroft, 'and, well, let's just say he's not quite himself.'

'Oh no,' said Ox. 'They let him visit Santa Claus with the kids.'

'Well, that explains that.'

Ox looked around. 'Which means Clint is probably here somewhere as well.'

'Seems like every kid in Greater Manchester is, too.'

Ox came to an abrupt halt. 'Wait a second. What about Grace?'

63

Hannah, Reggie and Stella had managed to pin Grace up against the wall just beside the lift, while confused members of the hospital staff looked on.

'Grace,' shouted Hannah. 'Grace, it's us.'

'I'm assuming she is not herself,' said Reggie, 'as I'd like to think that if she was, she probably wouldn't be trying to knee me in the gentleman's reproductive region.'

'That,' said Stella, 'and the glowing red eyes.'

'I've really been more focused on the groin thing.'

'OK,' said Hannah, 'maybe we could—'

She was cut off by a foul-smelling cup of something being thrust between her and Reggie and placed under Grace's nose.

'What the . . .'

After a second, Grace stopped struggling, blinked a couple of times and suddenly went back to being Grace again. 'What in the name of the good Lord?'

Reggie and Hannah released their grip on her and took a step back. Hannah turned to see Dr Black standing close by, holding the cup and, even for him, looking smug.

'You're welcome,' he said.

'How did . . .' started Reggie.

Dr Black was already striding back down the hall. 'Genius, remember?'

64

As they neared Christmas Wonderland, Ox was finally able to make out more of what was going on inside the dome. He really wished that wasn't the case. 'I presume you're seeing that, too?' he asked Banecroft.

'If you mean the pyramid with what looks like a morbidly obese Santa Claus sitting on top of it, then yes, it has not escaped my notice,' his boss replied, trying for an air of nonchalance he couldn't quite pull off. 'If it's any consolation, I'm ninety-five per cent certain that isn't the real Santa Claus.'

'Oh, right. Who is it, then?'

'Almost certainly a demonic old god summoned here and intent on wreaking havoc and destruction on mankind.'

'To be clear,' said Ox, 'you thought I would find that comforting?'

All around them, the red-eyed horde had formed into lines that were radiating in all directions and slowly filing into the dome. Banecroft and Ox watched a young boy, hand in hand with a Tellytubby, walk into the wall of energy. The child passed through it as if it wasn't there, but the Tellytubby disintegrated into a shower of red sparks.

'That was Tinky-Winky,' said Ox numbly. 'He's the best one. Should we join a queue?'

'No. We're skipping to the front as I'm pretty sure we're going to need to speak to someone in charge.'

Ox should have felt terrified, and he did, but at the same time, the whole thing had the surreal feel of a dream brought about by excessive late-night consumption of cheese.

As they made their way closer towards the dome, Banecroft stopped. 'Am I going mad or is there a dinosaur standing in line over there?'

'Told you.'

'And is that Clint?'

Ox turned to where Banecroft was pointing and there stood Clint, eyes glowing red, a couple of women standing either side of him. It appeared he was the only child whose Christmas wish comprised two heavily chested women who had not dressed for the weather.

'Ugh,' said Ox. 'He really is the worst.'

'Should we try and save him?' asked Banecroft, shifting his grip on the Carcassonne box again. The vibrations from within were growing stronger, to the point that he felt the need to hold the lid in place, in case an escape attempt was imminent.

'I think we'll need a team of therapists and one hell of a cold shower for that. But if you mean in the short term, if we touch any of the people with red eyes, the rest of them are going to turn against us.' Ox looked around again. 'I'm not loving our odds.' He pointed at the front of the line. 'Hey, look at that.'

They watched as children passed through the membrane

untroubled. When any adults reached it, however, they peeled off and formed a line surrounding it instead.

'Great,' said Banecroft. 'A human shield. I suppose it makes sense – Zalas wants only the true believers, so . . .'

'Children,' finished Ox.

'Children,' confirmed Banecroft.

Through the glowing membrane they could see children in their hundreds, possibly thousands, forming neat phalanxes, all facing the pyramid within the dome.

'Oh, look,' said Ox numbly, 'Santa's reindeer are up there, too.'

Banecroft tapped Ox on the shoulder and nodded in the direction of one of the queues to their right.

'Brian?' said Ox. 'Is he with a . . .'

'Three-foot-tall Santa Claus that has come to life?' said Banecroft. 'Yes, he is. Come with me.'

Being careful not to touch anyone, they moved between a couple of the lines of patiently waiting, demonically possessed children and adults. 'Still,' said Banecroft, 'look at all this orderly queuing.'

'Yeah,' marvelled Ox. 'Does kinda make you proud to be British.'

As he made his way between the lines, Banecroft banged into a man wearing a football strip. He winced and took a step back but the figure simply turned and smiled. 'Hello, I am Ronaldo. I am Darren's best friend.'

Banecroft looked back at Ox, who shrugged. "Guess it's OK to touch the magical friendies, just not their owners.'

Ox tilted his head towards Brian and his little friend, who

were only a few metres away now. The ghoul was standing there, lining up calmly along with everybody else. 'All right, what are we going to do? We can't try and pull him out of the queue or else it'll kick off.'

'I'm not going to do that,' said Banecroft, with a peculiar glint in his eye. 'Seeing as we're almost certainly about to die, I want to do a little bit of score-settling first.'

'Hang on,' said Ox, horrified. 'We're almost certainly about to die? When were you going to tell me that?'

'I'd have thought it was obvious,' said Banecroft. 'Now, do you definitely have the office key about your person?'

'Yeah.'

'Good.' Banecroft shoved the box at Ox. 'Take this, and if you hear any voices trying to tell you to do something, ignore them.'

The thing inside rattled about in Ox's hands as he accepted his new cargo, and he was pretty sure he could hear growling. 'Fuckin' hell.'

'Right,' said Banecroft, pulling a cigarette from behind his ear and placing it between his lips, before producing a lighter to ignite it. He then popped the cap off the petrol can he was carrying.

'Isn't that dangerous?' said Ox, taking a few steps back.

'That's what I'm counting on.' Banecroft raised his voice. 'Hey, Santa baby!'

The three-foot-tall Santa turned around. When he saw Banecroft he smiled, let go of Brian's hand and stepped out of the queue. 'Well, now, if it isn't that little boy I put on the naughty list.'

'Yes,' said Banecroft. 'I came here to see if you fancied check-ing it twice.'

Ox moved away even further as he looked back and forth between the two figures, his boss and a three-foot-tall Santa eyeing each other like gunfighters. The moment stretched out before them until suddenly, ho-ho-hoing all the way, the pint-sized Santa charged.

Ox glanced around. Thankfully, none of the red-eyed queu-ers were paying a blind bit of notice, their unblinking stares utterly focused on the pyramid. As the micro Santa grew closer, Banecroft tossed the contents of the petrol can at it. The little figure howled and raised its hands to its eyes, blinded by the liquid. Banecroft, meanwhile, with a matador-like flourish, took a deft step to the left and stuck out his foot, tripping his oppon-ent on its way past.

The mini Claus stumbled but executed a forward roll and regained its feet quickly before spinning around to face its adver-sary. It rubbed at its eyes and glared at Banecroft. 'Fighting dirty, I see.'

'I don't know any other way,' responded Banecroft cheerfully, before taking a quick drag and flicking his cigarette. 'Pressie for you.'

Ox watched the mini Santa Claus run off into the night between the oblivious queues of the demonically possessed, engulfed in flames and waving its arms about while screaming 'ho ho ho' at a screechingly high pitch.

'Y'know,' he said, 'of all the disturbing things I've seen in this job, I reckon your immolating Father Christmas is definitely the most messed up.'

'You're welcome,' said Banecroft. A deafening new sound behind them made him look up towards the sky. 'It would appear we're about to have company. Well, more company.'

Two large, military-style helicopters were approaching, their heavy blades fump-fump-fumping as they passed overhead.

'The army?' shouted Ox.

'I doubt it,' said Banecroft. 'At least not the British one.'

As the pair of choppers settled into a low hover, Ox and Banecroft braced themselves against the downwash. Almost immediately, figures kitted out in full black combat gear began parasailing down ropes at lightning speed.

'I recognize these pricks,' said Ox, whacking Banecroft's arm and shouting to be heard. 'They're the Founders' muscle.'

As soon as their feet touched the ground, the storm troopers took off at a sprint and formed into four groups before charging towards the dome, their futuristic-looking automatic weapons trained on the queues that showed no acknowledgement of their existence.

The figure in the Santa Claus suit sitting at the top of the pyramid stood up from his throne, his immense belly straining against the confines of his outfit's rapidly warping, thick leather belt. He reminded Ox of one of those blokes Channel 4 occasionally did specials on – the ones who couldn't fit through their own front door. All around him, Ox noticed the red-eyed gazes of the zombies shift slightly to keep him firmly in their view.

As the figure spoke, his voice carried across the ground at such a deafening volume that Ox felt it rattle his fillings. 'I see some-one has come to wish us the greetings of the season.'

The figure flung out his hands and four arcs of red light shot forth from them, obliterating each of the attack squads in the blink of an eye.

'Jesus!' exclaimed Ox.

Not even ashes remained where the storm troopers had been running just seconds before. Meanwhile, still oblivious, the queues continued to trudge forward steadily.

'Yes,' said Banecroft, shouting back at Ox. 'I was kind of hoping that would work.'

The box in Ox's hands started to buck and shake furiously. So much so that he had to struggle to maintain his grip on it. With-out warning, it became cold to the touch, fractals of frost forming on the cardboard, which started to warp under the strain. 'What are we going to do now?' he asked.

Banecroft looked down at the box and then up at Ox. 'You know how they say a bad idea is better than no idea? Well, we're going to put that to the ultimate test.'

65

Zalas stood atop his pyramid and roared with delight. With a flick of his wrists, he sent forth two more gouts of energy and the flying machines burst into flame before crashing to the ground. He bared his teeth then stuck out his tongue as he howled, drinking it all in. Vengeance. Glorious vengeance. Now was his time and it would be his time for evermore. The world of man was his to crush. Sweet nectar.

At his feet cowered the pathetic form of Claremont Dibner, clutching his red sack to himself.

Lined up before them stood legion upon legion of true believers. Little children, their faces aglow with the excitement of Christmas. Zalas already had more power coursing through him than he could have possibly imagined, with more and more flowing into him with every second that passed. He was unstoppable, and it was all thanks to the simple-minded fool he'd taken over and then allowed to fulfil his role. Poor little Neil – all he wanted was to be Santa Claus. Now, only now, did the pathetic creature realize quite what he had done. The only downside was that he was hard to silence, having been allowed free rein for so long. In the back of his mind, Zalas could hear him sobbing: 'Please, don't do this.'

'Stop your mewling, you wretched little creature.' Zalas spread his arms wide. 'Look at all these happy children whose wishes you made come true. And now you will make *my* wish come true, for already we have more than enough power to rip through the borders of this world and bring forth the howling legions from the void. It shall be glorious.'

Zalas clambered up to stand on the throne, which creaked under his weight as he raised his voice. 'My children, our time has come. I have given you all you asked for, and in return, you have given me everything!' He threw out his hands in triumph. 'I am now truly a god amongst gods! And I have chosen to make this world my bloody sacrifice so that I may grow yet more powerful and feed upon the very marrow of the universe. For this—'

An unfamiliar sound reached him from the ground below.

'Is . . . is someone booing?'

A figure stepped forward just outside the dome and waved. 'That would be me, O mighty Zalas.'

'And who might you be?'

'Vincent Banecroft, *The Stranger Times*. Would you mind if I asked you a few questions?'

Zalas laughed, causing the ground to shake. 'Can a gnat question a mountain?'

'Well, I wasn't going to mention your weight but, seeing as you asked, yes, a gnat can question anyone, if he or she has a National Union of Journalists press card. I was just wondering what it was like to be a fraud?'

'A fraud!' boomed Zalas.

'Yes. You see,' said the figure, 'none of these people – not the children, not the adults – actually believe in you, O mighty Zalas. They believe in Santa Claus, someone you are pretending to be. You're a phony. A cover act. A poor excuse for a stand-in. You are not Death, the destroyer of worlds, you're Bingo, the clown of children's parties."

'I am Zalas, reaper of souls, crusher of worlds.' His voice echoed off the very fabric of existence. The earth trembled.

When the tremors had died away, the figure below dared to speak again. 'Nah, you're just some loser in fancy dress.'

'SILENCE!' bellowed Zalas. 'I grow tired of your impertinence.' And then, with a flick of his wrist, he shot a bolt of energy towards the impudent fool who had dared to challenge him.

Ox hadn't stepped away from Banecroft deliberately, it'd just sort of happened. Then, his boss had completely lost it and started shouting abuse at the whatever-the-hell-it-was in the Santa outfit, sitting on top of the pyramid, and he was rather glad he had. He was beginning to think Banecroft had not had the happiest of childhoods, given his apparent issues with Santa Claus.

During the mini earthquake Ox lost his footing and ended up on his arse. Even for Banecroft, that was an impressive result in the pissing-somebody-off stakes. Ox didn't know who this Zalas lad was, but he and the bloke from the local corner shop clearly shared a similar opinion of his editor. He also didn't know if Banecroft had any kind of a plan, right until the moment it became apparent that he did. Even then, 'plan' was a strong word for what was more like assisted suicide with possible benefits.

The earth shook again as Zalas screamed and a bolt of energy like the ones that had eviscerated the storm-trooper dudes hurtled towards Banecroft. Exhibiting a similar level of the unexpected dexterity he'd used to trip and then immolate the mini-sized Santa, Banecroft whipped something from under his coat. As the bolt hit, Ox caught the briefest of glimpses of what it was. A book. He was holding up a book.

Then, in a day already filled to the brim with weird shit, a lot more weird shit happened at once. A massive explosion erupted with Banecroft at its epicentre, followed by a sound like the fabric of time and space ripping asunder. As Banecroft stood rooted to the spot, still holding the book aloft, a plethora of nightmarish-ness shapes erupted from it, filling the sky above. A confused mass of tendrils, screaming mouths, burning eyes, clawing hands. A swirling vortex of black shadowy forms streaming in all directions. A screeching noise filled the world, as if existence itself was protesting against this incursion.

The shadowy forms encircled the dome of energy like a swarm of locusts and devoured it in a matter of moments. Then, they coalesced around the figure atop the pyramid. Zalas. He was screaming a different tune now, one of sheer terror and frustration. The mass of tendrils picked him up and drew him towards the book, screaming all the way. 'No. No. Not again. NOT. AGAIN!'

He swam in the air, his arms flailing furiously like a drowning man, and for a moment it looked as if he might escape, but then, with a despairing wail, his resistance faltered and he was dragged ever closer by a swirling frenzy of spectral figures and clutching hands; a particularly nasty spider being flushed down a cosmic plughole.

In an instant, with a sound that could best be described as a reverse popping noise, it was gone. All of it. Everything. Zalas and the maelstrom of nightmares that had risen to reclaim him. All gone, leaving behind nothing but absolute silence. For a moment.

After a beat, Ox watched the world around him wake up from its nightmare. The glowing red light in the eyes of the assembled throng around him faded. Suddenly, they were ordinary people once more, looking around in confusion. It was as if all the many thousands of them had simultaneously walked into a room and forgotten what they'd come in for. The air of befuddled embarrassment lasted for a few seconds until the earth beneath their feet started to shake, and with a series of sudden cracks, the pyramid began to collapse in on itself. At this, the confusion turned to panic, and the lovely straight queues and neat phalanxes of obedient children devolved into a riot of screaming humanity fleeing in all directions.

Fighting against the tide, Ox had to bob and weave his way to where Banecroft was lying motionless on the ground, a couple of wisps of smoke rising off his suit that was now covered in ash — presumably all that remained of the book.

Another figure — a skinny man in his late twenties, dressed in a dirty Santa outfit — was lying a few feet away, blinking groggily as if he too were waking up from a dream.

'What the hell happened?' he asked Ox.

Ox ignored him. Instead, he fell to his knees and tried to pick up the limp form of Vincent Banecroft.

'Oh no, oh no, oh no,' he fretted. 'Boss? Boss?' He started shaking him. 'Wake up, you miserable sod. Don't you dare die before I get a chance to kill you.'

Banecroft remained unresponsive in his arms. Ox lowered him gently back down and turned to the skinny man in the Santa outfit. 'Do you know how to do the kiss of life?' The only thing he got by way of reply was a look of bewildered confusion.

Ox steeled himself. 'OK, then. Here goes nothing.'

He'd just started to prise Banecroft's lips apart when the editor's eyes shot open. 'Not until you buy me dinner first.' Banecroft pushed Ox away and pulled himself upright. Given that he had appeared all but dead seconds before, he seemed if not well then remarkably like himself. The one advantage to perpetually looking like you were auditioning to be your own corpse was that it didn't take much to make what amounted to a full recovery. 'What the hell happened?'

'I think you . . . sort of saved the world or something?'

'Sort of saved the world or something?' repeated Banecroft. 'As someone who employs you as a writer, can I point out how appalling a sentence that is?'

'Oh, shut the hell up.' Ox tried not to smile as a sense of relief washed over him. Banecroft, for better or worse, was still very much Banecroft. A fact he confirmed by raising one arse cheek off the ground and loudly passing wind.

Somewhere in the distance, Ox could hear sirens.

Banecroft noticed the skinny figure in the now grossly over-sized Santa Claus outfit stagger away, stopping only to pick up a red sack. 'Who the hell is that?'

'Who knows,' said Ox, standing up and offering Banecroft his hand, 'but leave him alone. I've already seen you immolate one Santa Claus today – that's my limit.' He heaved his boss to his feet then stopped as he felt something wet land upon his cheek. He looked up at the sky. 'Would you fancy that?' he said. 'It's gonna be a white Christmas.'

As the snow began to fall around them, the pair stood in silence, watching a bewildered man in a Santa suit stumble away into the night. It said something for how dazed and confused Neil was that it took him several hours to realize his sack contained enough money to make every day feel like Christmas.

66

Banecroft claimed he was feeling all right but he clearly wasn't. Ox could tell because for the first time ever, he'd been allowed to drive the Jag. It'd taken them quite a while to locate Brian and Clint, both safe and sound, and once the pair had been corralled successfully, Ox bundled them all into the car, where Banecroft had fallen asleep instantly. Ox had been both thrilled to find himself behind the wheel of Banecroft's beloved Jag and thankful that he'd managed to stop Brian from relieving himself on the back seat. He never would have lived that one down.

Once they'd parked up at the offices of *The Stranger Times*, Ox woke Banecroft and the weary quartet trudged inside. As they clambered up the stairs, Ox was grateful to find Grace, Reggie, Hannah and Stella waiting for them.

'Praise the Lord,' said Grace.

'Let's leave him out of it,' said Banecroft, focusing immediately on Stella. 'Are you OK?'

'She's fine,' answered Reggie. 'As is Grace, who took a funny turn.'

'I did not,' protested Grace.

'I'm afraid you did,' said Hannah.

'Don't worry about it,' said Ox. 'There's been a lot of it going about.'

'Where were you lot?' asked Hannah. 'We know something's been going on but social media's been an even greater shitstorm than usual. There's several people claiming dinosaurs once again roam the Earth.'

'People can be so dramatic, can't they? No, we were fighting off a demonic old god who was trying to destroy the world. Y'know, the usual,' said Banecroft. 'How was your last-minute Christmas shopping?'

'Ha ha,' said Hannah sarcastically. 'Obviously, I wasn't actually . . .' Her face dropped and she leaped out of her chair. 'Jesus!'

'Language,' exclaimed Grace.

'I've left Sturgess tied up in my apartment.'

'Well,' said Grace, 'I do not approve of that.'

Without another word, Hannah sprinted for the stairs, nearly knocking over Clint in the process.

'Hang on,' said Stella. 'You were fighting off some demonic thing and you took the kid with you?'

Clint gave her his best teenaged sleazy grin. 'I knew you cared, sweet cheeks.'

'Are you OK?' Grace asked him.

'No, he isn't,' Stella answered on his behalf, 'but he's just as awful as he's always been, if that's what you mean.'

'Don't hate the player,' said Clint, 'hate the game.'

'I think I can do both.'

Stella eased herself to her feet. 'Well, now that you're all back safe and relatively sound, if you'll excuse me, there's someone I need to go and have a chat with.'

'Are you sure that's a good idea?' asked Reggie.

'It's fine,' said Stella, before catching sight of Grace's worried expression. 'Honestly, it's absolutely fine.'

'I'll tell you what else is fine . . .' began Clint.

'Finish that sentence, Clint,' warned Stella, 'and I guarantee it'll be your last.'

Stella walked into the printing room and closed the door behind her. Manny was seated at his desk, absent-mindedly polishing a gleaming piece of the machinery in which she could already see his face reflected. As he noticed her, he stopped what he was doing and clambered awkwardly to his feet. He stood there before her, a wary look in his eye, and fiddled nervously with the rag in his hands.

'It's OK,' she said with a soft smile. 'I come in peace.'

She walked over, reached out and gently touched his arm.

'We . . .' began Manny. 'I . . . I don't know what to say.'

'That's OK,' said Stella. 'I understand now.'

Above Manny's head, the smoky swirl of the angel was starting to form. This time, the angel's face was not angry but rather an implacable facade, impossible to read.

Stella looked up at her. 'I understand now,' she repeated. 'He was in pain, so much pain, and you helped him. So . . . thank you.' As she spoke, faint echoes of the memories – Manny's memories – played through her mind, no longer the visceral nightmare but more a wistful tune, half remembered. 'You took it away. You saved him.'

Manny had started to cry and Stella smiled at him again. 'Here's the thing, though. It was never just your pain, was it?'

He shook his head.

'And now our . . . I mean *your* little girl, Dottie – she needs her daddy again, one last time.' Stella looked back up at the angel. 'Is there any way he could . . . Just for a little while?'

She was surprised when Manny spoke again, his voice somehow different – sombre. 'It doesn't work like that, chile, but no matter. Everything has its time. I was wondering, could you maybe call that nice Zoe girl? I'd like to meet her, properly.'

Stella nodded.

Manny turned and looked up into the face of the angel. 'Thank you, for all you've done for me. This is the right time. None of us can stay here for ever.' He smiled. 'Well, maybe you can.'

It was hard to tell, but Stella thought she saw what might just have been an angel shedding a tear. Manny was gently lifted into the air before her, and Stella watched as he was spun around gently, as if caught in one last, slow waltz.

When it finished, the angel placed him softly back on his feet. He was now wearing a suit which, with a jolt, Stella realized she recognized. She also realized that he looked older. Suddenly, there were wrinkles on his skin.

Stella gasped. 'Wait, what's happening?'

'S'all right, chile. Everyone has their time. It's been a long time coming.' Manny steadied himself against her and looked down at himself before giving her a big grin. 'Would you look at that – the old thing still fits.'

Thirty minutes later, all the members of *Stranger Times* staff who hadn't recently remembered they'd left an unconscious police officer tied up on their sofa were standing outside the front door to the Church of Old Souls. Nobody had suggested it and yet, somehow, they'd arranged themselves into a straight line. Like a guard of honour. Manny, with his great-great-granddaughter Zoe beside him, walked slowly between them, shaking hands and exchanging hugs. He looked even older than he had done just a few minutes ago – as if time was racing to catch up with him.

At the end of the line stood Brian. Manny stopped in front of the ghoul, placed a hand on his shoulder and smiled. 'You need to stand up proud now, my friend.'

For the first time anyone could recall, Brian did precisely that. It was amazing the difference the change in his posture made. Shoulders back, chin held high – he looked like a new man. Stella glanced across at Grace, who was already crying, but a smile spread across her lips, too.

Manny shook Brian's hand. 'You take care of yourself, my brother.'

Brian nodded.

'And her.'

He nodded again.

With that, Manny turned to the group. 'Thank you, all. It's been quite the ride. Now, if you don't mind' – he patted Zoe's arm – 'me think me like to go out for a walk now.'

67

The staff sat dotted around the bullpen, no one saying a word. Eventually, Stella broke the silence. 'I didn't . . . When I went to talk to him, I didn't think that was going to happen.'

Grace reached across and patted her knee. 'It's all right, dear. He seemed very happy, I thought. At peace.'

Stella nodded. 'I hope so.'

The room fell back into contemplative silence. Banecroft took another deep slug from the latest bottle of non-alcoholic wine that he was demolishing. Grace allowed herself the briefest of smiles.

'What did that mean?' asked Ox.

'What did what mean?' said Reggie.

'What Manny said to Brian?'

The group as a whole turned their attention to the other end of the room where Brian was sitting, playing Connect Four by himself. As if in answer to Ox's question, Brian got to his feet. Stella couldn't help but marvel at just how different he now looked. Still Brian but very different, too. Instead of the creature who scurried about, eyes downcast, he surveyed the room and smiled broadly before stepping forward. He closed his eyes for a couple of seconds and opened them only when the floor started to shake. Stella glanced at the glass of water on the desk in front of her as a vibration passed through it.

'What the hell is happening?' said Banecroft. 'We're not supposed to be printing anything.'

'I don't think that's the printer,' said Reggie.

The rumbling increased in intensity. Somewhere, something fell to the ground with a thump. Stella didn't see what it was — she couldn't take her eyes off Brian. She couldn't be sure, but it seemed as if there was now a glow in his eyes. He held out his hands, the wide grin still on his face.

The staff jumped out of their seats as smoke began to billow out of the floor. In truth, it was more like dry ice, except it wasn't coming from anywhere. It seemed to be coming *out* of everywhere all at once. As if the building as a whole was breathing it. Brian, still smiling, started to rise slowly off the ground as a wind began to whip around the room. An ecstatic look spread across his face, and he stretched out his arms as if trying to hug the sky.

Ox dived on top of his desk, trying and failing to prevent the one hundred seemingly random bits of paper – not to mention the rubbish that perpetually covered it – from taking flight. Grace went to take a step forward but Banecroft put a gentle hand on her arm to stop her. As she turned to him, he shook his head.

'Oh my God,' shouted Reggie over the noise.

Brian was now hovering a good ten feet in the air, arms still extended, looking up at the ceiling. He began to spin, slowly at first but picking up speed until he became a blur of motion. The wind was now so strong that Stella had to cling on to her desk, as did the others. Ox was still vainly attempting to snatch at various pieces of paper as they were whipped off his desk, like a gameshow contestant in one of those big glass boxes full of money or tokens.

And then, as suddenly as it had started, the tumult ceased and Brian descended slowly back to the floor.

He stood tall in front of them now, his stoop completely gone. He looked round the group and, with a broad smile, spoke in a deep voice with an accent Grace couldn't place. 'Merry Christmas, one and all.'

68

Tamsin Baladin was sitting at her desk, typing away diligently. His Lordship had asked her to prepare a report and it was going to take a considerable amount of time.

She paused, sensing a change in the air. 'I do wish you'd stop doing that.'

A figure stepped out of the shadows behind her. 'Forgive me, sister dearest, but it is such a cool trick.'

She turned around to look at her brother, disguising her revulsion behind a tight smile. Every time she saw him these days, he seemed to have changed even more. He now barely resembled himself at all. It wasn't even the more superficial changes – the paler skin, gaunt face, his unruly mop of hair now coiffed so much as to be unrecognizable. It was the eyes – there was a look in his eyes that was glassy, inhuman.

'Is the cloak really necessary, Alan?'

'Don't call me that,' he said. 'I no longer answer to that name.'

Tamsin was a little taken aback by the vitriol in his declaration. 'Sorry,' she said, 'I guess you'll always be my little brother.'

'By all of thirteen seconds.'

'It still counts.'

'Well,' he said, 'it seems our little project was a roaring success.'

'You say that,' said Tamsin. 'I'm reliably informed that we came precariously close to bringing about the apocalypse.'

Her brother shrugged in that infuriating way he'd always had. 'You asked me for chaos, I brought chaos.'

'Yes, well,' she said, 'moving forward, perhaps we need to be more careful.'

'Did it work, though?'

Despite herself, Tamsin smiled. 'It appears it did.'

69

Up on the roof of the former church that was now the offices of *The Stranger Times*, Vincent Banecroft lay on the rickety old sun lounger, his coat wrapped tightly around him, bottle of non-alcoholic wine in hand, watching the snow fall.

He heard a movement behind him. 'You'll catch your death sitting up here, Vincent.'

Dr Carter smoothed out her coat and perched on the wall opposite.

'Nah,' said Banecroft. 'I think I might survive this. Not to be rude, but don't I have to invite you in before you're able to cross the threshold or something like that?'

'Oh, please,' she said. 'Just this once, Vincent, try not to be so . . . you.'

'Rough day?' he asked.

Dr Carter looked at the bottle she was holding in her hand. 'You could say that.'

'Was that Zalas thing your lot?'

'Quite the opposite, I assure you.'

'In which case,' he said, 'you and the rest of the planet are very welcome. Don't mention it. Happy to be of service.'

'Yes,' said Dr Carter ruefully. 'I saw that. Your ability to annoy absolutely everyone does you great credit, Vincent.'

'Thank you.'

'Do you understand what happened today?'

'To be honest, despite being there for most of it, "understand" would be a strong word. Still, all's well that ends well.'

Dr Carter gave a bitter laugh, a million miles from her normal grating giggle. 'Would that it were the case. Today was what could be termed a fracture point. The façade of everyday existence was damaged, and I doubt if all the King's horses and all the King's men will be able to put it back together again.'

'I'm afraid you've lost me?'

'The public. The great unwashed. The man and woman on the street. Call them what you will – enough of them saw too much today. Convincing them to forget all about it may well be beyond the ability of anyone.'

'And that's bad news for your lot, is it?'

'It's bad news for everyone, Vincent. The Folk don't want that any more than the Founders do. Trust me, in that situation, nobody wins. Well, almost nobody. Clearly, somebody thought it was a good idea.'

'If I'm honest,' said Banecroft, after taking another swig from his bottle, 'you are rather wrecking my buzz.'

'Sorry about that. I am not my usual cheery self.'

'Why so? I mean, other than the whole cat being out of the bag thing.'

Dr Carter hefted her bottle and read its label. 'Let's just say I've been passed over for a big promotion at work.'

'Oh no, were you due to be made top villain or something?'

'Do shut up, Vincent. What are you drinking?'

'Non-alcoholic wine.'

'You're kidding?'

'No. A gift to my office manager.'

'Don't you mean from?'

'No – to. I've been letting her think I'm off the booze, which she seems to be oddly obsessed with. I've been secretly mixing it with poitín, of course.'

'Of course,' said Dr Carter. 'Do you mind if I join you for a drink?'

'Well,' he said, 'I am running low on alcoholic non-alcoholic wine, but I suppose I could spare a little.'

'Thank you for the sweet offer but, like all good guests, I've brought a bottle. A Macallan Valerio Adami nineteen twenty-six.'

'Any good?'

'I have no idea. I was saving it for a special occasion.'

'I did just avert the apocalypse.'

'True, but still – not what I had in mind. Having said that . . .' She held up two glasses she'd produced from somewhere and raised an eyebrow.

Banecroft shrugged. 'Well, it is Christmas.'

EPILOGUE

And there is our story, my fellow dead thing. A festive tale where a grown man immolates an undersized Santa Claus and casts an oversized one back to the hell from whence he was summoned. And a Merry Christmas, one and all. Let's see the Muppets do that one.

Still, I promised you story and we have had a feast of it, have we not? There were ups, downs, twists, turns, goodies, baddies, victims, victors – not much romance, I grant you. In fact, even now, as he is being untied and offered nonsensical justifications and apologies, a certain detective inspector is actively considering whether he can charge the woman with whom he has been romantically linked with kidnapping and false imprisonment – an unlikely scene for a Hallmark movie. But that is story for you – I never said it wouldn't be messy in places. That is because it contains people, and people are messy. And while we have tasted many flavours of story, we have not drained the last drop from it. Heavens, no. There is always more, especially around here.

Where to next for our fond family of misfits? For the girl who does not know who she is? And for those who would rule the world but do not realize that a certain twin sister and brother seem intent on tearing down their kingdom from within? Not to mention the city itself, for the genie has been let out of the bottle, and while you can fool some of the people all of the time, all of the people some of the time, and the readers of certain newspapers indefinitely, it's still hard to convince people that they didn't see a T-Rex stomping on a Tesla in Chorlton. A threshold has been passed and there is no going back.

Story is life – all of life. Even the end of it. For yes, there is a very definite ending still to be had. It is happening right now.

In a hospital room, a woman who has led a truly good life awakens. Her eyes are blind, leaving her lost in the cold darkness. Her mind has all but deserted her too, because sometimes life can be unforgivably cruel – robbing someone of their own story. A nasty disease reducing a strong woman to a frightened child, who wants nothing but her father to come and tell her everything is going to be all right.

'Daddy?' she says, every time she wakes. Normally, her question is only ever met by terrifying silence or confusing strangers.

But not this time.

A wrinkled hand pats hers and a voice she recognizes speaks softly in her ear. 'It's all right, my darling girl. Daddy is here.'

Tears of joy flow down her cheeks until a gentle finger ushers them away.

'I missed you, Daddy.'

'I missed you too, my angel, but I'm here now.'

'I'm frightened.'

'No need for that now. No need at all. Daddy is here and I'll be with you for evermore. I promise.'

'Are we going somewhere?'

'I think we are,' he said, 'but don't you fret.' A feeling of warmth spreads through her as he takes her hand in his and, in that soft, sweet voice, whispers in her ear. 'No need to worry at all, my darling.'

And she believes him, for what little girl can ever be frightened so long as her daddy is holding her hand and telling her everything is going to be all right?

Happy now, she closes her eyes. And then, in a tender voice, he sings, 'Hush, little baby, don't say a word . . .'

FREE GOODIES

Hi,

C. K./Caimh here—thanks for reading *Ring the Bells*. Would you like to watch an exclusive video, where I discuss world-building, sewage plants and all things Manny. Then scan the QR code below with your phone right now, or visit TheStrangerTimes.co.uk/HoHoHo

And if you'd like to receive some exclusive *Stranger Times* short stories, you can get them delivered straight to your inbox by signing up for my newsletter at TheStrangerTimes.co.uk

Also, check out the award-winning *Stranger Times* podcast, which is chock-full of short stories written by me and read by some of my former co-workers at the coalface of the British stand-up comedy circuit.

Sláinte and stay weird,

Caimh

ACKNOWLEDGEMENTS

In lieu of traditional acknowledgements, the author has contacted his good friend the REAL Santa Claus and asked him to confirm who's getting what – and why – this year. Take it away, St Nick . . .

Tremendous editor Simon Taylor has been a good boy this year, and so will be receiving a signed picture of Nana Mouskouri. I don't know if he likes her, but we've had it sitting here for years and it's taking up space.

Magnificent managing editor Judith Welsh gets a signed picture of John Krasinski, as I'm reliably informed the ladies go mad for him. She also gets a set of steak knives. You never know when they'll come in handy.

Irreplicable copy editor Rebecca Wright receives Jason Momoa. Not a picture, but the actual man. To be honest, I've no idea how I ended up with him. However, I need to give him to somebody as he's eating me out of house and home. Please remember never to feed him after midnight – bit of a *Gremlins* situation.

The wondrous Melissa Kelly from Marketing and the sublime Oliver Martin from PR will each receive a Clarify 5000 robot, which will follow them around at work, patiently explaining the difference between PR and marketing to fools who still don't get it. Basically, the former starts the fire and the latter shouts 'Fire!'

Production whizz Phil Evans gets a very large Lego set, as he strikes me as a man who secretly really wants Lego, and no one is providing him with any.

Audio dynamo Tom McWhirter receives a fondue set and a forty-by-thirty-foot reimagining of Michelangelo's *The Creation of Adam*, featuring world-beating, legendary narrator Brendan McDonald and producer extraordinaire Paul Fegan. Paul and Brendan, for their shared gift, finally get rid of that bloody painting they had commissioned while on a regrettably good night out.

Every member of the UK and International Sales team will get a large box of chocolates, each one hand-delivered by a member of nineties boy band 5ive (please note Jason/J can't do every other Tuesday as he's got five-a-side). Lewis Cain, for the frankly extraordinary and spectacularly ill-judged feat of having the cover of *This Charming Man* tattooed on his calf, gets a set of those Oscar Pistorius bouncy metal legs – just in case that thing turns septic.

And finally, dynamic, hard-working agenting duo Ed Wilson and Hélène Butler are gifted a cricket ball each. Ed because he has been good; Helen because she has been bad.

ABOUT THE AUTHOR

Born in Limerick and raised in Dublin, C. K. (Caimh) McDonnell is a former stand-up comedian and TV writer. These days he dedicates all his time to writing books as his dogs don't like it when he leaves the house. As Caimh, he published his first book, *A Man With One of Those Faces* – a comic crime novel – in 2016 and it has gone on to spawn the bestselling Dublin Trilogy books and the spin-off McGarry Stateside series. It is being adapted into a TV show called *Tall Tales & Murder* which will be screened in 2026.

As C. K. McDonnell, he is the author of *The Stranger Times* contemporary comic fantasy series including the many short stories that appear on *The Stranger Times* podcast. He has also co-written *Ursula and the V-Team* with his wife, Elaine Ofori. It is set in Cologne, and its primary purpose is to make his agent's life difficult.

Caimh lives in Manchester and is a proud supporter of Dogs4Rescue, a kennel-free dog rescue.

To find out more, visit whitehairedirishman.com